SPOCK STRUCK THE FLOOR HARD . . .

He twisted his body to catch at any handhold he could reach. Behind him the Vulcan could see the wet gleam of an eyeless, narrow head, and the wet star of writhing tentacles that reached for him. The tentacle that had seized him ended in a double-padded grip; the next nearest one ended in a razor-sharp mouth.

Spock snatched his phaser from his belt and fired into the center of the black, slippery tentacles. It had no effect. The creature's gaping maw moved toward him. . . .

Look for STAR TREK Fiction from Pocket Books

Star Trek: The Original Series

Star Trek: The Next Generation

Star Trek: Deep Space Nine

STAR TREK®

CROSSROAD

BARBARA HAMBLY

POCKET BOOKS

New York   London   Toronto   Sydney   Tokyo   Singapore

This book is a work of fiction. Names, characters, places and incidents are products of the author's imagination or are used fictitiously. Any resemblance to actual events or locales or persons, living or dead, is entirely coincidental.

An *Original* Publication of POCKET BOOKS

POCKET BOOKS, a division of Simon & Schuster Inc. 1230 Avenue of the Americas, New York, NY 10020

STAR TREK is a Registered Trademark of Paramount Pictures.

This book is published by Pocket Books, a division of Simon & Schuster Inc., under exclusive license from Paramount Pictures.

ISBN: 0-671-79323-3

First Pocket Books printing September 1994

10 9 8 7 6 5 4 3 2 1

POCKET and colophon are registered trademarks of Simon & Schuster Inc.

Printed in the U.S.A.

For Erina
Wherever she may be

CROSSROAD

Chapter One

IT HAPPENED SHORTLY AFTER the start of the evening shift.

Later on, everyone agreed on that.

At nineteen hundred hours, forty minutes, on Stardate 6251.1, Captain James Kirk was in the gym on Deck Eight of the *Starship Enterprise,* sparring with Ensign Lao Zhiming—twenty-one, compact of build, his reflexes as quick as his mind—when the whistle of the comm link sounded and one of the basketball players down at the other end of the big, curved room went to get it.

A moment later the man called out, "Captain?"

Kirk ducked a kick, backed off, his hand still raised to guard, panting; Lao relaxed with a grin and teased, "Saved by the bell, sir."

"Me or you?" Kirk grinned back and lightly ran to the comm link nearest them—there were eight in all in the big, echoey chamber, which curved in a quarter section around the ship's main hull. He did notice that the basketball players hadn't resumed their game. They were inconspicuously loitering, bouncing the ball on the highly polished floor or doing ham stretches on the ribstalls with the air of people not quite eavesdropping, but waiting; just a little— just the tiniest bit—nervous about what it was that the

1

bridge had to convey to the captain after he was off duty for the day.

As he slapped the comm button, Kirk was conscious that he, too, felt the twinge of adrenaline, over and above what the sparring match had roused.

Lao kept his distance, but he was listening, too.

"Captain?" Mahase's deep voice sounded completely neutral, as if it were none of her business. "First-line guard buoys of the Federation proximity zone around the Tau Lyra star system report an unidentified vessel."

"That's impossible," said Lao.

Kirk glanced back at him. The boy pushed his straight, sweat-drenched black hair back from his face, his forehead bunched in a frown at the inconsistency of data.

"We ran scans of the whole quadrant three hours ago, sir, just before we came off shift. You saw them. It's a deserted area. No shipping, no mining, no starbases . . . No civilizations at all, except what's on Tau Lyra Three. Nothing could have come in range of the buoys in that time. Nothing's that close."

"Except the Crossroad." The sweat drying stickily on his chest in the open front of his gi chilled Kirk slightly. There was certainly no other reason to feel cold.

"But there's . . ." Lao broke off. He was young, a midshipman, just out of the Academy. One day, Kirk knew as surely as he knew his own name, he would be one of the finest captains of Starfleet.

"There's nothing in the Crossroad Nebula?" Kirk finished his protest for him and gave him another lopsided grin, wry this time, as much at his own memories as at the young man's assumptions about how accurate readings were on the fringes of unknown space. "That we know about, Ensign. That we know about."

He turned, and slapped the comm button with the heel of his hand. "We're on our way."

"It's a vessel all right, sir." Lieutenant Tonia Barrows punched up maximum magnification on the long-distance readout, and Kirk tapped the code to put it on the miniature strategic screen on the arm of his command chair. This proving too small to be satisfactory—the strategic readouts had a sublime disregard for anything beyond the range of a photon torpedo—he rose and stepped down to the evening-shift navigator's side. Mr. Spock, who had been reading in his quarters when news came of the potential violation, descended from his position at the Central Computer station to join them.

Green lights floated in the onyx abysses of the screen. Dim yellow haze marked the first, far-off effects of the star Tau Lyra's cometary field, though the star itself was too distant to show on the screen. The tiny pinlight was the drone buoy that had sent out its alarm, out beyond even the comets; the moving, antlike glow, the approaching craft.

"Looks like they're heading for Tau Lyra, all right, sir," said Barrows, looking up at Kirk. She was a dark-haired woman, pretty and competent, reputed to play a mean game of poker. In the four years, nine months of the *Enterprise*'s mission, crew members had come and gone, but Barrows was one of the moderate-sized group of those who had been on board from the first.

Evening shift being smaller, the duties of navigator and helm were combined. "Can't tell for certain, but there's sure nothing else around there that they *could* be making for. High sublight speeds."

"Point of origin?"

"Crossroad Nebula, sir."

Kirk was silent a moment, gauging, measuring in his mind. He could feel the tension go through the bridge crew; less familiar to him than the day-shift gang, though he made a point of spending several hours each evening on the bridge when he could. He knew that the big, easygoing engineering lieutenant Winfield essentially ran the bridge in his absence; he could see him now, trading a worried glance with Lieutenant Mahase, could sense the weight of the silence in the way Dykstra continued to work at the ops station. It was as if he could hear the pulse of each person in the room—

3

with the possible exception of the unflappable Mr. Spock—slightly quicken.

He returned to his seat, the Vulcan moving quietly at his heels. "When did the last ship vanish in the vicinity of the Crossroad Nebula?"

"Three point seven standard years ago, Captain. It was the Federation scout *Harriet Tubman,* with a crew of twelve, out of Starbase Twenty. Prior to that there is an unconfirmed report of the free-trader *Sagittarius,* last reported in this vicinity. In addition, three of the Federation observation buoys placed on the outer perimeter of Tau Lyra's proximity zone have disappeared, as have three automated drones sent into the nebula by the Federation Science Institute to determine whether there is, in fact, a Turtledove Anomaly Point within the nebula."

"And you know all that off the top of your head?" The turbolift doors whooshed softly shut as Dr. McCoy descended to the other side of Kirk's command chair and fixed the Vulcan science officer with a bright, sarcastic blue eye.

Spock drew himself up a little and replied, "As our current assignment is to release yet another series of instrument packets into the nebula, it seemed logical to familiarize myself with the potential hazards of the phenomenon. Quadrant Six is largely unexplored. The charts we made this morning are the first since the early Vulcan readings five centuries ago, which also marked the region as *p'laaka*—prone to unpredictable events. Since that time the Crossroad Nebula does not seem to have enlarged nor unduly shifted position relative to its surroundings. An anomaly, but not a danger."

"Unless you happen to get too close," muttered McCoy.

Spock elevated one brow. "The same may be said of a slime devil in one's bathtub. Though data is fragmentary, there is reason to believe that the region was marked on the ancient charts because of unexplained disappearances. Following the disappearance of the *Harriet Tubman,* the Federation declared the nebula a Standing Hazard. Hence the exploratory drones."

Not to mention, thought Kirk uncomfortably, the standard warnings in force concerning all planets, inhabited or otherwise, within five parsecs of Anomaly Points.

"There's an organized exploration slated to begin the year after next," said Ensign Lao. He'd come onto the bridge only moments behind Kirk, like Kirk still shrugging his gold command shirt straight, his wet hair sleeked back and his eyes alight with enthusiasm at the idea of such a mission. "Personally, I want a closer look at that planetary system that showed up on the edge of the nebula this morning. If they'll take me."

Kirk grinned at the buoyant eagerness in his words. "Well, since you're probably one of the few midshipmen who's even been within spitting distance of an Anomaly, they can hardly leave you out."

"If Starfleet can budget the funds," grumbled McCoy cynically.

"Naturally," Spock said, "I have no data on Fleet budgetary projections. And until such an expedition can be mounted, our information must remain fragmentary."

"But they have found debris," Kirk said.

Spock inclined his head. Any of the bridge crew—or indeed, most of the four-hundred-odd men and women aboard the *Enterprise*—knew about the debris. Whatever had produced those disturbing fragments of metal and porcelain the *Tubman* had reported picking up on the fringes of the nebula, four or five hours before it had vanished itself, had—Kirk was willing to bet—been in the minds of every suddenly idle basketball player in the gym, as it was now in the set of Barrows's shoulders, the angle of Winfield's head. The report was in the central computer and had probably been scanned by everyone on board.

Technology unknown, it had said.

Now, for the first time in five centuries that anyone knew about, a ship had emerged from the dark heart of the gas veils, the clouds of glowing dust, the fluctuating screens and fields of mu-spectrum radiation that made the Crossroad almost impenetrable to any form of scans. A ship heading straight for the unprotected, prespaceflight world of Tau Lyra III.

"We're getting a reading," said Barrows. "Same mass as the *Enterprise* but a much smaller power output. It looks like the power's falling even now."

Across the bridge someone said, "Not the *Tubman . . .*"

"Power readings?"

"Anomalous." Barrows double-checked her data, perplexed. "Looks like some kind of matter-antimatter drive, but the burn rate's lower."

"Got them on visual," Lieutenant Mahase started to say, then broke off with a gasp. Her eyes widened and she looked helplessly across at Kirk, shaking her head. It took a lot, Kirk knew, to unsettle Mahase.

"Put it on visual, Lieutenant."

She whispered, "I don't believe it," even as her fingers tapped in the magnification code.

The alien ship, the intruder from the secret hidden within the heart of the Crossroad Nebula, was a Federation starship.

It was painted a matte, dead black, nearly invisible against the velvet pit of space. Only the trapped glow of ambient light in the dust curtain of the nebula backlit it and made it visible at all.

The viewports across its sides were dark. Dull ruddiness flared in the engine ports, but that was all. Other than that, they might have been looking at a mirror image of the *Enterprise,* or any of the other eleven Constitution-class starships, save for the stained and rust-streaked black paint. Battered, meteor-dented, and burned, the triangular arrangement of the nacelles, the shape of the command saucer, and the sleek, familiar lines were unmistakable.

"Fascinating." Spock clasped his hands behind his back and studied the screen.

"Well, I'll be a pink-eyed mackerel," whispered McCoy, and so absorbed was Mr. Spock in contemplation of the dark ship on the screen that he forbore any obvious rejoinders to this piece of reincarnative speculation.

"It's . . . it's one of ours." Barrows sounded absolutely stunned. *As well she might,* reflected Kirk.

Behind him, Lao was staring, openmouthed—being too

young to have learned, Kirk thought, that anything was and could be possible in the dark starfields that were their unknown world.

"ID code?"

"Too far away to tell, Captain. I'm not getting anything, not even static."

Kirk's eyes hardened. "Then open a hailing frequency. Mr. Winfield, deflector shields up."

He glanced at his own readouts, more numerous and accurate as the distance between the dark ship and the *Enterprise* decreased. "Their power's falling, but they might have enough reserve to get off a shot or two." God knew, he added to himself, he'd wrung enough last-gasp bolts from the *Enterprise* not to trust even the feeblest of crippled starships. And even without phaser reserves, there were still photon torpedoes to be reckoned with.

They were near enough to the other ship to be able to pick it up without magnification now. Streaks of rust and smoke fouling, the silvery pitting of meteor debris, the long burns of battle covered the black-painted hulls. Under the paint, thick and numerous patches could be seen in the metalwork itself. Whatever serial numbers or names were once there had been scorched and battered away long ago.

How long? Kirk cast his mind back, trying to call to memory early losses among the starships of the Fleet. This one had clearly been out in space and taking a hell of a beating for decades. Yet the Constitution-class ships were only twenty years old. In a high-stress environment, perhaps . . .

But it gave him an eerie feeling, such as he had felt when, during the Gamma Hydra II incident, he had looked into the mirror and seen that aged face staring back at him, had known it for his own.

Against the faint glow of the far-flung nebular gases, the other starship veered, swung away. At the same moment, Barrows reported, "They're evading . . ."

"Stay on them."

Even as Kirk gave the order the navigator was swinging the helm. The image of the star Tau Lyra, no bigger than a yellow pinhead at this distance, fell away into the inky pit. Ahead, the dark starship was accelerating spongily. Kirk's practiced eye marked the brightening and dulling of the engine glow that told that the matter/antimatter flow was ellipsing. His glance cut back to Spock, bent over his computer again, Lao at his side. "Didn't the drones that vanished into the Crossroad report a power loss?"

"Affirmative, Captain." The blue light of his station wavered over the angular features. "The *Tubman* reported anomalous effects up to two parsecs from the edge of the nebula itself. Our own readings of the planetary system we charted this morning were affected by it. I suggest that if the starship approaches it any closer, we exercise extreme caution in pursuit."

"To hell with caution," muttered Kirk between his teeth. "I want to know who they are and what they're doing with a starship." He knew that Spock was, of course, right. He had no business being drawn into a dangerous pursuit based sheerly on his own impatience, his own need to crack the mystery—particularly in view of the standard warnings in force in this area. There was an outside chance that the black starship was a decoy, sent to lure the *Enterprise* back into whatever dwelled in the heart of the Crossroad—into whatever caused the strangely variable readings and un-known energy spectra known these days, for lack of a term better than their discoverer's name, as Turtledove Anoma-lies.

Spock, who had the excellent hearing of Vulcans, raised an eyebrow. Nobody else heard. Before them, the black starship swung again, headed for deep space this time, away from the hazards of the nebula, the forbidden Tau Lyra system. Barrows nipped the *Enterprise* around, cutting down the distance still further. To McCoy, Kirk muttered, "If they think they can flog that thing into warp speed I'd like to see it. . . . Mr. Spock! Names of all Federation starships out of service. . . ."

"The *Constellation, Valiant,* and *Intrepid* were all de-stroyed at a recent date—definite evidence of their destruc-tion. In fact"—the Vulcan straightened up and glanced

from Kirk to the dark shape on the screen before them—
"there has never been a case of a Constitution-class starship
simply vanishing without a trace."

"Then who the hell are they?" demanded McCoy, and
Spock gave him the eyebrow again.

"I trust that is a rhetorical question, Doctor."

"They're losing power, sir," cut in Barrows, and Kirk
could see the reddish glow of the other system's engine's
waning visibly. "Sensors indicate internal systems may be
breaking down. It's hard to tell, there's some weird shielding
there."

"Hailing frequency open, Captain."

Kirk cut in the mike. "Then let's see what they have to say
for themselves."

The carrier signal was bad, drowning in a flux of static.
Kirk sharpened his voice to the hard edge that had the best
chance of being heard, and said, "This is Captain James T.
Kirk of the United Federation of Planets *Starship Enterprise*. You are in violation of Federation shipping regulations and of the Federation Prime Directive. Please display
identification codes and state your name and your business
in Federation space."

The static swelled, filling the bridge with its harsh crackle.
For a long minute there was silence, though Kirk sensed a
listening, as if he could see someone standing as he stood, in
the darkened bridge of the craft silhouetted against the
luminous veils of shifting dust.

"Are they reading us?" he asked softly.

Mahase touched the comm set in her ear. "They should
be."

"If there is an energy drain," surmised Spock, glancing up
briefly from his station, "the life-support systems may well
be affected. The last transmissions from the *Harriet Tubman* indicated not only power loss but a series of unexplained power surges and overloads once they came within
the nebula itself."

"There's someone alive over there, all right," said Barrows suddenly. "They're making a run for it."

On the front screen the black vessel heeled and dropped,

trying to plunge beneath the *Enterprise* and away to safety. Kirk snapped, "Get a tractor beam on them, Mr. Dykstra!" even as Barrows hit the helm, dropping the starship downward like a guillotine blade toward the fugitive vessel. The unknown ship veered, banked, trying sluggishly to stay out of the limits of the beam. But its reserves were depleted, its pilot at the limit of endurance.

"We've got them, Captain," Barrows reported.

"Put her in reverse, then," said Kirk. "Let them tow us for a while."

The dark ship's engines glowed, flared. Then there was a spurt of red from the nacelles, and their brightness dulled from red to brown as their inner heat bled away into the cold black of vacuum. Spock reported, "Interior power in the ship exhausted. Life-support systems closing down."

Kirk leaned to the transceiver on his chair arm and spoke again over the sea-roar of static. "This is the Federation *Starship Enterprise,* repeat, this is the *Enterprise.* Come in."

"They're drifting, Captain," reported Barrows. "Engines dead."

"Maybe more than the engines," Mahase added softly.

"Are you getting any life readings?" Kirk glanced back at Spock.

The V of the Vulcan's slanted brows deepened. "Unclear, Captain. The ship is, as Lieutenant Barrows observed, very heavily—and rather oddly—shielded. Moreover, what readings I get are extremely unusual and warped by what appears to be mu-spectrum radiation originating from a point within the ship."

"Mu-spectrum?" Lao looked sharply up from the post he had taken at the weapons console. "But that's . . ." He cut himself off, conscious he had broken into the conversation of his commanders.

". . . highly characteristic of the Turtledove Anomalies," finished Kirk thoughtfully.

Then, over the buzz of static, a man's voice, hoarse with strain as if fighting for air to speak. "Federation . . ."

"Do you copy?" demanded Kirk. "You're in serious trouble. Prepare to beam over."

"No," whispered the voice. There was another sound, another voice perhaps, and the violent hiss of steam.

Coolant in the console coils, thought Kirk. *The whole bridge system must be rupturing.* The static peaked, swamping that exhausted voice as it gasped again, "Never . . ."

Kirk traded a glance with Spock. "Cyanotic disorientation?"

"Or one hell of a guilty conscience," put in McCoy.

On the screen before them, the dulling engines of the black ship flared again, sharp and orange. Kirk felt the vibration of the tractor beam through the decking as the other ship made one final, futile effort to break free. Then the brief glow died.

Kirk hit the toggle of the comm link. "Mr. Organa, prepare a boarding party. Full combat and environmental protection. Dr. McCoy, get Nurse Chapel and yourself suited out and join us. . . ." He flipped the toggle to the ship-to-ship link. "Unknown Starship, we're going to board you and take you off, if you won't come of your own accord," he said.

There was silence. Kirk nodded to McCoy, who turned to leave the bridge. Then, with agonizing slowness, the voice spoke again over the subspace link. "Surrender," it said thickly. "Beam us . . . coordinates . . ."

Kirk was already on his feet, speaking down into the comm link to Transporter. "Get a fix on them; I'm coming down. Security to Transporter Room Two. Mr. Winfield, you have the conn."

"Is there anything in any of the standard warnings about this area that concerns—well—any of this?"

Lao's question broke the uneasy silence of the turbolift as the lighted bands of floors flashed across the lift's dark viewing bar. Kirk, absorbed in his own speculations, looked at him in momentary surprise: Lao's brilliance, his expertise with computers, and the obviousness of his mechanical and physical abilities sometimes masked his youth and inexperience.

A curious thing, thought Kirk, being a mentor. It didn't

make him feel old, precisely, but it did make him realize how far he himself had come in the almost five years of the *Enterprise*'s mission. It did make him aware that instead of being thirty-four now, he was only a few months short of forty.

"Not . . . as such."

Lao's brows descended, baffled. Spock explained, "The standard warnings in this sector deal with probabilities of the unexpected. Within five parsecs of any proven or suspected Anomaly Point, there seems to be a higher percentage of unlikely occurrences: a seven percent increase in computer malfunctions not provably due to operator or mechanical error; a four percent increase in overall statistical variation of biochemical experiments . . ."

"And most incidents of infestation by yagghorth," said Kirk quietly, "seem to take place within five parsecs of Anomaly Points."

Lao flinched. As well he might, Kirk thought. He himself had never seen a yagghorth—some ascribed the name to some ancient reader of H. P. Lovecraft in Starfleet, but there was disturbing evidence of different origins—but he'd been on board vessels that had been infested, and had helped retrieve the remains of crewmen from the vent tubes and ducts where the creatures customarily stored their prey.

And he'd seen the tapes. In the past few weeks, he was positive that everyone on the ship had seen the tapes, just as they'd read the reports about the *Tubman*'s disappearance. Even the best of them was unclear, having been found in a jettison pod in Sector Eight; it had been made after the ship's power had blown, and the skeletal shape, the gleaming, squidlike head and dripping tentacles, had been lit only by the fires of the unknown merchant vessel's burning engine room. But the image itself—eyeless, hissing, swaying as it ripped bodies open with the neat ghastliness of a razor—was the stuff of nightmares, like an escapee from the blackest pits of Hell.

"One couldn't get in through our shielding, could it?" Lao tried very hard to sound casual. "I mean, Constitution-class starships are pretty much proof against anything, aren't they?"

The door slipped open before them, to the cool, even lighting of the Deck Seven corridors, the bright uniforms of the men and women of the second watch as they went about their jobs.

"Ensign," Kirk said, "the first thing you're going to find out about deep space is that nothing is proof against everything that's out there—and that what we can imagine is not how it's going to be."

Chapter Two

THE GOLD SHIMMER of the beam chamber was solidifying into humanoid shapes as Kirk, Spock, and Ensign Lao entered Transporter Room Three. Dr. McCoy and Christine Chapel were already there, unshipping the collapsible gurney from behind its magnetized wall panel. Injectors of tri-ox, adrenaline, and antishock were already laid out. Mr. DeSalle was there, too, with a couple of burly redshirts. At the transport console with Mr. Kyle—making adjustments to allow for the peculiar shielding on the black ship—Mr. Scott reported, "There's only six of them, Captain."

"That doesn't mean they won't come out shooting." Kirk had picked up fugitive crews before. Besides, these people had been ready to choose death in the cold of space before surrender to the Federation. It argued, as McCoy had said, for fairly guilty consciences.

"Phasers on stun, Mr. DeSalle."

The sparkling columns of gold coalesced.

Humanoid, at any rate.

Beside him, Nurse Chapel took an involuntary step forward.

One of the fugitives, a Vulcan boy in late adolescence, was unconscious, supported by the small, thin man in the center

14

of the group. This man made a swift move, swiftly checked as Chapel halted like one not willing to startle a frightened, and potentially dangerous, beast. The other members of the newcomer crew closed defensively around them, but Kirk knew instinctively that that thin, nondescript individual, with his burned hands and baggy, cinder-colored clothing, was their leader.

Kirk stepped forward. "You are under arrest on suspicion of piracy. I'm Captain James T. Kirk; you're aboard the Federation *Starship Enterprise.*"

The reaction was the last thing he expected. One man— tall and lanky with dark hair stiff with sweat—laughed, a cracked bark of overstrained nerves. The curvaceous Orion woman widened her eyes in astonishment and glanced across at another crewman, short and dark and cherubic, who started to speak, a look of protest in his eyes.

The fugitive captain said, "Not now, Thad."

The tall Klingon woman behind him stepped forward and put a supporting arm around the unconscious Vulcan boy's waist.

The leader held up his hands to show them empty. "I'm Dylan Arios," he said. His hair was green, hanging in stringy points against the prominent cheekbones and square, fragile jaw. The hue of the discolored flesh around the watchful green eyes, the stains on the makeshift bandages that decorated his fingers and wrists spoke of alien blood.

McCoy looked up from his tricorder. "Get that boy on the gurney," he ordered shortly, and after a moment's hesitation—and a nod from Arios—the Klingon woman half-carried the Vulcan boy forward, Chapel stepping up onto the transport platform to help.

The three remaining on the platform—the Orion girl, at whom Lao and every other man in the room were gazing with frank admiration; the young man called Thad; and the tall, scar-faced man who had laughed—stirred among themselves as if they would speak, but Arios held up his hand again warningly and said, "Not now." His voice was the light, scratchy tenor Kirk had heard over the roar of static from the black starship's bridge. Turning back to Kirk, he explained, "We had a leak in the subsidiary reactor. Our med section went down."

"That your whole crew?" McCoy adjusted oxygen over the boy's waxen face, ran a scanner quickly along his chest, and noted the dangerous levels of toxins in the blood, the shock, trauma, exhaustion. "The six of you?"

Arios nodded, after a fraction of a second's hesitation. "Stay with Sharnas, Phil," he said, and the tall man stepped down from the platform.

"Will do, Master." He caught very briefly at the corner of the gurney to steady himself, but let it go immediately.

DeSalle cast a quick glance at Kirk as Chapel pushed the gurney toward the turbolift doors, Phil following in her wake; Kirk nodded, and DeSalle signaled one of the redshirts to join the little procession down to sickbay.

"We couldn't get your readings clearly," explained Arios, folding his arms and stepping back as McCoy aimed the scanner in his direction. "We were attacked in the nebula by a ship we barely saw. It put out our visual, so all we were getting of you was your mass and power readings, and they were close to our attacker's. Our power was almost exhausted. Flight was our only recourse."

"You couldn't . . ." began Lao, but Kirk signaled him silent.

Kirk could feel through his skin that the man was lying, and knew that an inquiry as to why Arios had refused surrender even after his pursuer was identified as Starfleet would only get him another lie. All he said was "I see." At his nod DeSalle and his remaining guard stepped back and clipped their weapons.

Arios gestured with fingers like knotted grass stalks under the bandages, to the others still standing on the transport disks. "Adajia of Orion," he introduced. "Raksha . . ."

"Pleased," murmured the Klingon woman, coal eyes taking in not only the room but the men in it with the speculative air of one working out some mathematical puzzle in her head. A renegade? wondered Kirk. Or a watchdog for the real masters, whatever Arios's crew might call *him?* The Vulcan boy—Kirk didn't think he was a

Romulan—looked young to be a renegade, but it was within the realm of possibility.

"Thaddeus . . ." There was a moment's pause while Arios fished almost visibly for a name. ". . . Smith." The cherub-faced young man opened his mouth to protest, but Raksha kneed him sharply in the side of the leg. During the rest of the conversation Kirk was peripherally aware of Thad soundlessly repeating the name "Smith" to himself to remember it.

"The Vulcan's name is Sharnas T'Gai Khir—his *akhra-*name, that is."

His real name, Kirk guessed, like Mr. Spock's, would be unpronounceable. He was interested to see his Vulcan science officer's left eyebrow cant sharply upward, but taking his cue from the captain, Spock made no comment. Kirk thought Mr. Scott, finished now with double-checking the console readings, might have said something; the engineer was watching Raksha, the Klingon woman, with wary suspicion at the way she was observing every detail of the room around her. Kirk himself was more interested in the others: the way Adajia was staying as close to Arios as she could, and the blank, barely controlled dread in Thad's eyes.

"That's Phil Cooper with Sharnas," Arios went on. "My astrogator and supercargo. We're free traders."

There was a saying in Starfleet: *Every smuggler is a free trader to his friends.* But again Kirk only nodded. By their oddly assorted clothing—to say nothing of a Klingon and a Vulcan in the same crew—this scruffy rabble could have been free traders, but they lacked the typical free traders' air of careless outlandishness. The black starship might, indeed, have carried smuggled goods—something Kirk intended to find out at the earliest possible moment—but his instincts told him there was something else afoot.

Softly, Mr. Scott said, "For free traders, ye've got the weirdest engine readings I've ever seen," but despite Raksha's sidelong glance, Arios made no sign that he heard.

"You can talk to 'em now, Jim," said McCoy, making a note of his scanner readings and slipping the instrument back into its pack. "But I want to see every single one of these people in sickbay inside two hours." Raksha angled her head to look down over the doctor's shoulder at his tricorder, calculation in her narrowed dark eyes.

"We found the ship derelict on the fringes of the Crossroad Nebula," Arios said, limping a little as he followed Kirk from the transporter room and around the corner to the briefing room next to the brig. DeSalle and his stalwarts trailed unobtrusively behind. "Her ID codes and log were wiped. We call her the *Nautilus.*"

Kirk recognized the name of the first atomic-powered submarine on Earth, and deduced that someone on board was an enthusiast, like himself, of old-time naval history. At a guess, he reflected, that would be Phil Cooper. Despite his battered, makeshift clothes, that young man still had military bearing.

"When was this?"

The door of the briefing room slid open before them. Arios and Raksha passed through on Kirk's heels, but Kirk was interested to notice that Thaddeus and Adajia hesitated, glancing first behind them at the two armed security officers, then, as if for reassurance, at their master. The Orion girl was keyed up, ready to flee or fight like a wildcat. Thaddeus was frankly, almost pathetically, scared, dark eyes flickering here and there like those of a small animal in a trap, sweat trickling down the black stubble of his round cheeks. At a nod from Arios he edged into the room and took a seat beside Raksha, who was examining the triangular viewscreen in the center of the table as unobtrusively as possible.

Kirk took a seat at the head of the table, Mr. Spock to his left and Arios to his right, Scott beside Spock and Lao at the far end with a small recorder and a log pad. The door slipped soundlessly shut, and DeSalle and his men made themselves as inconspicuous as bodyguards can. Under the table, Kirk touched the signal button to request additional guards outside the door. He had the feeling both Arios and Raksha knew he did it.

Picking his words carefully, Arios said, "We found the *Nautilus* four, maybe five days ago." Too recently, Kirk could almost hear him thinking, to have reported the find to authorities.

"And you left your own ship?"

"We had it in tow until we were attacked in the Crossroad." Dylan Arios had the most wonderful air of elflike innocence Kirk had encountered since his last brush with that redoubtable conman Harry Mudd. "The aft tractor beam went out and we lost it."

"We've been observin' the Crossroad for days now," said Mr. Scott, folding his hands and keeping the same watchful eye on Raksha. "I'd take oath nothing went into it from this side, and so far as anybody knows, there's nothing out there to go into it from the other side."

Arios only shook his head. "We never got a clear look at them," he said. "The first shot came out of nowhere and took out our visual. From then we were running blind."

"And you were headed to Tau Lyra Three for refuge?"

He caught the glance that went between Raksha and Adajia, saw the Orion girl's eyes widen. *"That* was . . . ?"

"We weren't sure." Arios's voice cut smoothly over hers.

A little sharply, Kirk said, "The Tau Lyra system is marked on every star chart, and in the guidance computer of every Fleet ship. And it's marked, incidentally, as Protected. There are warning buoys posted—you passed the first line of them. Landing on the third planet, orbit of that or any other planet in the system, or approach closer than the inner planets of the system, by any spaceflight civilization, even in case of life-threatening emergency, can be construed as a violation of the Non-Interference Directive. If you've received enough training to pilot a space vessel of any kind, you'd have known that."

Raksha's mouth curved in an expression of irony; Adajia was frowning protestingly. Thaddeus, baffled, began, "But the Federation . . ."

"Shut up, Thad," snapped Raksha, and Kirk's gaze snapped to the little man.

"The Federation?" he prompted.

Thad shrugged, with an ingenuous grin. "I forgot. Sorry. I'm only a Secondary."

Kirk turned back to study Arios for a time in silence. "The name and ID number of your own ship?"

"The *Antelope*," said Arios, his eyes resting speculatively on Kirk's face.

"Registration numbers?"

Arios made no reply. After a moment Spock looked up from the central table terminal and said, "There is no record of any vessel of that name in Starfleet records."

Watching their faces, Kirk saw that Thad was startled, Adajia puzzled. Raksha's mouth quirked in a kind of wry satisfaction, like that of a prophet who has pronounced the doom of a city and seen it burned before her. Arios only nodded, thoughtful.

Thad began protestingly, "But Master, the . . ." and received a sharp glance from Raksha.

Kirk's eyes returned to the fugitive captain again, noting once more the odd, alien bones that seemed to have more joints than they should have, the grass-colored hair. "Have you any explanation for this?"

The green eyes met his: then Arios shook his head. His eyelashes were green, too. "Not at the moment, no."

"Nor for the fact that no Federation starship is listed as missing?"

"Convergent evolution?" suggested Raksha snidely, and Thad began, "What's convergent . . . ?"

Arios signed them both silent. "I don't understand it either," he said, with a good imitation of frankness. "But we did find the vessel derelict. We have done nothing wrong."

Thad startled noticibly and Adajia became absorbed in turning one of her jeweled bracelets to the proper position on her slender wrist; the Klingon, Kirk observed, was watching the faces of those around the table intently from under long black lashes. For what, he would have given a good deal to know.

Arios continued quietly, "If you wish to hold us and check for criminal records with the Federation, by all means do so. . . ."

Thad blenched but said nothing.

". . . but you'll find that none of us has a record of any sort."

Kirk's eyes narrowed. "You may not have," he said. "But as of now you're detained pending investigation of charges of piracy and suspected intent to violate the Prime Directive. Mr. DeSalle . . ."

The security chief stepped forward, and Arios rose, signaling the others to do the same.

"Place Captain Arios and his crew in the brig. Send in Dr. McCoy to see them under appropriate guard. Mr. Spock, prepare to come with me over to that ship . . ."

"NO!" Arios, Raksha, Thad, and Adajia almost overset their chairs springing up; Arios caught Kirk involuntarily by the sleeve. Then the *Nautilus*'s four crewmen looked at one another hesitantly, not sure what to say next.

"Probably not a good idea." Raksha leaned casually on the end of the table, trying to pretend that no one had seen the momentary alarm and horror in her eyes. "We had trouble with built-in defenses on the ship. It's honeycombed with booby traps . . ."

"And stinking with reactor fumes," added Adajia brightly, unhooking a raven curl from where it had tangled in an earring.

"Captain Kirk," said Arios, "I'd advise against it." The hand that he'd put on Kirk's arm, as if to forcibly keep him from going out the door, he removed now, but Kirk could see the bandaged fingers shaking with exhaustion and strain. "As Raksha says, when we went aboard we found some pretty nasty defenses built in. We haven't had nearly time enough to explore the ship, let alone disarm half the defenses we *did* find. If you're going on board, take me along."

Kirk studied him for a long moment, trying to fathom the genuine fear he saw in the Master's green eyes. Beyond him, he was aware that Raksha had lost her air of cynical detachment; there was fear there, too. Surely more fear than of discovered contraband? And what contraband would be worth death by cold and suffocation in a dying ship?

Fear of what?

"I'll take that under advisement," Kirk said thoughtfully. "Mr. DeSalle, take them away."

"Promise." Arios pulled away from DeSalle's hand on his shoulder. "Don't go on board the *Nautilus* without me or Raksha. Please."

"Lock them up," Kirk said. "Raksha and Arios in separate cells; Adajia and Thaddeus can stay together." Both of them had given him looks of appalled horror, and Adajia, further, backed a step toward the corner as if she'd make a fight of it. "Mr. Spock?" He turned to the Vulcan as the crew of the *Nautilus* was led from the briefing room.

Mr. Spock, while everyone else had been grouped around the door, had remained seated, flipping screen after screen of information through the terminal on the table. Now, as the others departed he looked up, the reflected blue glow highlighting the odd bones of his face.

"No record of any ship—Federation, free trader, ally—named the *Antelope*," he reported. "As previously noted, no record of any starship missing, nor of any partially constructed but uncommissioned starship unaccounted for. Analysis of the *Nautilus*'s outline indicates the most recent innovations in starship design. No match on retina or DNA scans of either of the men calling themselves Phil Cooper or Thaddeus Smith; naturally, no records available on either the Orion or the Klingon; preliminary scanner analysis of Captain Arios indicates human-alien hybrid with some as yet unknown alien race. And the T'Gai Khir," he added, steepling his long fingers, "are relatives of mine, the affilium currently entitled to use the name consisting of five ancestors over the age of two hundred and fifty, a matriarch, four daughters, and a son in the Vulcan Science Academy who is forty-seven years old, unmarried, and whose name is not Sharnas."

Chapter Three

"HE'S RESTING EASIER NOW." Christine Chapel touched a stylus point to her log pad to note the readings on the diagnostic above the sleeping Vulcan boy's head, checked the feed gauge on the measured dosage of antishock, and turned back to the lanky young man slumped in the chair against the wall.

Phil Cooper's head jerked up sharply. He'd been dropping off to sleep. "Good." He rubbed a hand over his unshaven face. "God knows he took the worst of it, when the coils blew. At least the rest of us were on the bridge."

"What was he doing down in the engineering hull?" asked Chapel softly. Even with him in deeply sedated sleep, the ghost of pain shadowed the boy's bruised eyelids and odd-shaped lips. His hair, long enough to braid away from the narrow temples, framed a face that had the yellow-green cast Mr. Spock's did, when Spock was hurt.

"I've heard of boys that young being apprentice engineers, but he should never have been down there alone."

"No . . . I mean yes. I mean . . . Sharnas is . . . is sort of an . . . Well, he had to be down there." Cooper shook his head tiredly. "Dylan—the Master—is the engineer, but he had to be on the bridge, you see. He's kept that impulse

23

drive together for two years with engine tape and spit, but coming through the Crossroad was like being rolled down a hill in a barrel of rocks." He rubbed his face again, his hand shaking with fatigue. His color was bad, too, his brows and the dark stubble of his beard standing blackly against a bloodless, exhausted face.

Chapel made no comment on the discrepancy between the Master keeping the *Nautilus*'s impulse drive together for two years with engine tape and spit, and the Master's own contention that he'd found the black ship four days ago like a bottle half-buried in sand at the beach.

"Nurse Chapel." McCoy came in from the lab next door, the colored sheets of digitalized internal photographs in hand and an expression of bafflement on his face. He halted for a moment, studying Cooper, then said, "I think you could stand a once-over yourself, Mr. Cooper."

Cooper waved dismissively. "I'm fine." He was younger than he looked, thought Chapel, studying his face in profile. The gray eyes were already netted with deep-cut lines of strain as well as laughter, and there was gray in the stiff brown hair.

"The hell you are." McCoy handed Chapel the sheaf of IPs and brought up his scanner. Cooper stiffened, as if in spite of being at the limits of his physical endurance he was readying for an attack. "This shows you're suffering from low-level rhodon poisoning and borderline shock due to trauma. Burns, from the reading, and pretty severe ones . . ."

The young man flinched back as McCoy moved toward him, and said again, "I'm fine. The Master told me to look after Sharnas. . . ."

"We'll look after Sharnas," said McCoy firmly. "It's our job. You need rest, and if I have to use a jolt of lexorin to give it to you, I will."

Chapel, who had been looking at the top shot of the pile, raised her head, baffled. It was a readout of the Vulcan's nervous system, an early one taken—by the look of the electrosynaptic patterns—before the antishock and relaxants had gone into effect.

24

But it wasn't the blurry galaxy of synaptic firings that caught her eye. Among the pinks and blues of the central nerve column itself could be seen a series of white dropout shapes, spreading out into a mesh of threads in the medulla and up into the cortex itself.

Cooper, who'd started to his feet as McCoy came toward him, settled back on the lab stool where he'd been, but he still looked ready to attack if McCoy got within arm's reach of him, which, Chapel noticed, the doctor was careful not to do. For a man with as good a *shucks-I'm-just-a-country-doctor* act as McCoy had, her colleague had picked up a fine-tuned reflex for self-preservation in his four years on the *Enterprise.*

McCoy looked up from the tricorder, his blue eyes narrow and hard. "Turn around," he ordered.

Cooper only regarded him warily.

"Turn around," McCoy reiterated. "I want to see what that is on the back of your neck. Your friend there has it, too . . ." He nodded toward the sleeping Vulcan. ". . . and from the preliminary readings, so does Captain Arios, so turn around and let me look at it or I'll call Yeoman Wolfman in here and have him turn you around."

Cooper's hand slipped down to grasp the leg of the stool, and for a moment Chapel, gauging the distance to the Emergency button that would have summoned the security officer in the next room, thought he'd start swinging. McCoy didn't move, nor did his eyes flinch from his patient's. Then Cooper relaxed, and said quietly, "What the hell. You've probably guessed anyway."

He turned around on the stool and bowed his head, his arms folded across his chest. Where the dark hair parted to fall on either side of his bent neck Chapel could see a chain of ragged, X-shaped scars and the dull glint of metal protruding from the skin.

"It's Fleet issue," Cooper said in that same low, resigned voice. "The Master keeps it open and short-wires the receptors every couple of months. He does it for Sharnas, too, as well as he can." He turned his head slightly, and in spite of the sweat that stood suddenly on his face, and the chalky grayness of his lips, there was a gleam of cynicism in his eyes. "But if you want my real name and my Starfleet ID number you're just going to have to run a DNA scan."

McCoy stared at him, nonplussed. "You're telling me *Starfleet* did that to you?"

"It wasn't the fairies at my christening." Cooper turned around and leaned his shoulders against the wall again. His eyes were slipping shut; he shook his head sharply, to keep from nodding. "How else are they gonna keep folks like us in line?"

McCoy sprang forward as Cooper began to slip sideways; Chapel dropped the charts and strode to help him. The *Nautilus*'s astrogator didn't even open his eyes as Chapel and McCoy carried him to the other bed; McCoy dug out his hypo and administered a dose of antishock, checked his tricorder readings, and said, "Get me a vial apiece of masiform and dalpomine, and the burn kit."

When Chapel came back, McCoy had rolled his patient over and stripped off his shirt, revealing, as he'd guessed, that the trauma readings resulted from two long strips of blistering flesh across the right shoulder and down Cooper's back, the sort of burns that result from falling cables in a blowout. As she helped McCoy strip the makeshift bandages someone had put on them back on the *Nautilus,* Chapel's eyes were drawn once again to the half-healed line of slashes and scars that ran from the first thoracic vertebra up through the cervical and into the sweat-damp hair.

"Starfleet . . ." she said softly. "Doctor, experiments in neurological control—if that's what that is—are outlawed."

"Even if they weren't," replied McCoy, spraying the burned area with traumex and neatly cutting feathercap dressing with the eye of an artist, "those implants are so far beyond anything I've even heard of that I'm not sure how they'd work. His look simple—I'm going to run another scan of them while he's out—but by the look of the IPs, the boy's run on up into the conscious centers of the brain. God knows what they're for."

He stepped back, surveying his patient, then turned and

looked over his shoulder at the bobbing golden triangles on the readout above the Vulcan boy's still form.

"But either he's run into an alien civilization that has convinced him—or programmed him—to lie . . . or there's something very strange going on in Starfleet."

Clothed in close-fitting black exercise togs, his sweat-damp black hair hanging in his eyes, the *Enterprise*'s first-shift helmsman looked very different from his usual efficient self on the bridge.

TAU LYRA III
Status—Level 1 Protected
Highest technological level—Electricity level 3
General technological level—Steam level 5
Civilization Class K—Unified-diversified
Planetary type M
Cultural zones—20
Radio linguistic count—8
Climate—Moderate polar/tropical
Forest cover 45%
Water cover 73%
Sentient Civilized species—1
Sentient Noncivilized species—2–4 (?)

All information based upon flyby probes (SD 1547.8, 1790.11, 2018.3)

Planet Tau Lyra III was flagged as potential protected SD 1798.9 on the basis of radio signals, granted Federation Level 1 protected status, standard proximity zone established at cometary field. (See minutes, Prime Directive Committee, Federation Council, 9-7-2261 and Promulgations, 2261.) Sentient Civilized Species refer to themselves as Yoons, planet most commonly referred to as Yoondri in radio broadcasts. (See broadcast analysis report #3—Tau Lyra III). According to Dr. Feshan Kznith of the Vulcan Science Academy, analysis of radio signals is difficult because of suspected high telepathic component of the language. In the twelve standard years of observation no major conflicts have been observed, and flybys indicate no evidence of major military violence for at least fifty standard years, perhaps two or three times that long. Neither have any major advances in technology been reported or observed, though because of telepathic component of the language it is difficult to determine this.

Tau Lyra III has no strategic, military, or commerical importance. Location could possibly be used should observation of the Crossroad Nebula become necessary, but artificial station in cometary field is at least as economically feasible, depending on cultural receptivity of the Yoons.

Standard warnings apply to all planets in the system. See journal articles . . .

"So what would they want there?" asked Mr. Sulu, flipping a screen-split and touching in the code for the well-circulated files concerning standard warnings, Standing Hazards, and the *Harriet Tubman.*

Navigator Pavel Chekov came back from the rec room's dispenser with three cups of coffee balanced in his hands. "Just our luck that it happened off our watch."

He shook his head, and Lieutenant Uhura, graceful in her bright-colored warm-up tights, pointed out, "Tonia and the others should be off in an hour. We can ask them."

In the far corner of the almost deserted rec room, Christine Chapel all but felt the young navigator's glance cross to her, but Uhura raised one slender finger, stilling whatever suggestion Chekov would have made about questioning her. For that she was grateful. McCoy's speculations —and her own, regarding what Cooper had said, the readings she'd been getting on the IPs and delta scans of the two strangers in sickbay—had troubled her deeply.

For four years now, Starfleet had been her home, the only place she had left, it seemed. It contained her only friends— and the man she loved. She wondered what the information —the ambiguous possibilities that those fragments of speculation had revealed—meant to the choice that was coming closer and closer.

She looked wearily at the reader screen in front of her.

RETURN TO CIVILIAN STATUS?
  ○ Yes   ○ No

DESTINATION OF OUT-MUSTER?
  ○ San Francisco—Earth
  ○ Memory Alpha
  ○ Vulcan—Central Port
  ○ Other _____

PREFERENCE FOR REASSIGNMENT?
  ○ Planetary (list in separate annex file in order of preference)
  ○ Starfaring (list in separate annex file in order of preference)

There's something very strange going on in Starfleet....
At this hour—shortly after 2230—the big rec room on Deck Eight was clearing out. Small groups sat around the scattered tables, playing cards or eating a late dessert, some in uniform if that was their habit, others in exercise clothes, or the civilian togs from their homes. Quite a number, Chapel saw, were occupying the reader screens.

Three months, she thought, and the voyage would be over. The five-year mission would be done.

They would all have to choose anew.

On the viewscreen above the table where Uhura, Chekov, and Sulu sat, the piped-in image of the *Enterprise*'s main viewscreen hung like a square of diamond-studded velvet, the black shape of the *Nautilus* a nearly invisible riddle in the darkness.

"There's no dilithium reported on the planet," Sulu was saying. "No metebelite, no brain-spice, no rare elements at all. From any starting point you care to name, it's a backwater, the end of nowhere."

"Could be a smuggler's drop, maybe?" suggested Chekov, putting a foot on a chair and leaning his elbows on his knee.

"Why choose a system where the whole shebang is ringed in a proximity zone?" Uhura sipped her coffee, frowning a little at the screen. "There are other deserted worlds in this system with the same atmospherics and gravity, aren't there?"

"Gamma Helicon Two's almost identical," agreed Sulu.

"Almost." Chekov seized on the word. "Maybe we should see where the differences lie? That might have something to do with their choice."

"If they had a choice."

Chapel, her eyes already returning to the form on her own reader screen, almost laughed at the aptness of the phrase. *If they had a choice.*

The last definite choice she had made—to abandon her biochemical studies, to turn her energies to the painstaking, heart-killing business of searching for the man she had then loved in all the vastness of eternity—had ended for her in such bitterness, in such confusion and pain, that for years now she had simply drifted.

Would she have been better off, or worse, if the *Enterprise* had never made planetfall on Exo III? If she'd never known whether Roger Corby was alive or dead? If she'd never found him? At least, she thought wearily, she'd still have the search.

She'd made friends on the *Enterprise*. Uhura, jigsaw buddy and confidant of a thousand late rec-room nights. Dr. McCoy, more a friend than a boss—she wondered where he would be signing on again. If he'd mind her continuing as his nurse, his second-in-command of whatever ship's medical department he wound up leading . . . *If* he chose Starfleet again.

Spock . . .

Her heart seemed to squeeze up inside her, as if crushed by a giant fist, and she felt defeated and utterly lost.

Her biomedical credential incomplete, she was only borderline qualified for a Science Department position—and there was no guarantee that if she asked for the ship of his next posting, she'd get it.

And she knew it was a childish thing, a schoolgirlish thing, to do anyway.

Follow your heart, Uhura had said to her once—more than once. Only Chapel suspected that her heart had a broken navigation computer.

"Could they be tracking some kind of space debris?" Uhura suggested, leaning forward to study the map Sulu had called up to the single—and now badly overloaded—reader screen beneath the dark viewscreen of the silent ship. "Maybe they're following some kind of unknown component, like the *Tubman* reported finding, and it drifted down to Tau Lyra Three. . . ."

"And didn't burn up in the atmosphere?"

"Come on, Pavel, you have no idea what kind of shielding it might have!"

"Christine?"

She looked up quickly, to see Ensign Lao Zhiming standing at her side.

He was still in uniform, his log pad still under his arm. He must have just come from the captain's second briefing with Spock and Mr. Scott—probably covering almost the identical points of speculation being indulged in around the reader screen by the first-shift bridge crew at this very moment. There was a slight line of worry, of concentration, between his brows.

"Anything decided?" she asked. "Or did they ask you not to say?"

Lao shook his head, pulled up a chair beside her. "I don't think it's anything classified," he said. "They're going to run scans on the ship before going across—Mr. Scott brought out his whole collection of schematics for Klingon booby traps, and with the shielding on that ship there's no telling about some of them. But in the end someone's going to have to go over."

He sounded hopeful. Chapel had to smile.

"Has Dr. McCoy examined the others?" he asked, after a moment's hesitation. "Or—questioned them? About what they're doing on that ship?"

Chapel shook her head. "Tomorrow," she said. "Most of them dropped off dead asleep the minute the doctor finished the preliminary scan." She frowned, seeing the worry in his eyes and remembering . . .

"Thad," she said, suddenly understanding his concern, and what it was he was trying to find out.

He nodded.

"He doesn't have any of the DNA markers for Pelleter's syndrome, or Tak's," she said, a little diffidently. "I understand those are the only two kinds that they haven't found a way to treat."

"Yet." He raised his head, and his eyes were bright with a kind of defiance, hope, and anger mingled—anger at fate, at those who accepted fate. "Yet." Then he sighed, and some of the banty-cock flash of energy seemed to go out of him. He folded his arms around the log pad and looked down at the floor for a time.

"Your brother has Pelleter's syndrome, doesn't he?"

Lao nodded. Chapel remembered going with Lao on a massive raid on a toystore on Andorus, watching the young man buy everything in sight with his usual delighted ebullience—a scene that would have been genuinely funny had not the intended recipient of the toys been thirty years old.

"Smith doesn't seem nearly as bad as Qixhu," he said, after a time. "He might have started off worse but have a condition which can be augmented up, but the thing is, I've got no idea how he could have ended up in a spacegoing crew. Even somebody like Smith would be kept an eye on by Assist Services, to make sure nobody takes advantage of him. A smuggler or a pirate crew would have to go to a lot of trouble to get someone like him on board."

Something very strange . . . McCoy's words flashed through Chapel's mind again.

Lao was looking at the re-up form on the reader screen, his dark, straight brows drawn down with something akin to pain.

"My mother says he asks about me every day. When am I

coming back? How long have I been gone? He doesn't understand."

He shook his head. "He never could understand why I could go into space and he couldn't. He didn't like the training to operate a machine—which is all he's able to do, really—and the drug therapy made his head hurt. He used to cry when they wouldn't let him follow me to school."

He was silent, as if, through the darkness of the screen, he was looking to some other scene: to a big, awkward boy in a padded blue coat, standing in the Beijing snowfall, watching his small brother walk away from him.

"I didn't like to leave him on Earth. I know Assist Services takes good care of him, and he has a job, and people to look after him . . . but it isn't the same. I know it isn't the same." His eyes closed, as if he could not look at that scene, could not look into his own guilt. "But I had to make my choice."

"We all do," said Chapel softly. She reached over, and flipped off the reader screen, unmarked, unchosen, unsaved. "We all do."

Chapter Four

THE FIRST THING Yeoman Wein of Security knew about Dylan Arios's escape from the brig some eighteen hours later was when he heard, in the corridor behind him, the hissing breath as one of the security doors slipped shut. Startled, Wein sprang to his feet. He was conscious that he'd drifted into momentary reverie triggered by the sight of the lovely Yeoman Shimada turning the corner into the Security lounge a few minutes before, but knew his mental abstraction hadn't lasted long. Besides, how on earth could Arios have escaped and where could he have gone?

The brig corridor—at whose head the guard had his small desk—was thirty meters long and bare of cover, curved just slightly with the hull but not so as to provide any place that was out of the desk guard's line of sight. Wein went to check the first door opposite him. Through the crystal-hard plex of the door he saw the Klingon Raksha inspecting the cell visicom: an independent unit unattached to the central computer, for obvious reasons.

The second cell, in which Arios had been incarcerated, was empty under the soft white glare of its floodlights, save for something that gleamed on the floor just to the left of the narrow bed.

With a startled curse, Wein hit the door combination and strode in.

When he came to in sickbay afterward, Wein admitted he should have punched the Backup button at his desk first, *then* gone into the cell to check how Arios had escaped and what it was that he'd left on the floor. Wein had no explanation for why he hadn't noticed that Arios had not, in fact, left the cell; at least, he hadn't left it at that point. In fact, Arios *did* leave the cell within moments of Wein's opening the door, just as soon as he'd manhandled the security officer's unconscious body onto the bed and covered him with the light blanket, relieving him in the process of his phaser.

There was, of course, no small, shining object on the floor, nor had there ever been.

"ChadHom . . ." Arios pressed up against the communications grille of the security cell, whispered Raksha's pet name even as he was pulling the faceplate off the touchpad. He'd already raided the drawer of Wein's desk for a cable, which he hooked into the terminal. Through the hard crystal of the door he saw her step close.

"Try IMP/RAN/NUM," she breathed. "And don't call me *chadHom.*"

Arios stepped back to the terminal, rapped out the commands quickly, shook his head.

"IMP/RAN/NET."

Another blank, and Raksha muttered, "Animals copulating all over the place," in Klingon. She thought a moment, then said, "NET/TEST."

The door hissed open.

"I told you it was magic," said Arios, as Raksha strode to the terminal, ripped free the cable, and began rapping out swift strings of commands. "All you've got to do is say the right spell."

"Remind me to explain the extent of your errors the next time we have three uninterrupted days." The black stormcloud of her hair fell forward over her face as she worked, big hands pecking swiftly, delicately over the keys.

Arios took two steps down the corridor, then stepped back to gather her hair into his two hands and bend to kiss the nape of her neck.

"The time after that," he suggested, and she looked back and up at him, into eyes bright as sunlight laughing through leaves. Her own smile turned her face briefly beautiful, and briefly young.

Then he strode off down the corridor, slapping through the code on Thad and Adajia's cell—which Raksha had gotten out of the computer moments before—while the Klingon pulled tight the belt on her doublet and shoved into the resulting pouch not only the cable, but every tool and piece of replacement hardware in the desk drawer. Adajia leaped up from the floor where she'd been sitting—having learned the uses of chairs only recently and not very completely—as the door slid open, and Thad almost flung himself into Arios's arms with a hug of desperate relief. Neither spoke, both having a healthy distrust of hidden microphones; by the time they reached the door of the brig corridor itself Raksha had cross-coupled the programming on the visual pickup to display its own loop, and the four slipped past the door of the Security messroom—contrary to Wein's belief, quite empty—and around the corner to an inspection corridor that would lead, eventually, to Engineering and its attendant shops.

Dr. McCoy stood for a long time looking from his two charges—prone, unconscious, and still naked to the waist from his examination, on the dark plastette of the diagnostic beds—to the bright-colored rectangles of the schematic display, which glowed like the windows of some bizarre cathedral on the screens beside each bed.

He had, quite literally, never seen anything like it in his life.

Under the burn dressing, Phil Cooper's ribs rose and fell gently with the rhythm of his breathing. Eighteen hours of rest and semisedation had stabilized his readings considerably, and his system was starting to respond to the hyperena and other metabolic accelerators. Sharnas T'Gai Khir still barely seemed to live at all. Only the steady movement of peaks and valleys of the brain-wave and heartbeat monitors showed that the boy was not, in fact, the corpse that he looked. His long hair had been brushed aside, and the pattern of messy olive green scars, like the spoor of incompetent butchery, ran from between his shoulder blades up to the base of his skull. Only when studied closely did the delicacy of the technique reveal itself, the sureness with which the incisions followed the nerves themselves. Arios, if it was he who had done this, had known exactly what it was he was looking for and where to look for it . . . whatever it was.

According to the delta and IP schematics, the wiring in both men extended beyond the cut zone, merging with breathtaking imperceptibility into the spinal nerves themselves. Even after nearly a day of continuous study, McCoy wasn't certain how to enter his observations in his log.

God knew what it was for.

It's Fleet issue, Cooper had said, and the weariness, the resignation, in his voice had shocked the doctor almost more than the implications of the implants themselves. The unspoken, *Oh, that stuff.*

You guessed it. You've seen it before. Therefore, you should know who I am.

According to his tricorder readings, taken during the morning's medical exams in the brig, Arios was also heavily wired—and scarred along the back of the neck—and there were some kind of implants in Thad's brain as well.

Some forms of retardation, McCoy knew, were correctable by implant. But the implants themselves were exterior, smooth metal casings several centimeters thick and about a third the area of a man's palm. The technology required to install an interior implant, much less communicate with it, would be extraordinarily advanced. In any case, it didn't seem to have eliminated Thad's condition, though it may have allieviated it—if that's what it was for.

McCoy wasn't entirely sure of that.

The door shut behind him and he returned to his office, where copies of the IPs he'd taken last night and today lay on his desk along with every kind of analysis and schematic he could come up with regarding Arios's physiology, DNA, and probable ancestry.

Those, too, were deeply disquieting in their implications.

"Journal digest," he said to the computer, settling into his chair and reaching for that morning's now-cold coffee.

The screen brightened at the sound of his voice, a plain, blank silver, unbesmirched by letter or line.

"Journal digest," repeated McCoy irritably, glancing at the chronometer. Lags occurred seldom, and only at times of absolute peak use, usually two to three hours into the first two shifts.

It was an hour from the end of the first shift. Everybody would be closing down recreational readers or games now, or gearing workstations over to evening shift. There should be no problem.

"I'm sorry," said the computer. "Please repeat request."

McCoy repeated himself, and the screen blossomed with the red and blue lettering of the index of journal digests. "Give me anything you've got on nanosurgical neurology over the last three Standard months," said McCoy, realizing despairingly how long it had been since he'd had time to thoroughly scan the digests, let alone study the articles themselves.

During his first year on the *Enterprise* McCoy had managed to keep up with them fairly well, as the computer absorbed the stacked and zipped transmissions every time they made port at a starbase and everyone read through the journals and digests at their leisure in between times. But—and McCoy was aware that Chapel, Paxson, and the techs had this problem, too—during the months and years of the starship's voyage, so much new information came in from the exploration of new civilizations, new biospheres, that had to be written up, studied, catalogued, transmitted, that current research by others tended to slip more and more by the board.

Given a choice between reading about someone else's research on genetic manipulation, or artificial optics, or improvements in warp drive physics, and studying a tankful of Kurlanian seedfish, or the fossilized remains of an Elthonian android's eye, McCoy knew what choice he'd make. And had made, repeatedly, over the past four years.

There were only so many hours in a day.

In three months the *Enterprise* would be returning to Earth. Then he'd be faced with the real decision: to re-up for another five-year mission, or to settle down at one of the major universities for the years it would take to analyze and study all that he'd gathered.

He found he didn't like to think about what settling down would mean.

Almost without thinking, he said "Come" to Chapel's signal; the tall woman stood behind his chair, looking over his shoulder at the listing of articles in the digest index. She held a log pad cradled in one elbow, with her own copies of the schematics. He hadn't seen her so fascinated, and so troubled, by a problem in years.

"It might be something so new that it isn't in the journals yet," she surmised, after it became clear to them both that no digest mentioned anything about radically new techniques of central nervous system augmentation, or neurological control, or whatever it was. "And it might be classified, if Starfleet is behind it."

She hesitated a moment, then asked, "That couldn't be true, could it?"

McCoy looked up at her, startled.

"Roger . . ." She brought out the name of her dead lover and mentor—"the Pasteur of archaeological medicine," he'd been called on the infovids, the man for whose sake she'd given up her own career in biomedicine—uncertainly, syllables she hadn't spoken since that weird, terrible, claustrophobic confrontation with what was left of the man on Exo III.

"Roger told me once about . . . I don't know, what he called 'conspiracies' in Starfleet. People who'd take any development, any knowledge, no matter how good or life-saving it was in itself—and use it to add to their own power. I never knew how much of that to believe." Her quick, rueful grin vanished as swiftly as it appeared.

"At the time it always seemed to be conspiracies headed by other scientists to take away credit from Roger's discoveries. But could there be . . . some kind of conspiracy to establish neurological control over members of Starfleet?"

She sounded troubled, as well she might, thought McCoy. For four years Starfleet had been her refuge, her home, the only place she had left to go after Roger's death.

McCoy, who had been in a similar position after his own divorce and the collapse of his life, knew exactly how she felt.

"If it were, Chris . . ." McCoy shook his head, touched the screen-through key. "Technology like that would show up somewhere. It would leave tracks. Not the neural wiring itself, but the manufacture of the wire, the research and development that created it, if it is wire. Even a conspiracy couldn't cover that. And it's not reading like any metal I've ever seen on the IPs. You'd see improvements in hologame design, in security system monitoring, in autocleaning of microducts. Something. Somebody didn't carve that hardware out of a bar of soap. Whoever's selling nonferrous nanotechnology that fine, and that efficient, to Starfleet would be selling it elsewhere, for other purposes. Analysis of the wiring itself shows it's literally growing, remaking itself out of minerals in the blood. . . ."

"Please repeat request," said the computer.

"What the hell's the matter with this thing today?" muttered McCoy.

"Please clarify question."

"I wasn't talking to you," he snapped. "Just give me listings on nanosurgical neurology for the past three Standard months. . . ."

After that, the computer appeared to behave, and McCoy —taken up with the problem of where Starfleet might have gotten the wiring from in the first place, much less why it had done what Phil Cooper claimed it had done—thought nothing further of it.

"I can't believe these safeguards." Raksha tapped neatly through the two double-wired keyboards in the safety of the Number 7-3 storage hold, which backed onto the branch line that fed the computers of the portside engineering workrooms. "Hasn't anybody told these people that you don't keep ferrets out of a building by lowering a portcullis?"

"Maybe it's a trap?" suggested Adajia, looking up from the weapon she was making out of engine tape, a small pry bar, and spare wire-stripper blades she'd found in a work-bench drawer.

"I didn't know they allowed ferrets on starships," said Thad worriedly. "The Consilium wouldn't let us have cats in our quarters at the Institute. I thought that was mean of them."

"It was mean of them," agreed Adajia. "The Consilium are mean people, Thaddy. Almost as mean as Klingons."

"Naah." Arios emerged from a small access hatch in the wall, pin welder in one hand and a straggling bundle of spare wire wound like a stole around his shoulders. A night's sleep and a couple of meals had taken the tremor out of his hands, but he still looked close to spent. "Nobody's as mean as a Klingon."

"You're straight on course about that, *puq*," agreed Raksha mildly.

"I'm convinced," said the Master, crossing to Raksha and considering the pin welder he held in his hand. "This really is the *Enterprise*. With that wiring it couldn't be anything else."

"We're just about done here." Raksha put the final touches to her codes, began disconnecting the keyboards. "Where's the most inconspicuous plexus on the main trunk for doors, lights, and gravity control?"

"Bowling alley," said Arios. "Deck Twenty. We can get there through the central dorsal vents."

"What's a bowling alley?" inquired the Orion, testing the balance of the quite savage-looking weapon she had made, then spinning it lightly around the sides of her hand.

Arios explained, "You balance pieces of high-impact plastic up on end and then try to knock them down from fifty feet away by rolling a ball at them."

"What if you can't get them to balance?" asked Thad, still worried, and Adajia said, "The Federation conquers the galaxy, crosses the stars, and fights the Romulans to a standstill, and they occupy themselves with *that* in their spare time?" Her earrings glittered as she tossed back her hair.

Arios grinned, shoving wires in his pockets. "The bent area on the *Nautilus* used to be the bowling alley," he said, irony bright in his green eyes. "But on this ship, it should be perfectly safe."

"Please repeat request."

Spock glanced from the starfield analysis hardcopy he was studying with a frown. "High-band scan results of sensor readings on the *Nautilus*, broken down in incremental bandwidths." He had always considered the whole voder-activated command system on the computer inadequate to the needs of any civilized intelligence, and this afternoon's particularly bad performance seemed to him typical of the kind of problems that could evolve in such a system. Humans, he reflected, seemed willing to go to almost any lengths to avoid specifics in their dealings either with one another or with machines. . . .

His quick ears picked up a familiar tread slowing down outside his door, and the word "Come" was out of his mouth almost before the chime sounded. "Captain," he greeted his friend.

"What've you got?"

The lab-quality display screen above Spock's desk had already manifested a proof sheet of sensor schematics, augmented where possible to adapt to the black ship's shields. Captain Kirk folded his arms and considered the images over his first officer's shoulder, noting differences between the designs of the *Enterprise* and the *Nautilus* that had been less obvious through the viewscreens against the blackness of space.

"Unless I'm mistaken," he said softly, "I've seen that shorter hull proportion on the very newest designs, stuff that isn't even off the drawing boards yet. But that's years' worth of pitting on that thing—decades' worth. Even on the places where the saucer's been repaired."

He was silent for a time, studying the repeated images: green shadows on one outline, yellow on another, depending on what the sensors were picking up. Several of the schematics showed no more than the bare, pale blue skeleton of the ship itself, either because the sensors found nothing of what they sought, or because that oddly massive shielding cut out all trace of certain bandwidths.

The *Enterprise* had looked like that, he thought, to all those who had studied her—and humans—for the first time.

The first Federation starship, shaped like a massive globe. The vicious but ultimately communicable Gorns. The Romulans, playing their silent game of cloaked chess.

To seek out new life, and new civilization, thought Kirk. And what had that new civilization thought, in all these five years, about being sought out?

"That's a lot of ambient heat they've got in the nacelles," he remarked at last. "Even given the fact they blew their coolant system."

"The pattern is a common one for derelicts in which life-support remains operant." Spock touched through a series of commands, and that particular schematic, with its cloudy patterns of yellow in some unexpected areas, enlarged itself to take up most of the center of the screen. Another chain of finger touches—Spock did it without even looking at the keyboard: "for swank," Kirk could almost hear McCoy saying—took the schematic forward through time, showing no change in the heat distribution.

"Fungus, mostly," said the Vulcan. *"Vescens ceolli* or

zicreedens. It generally indicates that areas of the ship have been out of use for two years or more. This was the reading I wished you to see."

Another schematic enlarged. Red pixels shifted as the computer framed the image forward through time. Kirk's mind snapped back from the puzzle of the huge amounts of yellow on the preceeding diagram to the changing pattern of the red on the current one.

"What *is* that?"

"Mu-spectrum energy, Captain." Spock settled back in his chair, folded his arms, and tilted his head a little to one side. "Neither light nor heat, though some species seem able to detect it as color, others as sound. It is, as you noted earlier, characteristic of the Turtledove Anomalies."

Kirk watched the zones of red slowly broaden through the engineering hull and the nacelles, then contract. Broaden and contract. Broaden and contract, like the bloody beating of an alien heart. "Is that surge effect mechanical?"

He didn't know why he knew that the answer to that question was no. Certainly Spock would say that he had insufficient data.

But for a long time the Vulcan did not reply at all.

Kirk let the silence run, sink. Spock's hesitation to answer was significant. Before them the color spread, shrank; spread, shrank.

"Is that real-time forwarding?"

"Affirmative. You will observe there appears to be no time lag."

Kirk nodded. The bloom started in the nacelles at the exact moment it began in the engines. "Can you get me a finer time breakdown on that?"

"Time increment to point five," instructed Spock. "Two-second freeze." But his hand strayed toward the keyboard as if subconsciously ready to back up with more specific instructions.

They studied the slow blink of the schematic. Kirk thought about the thin, green-haired young man who had lied so calmly to him, prisoned behind the crystalplex doors of the brig. The Klingon woman with her watchful eyes and her air of having seen everything before. *Don't go on board the Nautilus without me or Raksha with you.*

Booby traps, Raksha had said. DeSalle had produced reports and examples of lethal sheaves of them.

He wondered if he was looking at one now, or at something else.

"Increment to point one," said Kirk.

The color still started at exactly the same moment.

"That's a hell of a synchronization."

But it wasn't, he thought. The energy in the engine deck was the source of the energy in the nacelles. He didn't understand why he was so sure of that.

"Any theory?"

"Negative, Captain."

"But something's bothering you."

Spock looked up at him in surprise. "It is a capital mistake to theorize ahead of one's data," he said. "At the moment, the data is insufficient and the patterns apparently contradictory."

"Subliminal clues are data, too." In four years, nine months of dealing with his literal-minded science officer, Kirk had learned to avoid the word *hunch.* "Do you have the —illogical—feeling that the source of that energy is organic?"

Their eyes met. Spock's dark gaze was usually inscrutable, but far in the back of it, Kirk could see the Vulcan adding the fact of Kirk's conviction—equally baseless and illogical —to the fact of his own.

Then the screen before them flickered and blanked, like a window whose view has suddenly been jerked far away into a single spot of fading brightness. The bland contralto voice of the computer said, "Please repeat request."

Spock's eyes sharpened and hardened as he swung his head around to suspiciously regard the screen.

During the last hour of any shift, the bowling alley on Deck Twenty invariably closed down. The cleaning of the snack bar and hologames area, and the waxing of the lanes, could have been easily done without completely closing the place, as during that last hour even such diehard bowlers as Jefferson and the two Adamses—the cargo chief and his brother in Astrophys—went to shower, eat, and change their shoes preparatory to going on shift. But Lieutenant Mbu was fond of neat edges and routine, and so she had the place closed. She would reset and check the line of hologame terminals, adding up the totals played to make sure that those which had fallen from popularity were replaced, and then retire to her office to write up shift logs and time-and-motion analyses for the massive study she was doing on recreational patterns in Starfleet, leaving Yeoman Effinger to check the pin setters and wax the lanes.

The pin setters, of course, had self-calibrating and self-correcting modules, and the *Enterprise* bowling alley possessed two very efficient Dack and Homilie waxers—the lanes being highest quality Martian quasi oak and cared for old-style—but Effinger, though he had no mistrust of machinery per se, did not trust it one hundred percent. Digital settings were accurate to program, but they lacked, in his opinion, the fineness of human artistic judgment. It was his custom to tinker with the setters manually two or three times a week, to perfect tolerances too delicate for the self-correct modules to read, and when he followed the waxers onto the lanes—in his stocking feet, naturally—he would frequently kneel to add extra polish to the right-hand side, where the majority of bowlers landed their strokes.

This was what he was doing when he heard a voice call out from the direction of the doors, "Piglet!"—his old nickname, spoken in tones of amorous delight. Looking up, he saw Yeoman Shimada—who *never* bowled—coming toward him, holding out her hands and smiling, beautiful as a little porcelain doll with the winter-night torrent of her hair unloosed from its customary clips and shivering around the hemline of her short red skirt. The look of pleasure in her brown eyes almost stopped his breath.

The next minute his breath *did* momentarily stop, as

Adajia of Orion's green hand and arm appeared from out of the suddenly opened air duct in the ceiling overhead. Whatever else could be said about her—and a good many things could—Adajia was a deadly shot with a phaser.

Arios, Raksha, Thad, and Adajia dropped one by one from the duct into the alley inhabited by no one now except the comprehensively unconscious Yeoman Effinger. The illusory Yeoman Shimada had vanished in an eyeblink. Arios and the Klingon went straight to the rank of hologames while Thad and Adajia used engine tape to tape Effinger's mouth and eyes shut and fasten his hands around a stanchion of the alley railing; it took Arios only moments to pull the main hatch cover behind the games.

"Which one of these you leaving me?" asked Raksha— unnecessarily, as the lights on all but one of the brightly colored screens went dead. She perched on the seat and spent all of about a minute shortcutting the game itself and slicing into what the game module really was: a very elaborate lab-quality terminal.

Thad had already taken off his boots and was making long, experimental dashes to each of the alleys in turn, for the sheer joy of sliding down the waxed quasi oak in his stocking feet.

"System error check," said Spock. "Display."

Columns of blue lettering poured upward against the silver of the screen: communications batch files, execs that regulated the rate of matter-antimatter conversion in the pods, flavor-mix documentation for recycling, temperature-regulation parameters for every lab, stateroom, and shower cubicle on the ship, including the swimming pool on Deck Twenty. Holoshows, novels, letters, scientific and technical journals, logs of every imaginable section chief and auto-mated system, backup logs of the logs. Monitors of beds in sickbay and cells in Security. Internal sensor readings from the lowest cargo holds to the bridge itself. Regulations as to the amount of wax in the bowling-alley waxers, the bright-ness of the sun lamps in the rec room, the strength of the coffee in Captain Kirk's cabin tap, and the power of the magnets holding shut the hatches of every supply cupboard and the cover plates of every manual door release on the ship.

"No error in any system," said the computer in a voice that Captain Kirk thought sounded just slightly smug.

Spock shook his head, puzzled. "Cause of . . ." he began, and Kirk said, "It's lying."

The captain turned, strode to the door, and had to pull up short to keep from smacking himself on the nose when it didn't open.

"Maintenance! Maintenance!" Dr. McCoy abandoned the comm link on the wall—which had the slight ambient echoic quality of an open line but which wasn't receiving anything at all—and slapped the recalcitrant office door with his open hand.

Not much to his surprise, that didn't cause it to open, either.

"Och, hell," said Mr. Scott. The doors of even the smallest rooms on the *Enterprise*—and he was in one of the smallest rooms on the *Enterprise*—all had manual backups, but the magnetic catch on the discreet cover plate that hid the one in front of him seemed to have spontaneously glued itself shut.

A malfunction in the current controlling the strength of the magnet, Scotty guessed. Who'd have thought it?

He touched the comm-link button, knowing he'd get the ribbing of his life about this one. "Maintenance, this is Mr. Scott. There's a jam on the door of latrine number. . . " He checked the serial number above the transcom. ". . . latrine number fourteen-twelve. Maintenance? Maintenance?"

There was no reply.

Instead a light, slightly gravelly voice, which Mr. Scott vaguely recognized, came over the comm. "Captain Kirk? This is Dylan Arios." There was a momentary pause, during which Mr. Scott wondered, for just a moment, whether the malfunction that had quadrupled the magnetism in the manual cover-plate catch had also crossed the wires of some private communication.

Then Arios went on, "We've—uh—taken control of your ship."

Chapter Five

"*The hell you have!*" roared Kirk, pounding the comm button with the hammer of his fist. "Where the hell . . . ?"

The husky, slightly hesitant voice came on again. "You can reach me on direct comm at—uh—the Deck Eleven lounge. It's the only comm line on the ship still open."

"Deck Eleven lounge," repeated Security Lieutenant Organa, scrambling lightly down the pyramid of tables that had been erected—with startling speed and efficiency, considering how astonished everyone in the rec room had been—to bring her close to the air ducts in the ceiling. "Shimada, there'll be degaussers in Engineering. Once we can get the manual cover plates off, we'll be able to move. Anybody know the schematic of the air vents between here and Engineering?"

They had already ascertained that the computer wasn't giving out files of anything anymore.

"I do." Ensign Lao turned from his puzzled tapping at the keyboard of one of the rec-room visicoms, designed to access the library but, under Lao's expert manipulation, displaying some very strange data indeed. Across the room,

Second Engineer Danny Miller was investigating the stubborn cover plate on the manual release. Like most of those trapped in the rec room, he was in uniform, red engineering coveralls in his case, but the pockets had not contained a degausser, simply because such devices frequently—despite safety catches—tended to disable the programming of other electronic hand tools.

"But they're lying to you about the Deck Eleven lounge," went on Lao, crossing to the pile of tables. "They've got to be doing this from a lab-quality terminal and there aren't any on Deck Eleven. They must have cross-wired the comm stations."

He nodded back toward the visicom. "It looks like they've sealed all the blast doors in the corridors as well."

"But we got the league bowl-off tonight!" protested Yeoman Jefferson. "They keep us from whippin' those slime devils in Engineering . . ."

"You watch who you're callin' a slime devil, mold frog," retorted Miller good-naturedly.

"So they could be anywhere," said Organa in disgust.

Abruptly, the lights went out.

"I'm monitoring sickbay," Dylan Arios went on. "I'll know if anything happens to either of my men there, and believe me, Captain, I'll start shutting down life-support. We're real desperate, and I'm sorry, but that's how it is right now. All right?"

Kirk groped for the comm pad, cursing. At the Academy he'd taken the required survival courses, but it had been a long time since he'd even *thought* about touching through pad numbers without looking at them. Fortunately the Deck Eleven lounge was an easy one to remember—11-1. He didn't want the entire ship privy to the remainder of this discussion.

"What do you want?"

Behind him in the darkness he heard the rustle of Spock's clothing, then the biting whine of static as Spock flipped open his communicator. Arios, and whoever was with him, must have wired through the ship's pickup system to lay down a blanket field of electronic flak.

"We want you to take us to Tau Lyra Three," said Arios.

"Can you get a fix on him of any kind?" Mr. Sulu glanced over his shoulder, to where the dim glow of an emergency-kit flashlight outlined Lieutenant Uhura's long legs, projecting from beneath the communications console. At any other moment, he reflected, the view would have been worth lengthy contemplation.

She shifted uncomfortably, and Lieutenant Dawe—holding the flashlight for her since his operation systems monitor stubbornly continued to insist that absolutely nothing was wrong anywhere on the ship—tried to give her a little more room in which to work.

"Not much." Her voice sounded both muffled and distracted, and she wriggled again, trying to ease the awkward positioning of her arms as she worked from cable to cable of the impenetrable maze beneath the console with a single-pin pickup in quest of any clue to tell them what was happening elsewhere on the ship.

Even the emergency lighting had gone from the bridge. By the low glow of individual station lamps, the big, circular chamber had the appearance of some prehistoric cave dwelling, looming with eerie shadows thrown by illumination barely brighter than that of tallow-soaked reeds.

Against that heavy darkness, the starfields on the viewscreens blazed with heart-shaking clarity. Standing in the dark beside the turbolift door, Sulu reflected that he'd nearly forgotten the utter beauty of that cold, endless night, and had the danger been less, he thought he could have sat for hours in the darkened bridge, gazing into infinities of nothing and light.

Speed had been cut to slow cruise instants before the lights had gone—the moment, in fact, that Sulu had realized that someone had managed to cut through the double and treble defenses on the computer. Chekov, bent over the navigation console, was compensating and correcting the course still further, hoping to hell that what the computer was telling him was correct, that what he was telling the computer was getting through, and that some other disaster wasn't about to befall.

"But he's not in the Deck Eleven lounge," added Uhura around the stylus clamped in her teeth. "They've got the wires crossed somewhere."

"Can you do anything about the communicator static?" asked Chekov. "If we could just get in touch with somebody . . ."

"Got it!" Sulu felt the cover plate give under his fingers. He shoved the degaussing pencil back into his belt, ripped the plate itself away from the manual crank for the turbolift door, twisted the geared handle within. Unwillingly the laminated silver panels of the doors parted, to reveal a narrow rectangle as black as blindness, in which the dim reflections of the makeshift lights on the bridge picked out the amber line of the safety cable like a single stroke of gilding on velvet.

"Hmm," said Sulu. From the bridge, there was nowhere to go but down.

"Master . . ."

Raksha put her hand on Arios's shoulder. He covered the comm pad with his palm, glanced up at her, green eyes weirdly luminous in the glow of the flashlight taped to the game console before him. Thad was still happily playing slippy-slide on the newly waxed floor of the bowling lane. Adajia, Yeoman Wein's phaser in hand, sat close to the outer door at the far end of the long room, nearly invisible in the darkness; the air was filled with the smell of the bowl of popcorn at her side, which she was devouring, licking her fingers like a greedy child.

"If this is the *Enterprise*," said the Klingon softly, "your best bet would be to kill the life-support. You know that."

Arios's mouth flinched. A mouth too sensitive, Raksha thought dispassionately, in a face whose thinness rendered it almost fragile-looking, like a skeletal moth. Among her own people such a man would not survive.

"I know that."

Their eyes held for a long time.

She asked, "You know who is here." It was not a question. "I don't know his name, but you do."

He nodded, once. "I do."

"Then make him part of your terms. Ask for him as hostage and lose him out an airlock. Shoot him trying to escape. Say Adajia or I went berserk on you and cut him into little bitty pieces. I'd even do it."

The green eyes shut; he averted his face. "I can't." He drew a deep breath, as if against some terrible weight, and his voice became cheerful and light. "You'd better get going if we don't want Kirk to guess . . ."

Her brown hand caught him under the chin, forced his head back around so that his eyes had to meet hers.

"Whoever it is," she said evenly, "he's responsible for what they did to you."

Arios said nothing.

"He's responsible for Sharnas having a central nervous system like the main lode of a Denebian silver mine; he's responsible every time you have to strap Phil down and short out his implants; he's responsible every time you wake up screaming from nightmares . . ."

"Not every time," Arios said quietly.

Her mouth hardened, a bronze line like a bitter poem, and her fingers shifted where they still gripped the pointed chin. "Kill him. Whoever he is."

"I can't."

"Then tell me who it is and I'll kill him."

A bowling ball rumbled down the alley. Thad, who had flung it, made a running start after it, then slid in a neat intercepting arc, a child playing a game. Raksha's eyes followed the little man, and for the first time a glister of tears brightened them.

"He's responsible for Thad."

Arios wrenched away from her grip, looked down at the maze of keyboards and makeshift screens before him. His hands trembled a little, and he caught them quickly together so she wouldn't see. "I can't. It's not possible." He did not meet her eyes. "You'd better go."

She turned away. "Thad," she called out. "Thaddy, get over here, we're putting you on guard duty."

"With a phaser and everything?" His face illuminated with delight; then he stopped in his tracks, anxiety blotting all his momentary pleasure at their trust.

"Phaser and everything," said Raksha. "I have to take Adajia with me. You keep an eye on that door and listen, listen to everything. Any weird noise, any strange feeling you get that something may be coming out of the darkness . . . you've got to take care of it."

His dark eyes widened, scared. She pressed the second phaser, the one they'd gotten out of Wein's desk, into his hand, and nodded back at Arios, who had returned to speaking into the comm link. "You've got to protect him," she said.

And she added, in Klingon, as Adajia fell into step behind her and they moved once more toward the blind black eye of the open vent hatch, "Spirits of the lightning, protect him, too."

"I understand Tau Lyra Three's under the protection of the Prime Directive," went on Arios's light, scratchy voice. "Nevertheless we have business there. We mean no harm to the planet, nor, for that matter, to you or your crew. We're really not space pirates or anything, Captain. But we need to be taken to Tau Lyra as soon as possible, and we'll need repairs on our ship."

Kirk's mind was racing, as more and more frightful possibilities presented themselves. What the hell was happening on the bridge? Had engine and warp-drive controls been cut? The comm link was near the door of Spock's office, and through it—for the soundproofing on the starship was never a hundred percent—he could hear a mutter of voices, the occasional dim pounding as someone tried to get out of the shut library next door.

"One of my crew will take Mr. Spock over to the *Nautilus*," went on Arios. "I hope he understands that the internal monitoring devices implanted in some of my crew members give me complete awareness of what's happening to them. As I said, I don't want to start shutting down life-support systems, but I'll do it. And I can do it, from where we are. I hope you believe that."

"Can he?" Kirk put his hand over the link.

Spock's voice came from another part of the darkness than it had before. From the location, Kirk guessed that the Vulcan was trying to get enough purchase under the edge of the wall hatch that covered the emergency kit, which would contain, among other things, a degausser. Had the panel not fit flush, Spock's hands were probably strong enough to bend the metal aside, but without a handle to grip, his strength was useless. *Five years on the voyage,* thought Kirk irritably, *and nobody's ever thought to ask what would happen if something went wrong with the magnetic catches.*

"He appears to have tapped through to the main computer from a lab-quality terminal," replied the science officer's austere voice. "Although the core programs which control life-support—and the minutiae of ship operations—are theoretically shielded from tampering at this level, we are quite clearly dealing with technical knowledge far greater than our own."

"I take it that's a yes?"

"I have no precise knowledge of Captain Arios's capabilities, Captain." Despite Spock's claim of freedom from all human emotion, there was a slightly aggrieved note in his voice. "I would venture, however, to postulate a high order of probability in that direction."

Kirk swore. "Then I suppose the real question is, Would he?"

But to that, Mr. Spock had no answer at all.

"Will you be okay, Zhiming?" Lieutenant Organa took the damp moisture filter that was passed down to them from the open ceiling vent, handed it on to others waiting on the floor. A dozen bowls of vegetable oil ringed the stacked tables like a ritual altar, glimmering with the burning yarn of makeshift wicks. There were, Lao knew, three boxes of candles in one of the rec-room cupboards, but it, like everything else on the ship, had magnetic catches. The vegetable oil had been Ensign Giacomo's idea, and fortunately the group in the rec room had included Yeoman Brunowski, who programmed the food synthesizers.

At the moment Giacomo, Jefferson, and Emiko Adams were unraveling all the crochet yarn, embroidery floss, crewel-stitch, and macramé cord from every needlework project still in train when the lights had gone out, and fortunately needlework was a form of recreation much in vogue among the *Enterprise* crew. If they'd had access to everything cached behind the magnetic hatches around the walls, of course, they could have run guide threads through every ventilator duct and power conduit on the ship six times over, let alone down into Engineering, but reviewing the schematic of the vents in his mind, Lao thought there would be enough as it was.

"I'll be fine as long as there isn't something living in the vent shafts," he joked, and there was an uneasy laugh. Yagghorths weren't the only recurring nightmare starfaring crews had about picking up alien life-forms. Only a month ago a derelict free trader had been discovered by the *Kreiger* close to the Beta Lyrae system, the space between inner and outer hulls packed tight with the desiccated bodies of Udarian blood maggots, every chamber and hold of the ship drifted knee-deep with them, even the engines clogged. The salvagers from the *Kreiger* had to use chemical sensors to find the bones of the crew.

"You mean besides the mice?" joked Brunowski.

Lao walked over to the visicom, where Miller was still trying to work his way through the bizarre schematic of the guards on the slicer program. "I can't understand how they got through the safeguards," said the engineer, rubbing a hand over his head until his brown hair stood up like the crest of a startled cockatoo. "I put them on myself last year—not just a blanket program, but a system-by-system tailoring."

"It almost looks like they found a way to bifurcate each bit, and slip past the guard on a bit-by-bit basis." Lao folded his arms and studied the screen by the flickering glow of the smoky, smelly lamps.

"Is that possible?"

Lao shrugged. "No," he said cheerfully, and returned to the pile of tables. Organa handed him the only flashlight in the room—Miller had had one in his coverall pocket—and the end of a long, and rather kinked, swatch of yarn. Lao tied the yarn around one ankle, mounted the tables, and from there scrambled into the narrow square of the vent. Lao's memory was good, and he had studied the ship's schematics thoroughly in the five months he had been on board. While Giacomo was unraveling yarn for wicks and Brunowski and Miller were fiddling with the programming on the food slots, trying to convince them that what they really wanted was bowl after bowl of grease, Lao had sketched what he recalled of the vent system from memory, counting turns and branchings, hoping he wasn't leaving anything out.

"What if they're in Engineering?" Giacomo asked worriedly, coming to stand beneath the vent.

Lao adjusted the flashlight in his left hand. The vent shaft was only about fourteen inches square, cramping his arms and shoulders. Not the place, he reflected wryly, where one would care to meet a yagghorth—or even a mouse, for that matter.

"I guess I'll figure that out when I get there," he said, and set off, pushing himself carefully by elbows and toes through the dark.

"All right," said Kirk. "You win this round. I take it the lights are out all over the ship?"

It certainly sounded like Deck Seven was dark in the immediate area of Mr. Spock's quarters. It was one of the quietest areas of the ship, situated between the room of visicom cubicles and the ship's library, but even so, there was the rustling suggestion of activity vaguely sensed through both walls. Kirk wondered how McCoy was faring in sickbay. Wondered again, almost sick with anxiety, what was taking place on the bridge.

Minutes stretched without a reply. Kirk heard the almost soundless murmur of Mr. Spock's clothing as the Vulcan moved about, like a big cat in the darkened room, the steady whisper of his breathing, not even deepened with anger or frustration. With access to the specialized—and allegedly double-guarded—directories, Arios could have blanked out the lighting and door panels in selected areas of the ship, but at a guess he'd done it everywhere. At least, thought Kirk, that's what he himself would have done, to cut the crew off from each other and from any possibility of a general search.

"Listen," he tried again. "Clear the comm long enough for me to tell my crew to stay where they are. I accept your assurances that all you want is your ship repaired, and transport to Tau Lyra Three. I can't permit you to land on a protected planet, but I will help you repair your ship. What you do from there is your business." He hoped that sounded sufficiently casual, sufficiently thoughtless.

"But let me talk to my crew. Somebody's going to try to find you, and I want to minimize injuries in the dark. And if they *do* find you, I want to tell them that I've made a bargain with you, that neither you nor any of your crew is to be injured."

"They won't find me, Captain," came Arios's voice. "And I've already told them we're not to be touched. It's not that I don't trust your word. You had . . . have . . . a reputation for keeping it. But I know also you'd never let a bunch of problematical space pirates make a landing on a protected planet. I'm sorry about this, but I really can't take any chances. And I mean *any* chances."

"But you already have."

Kirk startled and looked—illogically—over his shoulder at where Spock's voice had sounded suddenly close. He felt the warmth of the Vulcan's body brush his arm.

"From what I overheard of your conversation with Rakshanes . . ." He used the polite Klingon honorific. ". . . you have already refused to wipe out the crew of the *Enterprise,* against her advice, although by doing so you believe you would destroy a crew member who has . . . wronged you. Injured you and your crew. This would indicate that a compromise is possible."

There was long silence. Kirk wondered what it was that Mr. Spock had overheard, for his own ears had brought him only the dullest of muffled mumblings over the comm. Faintly he heard a light male voice—Thad, he thought, that curiously childlike young man—say anxiously, "But how could he hear?"

"Spock's a Vulcan, of course he could hear even though I had my hand over the comm link. We knew they were in Spock's cabin. . . . I'm sorry, Captain." Arios's voice came back clearly again. "And Mr. Spock. I've taken enough chances. I can't afford to take any more. Some of us have our own Prime Directives. You'll need to . . ."

There was a sudden, scratching grate outside the office door, the sharp click of a cover plate being put back, then the grind of a manual release. A slit of yellow light, brilliant after the long minutes of darkness, gashed Kirk's sight, broadening into the doorway. Behind the light could be seen two forms, women, the dark-faced Raksha, her doublet winking with metal and leather, and the graceful houri Adajia.

Adajia had a phaser, and a horrific-looking weapon made of razors. Raksha held a metal pry bar in one hand like a club, and over the other shoulder hung a large tool kit stamped with the Starfleet emblem and the serial number of the *Enterprise.* Most such kits had the department they came from written on the side—ENGINEERING or GEO or whatever. Someone—probably Raksha—had put a couple of strips of engine tape over this one.

Adajia's phaser, Kirk noted, was Starfleet issue. That meant they'd taken out one security officer, probably whoever had been on guard in the brig.

"Captain," said Raksha, keeping a wary distance from the door, "we're going to need you along as a hostage for a short time as well. Now, you can let me tape up your wrists . . ." She held up a roll of silver engine tape. ". . . or I can have Adajia hit you with a very mild stun charge and *then* I'll tape up your wrists, which will waste time and give you a headache for the rest of the day. If necessary, Adajia can take out both of you, but then I'd have to go find somebody else to help me fix the *Nautilus*'s engines and computer. Okay?"

"I've already offered to cooperate," said Kirk, holding out his hands, wrists together.

"Mr. Spock . . . far corner, please. Away from the desk."

Spock retreated. Adajia remained in the doorway, keeping an eye on both him and the darkness of the corridor outside. Raksha turned Kirk roughly around, taped his wrists behind him instead of in front.

"Do you have all the repair equipment you require from Engineering?" inquired Spock politely. Beyond Adajia, the corridor was black and utterly silent—Kirk had had the impression of voices out there during the earlier minutes of the darkness. He could still hear, if he listened, occasional muttering from the library next door. Soundproofing, an expensive luxury aboard any spacegoing vessel, had been proven critical on starships with their long mission times and weeks—sometimes months—of isolation, but it was far from perfect.

"Most of what we'll need is on the *Nautilus* already," said Raksha, speaking past Kirk to the Vulcan. "We're going to need engine/computer interfacing work, which is why you got elected and not Mr. Scott—aside from the fact that we haven't been able to locate Mr. Scott. Now you, Captain, out the door. I think we're going to use the starboard transporter room instead of the one right next to Security. This way."

Her soft boots made barely a sound on the metal laminate of the deck. The glow of Adajia's flashlight beam passed briefly across the bodies of those unfortunate enough to be in that corridor when the lights went out. Kirk saw Gilden from Historical—who had his quarters just around the corner—move a little and moan as they went by, and breathed easier. It was clear the two women had fired heavy stun charges into every human being they'd met, and looking at Raksha's face, beautiful and utterly cold, Kirk was only glad it had been no worse.

He was interested to note how familiar they were with the

ship. True, their own was nearly identical, but the familiarity in her voice as she spoke about Scotty flagged something in his mind, gave him the uneasy sense that she'd been briefed on the personnel of the ship.

"Here's where we leave you." Her voice echoed slightly in the gallery between the two starboard transporter rooms. "After we transport Mr. Spock back and bring the Master and the others over, we'll tell people where you are. I'm sorry we have to do it this way."

She might actually have been sorry, thought Kirk, but she didn't sound like she was going to stay up nights soaking her pillow in tears over it.

"This may not be the only way you have to do it," he said. "Tell us who you are, and what you're up to, and . . ."

She uttered a brief, barking laugh. "Captain," she said, "believe me, you don't want to know." Her eyes met his, bitter and dark as Turkish coffee, haunted with old anger, old pain. In a quieter voice she reiterated, "You truly don't."

A line of cargo holds lay just beyond the starboard transporter rooms. She degaussed the magnetic catch on the cover plate of the nearest door, worked the crank enough to open the door a crack. As a final precaution, she tore a strip of engine tape and affixed it over his mouth, then pushed him through into darkness. His shoulder jarred bruisingly against something—a box or carton—but by the time he'd used whatever it was to work himself to his feet again the door was shut.

Through the metal he heard the whine of a phaser as she fused the mechanism.

Barely audible, her voice retreated down the gallery toward the transporter room. "That's seven-one-twelve, Mr. Spock. He'll be fine in there till you get back."

Kirk kicked the box behind him. God knew what was in it. It could be anything from soil samples to archaeological discoveries to unknown alien artifacts. Slowly, patiently, he turned his back on it and began to explore the edge with his fingers, seeking any sharp corner or projection that could be used to pick at the tape in the hopes of freeing his wrists.

* * *

"T'Iana . . ."

Christine Chapel turned sharply at the sound of the chemical-scorched whisper from the bed. Station lights called a thread of illumination from the claustrophobic darkness. The orange glow of the illuminated markers on the diagnostic board above the beds was barely strong enough to outline the coarse brush of dark hair on the one pillow, the thin, patrician features on the other. For several hours now the Vulcan boy Sharnas had lain unmoving, his features in repose like a statue's. Now his breathing quickened, lines of pain etched themselves into the sides of the mouth, the bruised, sunken flesh below the eyes. His hands, long and fine and uncallused, twitched and trembled on the coarse, sparkly fabric of the coverlet, and under it his feet jerked as if trying to escape red-hot needles.

"T'Iana," murmured the boy again, desperation in his tone. "Don't let them. I don't want to. They kill . . ."

His hand moved spasmodically, trying to accomplish some dream task; as Chapel knelt beside the bed to take it she saw the thin wrist, the pads of the palm and fingers crossed and covered with pale green cuts and scars of varying ages, some of them running right up under the sleeve.

For reasons of her own Christine had, for three years, studied the complex tonalities of the Vulcan language. This was the first time she'd spoken it to something other than the teaching computer. "It's all right," she said, hoping her pronunciation of the simple phrase was correct. She collected the clutching fingers in her own, held them still. "You're safe."

Safe from what? Was T'Iana a clan matriarch? The boy's mother?

Sharnas thrashed his head back and forth hectically, a thin noise of pain dying in his throat. "Don't let them," he begged, all logic, all Vulcan calm drowning in terror. "Don't let them do it, T'Iana, I don't want to . . ."

"You're safe," said Christine again, wondering if that was

true. The lights had been out for just over thirty minutes. After that single exchange of voices between Dylan Arios and Captain Kirk, audible over the comm to everyone on the ship, the security ward had been utterly silent. The waiting room, an office, and a good stretch of corridor separated the ward from McCoy's office or any of the labs, and strain her ears as she might, she had heard nothing save, early on, stumbling feet passing in the corridor, and the thump of a body against the wall, which had told her that the rest of the deck, at least, was as blind as she.

She wondered how long the batteries on the station lights would last, or whether desperation would, in fact, prompt Arios to make good his threat about shutting down life-support. She wasn't sure—her glimpses of him last night and this morning had been brief, and under adverse conditions, certainly as far as he was concerned. She had not had the impression of a cruel man, but it did not take cruelty, she knew, to kill large numbers of people.

Only a sense of duty.

Sharnas twisted under her touch, struggling against some unknown foe. "Please," he whispered. "It will . . . devour. Don't make me . . ."

There was a sedative, overdue; at her duty station behind the sealed and unresponsive door, naturally. She stroked the beardless cheeks, clammy with sweat, brushed back the raven wings of hair from his temples. "It's all right," she said, aching with pity for the boy, trying desperately to reach him, to make him understand, to ease his fear. "Nobody will make you do anything you don't want to do." The sentence was a complicated one in Vulcan, and she wasn't sure if she'd said it correctly, or if he heard.

A nightmare rising out of the black ocean trenches of inner fear? Or the replay of some event that had actually happened?

His voice came out twisted, a violin string of horror. "T'Iana . . ."

Then he sat bolt upright, throwing her hands off him with

the frightening strength of Vulcans, his black eyes an abyss of terror, staring into the dark. "It's in my mind!" he screamed, wrenching, clutching at his head, bending his body forward and gripping his temples as if he sought to crush his own skull. "IT'S IN MY MIND!"

And his voice scaled up into a despairing scream.

Chapter Six

THE FIRST THING Spock noticed, in the *Nautilus*'s engineering hull, was the smell.

It was perceptible over the faint sweetness of leftover rhodon gas, drifting through the cavernous darkness of the shuttlecraft bay, the stench of burned insulation and smoke: a slight fishiness, with an underbite that even through the filters of the mask lifted the hair on his nape. He checked his tricorder automatically, but the life-form readings everywhere were thick. Fungus and cirvoid growths blotched the pipes and conduits high overhead, and the sprinkling of dying reddish power lights showed him the furtive movements of rats and boreglunches in the corners of that vast chamber. Many bulk cruisers picked up that sort of small vermin from their cargoes if they weren't kept properly swept; Starfleet quarantine procedures precluded them almost automatically, but most of the crews on the independents weren't large enough to do proper maintenance, and frequently the transport filters on shoestring vessels were allowed to slip out of perfect repair. Free traders throughout the Federation and along its borders were frequently filthy with such things, and worse. It was one reason the Federation frowned upon free traders.

"I'm telling you this for your own good, Mr. Spock," said Raksha softly, and her voice echoed in the vaulted spaces above them. "Don't separate from Adajia and me. Don't try to overpower us and explore the ship. Don't get out of our sight."

He studied the two women for a moment, the Klingon in her metal-studded doublet with the pry bar over her shoulder like a bindle stiff's, the Orion swinging her razor weapon in one delicate hand. Did the threat come from them, he wondered, or from the booby traps that Raksha claimed riddled the ship?

If the latter was the case, with most of the power gone, how dangerous would such traps be?

The smell troubled him, half-familiar and repugnant as the smells of alien enzyme systems frequently were. He looked around him at the hangar again, noting all signs of long disuse. Dark streamers of leaks wept from every air vent, and the coarse purplish fuzz of St. John's lichen was slowly corroding the decks where oil patches had been. The Enterprise's sensors had showed widely varying zones of cold and heat—a sign of malfunctioning life-support systems—and here in the deeps of the engineering hull the very air seemed to drip with a gluey, jungly heat that stuck his shirt to his back and made stringy points of the women's long black hair.

Residual power fluttered at minimal efficiency in walls, pipes, hatchways. Oxygen levels were low, and he felt the queasiness brought on by fluctuation in the main gravity coil. Without the heavy throb of the engine, the ship seemed horribly silent.

His fingers moved a tricorder dial, and the alien colors of the mu spectrum blossomed across the small screen, throbbing like a sleeping heart.

"This way." Raksha's cat-paw step made no sound on the pitted and filthy deck. She twisted her black hair up in a knot, pulled a sheathed stiletto from her boot to fix it in place. "We'll need to get the pumps fixed and oxygen back in production before anything else. Adajia, keep an eye on him. I'll be up in the computer room, reestablishing the link-throughs as you get the wiring repaired."

She paused in the open doorway—all the doors on the ship seemed to have jammed permanently open, or perhaps there had been so many malfunctions that the Master and his crew had simply left them that way. Her eyes gleamed in the glow of Adajia's flashlight, under the knife-slices of reflection from the steel in her hair.

"And, Mr. Spock," she said quietly, "I wasn't lying about . . . defenses on this ship. You wouldn't make it to the transporter room. And even if there are only the . . . three of us . . ." He wondered why she hesitated on the number. ". . . aboard, believe me, you wouldn't be able to hide."

Spock raised an eyebrow as Raksha strode away into the dark. "Interesting."

"Sharnas says that," remarked Adajia, leading the way along the opposite corridor and down a gangway whose walls seemed crusted with a green-gold resin that gleamed stickily in the flashlight's tiny glare. "Do you quote odds and tell people what they're doing isn't logical, too?"

"Should the situation warrant it." The smell on the deck below was stronger, perhaps because of the increased heat, and the magenta glare of the mu-spectrum markers glowed up from his tricorder so strongly as to stain the fouled walls. He was interested to note that the engine chambers of the auxiliary hull had been moved down to these lower levels, and wondered why. Structurally the arrangement bore all the appearance of a makeshift job, jury-rigged a long time ago.

Interesting, too, that Raksha had taken the computer end of the job of relinking the engine systems. If she was the computer officer of the crew—and therefore the one who had created such havoc in the systems of the *Enterprise*—it was no surprise that she'd want to keep him out of contact with the *Nautilus*'s . . . but he wondered if there was another reason. Something about the computer systems themselves that she did not want him to see.

He reached out to touch the wall again, theory that

bordered upon certainty forming in his mind, and he murmured again, "Most interesting."

It did not take long to repair the oxygen feeds and pumps, and to realign the interface with the ship's central computer, which Spock guessed to be also in the auxiliary hull. Over the communicators, which did temporary duty for the silent comm link, Raksha reported clean air coming through within minutes, and by the time Mr. Spock reached the engine room the air there was sufficiently breathable to permit him to remove his filter mask.

This was fortunate, since the engines themselves were configured very differently, cramped and stacked and much smaller and less powerful than those of the *Enterprise*—a curious situation, considering the *Nautilus*'s more advanced design. Dark tanks and coils of unknown use clustered where the main warp-drive amplification units should have been, and in place of Mr. Scott's monitor console, there stood instead a sort of egg-shaped plex bubble, once crystal-clear but stained with yellows and greens and browns, and dribbled all over with the resin that seemed so stickily ubiquitous on walls, floors, tanks, railings. The fishy, alien smell was thick about it; thick, too, in the intense shadows among the tanks, the cavernous darkness beyond them. Spock found himself listening intently to the silent ship as he stripped and patched the great, dead, burned-out coils of the main generator, listening for some sound other than his own breathing and Adajia's, and the small, tinny voice of Raksha coming from the communicator on the floor at his side.

"You showing any light in the guidance system?" she asked. "That unit on the left," she added, as if she could see his momentary puzzlement. "With the tubes around it and the domed top."

It took him a moment to deduce the systems with which he was familiar from the mass of dark rhodon tubes and the sleek ranks of serial-racked wafers on the left, and his eyes narrowed as he glanced across at Adajia again, perched cross-legged on a rusted-out signal modulator with the phaser held loosely in one hand.

"I see no light anywhere," he reported into the communicator.

"There's a row of hatches along the bottom. Check inside for charring on the ports."

Spock obeyed and found a short in the line. While Raksha was running an interval check he removed his blue pullover, pushed up the sleeves of the thin black undertunic he wore for warmth on the *Enterprise,* which like all primarily Earth-human vessels was uncomfortably cold by Vulcan standards. Except for the humidity, which he considered excessive, this portion of the hull was more comfortable for him than he'd been in years, and he wondered if Adajia— the child of another desert world—felt the same.

And while he worked he listened still, straining his ears—wondering what was wrong. It took him a moment to realize that down at this level he had heard no scutter of rodent claws on the metal of the pipes, no scrape of boreglunches slipping under the floor.

Chance? The effects of the rhodon gas?

"Your captain said he also acted as engineer?" he asked at last, running a sequence check to align the impulse power with the channels Raksha had reestablished.

Adajia nodded. "He was trained at the Academy, after he got out of the Institute; he's kept this vessel together for many years. Myself, I know little of it. My clan lord only presented me to him last year, after the uprising at the Feast of Bulls, but I know he met Sharnas in the Institute, and Phil at the Academy."

Spock nodded, logging unfamiliar terms in his mind and noting that no uprising had occurred in the Orion systems for at least fifteen standard years. He wondered what service the Master had done for an Orion clan chief, to be presented with what was obviously an expensive concubine, but was aware that his curiosity was frivolous at best.

"And Mr. Cooper was trained as an astrogator?"

He was head and shoulders in one of the repair hatches; he heard her walk closer to him to be heard.

"Yes. The Consilium thought the Master should be trained as an astrogator, too, though he's a better engineer;

anyway, that's where he met Phil. They ran together, then went back for Thad. Thad helped get Sharnas out, which I guess surprised the hell out of McKennon."

"McKennon?"

She shivered. "Somebody you don't want to meet." She settled her back against the tank behind her; Spock could see the long, green curve of her leg from where he worked, the phaser on her belt and the gleaming razors of her makeshift mace lying like a long-stemmed rose in her hand.

"One of the Masters at the Institute," she went on after a moment. "They were going to kill Thaddy," she added softly, with a combination of wonder and loathing in her voice. "A *chuulak*—just for dereliction of duty."

"Who were?" He worked himself out from under the burned-out heat filter. Power had returned to some of the lamps, though they were still far from full. Those in the engine room had been quite visibly wired to augment their brightness, for it was obvious that those in the rest of the ship never got brighter than the murky, brownish semiblindness through which they had come to the engine room from the hangar. It was quite clear from Raksha's rerouting of the signal links that whole lines of power transmission had had to be abandoned.

"McKennon," said Adajia. "And the Masters. The Masters of the Consilium, but they do what McKennon says."

Upon a number of occasions over the past five years, Spock had seen Captain Kirk utilize a maneuver that he had, at the time, admired for its usefulness, though his own attempts at it had been less than convincing and he doubted he would ever attain his commander's smooth facility at the nonverbal lie. Still, he judged the time to be right. He looked up with what he hoped was convincing suddenness at the doorway of the engine room, which lay beyond Adajia's line of sight where she sat with her back to the tanks. The Orion girl quite gratifyingly spun around, phaser at the ready, to meet whatever threat she considered likely to be roving the corridors of this lightless and near-derelict ship.

Mr. Spock reached out and pressurized the brachial nerve plexus. He caught her as she fell, the phaser ringing noisily

on the metal deck, causing him to wince though he knew
that the hearing of Klingons was far less acute than that of
Vulcans and there was little more than a ten-percent chance
of Raksha hearing it over the renewed rumble of the engine.

His first impulse was to tie Adajia, to prevent too swift a
pursuit from impeding his investigation of the black ship's
final secrets. But as the rhodon gas dispersed the sweetish,
dirty-clothes smell of rodents, the filthy stench of
boreglunches emerged more strongly. On other derelicts
Spock had seen some of the latter nearly the size of his hand.
Instead he simply lifted her onto the old signal-modulator
console, where the vermin would be unable to reach her,
and left her lying unconscious, like a sacrificed virgin, with
her hair coil of sable silk trailing almost to the floor.

Chuulak, she had said. If he recalled his Orion
backcountry dialect correctly, the word referred to public
execution by torture for the purpose of discouraging other
possible miscreants.

A somewhat severe penalty for dereliction of duty, particularly for a young man of Thaddeus Smith's obviously
limited capabilities.

Readjusting the tricorder to home on the mu-spectrum
energy source, Spock set off in swift silence through the
gloom, his mind burgeoning with speculation concerning
who these people were, and how they had, in fact, come by
the black ruin of a starship of the very newest design.

Two turnings had branched off to the right, neat black
holes in the wan flashlight gleam. Ensign Lao wondered if
he'd actually seen two branches on the schematic, or three.
It all reminded him very strongly of the survival and
intelligence tests they'd run them through at the Academy
—that, or the more demanding type of fun houses he'd gone
to at carnivals. He wondered also what there was about the
circumstance of being trapped in a position wherein it was
impossible to scratch one's feet—for instance, crawling
with one's hands straight forward in a conduit barely the
width of one's shoulders—that automatically triggered in-
human itching in that part of the body.

He'd have to ask Dr. McCoy about that, he thought, with a wry inner grin. Possibly it had a scientific name.

He was speculating about it when the first wave of suffocating dizziness struck.

It took Kirk ten minutes of patient rubbing, scraping, and twisting at the edge of the crate behind him to work loose a corner of the tape that bound his wrists. It seemed like much longer. All the while he was listening, straining his ears in the direction of the unseen doorway—or the direction that he had mentally marked as the doorway before Raksha had shut him into darkness—seeking the smallest sound of voices or movement outside.

There was none. The blast doors designed to confine pressure loss had sealed one section of corridor off from another, and Raksha and Adajia had been quite thorough with their phaser fire. He worked slowly, trying to still the rage of impatience in his heart at the knowledge that his crew would be at large in the blacked-out ship, looking for him, or for Dylan Arios. Looking despite the fact that, with only a few exceptions, they were less familiar with its layout than he was, and more likely to run into open gangways or whatever obstructions Arios himself had arranged.

As he worked, he ran over in his mind every word Arios and his crew had spoken, every detail of their clothing, their behavior, their speech. There had to be a clue there some-where, something to tell him who these people were and what it was they wanted.

Why Tau Lyra III—called Yoondri by those who lived there, and by all accounts a harmless world of peaceful farms and city-states that hadn't had a major war in decades, perhaps centuries?

Raksha and Adajia had taken Spock, presumably over to the *Nautilus;* according to Dr. McCoy, Sharnas of Vulcan was far beyond being able to stand and Phil Cooper was heavily sedated.

That left only Arios himself at large, and Thad Smith—if Smith was his real name. What was that round-eyed, rather sweet-faced young man—clearly mentally impaired in some fashion—doing with that pack of pirates? Or the Vulcan boy, either?

Why was there no record of the *Antelope,* of the mysterious black starship, of Arios himself? A half-caste, like Spock, but half-human, half . . . what? McCoy hadn't known.

Ships had disappeared, of course, in the early days of deep-space exploration, even as they disappeared now. A mating with some still-unknown race wasn't unlikely. Still . . .

It took some backbreaking maneuvering to kneel and get his boot toe on the corner of the tape, slowly working and wrenching until a few inches of tape were pulled free, enough to catch and wedge on the corner of the crate. Once his hands were free it took another patient, groping search of the wall to locate the half-open cover plate of the fused door mechanism. From there he used the tape like Ariadne's thread, sticking one end to the cover plate and holding the other in hand while he explored along the walls of the hold in both directions, until he found what he sought: a cargo dolly of the manual type, with detachable handles.

The handles were metal, sections of hollow pipe. The diameter was large enough to fit on the dogged plastic wheel of the door crank and force it over, against the fused mess of machinery and wire on the other side of the wall. With the aid of the lever he managed to push the door open eight inches before it jammed hard.

Cursing—and thanking his lucky stars he'd been diligent in the gym—Kirk slipped through into the blackness of the corridor. "Can anyone hear me?" he called into the silence. "This is your captain."

Descending via the gangways was slower and more troublesome than via the turbolift shaft. But, reflected Mr. Sulu as he degaussed the third cover plate and laboriously cranked the protective blast door aside, probably far safer. If nothing else, there were the turbolifts themselves to be considered. The power might return at any time, as unexpectedly as it had been cut, and then the cars would come whizzing back up the narrow shafts at speeds no one could avoid.

"Of course there was no degausser available in the lab," flustered Lieutenant Bergdahl, the Anthro/Geo lab chief, trotting down the gangway in Sulu's wake. In the dim glow of the flashlight Sulu carried, the lab chief's balding forehead was rimmed with a glittering line of sweat, and his eyes flashed silvery as he glanced repeatedly behind him in the utter dark. Not, reflected Sulu, that there was any possibility of unknown assailants on the two decks above them. Deck Two contained precisely three labs, Deck One nothing more than the bridge. "We keep such things very properly under hatches, unless of course Ensign Adams has been careless again." He glared back at his diminutive clerk, one of the group Sulu had collected in the Deck Two labs.

"I was trying to link into Central Computer," added Lieutenant Maynooth, shambling anxiously in the rear as they descended the next gangway. The yellow glow of the lamps they bore bobbed and swayed eerily, monster shadows crowding behind them: Sulu had taken the battery-operated emergency lamp from the helm console, to which floodlights had been added from the lab emergency stores.

"There are some quite startlingly sophisticated program locks in place," the physicist went on approvingly. "Truly beautiful programming; I must admit I kept getting distracted, taking handwritten notes . . ."

"Does it look like Arios and his crew are in Central?"

"They could well be." Maynooth pushed up the thick-lensed spectacles onto his birdlike nose. He'd had four operations already to slow the deterioration of his eyes and had long ago become allergic to retinox; in the half-darkness, with his spindly arms and the myopic poke of his head he resembled a six-foot praying mantis in a blue lab smock. "All communication, of course, is cut. They'd need to be somewhere on the main trunk line, and have access to a lab-quality terminal, which limits the places where they *could* be."

"Considering the lax fashion in which Security operates," Lieutenant Bergdahl added crisply, "I am not surprised they had so little trouble in . . ."

The Anthro/Geo chief halted, gasping, hand going to his chest. At the same moment Sulu's vision swam in the feeble lamp glare. He threw out a hand, catching the wall as his knees turned to water under him. Maynooth, Adams, and Dawe sprang forward to catch Bergdahl as he staggered, and Dawe made a hoarse noise of shock, trying to draw breath. Sulu, eyes blurring, felt the cold in his chest at the same moment he was aware of sweat breaking out all over his body.

He managed to croak "Back . . ." and they all stood dumbly, staring at him in the chiaroscuro of patchlight and dark.

"Back," he repeated, trying to get leaden feet up the metal steps. "Gas . . . gangway . . ."

Bergdahl made a noise like a small engine lugging and slumped limp into Dawe's arms, nearly taking the Ops chief down with him. Adams held her breath and sprang down the two steps that separated her from them and hooked a shoulder under Dawe's armpit to drag him back, and in the yellow glare Sulu thought she, too, looked gray-faced and ill. They backed up the steps together, Sulu feeling better immediately and Dawe recovering quickly enough to half-drag Bergdahl, although Bergdahl himself moaned and gasped and begged for oxygen and first aid just in case.

They clustered for a moment by the doors leading back onto Deck Two, looking at one another, then down into the pit of the gangway. Then Sulu advanced cautiously again, a step at a time. Four steps down he felt blinding dizziness overwhelm him, sickness and cold and a sensation of suffocation, a feeling of being about to fall. He reeled back, catching himself with his hands on the steps as he did fall; Dawe steadied him, drew him back. He heard Adams say, "I'll get a tricorder from the lab," and Sulu was dimly aware of her boot heels clicking sharply on the metal steps.

"There couldn't possibly be gas," Maynooth said. "Where would it be coming from?"

His head between his knees, his consciousness still swimming in a strange sensation that was not quite anoxia, Sulu managed to mumble sarcastically, "Maybe it's a figment of my imagination."

Maynooth sniffed at the darkness, the remaining flashlight making huge yellow circles of his spectacle lenses. "Maybe it is," he said. He sounded pleased.

"Zhiming?" Lieutenant Organa scrambled up to the table in the lamplit, smoky gloom of the rec room, caught the edge of the open vent. "Zhiming, are you there?"

The yarn thread hung unmoving beside her.

There was definitely a life-form moving down there. An alien, certainly, thought Spock, remembering the smell that had tensed the muscles of his nape. In spite of the heavy concentrations of mu-spectrum energy, Spock could see it, a blurred and fragmented shadow on the digital. Evidently, even heavy concentrations of mu-spectrum energy were not inimical to life per se.

That was comforting to know.

On the other hand, he reflected, it would be comforting to know also if the life-form were carbon-based and more or less humanoid, since an unknown energy might well be absorbed with impunity by a silicon-based life-form and still be capable of doing serious damage to a Vulcan. As he keyed in a Hold on the mu-spectrum settings he reflected that clearly the ship's extraordinary shielding had prevented readings coming through on at least one member of the pirate crew—guessing from the size and mass of the life-form—and possibly more. And if that was the case, Dylan Arios might well be sending for reinforcements.

The mass was twice average human, and far differently configured. Metabolism readings different, of course. The tricorder's small memory might not be able to give a clear reading if, like Arios's unknown ancestors, the alien was of an unknown race, but . . .

The correlation program flashed its best guess on the small digital, as well as the parameters probability.

Parameters probability was over ninety percent.

Spock felt his hands grow cold.

The program's best guess, from information received, was that the creature two decks below him was a yagghorth.

The *Nautilus* had picked up a yagghorth.

No wonder, thought Spock, Raksha and Adajia had told him to stay with them. No wonder Arios had been desperate to keep any of the *Enterprise* crew off the ship. Not primarily to conceal, but out of genuine concern for their safety. On the other hand, whatever they were hiding on board the *Nautilus,* it must be desperately important to prevent them from simply abandoning the vessel at the first opportunity.

Six people could conceivably share a Constitution-class cruiser with a yagghorth for a certain period of time and not come to harm, particularly if they set the food synthesizers to spew the equivalent of fresh meat and blood every few hours in the lower holds to prevent its hunting on the upper, but it was not a situation that could be kept going very long. Uneasily, he switched back an overlay to recheck the position of the thing as well as he could.

But they had succeeded so far, which put them far ahead of most crews in similar circumstances, and it crossed Spock's mind to wonder, as he slipped through a half-open blast door and down the narrow, boreglunch-smelling gangway into the rising steam from below, whether there was someone or something on Tau Lyra III—perhaps the psychically active savants the planet was supposed to have—capable of dealing with a yagghorth. Considering the proximity of that world to the Anomaly in the Crossroad, it was a possibility.

In spite of the tightening in his chest with every step of descent, Spock found himself prey to an almost overwhelming curiosity.

He had said that it was a mistake to theorize ahead of one's data; nevertheless, his mind teemed with alternatives. There was a source of the mu-spectrum radiation on the ship. Somehow they had picked up a yagghorth—though larval infestation was usually postulated, there was, in fact, no case that provided proof—which prevented them from getting to the energy source. . . . Given that seventy percent of the admittedly small sample of known yagghorth infestations occurred in sectors where Turtledove Anomalies existed, thought Spock, moving cautiously through the dripping mazes of old crew quarters, it was conceivable that yagghorth had been drawn to the source of an energy typical of the Anomalies.

We're real desperate, Arios had said.

And Raksha had repeated several times, *Don't get out of our sight.*

He felt a sudden pang of concern for Adajia, lying unconscious on the deck above.

But according to the tricorder the yagghorth was still below him, as he stood at the head of another gangway down into darkness. Films of mold covered the metal walls in the gluey heat, fungus clustering in the corners of the stairs. Here and there a lumenpanel survived, shedding a grimy glow that only served to show up the desertion of the place, its utter neglect.

The source of a mu-spectrum energy generator on board was, of course, thought Spock, only of secondary importance. But it might hold some answers, hold the proof to the theory that had been forming in his mind since he had first seen the engine chamber, first spoken to Adajia there.

Another thought came to him. He turned from the head of the gangway, his sharp hearing stretching to its limits in the silent ship around him, and walked a few paces down the hall to the open door of one of the empty crew staterooms. Boreglunches scurried through vents long corroded, red-black backs gleaming and long, threadlike antennae projecting from the dark squares of the openings as Spock searched rapidly through the empty drawers of the built-in desks.

The first room yielded nothing. In the second he found a few small plastic cubes, three centimeters square, which he dropped into the utility pocket of the tricorder case.

He checked the tricorder again, paused to listen, picking out the scrabbling of small vermin in the darkness and wondering if he would be able to detect the movement of the greater thing lurking somewhere below.

He heard nothing that answered him. Taking the phaser from his belt, he moved silently down the steps.

There was even less light on the decks below. The heat was equal to anything on Vulcan, the moisture suffocating, clammy on his skin and condensing on the moldy walls. Fungal growths and heat-loving forms of simple life were rankly evident. The smell of the yagghorth was strong down here, like very old oil, resinous exudations thick on the walls. This close to the energy source, the mu-spectrum color blanked out everything on the digital; after vainly trying to catch a moving shadow, a fractionated form, Spock gave up and concentrated on listening.

It had clearly been hot and damp down here for a long time. A result of the mu-generator? he wondered. Or a necessity of its operation?

His mind went back over the articles he had read, articles speculating about the link between mu-spectrum energy and noninstrumentative transportation phenomena over huge distances. A link with the attenuated warp engines, the enlarged impulse drive of the *Nautilus* and its almost nonexistent power-source controls—controls that occupied huge percentages of the *Enterprise* engines—was almost certain.

The only question was . . . where had the *Nautilus* acquired a mu-spectrum drive?

Spock paused again, straining his ears, his mind. A scutter of claws—rats? Big ones, if so. But then of course they *might* be big ones. He'd seen engine rats on some tramp planet-hoppers not only grown to enormous size, but bizarrely mutated as well. He tried to adjust the tricorder to get a divided reading—half to alert for the yagghorth, half to register the proximity of the mu-spectrum generator—and received an error message and a polite request to recalibrate. The only person he had ever spoken to who had survived an infestation—Commander Kellogg of Starbase 12—had said that the creature was absolutely silent, but some of the visuals from surviving ships seemed to indicate a hissing, a rattle of chitin.

Adjusting the tricorder for the mu-spectrum lines again—since he had no idea what such a generator would look like—he set his phaser on maximum, and, listening to every sound in the silent darkness, moved forward again.

"They wired him when he was eight years old."

Christine Chapel turned sharply, her hands still covering the icy fingers of the Vulcan boy. Phil Cooper had dragged himself up a little in his bed, and was regarding her with drugged pain in his dilated gray eyes. In the near-total darkness of the security ward, his unshaven face looked battered and old beyond his years, and his head nodded with the effect of the melanex.

"They have to," Cooper went on thickly. "Trained as empaths . . . trained to the psion drive. The Vulcans make the best. Highest mathematical abilities. They need that. Have to understand what they're doing, bending space from inside rather than warping around it. They tried Deltans and Betazoids and Rembegils. The Rembegils all died. Little glass fairies, they looked like . . . big green eyes. Long green hair. The Consilium thought they had it made when they contacted Rembegil. Ran a colony of 'em for years, one of their biggest." He pushed a hand through his hair.

"It's the dreams, see. They put cutouts, limiters, to keep the dreams down. Works for Vulcans and Betas. Wiring . . . brings the dreams."

He sank to the bed again, closed his eyes. His voice was a slurry whisper. "Most people don't know that side of it. I don't know what they're telling you in the Fleet these days."

The floor hard beneath her knees, the darkness like a silent bubble, shutting her out from all sound, all contact with the ship around her, Chapel half-felt that she dreamed herself. Softly, she asked, "They did this to you when you entered the Fleet?"

Roger's voice returned to her, with the memory of moonlight shining on the pale V of his chest against the dark satin of his dressing gown; the smell of the university botanical gardens and the glinting jeweled eyes of Zia Fang, the Rigellian god of healing, whose lumpish stone statue sat in a niche among the wall of wafer storage, ancient scrolls, transcription equipment. *You have to realize that there's always a conspiracy somewhere, Chris,* he had said. *They'll corrupt anything, no matter how good you are, no matter what good you do or try to do. They'll take it over eventually.*

She hadn't wanted to believe it.

Cooper nodded, his eyes still shut. "Astrogator, impulse and warp. Put the ship in position for the jump and know where you are when you come out. Think about it. They can't let pilots start setting up on their own. Break the Consilium's monopoly on freight. The Master shorts it out. Nanological . . . repairs itself. Grows back."

They didn't carve those microservos out of soap, McCoy had said. By the scar tissue, the flesh around the minuscule line of metallic protrusions on Sharnas's neck had been cut many times.

After knowing Roger, Christine had never quite known what to make of conspiracy theories. She'd heard all the usual ones outlined by rec-room rebels like Brunowski and Bray: Kratisos Shah is still alive and tending bar on Antares IV; the Federation maintains a secret laboratory within a black hole for unknown purposes; certain historical characters (never the same ones) had been retrieved and cloned in hidden installations.

Even among those, she had never heard of anything called the Consilium.

Cooper tried to open his eyes again, but Chapel could see, even in the thick gloom, that his eyeballs were drifting, unable to focus. "You have a Vulcan," he mumbled. "Th'Master's mostly Rembegil, spliced onto enough human genes to take the stress. Consilium started doing that when the colony died off. Bred him, trained him for psionics. Served 'em right," he added enigmatically. "It's how he could break their hold on Thad. McKennon's tried to get it back two or three times. McKennon." His face twisted in momentary dread, or remembered pain. Then he shook his head. "McKennon. The Masters didn't leave Thad with much of a brain but he's got a hell of a heart. Consilium's quit growing them now—that strain. That combination. Too much trouble."

Chapel shook her head, baffled. "I've never heard of the Consilium," she said. "Who . . ."

Cooper blinked, trying to get her into focus, trying to see where he was. "Ah," he breathed at last, and the lines relaxed a little from his forehead. "Yeah. The *Enterprise.*" He shook his head. "Forgot where I was."

According to the readings on the tricorder, the mu-spectrum generator was somewhere in the vast darkness that had once been Recycling. Logical, thought Spock, his head still moving slowly with the attempt to distinguish sound, his eyes still trying to pierce the intense darkness that closed so thickly around him. Because of the needs of the food synthesizers, the main trunk of the computer lines ran through this section.

Some of the synthesizers themselves obviously still worked, at least to a degree. As he had surmised, the smell of rotting organics was thick in the air, bait to keep the yagghorth in this section, to keep it from wandering to the engine rooms above. It surprised him, however, that none of the doorways he had passed on his way here were barricaded.

Perhaps they simply knew that barricades were, in the case of a yagghorth, at best a temporary measure. The decking might be holed. It was often found to be, on infested ships.

Most of the square gray synthesizers were rank with ciroids, fungus, odd and mutant plants, the steamy heat aiding in the transformation of this chamber into an ugly, lightless jungle. Thready curtains of gray growths hung from the conduits that crisscrossed the ceiling, further shortening Spock's field of vision; one of the synthesizers had burst open, and a yellow-tentacled fungus—quite obviously car-

nivorous as far as rats and boreglunches were concerned—
grew from its heart to cover a good eight square meters of
floor and surrounding mechanisms. Moisture dripped from
the ceiling, and the scritch and patter of vermin sounded
everywhere, making it doubly difficult for Spock to listen for
the greater danger that lurked somewhere, very close now,
in the dark.

All around the synthesizer chamber the walls and floor
were crusted with resin, a slick laminate on the walls higher
than his head in places and gleaming vilely in the reflection
of his flashlight in the dark. In places it was still sticky—
outside in the corridor, he had passed a trail of it still wet.
The oily smell was everywhere.

He glanced again up at the main trunk of the computer
feed and power conduit. The central mixer board of Recycling was one candidate for a hook-in source to control the
mu-generator. Others on the main trunk might be the games
in the nearby bowling alley, or one of the computers in the
botany lab. He listened carefully, then stepped out into the
corridor again. Nothing yet, though he could feel his pulse
rate increase infinitesimally. The bowling alley was the
logical place to check next, he thought, replacing the phaser
in his belt to readjust the tricorder. The room itself was a
virtual dead end. . . .

He paused, looking at the readings in startlement, wondering if he had adjusted too high. . . .

The next instant he sprang away from the black mouth of
the open turbolift door as a striking tentacle jetted from the
darkness. Spock bolted back up the corridor, not looking
back, hearing the ghost-whisper of chitin and bone as the
yagghorth uncoiled and wriggled from the lift shaft where it
had been hiding. He heard it in the corridor behind him,
hideously fast; threw himself through the door into the
synthesizer chamber and twisted at the manual control.
Something fell against the closing door like a gelatinous
spider, and Spock leaped for the gangway at the end of the
room, only to have something catch around his ankle in a
biting grip that nearly broke the bone within the boot.

A force like a machine whipped him off his feet.

He struck the floor hard, twisting his body to catch at the hatch handle of the nearest synthesizer. Behind him he could see the black slit of the door, the wet gleam of an eyeless, narrow head trying to force its way through, the wet star of groping tentacles slobbering at the door's edges, the longer tentacles and two thin, multijointed legs squirming in the aperture. The tentacle that had seized his foot ended in a double-padded grip that was already working its way up his leg for better purchase; the next nearest one, not quite yet able to touch him, finished in a razor-toothed mouth.

The force of the drag was incredible. Spock held to the metal of the hatch handle with both hands, not daring to release even long enough to unship his phaser. He felt the sinews of his hands and shoulders crack. He hacked at the tentacle with the heel of his other boot, knowing it was a useless gesture as far as defense went. The thing shifted another coil onto his calf and made a grab with its rough-padded end for his other foot as well. The razored mouth had moved, groping now around the edge of the door and along the wall toward the manual controls, and Spock realized with surprise that the yagghorth understood how the door worked.

He released his grip with his right hand and snatched his phaser from his belt, firing even as the yanking strength of it nearly dislocated his left shoulder. He tried to pull himself free, and the jerk of it ripped the skin from his fingers and palm, his left hand slipping on the handle. He fired again, into the center of those black, groping tentacles, though in the darkness he could barely see his target. Pain sliced his left leg, his left shoulder. His grip clenched as hard as it could but the metal ripped from his bloody fingers and his body hit the floor hard. The next instant, it seemed, he was up against the twelve-centimeter gap of the doorway, a tentacle around his waist crushing his ribs, and he realized that the thing was simply going to pull him through the door slit, pulping the bones within the flesh as it did.

He fired the phaser again into the seething mass of bone

and organ beyond the doorway, felt it flinch, twist, then slam him furiously against the edges of the metal to drag him through.

Somewhere in the corridor he heard a woman's voice shout *"NEMO!"* And then, as consciousness blurred, he thought he heard her add, *"Zchliak!"*

Which was the Vulcan word for *friend*.

Chapter Seven

"WE NEED SOMETHING with a narrow end that won't bend under pressure." Kirk wasn't sure why he was whispering, but somehow in the darkness, the utter silence of the blacked-out ship, he hesitated to raise his voice. "Any suggestions? Anyone have anything?"

"Hairpin's too narrow?" came a female voice—Yeoman Wheeler's, of Security—and the next moment something about eight centimeters long and half the thickness of one of McCoy's tongue depressors was poked into his hand. "It's supposed to be titanium-finished."

He flexed it between his hands as hard as he could, and felt it bend. "Too weak. And now I'm afraid I spoiled it for you."

"I guess that means I'm never going to speak to you again, Captain." She took it back.

"I had a couple of styli in my log pad," offered Ensign Gilden, the assistant historian. "You put two of those together, it might work. The log pad should be on the floor here someplace."

There was a soft, deliberate scuffling as bodies hunched awkwardly and hands described large, cautious circles on

87

the floor. Kirk had found eight crew members slowly coming out of the effects of heavy stun in various portions of the corridors between Mr. Spock's office and Transporter Room Two, med or transporter techs or redshirts going on shift in Security, or those who, like Ensign Gilden, were simply unfortunate enough to have quarters in the adjacent corridors.

"How many of them are there?" asked Lieutenant Oba after a moment. The assistant transport chief's voice was soft, like Kirk's, as if he feared that somehow those who had taken over the ship could hear them through the disabled comm links.

And for all he knew, reflected Kirk, they might be able to.

"I don't know," said Kirk. "Scanner sweeps of the *Nautilus* showed no further human life there, but there was heavy shielding on the ship. Some areas didn't register at all. I don't think there's more than six of them all together. Four, now that two of them have gone back to the *Nautilus* with Mr. Spock. To the best of my knowledge two of those four are in sickbay."

And one of the remaining two, he added, *doesn't look capable of independent action.* And somehow, remembering the childlike dark eyes and sweet smile, Kirk didn't think Thad Smith was mean enough, or fierce enough, to kill. At least not on his own initiative. Maybe not at all.

And that left one.

Who could be anywhere.

"Got it!" came Gilden's voice.

"Over here," said Kirk.

Shuffling in the dark. Each stylus was eighteen centimeters long and two thick, tapered to a writing point at one end and a blunt, rounded key tapper at the other. They fit easily into the end of the dolly handle, held in place by the tape. Kirk knew the rooms and corridors of the *Enterprise* almost literally blindfolded, particularly those of the middle decks: the offices, transporter rooms, medical section, and Engineering of Deck Seven, the crew rec and Central Computer areas of Deck Eight, the officers' quarters of Deck Five above. He knew, almost without thinking about it, that there was an emergency kit next to the elevator around the corner from Transporter Room Two. It took him, Oba, and the beefy Ensign Curtis combined to lever loose the magnetic catch that held its cover, but the metal eventually bent and buckled, and they pulled out the long box within like treasure hunters who have finally achieved a pirate's hoard.

The kit contained, among other things such as medical supplies and a couple of oxygen masks, two flashlights and a degausser.

"Right," breathed Kirk. "Gilden, Oba, you both have second field experience in computers . . ."

"Not high-level stuff, sir," said Gilden. "I can untangle fragmentary historical files, but . . ."

"Doesn't matter. I don't know what you'll find when you get to Central." They were walking as he spoke, hurrying to the transporter room by the bobbing yellow gleam of the flashlights, where he degaussed the catch on the maintenance cupboard to remove more flashlights and another degausser. It was in his mind that there was a strong possibility Gilden and Oba would reach Central to find the entire staff unconscious—or worse—under their consoles.

"Butterfield, I'll need your phaser. Wheeler, go with Oba and Gilden to Central, see what's going on there. Get more flashlights and another degausser from the utility room at the end of that corridor there. Ensign . . ."

"If you don't mind, Captain," said Curtis, picking up the discarded yard of steel pipe they'd used for a lever, "I'll stay by the transporter room in case anybody else tries to get off the ship . . . or onto it." In the upside-down glow of the narrow light beams, his square red face was calm, with a very slight smile.

"Don't take chances you don't have to," he said— unnecessarily, he knew. They both knew. "And get yourself a phaser as soon as you can. I'll send back whoever I can to relieve you. All of you," he added, to the little group of Security redshirts and ad hoc computer draftees who followed him to the ship's central gangway, "I don't need to tell you to get into as many lockers as you can. Get demagnetizers, flashlights, phasers. We need to find where these people are hiding. They have to have access to lab-quality terminals, and they have to be somewhere on the main power trunk. Paxson, you go with the Central group, they may need medical attention down there. Butterfield, you go with them too, as a runner. I'll be on the bridge."

He killed and flipped the catch on the gangway's manual cover plate as he spoke, twisted the cog inside. Groaning, unwilling, the door slid back. He stopped on the threshold, his meager troop behind him, listening.

There were no voices from above.

Somebody—Sulu, probably—would have made the effort to come down. There were things on the bridge that could be used as levers, if no degausser was available.

Cautiously, Kirk flashed the light upward. Though there was no sign of danger in the enclosed blackness of the stairwell, only a faint glitter of residual moisture trickling down the side of a vent cover—the vent covers in the gangways weren't maintained as often as those on the rest of the ship—neither was there any sign that anyone had attempted to use the gangway in the nearly two hours that the lights had been out.

That was very unlike Mr. Sulu.

Kirk advanced a foot or so into the landing, shone the light down the metal stair below. Nothing. His boots chimed hollowly on the metal as he moved back around, to shine the light upward again.

Still nothing.

Very cautiously, he began to ascend.

"Do I have to mention that if you use that phaser again you're yagghorth chow?"

"Unnecessary, Rakshanes." Spock rolled over very gingerly and probed the zone of tenderness from pectorals to short ribs under his left arm, the sudden, flinching pain of the lowest two ribs on his right side. The tendons of his right hand ached at the movement of his fingers; his left palm, he saw belatedly, as sensation returned, was stripped of skin in patches, sticky with malachite blood.

The doorway was open before him. In the small glow of a hand lamp Raksha stood leaning, a bronze statue with a phaser in her hand and the garnets of her stiletto hilt glinting like blood droplets in her hair. Past the dark of her shadow something gleamed, too shiny, like wet cellophane or scar tissue: a squamous black hide stretched over uneven slabs of bone, salted with tiny flashes of gold; exposed organs pulsing thickly within the shield of hooked ribs and barbed legs. Black hair tousled silk, Adajia was making little pinch-and-scratch nips with her fingernails at the dripping masses of tentacles clustered at the front of the huge seahorse head.

At Spock's movement, fernlike growths slipped out of the leg joints and the small vents on the head's central ridge, pale yellows and whites against the thing's blackness in the sightless shadows, lacy as a vase of baby's breath on a Klingon mind-stripper. It coiled and retracted its tentacles, the foremost of the bony legs, holding them up mantis-wise, claws spread. As it did so the lamplight from Raksha's hand caught small points of metal along the central, ferny ridge, and down the back of the neck.

Spock leaned back on his elbows, the pain in his shoulders, his back, his hand and legs forgotten in that tiny line of spangling reflection. He was barely even conscious of deduction; certainly, at this point, not surprised. As if a final piece of data had emerged to link everything he had seen on the ship into a single, shining chain, he said, "People of your time have succeeded in docilizing yagghorth."

Raksha stepped forward, stooping carefully to pick up the phaser that lay beside Spock's bleeding hand. She tossed it to Adajia, who plucked it from the air like a thrown flower. The yagghorth retracted its sensory organs and hissed. Raksha put down a hand and helped Spock to his feet. His shoulders felt as if they'd been beaten with the blunt side of an ax.

"You don't know the half of it, pal."

"Is it permitted to request enlightenment?" He flexed his

hand gingerly, his body still reechoing with the aftermath of shock though his mind was striding quickly ahead. With the lamplight more steady upon it, he could see the creature clearly now, well over two meters tall in its current downslung position, but able to straighten, he guessed, to nearly twice that height, spiderlike legs tucked, vestigal wings half-spread, the three heavy tentacles more closely resembling spinal columns in their bumpy joints than limbs. Nobody had ever succeeded in killing a yagghorth in any fashion that left a skeleton intact; he found himself making mental notes on the anatomy, the forward-slumped stance, the way it kept moving its head, and the almost submarine waving of the sensory fronds.

He could see, quite plainly, the glint of metal on its spine, like the implants that glittered so evilly on Sharnas's back, on Arios's.

Raksha's eyes went from him to the yagghorth, suddenly old. "Sharnas tells me a story about a Vulcan master who met a god at the crossroads," she said. "He asked for perfect enlightenment. The god gave it to him. Gods do things like that. The Vulcan went and drowned himself, because it was the only logical thing to do." She leaned her shoulders against the door, brushed a coarse trail of black hair from her face. "Klingons have a reputation for being stupid. We treasure it."

Spock put his head a little on one side, his eyes meeting the ink-dark pits of shadowed grief, and for a time there was no sound but their breathing, the heartbeat of the engine, and the drip of moisture in the lightless belly of the haunted ship all around them. "Then you are from the future," he said at last, confirming what he had already guessed.

Raksha sighed. "Oh, yeah." She rubbed her forehead, her heavy eyebrows pulling together in pain, and shivered, as if suddenly cold. "Yeah. But it's not like you think."

"It's not a gas." Captain Kirk staggered down the gangway, stripping the oxygen mask from his face. In spite of the breathing apparatus, a few feet up the steps toward the deck above his breath had shortened and strangled, dizziness and weakness overwhelmed him. Wheeler and Gilden steadied him, looked at one another, baffled.

Butterfield said reasonably, "Could be why we haven't heard from the folks on the bridge."

Kirk walked slowly around to the door leading into the main hull's emergency bridge, a duplicate chamber directly below the main bridge six floors above. There was another such chamber in the engineering hull, surrounded, as this one was, with backup computers—a protected secondary heart and brain. He degaussed the cover plate and cranked the door open, stepped into the dark chamber, an eerie replica of that above, pitch-dark now that even the small red power lights on the overridden consoles were out.

The stubby finger of his flashlight's yellow gleam poked around the darkness, bobbed before him as he crossed the room, mounted the walkway to stand before the shut turbolift doors.

"I guess we have to do this the hard way," he said.

Thad Smith stood for some time in front of the long, metal-lined opening in the bright blue rec-room wall. He recognized it as a food slot—there was a metal counter in front of it for trays, and a series of buttons above it. Instead of the brightly colored pictures with which he had been familiar all his life, there was writing, as there was in the lounges of the Brass.

Though the Master and Phil had worked hard during the past year and a half to teach him to read, he still found it difficult to distinguish between *I*'s and *J*'s, *H*'s and *A*'s; difficult to pick out how the letters all made up the sounds of words. These were long words, too.

Still . . .

He glanced anxiously over his shoulder. By the glow of the small battery lamp, Arios sat unmoving at the table they'd dragged to the bank of games, his thin wrists one on top of the other in the semicircle of keypads Raksha had wired together, his green head bowed as if in sleep. Only his breathing, fast and shallow, told that he was not sleeping, but rather in the depths of a trance far longer, and far deeper, than Thad had ever seen him attempt.

Beyond the bright pond of lamplight the huge rec room was utterly dark, strange gleams lying like water on the glassy floors, the grinning machines. The other games, the comforting brightness of their lights quenched, stared at him with blank, demented eyes. No sound came from the corridor beyond the shut doors, save for the regular grumble of machinery in the other hold and the deeper, more soothing throb of the engines.

The thought of the engines made Thad shudder. If they didn't get away, if Raksha didn't get the engines of the *Nautilus* fixed fast, he and the Master would be caught, and very likely given to this ship's yagghorth. If the Master couldn't hold out the psychic defenses he'd set around this place, the illusion and interference he'd established between all the decks of the ship.

Thad was beginning to fear that he wouldn't. It was a huge ship, as big as the *Nautilus* and filled with people.

So, he returned to consideration of the food slot. He knew that sweet things—chocolate, or Klingon caramelized fruit—helped. Gave him back the energy that the illusion drained. Coffee, too. He thought he could spell coffee, but there were four different buttons with that word (only the spelling didn't look quite right) and there were other words besides. Any of them might have been poison.

Cautiously, he padded to the red-shirted Federation yeoman still stretched on the floor by the railings, his hands taped to a stanchion. Thad tried to think of a way to tear the engine tape off the man's mustache and mouth without hurting him, but couldn't think of any, so he simply grabbed a corner and yanked.

"How do you get chocolate out of the food slot?" he asked.

"Hunh?" said Yeoman Effinger.

"I need to get some chocolate out of the food slot, and it has writing instead of pictures, and I can't read that well."

At the Institute, of course, and in all the factories, the food slots in the Secondaries' room were all pictures, which in Thad's opinion were prettier than writing anyway.

"Oh," said Yeoman Effinger. "Uh—second bank of buttons from the left are all chocolate bars. First one's chocolate with almonds, second one has macadamias, third one's caramel and peanuts, fourth one's that kind of squishy orange nougat that's real nasty so don't eat it, and the bottom one's coconut marshmallow, but the synthesizer doesn't ever get the coconut right."

"Oh. Thanks. Are all the buttons with *coffee* on them okay?"

"Yeah. Top one's black, all the rest have stuff in them. Can you get me an almond chocolate bar while you're there?"

"I don't think the Master would let me," said Thad. "I'm real sorry. We'll let you go when we escape." He taped up Effinger's mouth again and went to get black coffee and two chocolate bars—macadamia-nut and caramel-peanut—from the food slot. Quietly, he stole to Arios's side.

"Master?"

Arios raised his head a little, though his eyes did not open. "Thad?" His lips formed the word without a sound.

"I got you some candy and some coffee."

Arios groped blindly for the coffee cup. Thad had to put it in his hand. "It's hot," he warned, but Arios sipped it anyway, then fumblingly broke off a piece of the candy.

"Thank you." His voice was thick and slurred, like a man speaking in deep sleep. "No word?"

"No."

"How long?"

Thad consulted the chronometer Velcroed to his wrist. Most Secondaries could not be taught to use digital readouts. His was an analog double circle, each face three centimeters across, one for day and one for night, the twelve segments of each brightly colored. It was a common Secondary design. The Master had to set it for him. "An hour and a half," he said, after study and counting.

Arios said nothing, but the muscles of his jaw clenched,

like a man who feels the cut of a whip. He sank into his trance again, his breathing labored, fine lines of pain cut deep into the soft flesh under his eyes. As quietly as he could, Thad took the coffee and the rest of the candy and returned to his post beside the door, consuming it thoughtfully as he listened to the dim echoes of the dark and sealed ship.

"Mr. Sulu!"

The voice echoed weirdly in the sounding column of the turbolift shaft, but it was unmistakably the captain's. Sulu flung himself to the open doorway, leaned down, and was rewarded with the sight of a small dot of yellow light below. "Captain! Are you all right?"

The others crowded up behind him—with the sole exception of Chekov, still at the helm, checking and double-checking the ship's slow movement against the position of the stars.

"Have you tried coming down the shaft on the safety cables?"

"Aye, sir," called Sulu. "Same problem as the gangways—I guess you tried the gangways? It isn't gas. . . ."

"No," said Kirk. "Or if it is, it got through our masks."

Sulu hunkered down on the threshold of that long, black drop. "Dawe's getting obstruction readings for seven or eight air-vent shafts on various decks. We think that's people who've tried to get through the vents, past the blast doors or out of rooms. They're not moving. We don't know if they're just knocked out or dead."

Kirk swore, wondering how many were lying dead in gangways throughout the ship; wondering what and how Arios had managed. "Any other in-ship sensors in operation?"

"Negative, sir. Dawe says Transporter Room Two activated about an hour ago. Three beamed over to the *Nautilus*."

"That was Spock, the Klingon, and the Orion. Have they returned?"

"Negative, sir."

"No indication of where Arios is?"

"Not a one, sir, except that it has to be somewhere there's a terminal."

Kirk was silent, looking up at that dark cluster of heads in the ocher square of the doorway light. "How far down did you get?"

"Deck Three, by gangways. Maynooth's up there now trying to figure out what Arios did to the computers."

"It's astonishing, sir," came the physicist's rather reedy voice. "Simply astonishing. They shouldn't be able to do the things they've done, slipping in and out of the defensive systems as if . . . Well, it's a marvelously sophisticated slicer program, sir. Orders of magnitude beyond anything I've ever seen." He sounded ready to marry the program's originator.

"Captain," said Sulu, and there was deep concern in his voice. "Captain, who *are* those people?"

Who indeed? An answer had occurred to Kirk already. He should have known, he thought, from the moment Cooper laughed in the transporter room.

He looked up again, gauging distances and the strength of his throwing arm. "Get down to Deck Three and open the lift doors there," he said after a moment. "Mr. Butterfield . . ." He turned to the security officer behind him, and held out the degausser. "Get to Security and bring me back some rope. Open every door you can find along the way and get enough people with degaussers and lights to make a general search of all the med labs and of Engineering. Find Mr. Scott if you can, or send someone to find him. And get me a report on those two we have in the security ward of sickbay. Mr. Wheeler, you go with her."

By the time the redshirt returned with the rope—and a half-dozen of her cohorts who reported that Mr. DeSalle had attempted to make an exit from the small Security messroom through the vent shaft and had not been heard from since—Kirk had gotten status reports from both Uhura and Maynooth, to the effect that the in-ship communication system was being "bled" for the ionization of all hand communicators, through a subtle cross-up of signals within the central computer itself. Like the cutting out of the doors and the lights, the blocking of the turbolifts and the quadrupling of the strength of all magnetic door catches on the ship, the reprogramming of that system was guarded with some kind of lock that left Maynooth speechless with admiration but utterly baffled.

"I'll get it, though," called down the bespectacled physicist cheerily. "Just give me some time. This is the most beautiful thing I've ever seen and I won't rest till I've conquered."

He sounded, Kirk thought with a smile, like half the male techs and redshirts on the ship upon their first glimpse of the lovely Yeoman Shimada. He wondered what Lao would make of the system.

Wondered where Lao was, and what had become of him. Not sitting around on his hands in the darkness, that was certain.

With Butterfield had come Yeoman Wein, released from a cell in the brig that had previously held Dylan Arios. The redshirt was unable to offer a satisfactory explanation of his inattention, but after the eerie phenomenon of the gangway, Kirk was not inclined to blame him.

"We've run into aliens who dealt in illusion before this," he said grimly. "If it is illusion we're dealing with and not something else. No, they got out, they did their preliminary setup at the terminal in the briefing room around the corner from the brig, then took off for somewhere they could fine-tune it in private."

He worked as he spoke, tying the end of the rope Butterfield had brought to the heavy metal ring from a tape dispenser found in the supply cabinet. "It took at least fifteen minutes for Raksha and Adajia to get from wherever they were to Mr. Spock's office, probably traveling by vent shaft most of the way. That says to me Arios is holed up somewhere in the engineering hull. Mr. Sulu?"

"Aye, sir."

"Catch!" He flung the ring upward and across the lift shaft with all his strength. It took him four tries to get his range, but on the fourth the helmsman caught the ring easily, hauling up a hefty bight of rope and fashioning a kind of body sling out of it, with the ring as a sliding bolt.

They were still discussing the logistics of lowering someone to the doors of Deck Eight when those doors opened beneath them, and Lieutenant Organa's voice called out, "Hello up there!"

"Do you have access to Central Computer?" demanded Kirk at once. "Is everything secure down there?"

"We've searched this deck," the assistant security chief called back to him. "There's some kind of gas in the gangways so we can't get up or down. It seems to go right through oxygen gear. Looks like it's in the air vents as well, but it doesn't come down into the rooms. Ensign Lao passed out in a vent trying to get to Engineering; we just located him a few minutes ago by tricorder. He seems to be okay but I'd feel better if Dr. McCoy took a look at him."

"I'm fine!" The broad-shouldered form of Lao Zhiming blotted the light behind her. "Captain, have you had a look at that programming? It's beyond anything I've ever seen, but it isn't alien! I swear it isn't alien! The logic systems are directly traceable. Could those people . . ."

"Stow it, Ensign," snapped Kirk. "No further speculation out loud—that's an order." There were two possibilities, and neither of them made him very comfortable.

He could hear the bafflement, the dawning understanding, in Lao's voice as the young man said, "Aye, sir."

"Keep at it," Kirk added, more kindly, not wanting to simply slap the young man's face to shut him up. "Find out everything you can, but report it to me."

"Aye, sir."

The weak glow of the flashlight gleamed briefly on his hair as he turned back in to the room.

"We'll send Maynooth down to you," promised Kirk to Organa. "Mr. Sulu, tie him in that sling and lower him as fast as you can. Mr. Organa, when he gets there, come up and take over the search on this deck, but I'm still willing to bet Arios is holed up somewhere in the engineering hull. Mr. Sulu, you have the conn."

"Aye, sir."

"Keep runners stationed all along the lift tube. If you need me, I'll be in sickbay. I think it's time I had a little talk with our remaining guests."

Chapter Eight

"THE FUTURE." Phil Cooper ran a shaky hand through his hair, regarded the men grouped around his bed with eyes that had long ago ceased to believe in anything they saw. Then he sighed, and looked away. "Yeah," he said. "We're from the future. If you really are who you say you are."

McCoy's mouth twisted in annoyance. "Who the tarnation else would we be?"

"Just who you are." Cooper's gaze traveled from the doctor to Captain Kirk, at the doctor's side; to Chapel, still kneeling beside the unconscious Sharnas; to Ensign Lao, armed and almost unseen beside the dark gape of the door. Lao, Kirk knew, had guessed—guessed that the *Nautilus* was either a visitor from the distant future or a Starfleet project so highly classified as to be unheard of even in rumors. In either case, whatever Cooper was going to say was nothing an ordinary security officer should hear.

"Starfleet," Cooper went on, and there was infinite weariness in his voice. "You'd have access to old uniforms, old ships, old visual logs about exactly how it was. Anything we've seen in the old logs, you could match. You could even doctor the starfields on the ports. And then I'd get all trusting and tell you about the rebellion, and where the

Shadow Fleet's hiding, and how the Master got in touch with them, and what he did to break the docilization codes the Consilium keeps on every captain and astrogator and psionic empath in the Fleet, and we all end up getting ripped to pieces on holovid by whatever alien predator is considered 'the ult' that week." The pulse-rate indicator above his diagnostic bed climbed slightly; clearly he'd seen such a holovid himself.

"If we wanted information," said McCoy, almost gently, "we could have pumped you full of lyofane or zimath, you know."

Cooper chuckled derisively. "Don't you think that's been tried? It's the one advantage I've ever seen in having had my backbone wired. That, and being able to catch the psion jumps before they happen. And to sometimes hear the Master's voice in my head."

He raised a hand to his temple again, closed his eyes, and bowed forward; a shudder went through him. With the addition of more battery lamps and a couple of flashlights, some of the intense darkness in sickbay had abated, but the room was still dingy with shadow. In the harsh half-light Cooper's face looked strained and old. "I'm sorry," he said after a time, his voice muffled. "You may be who you say you are. We may really have come through that Anomaly to the past, like the Master said we were going to, if we hit it right, if . . ." He hesitated, fumbling almost visibly for a lie, a cover-up, through the fog of leftover melanex. ". . . if all the calculations were correct."

If what? Kirk wondered.

Wherever he was on the ship, Arios would be tired, too. McCoy's tricorder readings had indicated fatigue greater than one day's rest could overcome. In time, he'd start making mistakes.

"They can be trusted." The voice from the other bed was barely a murmur; Chapel turned swiftly, reached out to touch the boy's hand, but drew hers back, remembering Mr. Spock's aversion to unnecessary contact. But perhaps because of his weakness, the boy didn't seem to mind. To Cooper, he said, "In my—dreams—she touched my mind, a little. She is not lying. She is not party to any lie. The Vulcan said to be Spock is in fact Spock of the *Enterprise*. Therefore, that is where we are."

Chapel felt her whole face heat to the collarbone and she looked away, profoundly glad for the darkness of the room. Blindingly, she remembered the Vulcan ability to make mental connection, and heard Cooper's voice saying again, *He was trained as an empath. . . .*

He knew. Knew not only that Spock was who he said he was—that there was no deception in the minds of impartial third parties—but knew also that she wasn't impartial. Knew of the love she had cherished, hopelessly, toward the impassive first officer for years.

For a moment she felt naked, as if the boy had revealed her innermost secrets to the men in the room. From the corner of her eye she saw Sharnas startle and realized that he had read her discomfiture as he had read her love. For a moment she met his eyes, filled with puzzlement and apology, and turning back with an effort, saw in McCoy's face, and Kirk's, and young Lao's, only curiosity about what Cooper had to tell them, not about her at all.

Sharnas began, "The Consilium . . ." and Cooper shook his head violently.

"No. The Master said no information. None."

The boy's slanted eyebrows dragged together. His voice, ragged from the corrosive gas, was surprisingly deep. "If they knew, they might be able to . . . to change it. To make it different."

"The Master said no," repeated Cooper, closing his eyes and leaning back again. "McKennon can use anything; you know she was on our trail. *I* say no."

"You've told us a good deal already," said Kirk, lifting a finger to silence McCoy's remark. "You weren't thinking very clearly at the time, but Nurse Chapel has a lot of what you said earlier down in her medical log. There's enough there for me to make some guesses. About who the Consilium is. About what's happened in the . . . how many years has it been?"

Cooper sighed, defeated. His body relaxed, as if only

tension and pain had been holding his bones together. "I was never real good at history," he said softly. "The Master and I ran from the Academy in forty-six. Twenty-five-forty-six. We . . . Most people don't believe what the Consilium's doing. Most people never come in contact with laserbrains or psis, or with the gene splicers. But you can't keep it from people in the Academy, no matter how strong the programming is. Everybody going for captain or astrogator is wired. We work with the psionics all the time, with the specials, with the tame scientists who've got tape loops for brain stems. We ran . . . two years ago."

"That's when you acquired the *Nautilus.*"

Cooper moved his head. "She'd been brought in to be junked. Obsolete after years of hauling ore in some backwater, but she'd been converted to the psi jump at some point, probably right after the Consilium gave the technology to the Fleet. The Master fixed her up."

"And what is the Consilium doing?" asked Kirk, his voice low. He glanced hesitantly at Lao, at Chapel, wondering just how many should know, and what they should know. *Three people can keep a secret. . . .* He pushed away the conclusion of the old saw.

"Who is the Consilium?"

Cooper only averted his face from them, lying as if for protection against the wall. Kirk could see the tension in the muscles of his back, the set of his shoulders, as if physically fighting the weight of the horrible decision involved in all temporal paradoxes: to do something or to do nothing, either of which might hasten the future evil.

It was Sharnas who spoke.

"The Consilium pioneered the entire technology of psychoactive neural enhancement through nanotech wiring," he said. He coughed, but winced only a little. The hyperena was finally beginning to take effect, healing as dalpomine lowered the stress level of his system.

"The earliest applications were to docilize the criminally insane," the Vulcan went on, as if speaking of some world other than his own. "Massive documentation, massive checks and balances; implants kept them calm, gave them a reality check when violence started cutting into their minds." He coughed again, pressing his scarred hand to his side. "But after the plague, there were millions, hundreds of millions, who would have died, or for whom there would have been no alternative to extermination, if it hadn't been for the neurological rewiring of their perceptions. It kept whole populations calm and in touch with reality. It saved civilization. Literally. Everywhere."

"Saved it," said Lao softly, into the silence. "Or . . . turned it? Turned it into something else. Something . . . that could be controlled." Already he could see what was coming. There was disbelief—or the hope in the possibility of disbelief—in his voice. *Tell me what you're going to say isn't true.*

"When you're being fed through the bars," replied Cooper, "you don't ask whether the hand that's passing you the food is clean or dirty. You eat and thank God."

Sharnas shook his head, his face grave but his eyes very sad. "For many there wasn't even that choice. Whole populations were wiped out, either by the sickness itself, or by the results of the neurosynaptic breakdowns that the plague caused, or by the fighting that followed, or by the . . . the things the wars did to the genetic material of those who survived. But twenty years later, it was Fleet captains who had been wired as children, and wired astrogators, who made the . . . the discovery that led to the psion jump. The literal bending of space to allow a ship to . . . to go around hyperspace."

"What?" Kirk tried to picture it and failed. "How? I mean . . ."

"What was the breakthrough?" asked Lao, and for a moment his usual eagerness broke through the dark silence that seemed to have settled upon him. "Research now points to a kind of wormhole theory, but . . ."

"Better not go into that," said Cooper, a little too quickly. "But it works. And it works faster, lighter, than anything that's been dreamed of now. It's a completely different principle. But it won't work unless you've got a wired astrogator and a wired empath . . . among other things. And that gave the Consilium control over the Fleet. Over all trade everywhere. It made the warp drive obsolete overnight. For the past sixty years Starfleet—and the Federation Council—has been in the Consilium's desk drawer. They get what they want."

"I suppose," said Kirk, into that terrible silence, "there are members of the Federation Council who are wired, too."

The rain-colored eyes glinted cynically up from the pillows. "You catch on quick."

They get what they want. Kirk had been around the sources of power, the governments of alien planets and small colonies and bureaucracies minor and major too long not to know what that meant.

Outside the open doors of sickbay, firefly lights flitted through the night-drowned halls. Voices called to one another, hushed with the curious impulse to quiet that all of them felt. Someone said, "He's up here," and there was a muffled clashing of metal as yet another enterprising soul was extracted with great care from the air vent he'd attempted to use as an escape passage from some sealed room or blocked corridor. Three such victims were already being gone over by the techs in ICU, apparently completely unharmed once they got out of the narrow space.

Narrow spaces, thought Kirk, with the part of his mind still functioning in the present, still working as the captain of a beleaguered ship.

But it was only surface reaction. In the battle of Achernar, Kirk had seen men go on running after taking a mortal hit.

Starfleet would become the private arm of a private power, used for that power's convenience. The Federation would end as an Imperial Senate at the subtle beck of an inner circle of those who could control other men's minds.

All he had worked for—all his own dreams of future worlds, future justice, future good. Gone.

Gone in slightly less than three hundred years.

If those who came after him wanted to follow his footsteps to the stars, they'd have to do it with wires up their spines and voices in their heads telling them what they must and must not do. Would and would not think

Sharnas had seen it. Cooper had seen it. The reflection of it was in their eyes.

Beside him, he heard Lao whisper, "No," like a man watching a holovid, watching people he'd learned to love and care about going up in a computer-digital holocaust.

But it was real. It would be real.

He turned, to see the arsenic corrosion of the knowledge at work in McCoy's tired eyes.

We all end up getting ripped to pieces on holovid, . . .

Hyperbole? Paranoia? Kirk didn't think so. There was darkness there he hadn't looked into yet, didn't want to look into.

"I'm sorry," said Cooper softly. "I shouldn't have told you all that. You did ask."

"Yes," said Kirk. "We asked." Why was it the nature of humankind to ask?

He took a deep breath. Like taking the first step with a gut wound. Like saying the first words to a woman after finding the tracks of the other man. "So the rebellion is centered in the Fleet?"

Cooper nodded. "The Shadow Fleet split off about three years ago. Junkers, mostly. We're the only psion jump-drive vessel they've got. The rest are outgunned and outmaneuvered."

A lie, maybe, thought Kirk, scanning the young man's face. He prayed Cooper was lying, anyway. Another part of him wondered why it was so important to him to believe that it was a lie. To believe that the Rebellion—the Shadow Fleet—was stronger than that. Was capable of winning.

What did it matter, if everybody in it had to be wired anyway?

Why should he care, if it would all happen years after he himself was dead?

"So what brought you here? Why Tau Lyra?"

Cooper shook his head. Sharnas drew in breath, and the astrogator said harshly, "No."

"But . . ."

"I said no! You trust them, Sharnas. You trust her." He nodded across at Chapel, still kneeling by the boy's bed in the semidark. "I don't. You've seen them program a holodeck. You'd be willing to swear you're eating dinner on the beach or tracking criminals with Sherlock Holmes . . . or having sex with a chained-up fourteen-year-old or getting your eyes and your entrails ripped out if someone in the Consilium doesn't happen to like you, for that matter.

"You've met Fleet captains McKennon's programmed to believe owe her their lives, so of course they'll destroy themselves and their men at her command. You've met people who've been programmed to believe that they owed their corporate Brass their lives, so of course they'd work sixteen hours a day or be on call or whatever was needed—people who've been programmed to believe their families were murdered by whoever the Consilium wants out of the way. Of course Nurse Chapel could believe that Vulcan guy is Mr. Spock and this is the *Enterprise.* McKennon could have figured that out when she sent her in here to hold your hand."

Sharnas said softly, "You're wrong. I'd know."

Kirk was aware of Lao's indrawn breath, of the shock in his eyes. *He's too young for this,* he thought. *He has ideals. . . .*

He only asked quietly, "And what have you been programmed to believe, Mr. Cooper?"

Cooper met his eyes, but made no reply.

Not unkindly, Kirk went on, "There's no chance your Master is going to get out of here and back to his own ship, you know. He's only got Thad with him now. We'll trace him down with tricorders, if nothing else. We have to know. They're innocent people on that planet, people who don't even know about spaceflight, about other worlds. Why Tau Lyra Three?"

Cooper turned his face to the wall.

"Don't ask him." Sharnas's voice was very low. "And don't ask me. I think he's wrong, but if he's right, what we've told you, McKennon would have known already. She's . . . the Consilium domina in charge of Starfleet. In charge of crushing the Shadow Fleet, of bringing us back into line."

The diagnostics above the bed showed heart rate up, blood pressure down, the returning symptoms of trauma and shock at the mention of her name. Chapel rose quickly. "Captain, I have to . . . to ask you not to question him any more. Either of them." In her own face was the shadow of everything she had heard, but with it, the determination to protect her patients no matter who they were or what they knew.

Kirk hesitated, then said, "It doesn't change the fact that we have to know, Nurse. Mr. Lao, get back to Central Computer. Break that block on the computers any way you can and get the controls back. And not a word to anyone—not *anyone*—of one thing you've heard. I don't think I need to add that goes for everyone in this room."

Lao nodded. Kirk could see in his face the reflection of what he knew was in his own: a hollow inside, a darkness where something had been taken away. Like Bluebeard's seventh bride, they'd opened a locked door, and what they'd seen beyond it couldn't be unseen. He felt as if some internal gravity had been switched off, leaving him to float.

"I'll be with the security party trying to get down the gangways in the pylon," he went on, with a certain amount of effort. He was, after all, the captain. Whatever the others guessed of what he felt—of the sudden death of all the promises on which he'd based his life—he still had the ship to run. The Prime Directive to obey, though it—and everything else—seemed now like some bitter joke.

He was aware, however, that he sounded very tired. "I'll leave Yeoman Wein here as a runner . . ."

"Captain . . . !" Sharnas's dark eyes snapped open again, and the diagnostic arrows leaped. He made a move to sit up—Chapel flung out her hand, staying him, forcing him down. "Captain, the Master . . ." Sharnas wet his lips. His words came slightly thick, a stammer and hesitation. "The Master wants to talk to you." The diagnostic arrows steadied, sank, as he bowed his head, folded his arms about himself as if for protection. When he looked up again, the calm, the logic—the *Vulcanness,* Kirk thought—had left his

face, replaced by that slight angle of the head, the slouch of the shoulders, that Kirk remembered from the briefing room and the brig.

"Captain, I hear Mr. Spock's finished with the engines on the *Nautilus*." Even the slight roughness was the same, different from the coolant's corrosion. "He'll be coming back . . . Transporter Room Two. After Sharnas and Phil are sent over to the ship."

"Captain Arios, I'm afraid that's not possible," said Kirk grimly. "Where are you? You can't hide forever, my men are . . ."

"Your men are running around in the dark with flashlights, and I promise you the ops programs on the lights and the doors are going to stay locked down until all of us are back on the ship and we're the hell away. I've got a timer lock on your tractor beam and your phasers and I'll put one on your main drive if I have to."

"Don't be a fool."

Sharnas's face broke into a curious, and very Arios-like, grin. "Captain, if I wasn't a fool six ways from Sunday you'd be in *real* trouble. We mean no harm. Not to you, not to anybody on Yoondri. I swear to you we're not going to tamper with their culture or tell them things they shouldn't know. But unless we get there . . ."

His voice broke off, stammering; Sharnas made a sudden, twitching movement with his hand. The arrows above the bed fluttered with the increase of the pulse.

"Unless we get there . . ."

"Jim, you can't . . ." began McCoy in soft-voiced protest.

"Captain, we're in touch with the engineering hull," whispered a voice. Turning, Kirk saw a panting Ensign Giacomo in the doorway. "We're lowering bottles on strings down the dorsal conduit to Air-Conditioning. There's gas in all the gangways and vents down there, too."

"Tell them to get a guard on the emergency transporter rooms on Deck Twenty-two *at once*." He kept his voice low, wondering how much Arios could hear through his mental link with the Vulcan boy. Wondering how much it mattered. "I don't care how they do it, just do it."

He turned back to Sharnas, who was staring blankly before him, as if facing something in some timeless distance that filled him with both horror and grief. Thin and without breath, he whispered, "Oh, dear God . . ."

The diagnostics peaked, slammed: shock, trauma, the onset of agony. "Dalpomine," snapped McCoy, and Chapel was already lunging for the open darkness of the door.

Sharnas's breath drew in . . .

And his face changed. He was Sharnas the Vulcan again, a look of panic in his eyes.

"What is it?" Cooper dragged himself to one elbow.

"He's gone." Sharnas was shaking all over as McCoy pressed the injector of sedative to his arm. "Fainted. Pain . . ." He looked about to faint himself.

Kirk wheeled, plunged through the open door and around the corridor to the emergency bridge, where a small group still clustered by the door of the turbolift shaft. In addition to the tunnel that led upward through all decks of the saucer, at this point it branched laterally, cutting across the hull to Engineering. Mr. DeSalle stood in the doorway, shouting along the echoing tube, "Just be glad there wasn't a vent shaft to tempt you into crawling out of there, Scotty!" He turned and greeted Kirk with a half-salute. "It's Mr. Scott, sir," he said. "He's been locked all this time in the port-side Engineering head."

"Come on." Kirk strode into the horizontal lift shaft.

The security chief caught him by the arm. "You want to take a rope so we can haul you back when you pass out?"

"Come on," repeated Kirk, jerking his head. "Lao, with me, we may need something on the computer. . . ."

DeSalle shrugged and stepped into the dark tunnel after them.

"Organa, hand me that rope. . . ."

It was forty-five meters along the shaft to Engineering. The redshirt runner who'd tried to walk it had keeled over four or five meters in and had had to be dragged the rest of the way. Kirk, Lao, and DeSalle covered the ground in sixty seconds.

"What the . . . ?"

Kirk turned to shout back down the shaft. "Mr. Organa, muster full security forces for a search of the engineering hull. All locations where there are lab-quality terminals, and extra guards on the emergency transporter rooms. You should be able to get down the gangways now. On the double!"

Lights swarmed along the dark corridors like torrents of luminous bubbles in a stream. At the head of a platoon of security officers, Kirk clattered down the echoing darkness of the gangways. He picked up more personnel at every level of the pylon; a few men and women had been in each of the dorsal lounges when the lights went out, drinking coffee and having a final chat before going on shift. Kirk briefed them on the run: lab-quality terminals, and someplace empty or nearly so in that last hour of the shift.

"How about the bowling alley, sir?" suggested a burly tech in maintenance coveralls. "Those games they have at the back are complicated enough, they have to have lab-quality circuits or better. Besides, the main trunk from Recycle leads right underneath."

"What games?" Kirk had visited the bowling alley maybe four times in his entire tenure as the *Enterprise*'s captain. He had a vague recollection of pinball and pachinko, but games and game technology were something that existed, in his mind, chiefly in terms of Academy trainers.

"Hologames, illo-spex," said Lao, springing along beside him like a young cougar. "The phantom-league baseball's been going for nearly four years. Mario's right, I've watched the techs reset those games. Those are lab-quality, and high-end at that. They could easily have cut into Central through one of them."

Serves me right, thought Kirk dourly, *for spending my off shifts playing chess with Spock in the rec room instead of hanging out with the beer-and-pretzels crowd downstairs.* He wondered what else he might have missed.

The engineering hull was always more sparsely populated than the main saucer, and there were huge sections where the blast doors were still down, where the population of technicians and researchers were still trapped in whatever small areas they'd been occupying when Raksha's locks had gone into the ship's internal systems. There was, Kirk noticed, very little panic. Lamps had been improvised out of oil in every rec room and mess hall that had access to food slots and enough string for wicks, and the whole ship smelled of burning grease. On Deck Sixteen, Lieutenant Bistie had rigged an electrical coil from a welder in one of the maintenance shops powerful enough to degausse the magnets on the cover plates. The staff in the backup computer room that surrounded the Deck Nineteen auxiliary bridge hadn't even tried to escape—Kirk and his party opened the doors to find them clustered around two or three terminals, working at the program locks and internal loops with the patience of the machines they cherished.

"We haven't been able to get anywhere with them, sir," said the thin, arrogant computer chief McDonough, who had happened to be trapped there when the doors locked up. For once he sounded, if not humble, at least awed. "This is stuff I've never seen before. It's like our own programs . . . I don't know, had holes in them or something. Their commands just slipped on through between the cracks. I've never seen something that sophisticated."

"Of course he hasn't," said Lao grimly, as he and Kirk strode on their way. "They've got a two-hundred-and-fifty-year jump on the defenses. What the hell kind of defenses must they have in the future, against systems like that?"

Throughout the engineering hull, they encountered small parties of rescuers taking people out of vent shafts, gangways, and both vertical and horizontal turbolift shafts—people who had attempted to move through the ship's smaller capillaries when the blast doors came down across every corridor. Narrow places, thought Kirk again. Some kind of psychic resonating field? The ability to project theta waves, enhanced by wiring, training, technology? He'd seen similar powers in alien cultures, seen what it did to civilizations where such powers had evolved.

No such wave effect occurred now.

They clattered down the final gangway, the huge cavern of Recycling picking up the ring of their boots on metal. The flashlight beams picked out the corners of row after row of synthesizers, grumbling to themselves, like unquiet tombs in the dark. Kirk wondered, unshipping his phaser, what they would meet. Even if Arios had regained consciousness, would exhaustion prevent him from using the full force of his mental powers, whatever those were? He had at least one companion with him, but it was a toss-up whether the young man would surrender, or feel himself obligated to fight to the death.

The yellow circles of flashlight beams converged on the cover plate next to the bowling alley's door. DeSalle degaussed the catch, and an officer stood on either side, phasers at the ready, as he cranked it open. From within a voice called, "Don't come any closer!"

The men stopped. Kirk leaned over to Lao, asked softly, "Would Arios have been able to rig some kind of fail-safe code on the computer that would let Thad trigger a life-support shutdown?"

The young man nodded. "If he could get into the base exec, he could do it with a batch program. He'd have to mark the keyboard with tape, so Thad would know which one to hit, since he probably couldn't remember under pressure. If Arios has known him for long, he'd know that about him. It's a possibility."

Kirk's eyes narrowed as he regarded the dim glow of lights beyond the slitted door. "With all the safety bulkheads opened there wouldn't be any danger of suffocation, but the gravity and the heat could give us problems."

"Just keep things calm and slow, sir," said Lao softly. "Don't panic him, and don't confuse him. And don't blame him for being what he is."

Kirk glanced at him, hearing experience in his voice—hearing, too, both concern and rage that anyone would make a pawn of someone like Thad. He walked forward to the door alone and called out, "Smith? Thaddeus?" He remembered Thad probably wouldn't recall that his name was supposed to be Smith. "Thaddeus, it's Captain Kirk."

There was a long silence, in which Kirk heard the barest

whisper from the echoing room beyond. "Master? Master, *please* wake up!"

He stepped through the doorway. DeSalle, Lao, and the guards remained where they were.

A yellow bubble of electric light illuminated one end of the bank of arcade games at the far side of the thirty-five-meter hall. Gaudy posters surmounted the game consoles. SMUGGLER'S TREASURE. ASTEROID MONSTERS. GALLERY OF AMAZEMENT. Three of the programming consoles had been unshipped from beneath the games and rewired in front of the largest of the game screens, the now dark NECROBLASTER 989. At this makeshift console, Dylan Arios was slumped in a chair, a scarecrow bundle of rags like a dead elf, graying green head resting on one crooked arm.

Thad straightened and whirled, phaser gripped in both hands, pointing toward Kirk in the shadows. The round, childlike face was sweat-bathed and grim, the dark eyes deathly scared.

"Stay back!" Stress cracked his voice. "I'll kill you! I really will!"

Kirk held up his hands to show them empty, though he had a phaser clipped to his belt behind his back. "I'm not here to hurt you," he said.

"That's what McKennon said. . . ." Thad's voice shook, and he forced it back under control. "That's what they always say."

Kirk looked over at the unconscious Arios. "What's wrong with him?"

"I don't know!" Thad sounded desperate, terrified. "He was talking thorough Sharnas, he'd just heard from Nemo on the *Nautilus* that the engines were fixed. . . ."

"The same way he talked to Sharnas?"

"Uh-hunh." The gun was shaking visibly in the sweaty hands. Kirk wondered what the setting on it was.

"Who's Nemo?" he asked, keeping his own voice conversational. Neither of the women had been wired, Kirk recalled. Scanners had shown no human life on the black ship, though with the shielding it was difficult to tell.

Thad said quickly, "No one. Uh—nobody. Uh—I meant he'd—he'd just heard from—from Adajia." He glanced back at Arios, his face twisting with anxiety and distress. "Then he just . . . he just collapsed. He said, 'Oh, my God,' and . . . and looked out, like he saw something, something awful."

"He needs to get to sickbay," said Kirk gently, feeling like a betrayer. "He needs to be taken care of. Neither of you will be harmed. I swear it, I promise. You can't escape anyway, you know," he added, as Thad looked from Arios around the dark cavern of the room, desperately trying to figure out if there was a way to escape. "My men are back in control of the ship. The only thing we can't do is turn the lights on." *Or make the turbolifts run,* he reflected. *Or operate the main computer, or communicate. But Thad doesn't know that.*

Thad looked almost in tears with indecision and fear, the success of what was obviously a desperately critical operation thrown upon him, knowing he was incapable of planning ahead.

"I'll let you keep the phaser," Kirk added. "How's that?"

The Consilium didn't leave Thad with much of a brain, Phil had said on Chapel's transcript. *But he's got a hell of a heart.*

And a hideous, all-consuming terror of the Consilium that had done to him whatever it had done.

Thad cast one more agonized glance at Arios, then looked back at Kirk, trying to come to the right decision and knowing that he couldn't. At last he said wanly, "All right." He looked around for someplace to put his phaser, then stuffed it awkwardly into the pocket of the baggy coverall garment he wore. Kirk hoped the safety was on.

"Mr. DeSalle," he called out cautiously, and the security chief appeared behind him in the doorway. To the chief's eternal credit, thought Kirk, he also had put his phaser out of sight. "We're taking Captain Arios up to sickbay. Post a man here to watch the setup and make sure nobody comes near it. I've told Thad he can keep his phaser for now."

Two more redshirts appeared, also unarmed. Thad watched in hand-twisting apprehension as they lifted Arios between them and started toward the door. "You'll be all right," said Lao gently, coming over to stand beside him. "You did the right thing. All the way through."

"Did I?" Thad looked wistful. "I'm not very good at it—I mean, I'm just a Secondary. Most of them didn't even want me in the rebellion. But I do try." They started after Kirk and his little procession. "He's probably gonna want some coffee and some candy when he comes to," added Thad, nodding toward his chief. "He does after the psion jump, usually, and he said this was going to be lots worse. Oh, and let that guy go." He nodded toward the single yeoman who'd been on duty at the bowling alley, sitting resignedly by the alley railing with his hands taped around a stanchion, trying to pick off the tape that had been slapped over his mouth.

It wasn't until they were carrying Arios into one of the convalescent wards in sickbay that he seemed to come around a little. Kirk had quietly instructed DeSalle not to let Thad or the Master have any contact with Sharnas or Cooper; they passed the door of the security ICU without comment and moved on through the dark to the corridor beyond. Through one open door—curious, thought Kirk, to see so many open doors, to hear the babble of voices— yellow flashlights glowed, and he heard McCoy say, "No, you seem to be fine, too."

"I told you I was fine," said Lieutenant Sue's voice.

DeSalle said, "Doesn't look like anyone who got caught by that . . . whatever it was in the gangways and vent shafts . . . was harmed."

"Oh, no," said Thad earnestly. "It was just a standing theta wave to keep everybody from moving around. The Masters can do that in closed spaces." He touched the back of his head. "With us it's worse. They can trigger the pain-center implant almost at maximum, and we're not . . . Secondaries can't shake it off, the way regular people can. It's got something to do with being smart. McKennon . . ." He flinched, and let the subject trail away.

Kirk put his hands on his hips, looked down at the little man. "So 'Master' is really a Consilium title."

Thad nodded. "Is Phil all right?" he asked suddenly.

117

"He'll be fine." Kirk flashed his light into an empty two-bed room, nodded to DeSalle. "Can your Master get in touch with the *Nautilus?* You said someone there told him the engines were fixed."

Thad hesitated, then said apologetically, "I'm not supposed to talk about it."

"Nemo?" Arios stirred, groped out with one hand as the officers laid him on the bed. Then, desperately, *"Nemo . . ."*

"Who is Nemo?"

"It's all right if you tell us," said Lao. "Sharnas looked into the minds of some people here, and he said we really are who we say we are."

Thad sighed but looked relieved; Kirk couldn't repress the thought that it was no wonder the other members of the Shadow Fleet weren't enthusiastic about the Secondary's inclusion in the rebellion. Then he said, "He's our yagghorth."

He sat down on the other bed, looked resignedly up at Kirk, who was staring down at him in horror and shock.

"Don't you have a yagghorth on the *Enterprise?"* Thad asked in surprise. "I thought that's what Mr. Spock did. That he was the empath who partnered your yagghorth."

And, seeing that everyone in the room was looking at him with baffled incomprehension, he said, "That's how the psion jump works. The yagghorths do it. They just take the ships along."

Chapter Nine

HALF AN HOUR LATER, Mr. Spock confirmed this. "It is not an unreasonable situation," he said, holding one hand out while Dr. McCoy sprayed the abrasions on it with plast that did not quite match his skin tone. The left was more thickly covered with permaskin, which also didn't match, and by the way he moved Kirk guessed McCoy had put some kind of dressing on the gashed leg and cracked ribs. He had returned to the *Enterprise*—scuffed, bruised, clothing patched with oil and mold—in company with Raksha and Adajia at the news that Arios had been taken. There had been no negotiation, though scans indicated that a new layer of shielding had appeared around the *Nautilus*—presumably one of Raksha's repairs—making it impervious to outside transporter beams. In spite of his injuries, Spock retained his air of prim neatness, as if it were human—and therefore a point against him—to appear ruffled or in deshabille.

Sharnas, sitting up in bed now with his long black hair braided away from his face, had the same air of catlike neatness, of being above disorder of any sort.

"It is, in fact, logical, once one examined all the elements

119

of the puzzle of the yagghorth themselves," added the boy. "The specimens examined were almost genetically identical, even though they had infested ships or colonies dozens of sectors apart; identical down to nonevolutionary traits like head shape and color bands and dancing behavior. Did you know the yagghorth dance? Yet no instrumentality for transport—not even evidence of sentience—was ever found. But once you had empathic races being wired for psychic contact—in the first instance, Betazoids who had been wired as children to repair the neurological damage caused by the plague—contact with the yagghorth became feasible."

Kirk shivered, recalling things his Academy buddy Maria Kellogg had told him about the yagghorth, and the one infested ship that the *Farragut* had picked up when he was a young midshipman, not yet out of the Academy. The yagghorth had been destroyed by the time the *Farragut* had picked up the distress signal—Kirk had helped in getting the bodies of three crew members out of the engine coils where the creature had shoved them. He still remembered the runnels of blood and resin trickling down the walls.

"It was discovered that yagghorth dream dreams about other worlds," Sharnas went on softly. "And go there . . ." He opened his fingers, like a man releasing a butterfly that has lighted on his hand. "Like that. All they needed, really, were referent points, a modulator coil, and a reason to take the ships with them when they went."

"Their previous referent points being the mu-spectrum energies emitted by Turtledove Anomalies," said Spock. "Energies which they themselves also emit. Fascinating."

"They're no problem as long as they're kept fed," added Adajia, seeing the expression on Dr. McCoy's face. "And Nemo's . . . kind of sweet."

Kirk felt himself inclined to agree with McCoy but didn't say so. The little band of travelers was gathered in the security ward, Phil Cooper dressed again—in the strangely dyed wool shirt and what looked like combat-fatigue pants in which he'd arrived on the *Enterprise*—and sitting in one of the ward's several duraplast chairs. Thad Smith was sticking as close to him as he could, his hand protectively over the phaser still in his pocket: Ensign Lao had convinced the Secondary to let him see it long enough to make sure the weapon was set for mildest stun, and that the safeties were on. Sharnas, looking small and thin and horribly young in the blue med smock, was propped on pillows in bed, but for the first time his eyes were clear and free of either pain or drugs. Adajia sat cross-legged in the shadowy doorway of the room next door, which had been left on Open even after the lights and door power had been restored. She kept glancing through to where Dylan Arios's still form could just be distinguished, lying in the bed with the light falling on one thin hand where it rested on his chest, his face in shadow.

Guards were posted outside both rooms, and Security Officers Butterfield and Shimada had accompanied Raksha and Lao to Central Computer, but on the whole, Kirk expected no further trouble from his guests. The ship was settling, rather shakily, into the second watch of the day. Scotty and his team were going over the ship inch by inch to make sure no damage had been sustained, and had so far reported none. Similar teams from Security and Engineering were shaking down the bowling alley, prior to the big upcoming match.

All things were returning to normal.

Except, thought Kirk, for what he now knew. With that knowledge, nothing would ever be quite normal again. Not for him, nor for anyone who'd been in that room.

Kirk had traveled enough in time to know that it was theoretically possible to change the future—if one knew what to change. He could not imagine what could be done at a distance of 250 years, to prevent the plague, to prevent the corruption of the Federation, to prevent the growth of the Consilium. Could not imagine anything that he could do to alter events the causes of which he was absolutely ignorant of.

It was never simple, and any event, building and multiplying through time, had such geometrically accumulating consequences as to make tampering frequently more hazardous than sitting still. Even his knowledge was, in a way, tampering, alteration—but knowledge wouldn't be enough.

He didn't know what would be enough. If anything would.

If, of course, Cooper—and Arios—was telling the truth. And how could he ever know?

"All it came down to, really, was convincing the yagghorth that the starships were in fact their eggs, and the empaths assigned to them their nestmates," Sharnas went on, as if the matter were the most reasonable in the world. "They link to the empath, and the modulator coil aligns them with the engine itself."

Spock remembered the modulator coil. It was one of the pieces of equipment Raksha had talked him through repairing without explaining what it was. "I was under the impression that the yagghorth were nonsentient," he said.

"It's a subject upon which there is little positive data," replied the Vulcan boy. "Yoruba's 2478 study showed . . ."

"Here." McCoy came in, trailed by Nurse Chapel bearing a tray with a hypospray and a blood-analysis cuff. "I've got a general gamma shot in case that thing was carrying unknown infections, but I'd like to borrow some blood first to run tests. You seem to be the first person in the history of xenomedicine who's simply been bitten by a yagghorth instead of disassembled into component pieces."

Phil and Thad both averted their eyes from the dark green blood filling the phials; Spock and Sharnas continued to discuss yagghorth as if the one had not almost been torn to pieces by the other's pseudonestmate.

"All straightened out." The door slid open and Raksha came in, followed by Ensign Lao. "Told you it wouldn't take long." The steel on her doublet glinted as she passed through the other door into the room where Arios still lay asleep. She said softly, "Hey, *puq*," in a voice Kirk hadn't thought Klingons possessed.

"As far as I could tell she didn't add anything to the existing programming when she took the locks out," said Lao.

He looked tired, thought Kirk. Driven. As if burning up

inside. As well he might. He was only twenty-one, young enough for anything to seem enormous, final, huge—young enough for the all-darkening despair of the young. Even with years of experience, Kirk was aware of his own sense of helplessness—only seeing the bleak defeat in the boy's eyes did he realize how far he himself had come from that young and passionate ensign on the *Farragut,* viewing, appalled, what the yagghorth had done. He remembered wondering, at the time, how Captain Gannovich could stand the horror of what they had found. Now he knew that one got used to it, and one went on.

Damaged sometimes—patched like the old black starship that had become the *Nautilus*—but one went on. One watched for the chance to do what one could.

"Not that I'd be able to tell." Lao passed a weary hand across his face. "I took notes. . . ."

"Destroy them," said Kirk quietly. "Don't even read them yourself."

Lao regarded him in surprise. Nearby, Phil was saying to Spock, "What surprises me is that Sharnas and the Master were able to talk Nemo into deserting and joining the rebellion with us. Because we couldn't have gotten a psion-jump ship without him. I still don't understand how they did that."

"We didn't," said Sharnas. "Nemo made the decision. On his own, for his own reasons—and *that* is what the Consilium does not understand."

"We're dealing with a temporal paradox," said Kirk in a low voice, pitched to exclude McCoy and Chapel, the guards outside the door, and the little group of rebels, with the possible exception of the Vulcan Sharnas, who was still deep in discussion with Spock. "I don't know what's going to come of it, at this point, but Arios was right when he insisted that information be kept to a minimum. I'm confiscating any notes Maynooth, Miller, or McDonough might have made as well."

He paused. In the other room, Raksha stood silent at the foot of Arios's bed, looking down at him with an impassive face and haunted, weary grief in her eyes. Watching Dr. McCoy and Chapel exit, Thad remarked wistfully to Spock, "You know, I like your Starfleet better than our Starfleet."

"Thad," said Phil patiently, "that's the *point* of the rebellion."

Lao smiled, and some of the weariness left his face.

Kirk went on, "Whatever they've told us about the rebellion—and it might even be the truth—they haven't told us what they wanted on Tau Lyra Three; what they're doing in this sector of the galaxy; why they chose this time; why it's so important that they get there. And no matter what their story is—even if we can verify it independently, which we haven't yet—our orders are clear. Tau Lyra Three is a protected planet with a sentient, nonspaceflight civilization. It is our duty to keep that civilization from being tampered with by *anyone,* for any reason. To allow that civilization to develop freely in its own direction, for as long as it takes them to achieve spaceflight capability. And what they've told us about themselves can't be an excuse to let them violate that responsibility."

"No, sir," said Lao. He hesitated, struggling within himself, as if seeking words to say, some way to frame his questions and his despair. "Captain . . ."

Kirk wondered how he was going to answer. *There's always something we can do?* How could he be sure that that *something* wouldn't lead to the very situation he sought to avert?

He couldn't. Nobody could. And hope—and despair—were factors like anything else, to be taken account of in the ripple effects of time.

He was spared the necessity of reply by the whistle of the comm link. "Captain," said Uhura's voice. "We have signals coming in from the buoys around the Tau Lyra system. They started while our communications were down; analysis has only caught up with them now."

"Signals?" said Kirk sharply. "What kind of signals?"

Her voice sounded flat, strangely dead. "An hour and a half ago, a major solar flare exploded from the star Tau Lyra. Most of the buoys themselves were scorched out, but according to the signals they picked up . . . all life on Tau Lyra Three has been destroyed."

All life.

James Kirk stood on the bridge of the *Enterprise,* watching the delayed playback of information that had reached the ship's paralyzed receptors ninety minutes ago. Saw the filtered yellow corona of the star brighten fitfully, like some huge beast twitching as it dreamed, then fade. . . . Five minutes. Ten. Then it brightened again, the glare growing rapidly, swelling from yellow to white to deadly incandescence as a flare swept out from its surface, blazing streamers of fire, as if the star's furnaces had redoubled their rate of burning, then redoubled it again.

All life.

On the planet, Kirk thought, people wouldn't have known what hit them. Heat and brilliance, driving them indoors . . . According to reports they'd built astonishing structures of stucco and iron-hard vegetable matter on the arching backs of the strange, banyanlike plants typical of the temperate zones. He had a pile of wafers on the arm of his command chair, a heap of pale green flimsiplast sent up to him by Historical. Articles, surmises, long-distance surveys taken by careful scholars whose life and treasure that planet was . . . who, true to the Prime Directive, had never set foot on it but looked forward to the day when they might.

Now the day would never come.

Vehicles stopping as animals shied. Arms thrown over eyes to protect them. Communications lines overloaded, breaking down as the insulation burned. On the nightside, those awake reading or singing or watching the odd little flat vids referred to in radio broadcasts, rushing to the windows, marveling as the moon swelled and blazed into unknowable brightness, then faded as the sky itself became lambent with killing light.

Ten minutes of growing panic, terror, prayer.

And then the heat came.

All life.

He closed his eyes.

All life.

It did not escape him that the small chrono on the bottom of the screen showed the identical time that Dylan Arios had passed out in his efforts to maintain the standing theta wave in all open passageways of in-ship communication.

Nor did he forget that the *Nautilus,* that shadow twin of his own ship, had been in the Tau Lyra system when the arrival of the *Enterprise* had caused it to flee. True, it had appeared to have only just entered the farthest outskirts of the cometary field, but there was the possibility that the ship had been coming from, rather than going to, the planet.

And Arios had been desperate to get there, or get back there—so much so that he'd risked his life to take on an entire starship.

How much of this could have been averted if he'd known earlier who and what these people were?

If he knew that, even now.

To what degree was he responsible for all those deaths?

He opened his eyes again, watched the display on the screen. It now showed the current status of the star Tau Lyra. The readout numbers of temperature and coronal activity were virtually identical to what they had been a week ago, a month ago, twelve years in the past when the planet had first been scanned.

Only, the inner four planets of its system were cinders now. The civilization the Federation had ordered him to protect—as a matter of course, as a courtesy extended to another sentient race—was gone.

Someone behind him exclaimed in surprise, then cursed. Kirk turned to find Dylan Arios standing behind his chair, with the air of one who had been there some time. Kirk raised his hand to signal the on-duty security yeoman—who was advancing purposefully but with a rather red face—to return to his post by the turbolift door. "It's all right," he said.

"I thought you'd want to see me." Arios folded his arms, canted his head a little to regard the screen before them. He looked exhausted and rather the worse for wear, but his eyes, in their dark rings of sleeplessness, were clear, and infinitely sad. "The rest of the gang are back in sickbay, by the way."

Kirk hit the comm link. "Sickbay," said Chapel's voice.

"Everything all right down there?"

"Yes," she said, slightly puzzled. "You mean with our—er—guests? They're fine." A pause, probably while she looked through a door or switched on a monitor. "Yes, they're all in the ward where you left them."

"Including Captain Arios?" He glanced at the young man beside him; Arios raised wispy green brows.

"I think so. I checked on him just a minute ago."

"The Masters bred me to do this kind of thing." Arios's grin was lopsided, surprisingly sweet. "Bred me and taught me and wired my brain when I was sixteen and would rather have been doing other things. Then they acted real surprised when I used it against them." He turned to watch the replay again: flare, dullness, the onset of hell. Even more softly, he said, "They're here."

"You're telling me the Consilium did that."

Arios nodded. Ensign Lao, working steadily, wearily, over the Central Computer console, half-turned in his chair and seemed about to say something, but turned away again, and resumed work.

"It is theoretically feasible to trigger a solar flare-up by firing sufficiently powerful fusion torpedoes into the heart of a star," said Mr. Spock, stepping from his station, where he had been watching a digitalized readout of the same scene, altering the spectrum analysis as he had earlier on the scans of the *Nautilus*. "Tau Lyra has always been an unstable star, with long-term cycles of core activity which have showed up on spectroscopic records for three hundred years. It would have erupted into flares eventually in any case."

"How soon?" Kirk felt weary to the marrow of his bones.

"Statistically, any time between tomorrow and the next two hundred thousand years."

"And just what were the odds," Kirk inquired savagely, "that the flares would erupt today?"

Spock regarded him in mild surprise. "The same as on any given day."

Kirk was silent.

"In our time Tau Lyra Three is a wasteland." Arios returned his gaze to the screen, the light of the ruined star harsh on the stress lines that webbed the corners of his eyes. "We knew it was destroyed around this time—records of your mission survive, and you report it destroyed. We came in when we thought would be a little bit before you arrived, hoping we could reach there before it happened."

"Why?"

Arios sighed; Kirk saw the quick jump of the muscles of temple and jaw. Then, looking up again, he said, "The old linguistics analyses pointed to a high level of psychic skills among the people there as a whole, and to some very high-level savants—Masters or above."

"So you went there looking for help against the Consilium." On the screen below the repeating image of the flares, small windows in the blackness gave readouts: spiking levels of radio activity as planetwide communications jammed; humidity levels rising as the oceans first vanished under blankets of fog, then began to boil; spontaneous fires sweeping the thick-growing forest that covered most of the planet's surface. A smaller readout showed Tau Lyra III itself, glaring white with a layer of heaving cloud. The surface would be a hot and rain-lashed Erebus.

All life.

Arios flinched and looked away at the harshness in Kirk's voice. "I thought we'd covered our tracks," he said softly. "We did take precautions not to be followed, you know."

Kirk remembered precautions he himself, and others, had taken, against Klingons, against infection and infestation, against ambush and attack on incomprehensible worlds. Sometimes, precaution was not enough. Sometimes nothing was enough.

"We need people who can stand up to a trained and wired Consilium Master," went on Arios quietly. "We need training ourselves. There has to be an alternative to wiring, to continue the use of the psion drive; there has to be some way of boosting, or training, psychic abilities without opening that door for psychic control. We can't destroy the Consilium—what the Consilium has done—if we continue using their technology, their way. All we'll do is become them, eventually."

"No," said Kirk, knowing that Arios was, at least partially, right.

"And we need some way to fight the wiring itself. We didn't know what we'd find there, but we . . . hoped. Maybe it was stupid of us."

"No." Kirk shook his head. "No, it wasn't stupid. Mr. Barrows? Lay in a course for Tau Lyra Three."

"Aye, sir." Her hands moved swiftly over the course computer; she looked a little rumpled from having spent nearly two hours passed out in a vent shaft when she'd tried to get from one sealed-off corridor to another, but perfectly alert. While some of the day-shift crew remained on the bridge to sort out the tangle of readings and overloads caused by the blackout, others—like Sulu and Chekov— had retired to belated dinners and the first of what would easily be weeks of postmortems, reminiscence, and horror stories about who was where when the lights went out, and what they did about it.

"What about the *Nautilus,* sir?"

"We can meet you there," said Arios. "Now that the engines are repaired and Sharnas is up to the jump, we'll make orbit around the planet and wait."

Kirk's jaw tightened. "The hell you will," he said quietly. "Mr. Barrows? Sublight bearing. Keep maximum tractor on the *Nautilus.* Notify me at once if problems develop with the beam."

"Aye, sir."

"Mr. Spock? Assemble all information about the solar flareup of Tau Lyra, and all information in the library computer about Tau Lyra Three. Meet me with it in the main briefing room at twenty-two-hundred hours."

Spock inclined his head and, turning, flipped the wafer of

readouts from his bridge station. The main viewscreen returned to the dark starfield, already moving laterally with the slow swing of the *Enterprise* as it responded to the helm.

"Lieutenant Uhura? Any pickup of radio signals from the planet itself?"

Uhura, who'd been briefing Mahase, looked around and removed the comm link from her ear. "I have recordings, sir, but they're zipped and garbled."

"How long would it take you and xenolinguistics to unzip and ungarble them?"

Without a blink—though Kirk realized several hours later that he'd just asked his communications chief to skip a well-deserved dinner after a particularly trying day—Uhura replied, "Depending on how much transcript is in the computer banks, between ten and twenty hours, sir."

"Get your people started on it," he said. "If you have anything before twenty-two-hundred hours, relay it to the briefing room. If not, let me know when they do have something."

He turned back to Arios, who still stood behind him, eyebrows raised but no surprise whatsoever in his eyes.

"Your crew has expressed a lot of concern about being deceived—about this ship and everything on it being some giant scam by this Domina McKennon to trick you into believing we are who we say we are," he said quietly. "That works both ways. I accept that you're from the future—those journal cubes Spock picked up in an abandoned stateroom on your ship don't leave me in much doubt. But as for the rest of your story—who you are, and what you were doing in the Tau Lyra system—I have only your word. The Consilium aren't the only ones who might have fired high-compression fusion torpedoes into the heart of that sun. I hope you understand that I'm going to have to keep you on board the *Enterprise,* and under surveillance, until I at least know whether a starship was in the Tau Lyra system when those flares began. A starship besides the *Nautilus,* that is."

Chapter Ten

HOT RAIN slammed like bullets into water the color of a bruise. Typhoon winds nearly took Kirk off his feet as he and the landing party stepped around the broken wall in whose shelter they had materialized. Above them, around them, the blackened arches of the Tree of Oobast groaned and swayed. Much of it had already fallen, a perilous mangle of wire, steel, glass beneath the carpet of stinking ash.

All life, thought Kirk, the words repeating themselves in his mind with the bitter taste of recrimination, of wondering what, if anything, could have been done. *All life.*

Towing the *Nautilus,* it had taken them three days to reach Tau Lyra at sublight speeds. During that three days Uhura, Gilden from Historical, and Lao operating the computers had put together as much of a reconstruction of the planet as they could, seeking out the likeliest places where some might have survived and running redoubled scans and probabilities in the vain hope of finding life. They had found none so far.

Uhura had also combed every piece of data, every spectrographic record, every transmission still extant from the burned-out buoys, in search of evidence that would point to

131

the presence of another starship in the Tau Lyra system at the operative time.

But there was nothing. Only the antimatter trails of the *Nautilus*'s dirty-burning impulse drive, and a track of engine residue leading back into the heart of the Crossroad Nebula.

"A psion-jump ship wouldn't have left any residue at all," Arios had pointed out, when confronted with the information. "Their impulse engines would be in better shape than ours were, after the pounding we took coming through the Anomaly in the heart of the nebula. A Fleet jumpship could have materialized inside the buoy ring, fired its torpedoes, and jumped out. They could be seven systems away watching you on a long-range scanner and never leave a swirl of dust."

Kirk still didn't know whether to believe him or not. On his orders, Spock had checked every torpedo tube in the ship, and found them choked with decades of ciroids and corrosion—but there were, he knew, other means of launching weapons.

The landing party consisted of Kirk, McCoy, Russell from Historical, Adams from Anthro/Geo, Ensign Lao with a vid pickup, three security yeomen, and Dylan Arios, almost unable to stand in the pounding wind. Fragmentary data put together by Gilden and Lao had indicated that only one of the large cities was still above water—Oobast—and that only marginally. "City" was probably not the best word. Analogs included "warren," "clanhold," "house," and "tree."

Cracked arches of burned wood curved blackly against the vicious roil of clouds. Most had been blown down already, lying like charred skeletons in the rising gray water, lashed by rain and occasional hail. Blue-white lightning stitched the sky; scattered fog ghosts curled wherever there was shelter from the hurricane-force blasts; in black distance, waterspouts wove drunkenly.

It was Hell.

Of the civilization that had made this world its home—of

the families that had made up the clan of the Tree of Oobast, listening to the oddly accented music or the incomprehensibly rambling radio plays—nothing remained. The sodden ground was a mangle of dead wires, cables burned free of their insulation, like a blackened mat of unbreakable vines; Kirk's boots crunched shards of porcelain and glass underneath it, and water squished thickly up through the mess. Mr. Kyle put them down on the high ground close to the city's western edge, where the Tree of Oobast had encroached over the ridge of hills that once had bounded it—the best-sheltered spot he could find. To the east, gray sheets of water lay only a few meters from the beam-down point, quickly lost in murky fog.

The water bobbed with chunks of burned stucco and plaster, with such fragments of wooden furniture as had not grown sodden and sunk yet; with bits of machinery and simple electronics. Ensign Lao, visual pickup on his shoulder, squinted around him into the pounding rain.

"I thought it'd . . . be worse," he said after a moment. "Where are the bodies?"

"Under shelter," McCoy said briefly. "Temperatures were up above five hundred degrees. The storms that kind of heat generates swept away everything that wasn't pinned down."

Kirk looked down at the pewter-colored sea stretching away before them at their feet. In spite of the hammering rain and tearing gusts of wind, white mist hung over it knee-deep, swirling around the melted spars of structural steel like the ghosts of everything that he and Starfleet had tried to protect here. A fragment of something bobbed ashore, smooth reddish wood, a tangle of copper wires with the remains of scorched cloth insulation clinging to them.

"Not even in the water," Kirk said quietly. "No bacteria —no internal gas."

They stumbled off, leaning against the wind, wading through standing water that hid debris and cables and things that gave and slithered underfoot, to explore. Where the curves of the hills sheltered portions of the original Tree from the wind—where thick masses of burned wood had fallen, bringing down the structural steel and glass of houses with it and burying all within, and where rising steam reduced visibility to a few meters—they found corpses.

Symmetrical primate analogs, Kirk deduced, peering through the twisted rubble at the barely seen bones: rounded rib cages, six limbs, flat, froglike heads. Early studies had postulated the same. Front-facing eyes. Three-fingered hands. McCoy and Adams from Anthro/Geo extricated two as best they could, Lao photographing them in situ. Russell, the thin, ascetic head of Historical, knotted yellow markers around the tree stalks, to mark the areas where he found bones.

Kirk was sharply aware that the "few scientists" of whom Mr. Spock had spoken—the ones who made Tau Lyra III and the Yoons their study—would be heartbroken to learn of its destruction, as if they had lost members of their families. As, indeed, they had.

They had lost the civilization that had been their distant study for the eleven years of the Federation's knowledge of the place. The civilization about which they had written articles, monographs, studies; which they hoped one day to live long enough to visit as messengers and emissaries of the Federation. The civilization they had fought to have recognized, put under Protected status, funded for surveillance.

Kirk understood that he owed it to these scientists to gather as much as he could from the ruins, before water and storm and seepage eroded it away.

"Any sign of life at all?"

McCoy shook his head. "The tricorder's set at maximum. There's a lot of electrical interference. But nothing could have survived this."

Distant barrages of thunder, and sky the color of Iowa tornado weather. No. Nothing could have survived. The big scanners on board the *Enterprise,* which could distinguish apple trees from orange trees kilometers above the surface, had been little use in the heaving washes of electrical interference generated by the storms. In spite of everything, Kirk had come down to the surface with some hope.

"Nothing." McCoy angled the tricorder in its plastic protector. "No animals, no insects—*were* there insects here?"

"Thousands of species." Arios knelt, head bowed, among the rubble. Water sluiced from his shining gray suit, from the polarized glass bubble that protected his head. Within that protection, his face was drawn with pain. "Birds . . . bird analogs, anyway. Slothoids, tree-runners . . . They kept tree-runners as pets." And, looking up, seeing the expression in Kirk's eyes, he said, "I . . . I feel this. It's like an echo rising from the ashes. Ghosts, like remembering a dream."

Kirk said nothing.

"I didn't kill these people."

Kirk still did not reply and turned away, staggering as another gust hit him.

Following Lao's analysis of Gilden's reconstruction of fragmentary data, they crossed the ridge, found what had been the center of the town. Some reports had indicated that there had been a high concentration of savants here, as if there were a university or some kind of psychic training facility. In extremis, the Yoons had used its underground rooms as a bunker, carrying chests of printed matter—awkward, bundled collections of pages bound with colored cord—of strange equipment, of pots and jars of what were probably medicines, down flight after flight of steps, until the heat overcame them and they died, huddled, crowded, contorted with their treasures still clutched in their withered hands. The lowermost of these underground rooms was already flooding, the ceilings sagging and creaking as the earth above grew sodden and heavy; every member of the party bent his back to lug the four unwieldy chests up flight after flight of steps to the surface again, and back to the pickup point for transport to the *Enterprise*.

Whatever the hell was in them, thought Kirk, as the boxes dissolved in swirls of golden dust, it was the treasure the Yoons most wanted to save. The least he could do was save it for them.

"The highest point in the city should be this way," said

Lao, who had worked with Gilden over the maps. In the electromagnetic chaos that was left of the stripped magnetic field, not even a standard compass would work; Lao held a terrain-orientation scanner, its uneven lines repeated in a ghostly network on his face shield. The young man looked shaken and had been very silent after the heaps of charred and sodden bones in the bunker. He understood, thought Kirk, as the guards and Russell did not, that he was looking not at the victims of a so-called act of God, but at murder.

"And the question is," Kirk said quietly, into the portable recorder he'd brought along, clipped to his belt, "just who the murderer is, and how the crime was committed. Because the possibility remains that the man who claims to be the star witness—and the star character witness—is actually the author of this catastrophe."

And there was no way to tell.

Yet, thought Kirk, subconsciously quoting Lao's stubborn hopes for his brother, for change against all possibility of Fate. *Yet*.

The highest point in the city—or what remained of the city—was a sort of pinnacle of blackened tree-stem arches projecting from the side of the rocky ridge that formed the backbone beneath the Tree of Oobast. Sheltered by the ridge, the arches remained more or less intact, though they swayed sickeningly in the gales that howled over the crest; Kirk found himself clinging desperately to the bent ironwork, the bunches of seared wire that hung down like crumbling vines. Far below, the water churned among the tree roots and debris, sometimes visible under the slashing rain, sometimes masked by drifting stringers of steam. Kirk was panting, his breath coming short in the heat, and under the protective suit his clothes stuck to his flesh with a clammy douse of sweat.

Arios wrapped an equipment strap around his waist, lashing himself to the strut of a twisted platform surrounded by dizzy mazes of black limbs, dangling cables, broken machines, forty meters above the hammering millrace of waters below. Folding his arms, he bowed his head in concentration, like a beggar in the rain, standing so for a long time while the winds hurled water around him, and he struggled visibly for footing amid the swirling steam. The rolling of the thunder was like the aftermath of Götterdämmerung, and lighting threw hard bars of whiteness across the landing party's gleaming shapes. Somewhere close by, a section of entangled limbs, structural metal, and messes of stucco plunged down into the maelstrom below. Beyond Arios, Kirk could see waterspouts weaving diabolically on the horizon through torn shreds of cloud and fog.

At length Arios turned back, unhooking himself from his support and almost falling. Lao and Kirk both sprang forward to catch him, Kirk knowing that protective suit or no protective suit, nothing would survive a drop into the flood below. Within the helmet, Arios's face was ghastly, and it came to Kirk what a horror it must be, to be a psychic, listening on a world whose entire population has been burned alive.

His voice gentle, he asked, "Did you hear anything?"

The Master shook his head.

In the briefing room, later, they reviewed the visuals Ensign Lao had taken, and those Yeoman Reilly had made of the other landing party's finds at the Tree of Ruig, half a continent away. Chapel and Sharnas had gone down with Gilden, DeSalle, and his redshirts. Chapel looked badly shaken, Sharnas ill.

Ruig was the only other major population center still above water at which Arios and Sharnas had deduced a concentration of savants. That Tree clung vertically to the end of an enormous box canyon in the mining districts of the mountains, and many of its inhabitants had sought refuge in the mines when the heat started to climb and the night skies to glow red. They'd been found—thousands of them—baked, withered, mummified by the heat, surrounded by whatever possessions they'd cherished enough to carry with them to world's end, anywhere down to seven hundred feet into the mountain.

The lower part of the mine was already deeply flooded. The playback on the briefing-room vidscreen showed the contorted froglike faces, the withered limbs and sealed eyes, of the dead. One child's breast and arms were covered with a puddle of melted wax that must have been a toy. Near the bird-claw hand of another lay the fragments of a bisque doll, cracked to pieces in the heat. Nearly invisible in vapor and shadow, Sharnas stood knee-deep in steaming water in the shaft, a flashlight raised in his hand, stretching out his mind to the flickering darkness, seeking some response to his silent calls.

There had been none.

"So what happens now?" McCoy asked, and his Georgia drawl was deeper, a sign of how deeply the visit to the planet had disturbed him. There was a dangerous glitter to his blue eyes, the barely contained, helpless rage of a man who has witnessed utter evil without being able to do one thing about it.

"You just going to hop into the *Nautilus* and fly away into the sunset looking for some other planet to help you with your damned rebellion?"

"You mean some other planet we can lead McKennon to?" Arios's sandpaper voice cracked with bitterness as he raised his head from his hands, meeting McCoy's eyes—it was the doctor who looked away, ashamed.

Kirk looked around the table. All of them looked like ten miles of bad road, even the imperturbable Mr. Spock, who had just spent the past three days alternately coordinating information on the solar flareup and assisting Arios and Mr. Scott—with a suitable guard of redshirts looking on—in further repairs of the *Nautilus*'s engines. Scott, the only one who hadn't been down to the planet and was in any case too pragmatic to worry about problematical futures, looked deeply troubled nevertheless.

But Lao, Kirk thought, looked the worst. He'd been in charge of the computerized reconstruction of everything concerning the planet Yoondri, putting together Uhura's final communication report and every unrelated bit of information Gilden could glean from the History Section's files, working far into the nights, sometimes straight through, as if the work were a drug to hold confusion and despair from his mind.

Kirk understood. His own nights had been sleepless, a prey to dreams of other eras, other futures, other pasts.

He scanned the faces around the briefing-room table: McCoy with his anger, Chapel leaning the bridge of her nose onto folded fingers as if she could not bear to see on vid what she had seen in person in the mines. Lao with his dark-circled eyes and the grooves that had formed from nostril to chin, turning his youth old overnight. Raksha and Cooper drawn into themselves, Thad looking worried as usual, and Adajia wary, suspicious. . . .

But they, at least, would say whatever Arios charged them to say. The programming Cooper had spoken of so casually worked two ways.

Kirk said, "If this McKennon you speak about really exists. If there is a Consilium." Raksha raised her head, her eyes flaring with anger.

"I've had about enough of . . ."

Arios lifted a hand. "No, it's a justifiable question," he said. "It's been . . . our problem all along."

"The technology of high-compression fusion torpedoes capable of triggering explosions and flares in an unstable sun has been postulated in scientific journals already," put in Mr. Spock, in his reasonable voice. "It is not illogical to wonder whether it is already in existence. Conceivably, a missile-delivery system could be evolved with current technology to put such a torpedo in the star Tau Lyra even from the extreme edge of the cometary belt; conceivably, that torpedo could have been timed to explode eighteen hours or eighteen days after it was delivered. You do not have to have been anywhere near the system when the star pulsed."

Raksha's lips thinned and her nostrils flared, like an animal about to bite, and Arios put a hand over her wrist.

"There's always conspiracy theories," he said to her. "You know that. Most people still don't believe the Consilium seeded the plague on Qo'nos and Khergos and Romulus, in order to get half the populations wired to control the effects. I thought it was damn far-fetched myself until that night you and I broke into the Consilium main computer and found the files."

He turned back to Kirk. "And I know most people blame the aftereffects of the plague, or the deterioration of the educational system, or the cloning process itself for the drop in the general level of education—not the fact that about seventy percent of the clone lines are genetically engineered to be Secondaries, because Secondaries cause less trouble about low-paying jobs. They make damn good workers." He smiled across the table at Thad.

"We make pretty good rebels, too," said the Secondary, with shy pride. "If somebody tells us what to do, I mean."

Lao sat up, staring at Thad, at Arios, in shocked disbelief, but Arios was still watching Kirk.

"I guess what happens now is up to you, Captain."

"And I guess this is where *we* find out," said Phil Cooper, "if you are who you say you are . . . or if this is all a Consilium scam to get us to tell you where the Shadow Fleet is hiding, and why a yagghorth decided to quit the Fleet and join us."

There was a short silence in the briefing room. The three screens of the triangular viewer had gone dark. Kirk found it difficult to remember that of the *Enterprise* crew, only those in this room knew the whole truth: about the future, about the Consilium, about the implications raised by the presence of these ragged and scruffy outlaws. Around them the ship was settling in its normal business, rec-room conversation over dinner, the never-ending quest to get decent chocolate or shirts that fit out of the synthesizers, the small politicking over storage space that had become acute in the last year and a half. Tonight was the night of the big bowling match between Security and Engineering; elsewhere on the ship there was going to be a screening of *Gargoyle Man*. People trying to come to decisions about what they would do when the five-year mission was over.

And always the question, thought Kirk, of what to do. Of what he *could* do, to alter a future so distant.

"Uh . . ." Adajia lifted her hand timidly. She'd gotten gold nail paint from somewhere, and jeweled combs to stem the storm surge of her hair. "Master, is there any reason why we couldn't just . . . just stay here? I mean, the Consilium doesn't even exist yet, so they can't be after us. You don't have a criminal record here. We've got the fastest, most accurate starship in the entire galaxy and the best computer tech. We could clean up and be rich."

McCoy started to speak but did not, his eyes on Arios. Chapel did not raise her head from her hands. Spock, likewise, was watching Arios, and one eyebrow tilted upward—curious, thought Kirk. Wondering what the Master would say. Beside Thad, Ensign Lao sat with closed eyes, his forehead on his fist, but the tension in his shoulders, the look of nauseated bitterness on his face, did not let Kirk deceive himself into thinking that the young man rested.

"It's all very well to talk about our duty to the Shadow Fleet, Master," went on Adajia. "But you know we're not going to win. The Shadow Fleet has about forty planet-hoppers and a couple of freighters and maybe a thousand fighters, and most of them are hiding out. Starfleet nearly got you back on Delta Seven, and the next time . . ."

The malachite-dark lips flinched, and she looked quickly down at her hands. "Do we really have to go back at all?"

"There are certain rules concerning temporal paradoxes," pointed out Spock gently.

"We wouldn't talk to anybody," the Orion girl promised, and made a backcountry sign of childish avowal. "And even if we did . . . we might be able to prevent . . ."

Lao raised his head, feverish intensity in his gaze.

"Well," Arios cut her off, with a small grin, "for starters I'd hate to see what kind of temporal conundrum we'd cause by introducing twenty-sixth-century technology into the twenty-third century."

"But it wouldn't be twenty-sixth-century stuff then," pointed out Thad. "It would be twenty-third-century stuff."

"And it might prevent the plague," added Adajia. "And cut off the Consilium before it has a chance to form."

"It might," agreed Arios. "And it might change the course of certain battles, and showdowns, and confrontations arising in the next thirty years or so with various other military powers in the galaxy so that the plague wouldn't spread because large segments of the population of every Federation or Klingon world had already been wiped out."

Adajia, Kirk could have sworn, looked across at him with startled enlightenment—memory of history still unwritten—in her dark eyes, and she said, "Oh. Er—yeah. *That,*" in a way that made him feel suddenly very strange.

"Second," said Arios, "in addition to having the only psion-drive jumpship in the twenty-third century, we have the only psion-drive jumpship in the Shadow Fleet."

"You think that's gonna make you points when Starfleet finally runs us down, I suggest you review the chapters about Starfleet in your handbook," remarked Raksha, a crooked expression on her mouth.

"And third," said Arios, folding his insectile hands, "the Consilium is here. McKennon followed us through the Crossroad Anomaly. She's already destroyed one planet, God forgive us. We've got to get her to chase us back through before she starts thinking *she* can go into the temporal-paradox biz."

He turned back to Kirk. "If it meets with your approval, Captain, I'd like the *Enterprise* to escort us back to the edge of the Crossroad Nebula. I'm guessing McKennon's ship will pick us up at some point and follow us. I'll show you how to adjust your standard shields so she can't just put a beam on your ship and snatch us if she shows up while we're still on board. On the edge of the gravitational well around the Anomaly, you pull the *Enterprise* out. We'll make a run for the singularity shear and hope their phaser targeting is thrown out of calibration by the gas clouds' ion fields long enough for us to make the jump. They'll have to follow."

Spock raised an eyebrow. "You display startling confidence in the structural integrity of your ship."

Arios smiled. "I display a startling grasp of the fact that there isn't a damn thing I can do about the *Nautilus*'s structural integrity right now."

Spock raised the other eyebrow concedingly.

"And what's McKennon going to do while we're escorting you?" asked Kirk grimly. "Sit back and watch? If your contention is correct, Captain Arios, she just destroyed a civilization of close to a billion innocent people. Shielding or no shielding, what makes you think she'll hesitate to attack a starship with weaponry three hundred years behind her own?"

Arios looked down at his folded hands. "They won't attack you."

"Is that a convenient way of saying we won't see them? That we'll still be without proof of their existence? Without any proof beyond your word?"

"I think you'll see them," said Arios slowly, with an air of a man picking his words carefully. "The reason they haven't shown themselves so far, at a guess, is because they didn't want to risk a battle; didn't want to risk damaging you. You should see them when they start shooting at us, the minute we're clear of the *Enterprise.*"

"The minute you're free of our tractor beams?" Kirk pressed him. "Free to go where you wish and do what you want? If these people are as evil as you say—if they have, in fact, done things like seed planets with diseases and genetically manipulate populations to make them more amenable to mental control—I have a little trouble in picturing them sparing their enemies out of consideration for the four hundred and thirty people on board this vessel."

"Well, for four hundred and twenty-nine of them, anyway," responded Arios, not looking up. "But you see, Captain, the person who gave the Consilium its start is one of your crew. And the Consilium knows it."

Into the shocked silence that followed this information,

the comm link whistled, and Lieutenant Uhura's voice came over the speaker. "Captain . . ." She sounded shaken. "A vessel has . . . appeared . . . in our sector. No warning, no . . . no sensor pattern, no antimatter trail, not even a hyperspace doppler. Just . . . here. They're hailing us on a Starfleet frequency. They say they want to talk to you."

Chapter Eleven

"CAPTAIN KIRK." The woman who had introduced herself over the viewscreen as Domina Germaine McKennon, small, delicately built, unbelievably pretty, held out both hands as she stepped from the silvery disk of the transporter. She bore no sign of Starfleet insignia, being clothed in what was possibly civilian attire of the twenty-sixth century: a smooth-fitting green dress whose full hem tuliped around her calves, and over it a white tabard of gauze-thin silk that billowed behind her like an enormous cloak. Her only jewelry was earrings—tiny roses of pink-tinted ivorene—and she wore no other decoration save the flower-sized bunch of green and white ribbons adorning the clip that held back the heavy copper waves of her hair.

"Thank you for permission to board."

Kirk found himself taking both of her hands, and a surge of protectiveness warmed him—not something he was used to feeling about women with sufficient authority to direct starship missions. Or at least, not in the past few years. But when he tried to examine the feeling it seemed to dissipate, leaving only the faintest fragrance in his mind.

McKennon smiled up into his eyes. "I did want to speak

with you, and as a commander you know how easily even coded transmissions get intercepted by the . . . wrong people. Forgive my paranoia." She smiled ruefully. "It's—well. Call it the result of dealing with . . . with unscrupulous enemies."

Her perfume was a reminiscence of something he had once known, then lost: a youth he had never been, perhaps. He had to concentrate to shut it out.

"You mean Dylan Arios."

A small crease marred the startled dove wings of her brows. "He is far from the worst."

Kirk turned, discomfited by her nearness. She was nothing like Arios had led him to expect, nothing like a woman who would order the carnage of Tau Lyra III. Gentleness and an almost spiritual sweetness seemed to radiate from her. Behind him, Mr. Spock and Dr. McCoy executed small, formal bows. "My first officer, Mr. Spock; Ship's Surgeon Leonard McCoy."

"Delighted." She did not say it effusively, but her smile beamed warmth. Kirk realized that, like Dylan Arios, she had probably seen all of them on the *Enterprise*'s visual logs, the record of this mission logged, like all missions, in Memory Alpha. Seen records of later missions as well, if there were later missions. If they all survived the next three months.

She would have seen them grow old.

She would know what Adajia meant by "Oh—Er—That."

The thought was disturbing; the knowledge that she knew what was going to become of him, of Mr. Spock, of McCoy . . .

. . . of whichever member of the crew gave birth to the Consilium.

He pushed the thought away. As he led her along the corridor to the briefing room, he was aware of the turned heads, the larger-than-usual number of crew members who found some reason to be in that part of the ship. Of the crew at this point, only a handful knew what was going on, but everyone knew that *something* was. The rumor of a ship appearing, literally without warning, without engine vibration on the sensors, without long-range effect on the fabric of hyperspace, had flown like lightning among the crew still speculating about the blackout, the *Nautilus,* the fate of Tau Lyra.

McKennon looked around her with frank interest, smiling a warm greeting to those they passed. "To tell you the truth," she said, as Kirk stepped back to let her pass before him through the briefing-room door, "there are times when I wonder whether Arios's espousal of the Schismatic cause isn't just a ploy of some kind, a means to get backing for his own ambitions within the Consilium itself. For all his charm, he has always been shockingly ambitious."

"Has he?" Kirk held her chair for her as she sat. *We could all stay here and be rich,* Adajia had suggested. And be three hundred years ahead of everyone. But it was conceivable that Arios's ambitions took a different form.

"He hides it well," she said, smiling up at him. "But surely you've seen the influence he wields over his crew— which is *not,* by the way, at all usual in the Fleet. A high-level Master—which is what he'd have become if he'd been willing to accept the discipline—can control not only the actions, but to a large extent the thoughts of his astrogator and his empath. To a degree, their emotions as well. Certainly he has that poor little Secondary he kidnapped completely brainwashed."

She frowned, a look of pain glimmering deep in the sea green eyes. "I expect that in the two years since he quit the Consiliar Institute in a snit he's managed to win a tremendous following among the original dissidents in the Fleet by the same methods. Most of them are wired; it would be pitifully easy for him to do. He likes control," she concluded dryly. "And he likes power."

McCoy and Spock traded a glance. They would be, Kirk knew, replaying every conversation with the Master in their minds, even as he was, looking for clues. For something to tell them where the truth might be found. From beneath her tabard McKennon drew a leather case no larger than her hand, which had been clipped to her belt. Fingers moving with neat precision, she unshipped a white plastic instrument, oval and smooth, and fingernailed one of its small gray buttons. She glanced at the briefing table's three-faced central screen, made another adjustment.

"I think you'd better take a look at this."

McCoy held up a finger. "Before we do," he said, "just what 'methods' are you talking about Arios using?"

McKennon frowned a moment, like a woman seeking the best and most understandable explanation. Watching her face, McCoy, too, was conscious of a sense of protectiveness, for she reminded him of the daughter he had not seen in ten years. Probably her diminutive stature, he thought, her air of fragility. Though there was something about the eyes . . .

"Bones . . ." said a soft voice behind his back.

And for one second, his wife was there.

Later, when he thought about it, he couldn't swear he actually saw her, though at the time he was positive he glimpsed her from the corner of his eye. But recognition knifed him in the heart. Sweetgrass perfume, and the deep garnet color of the dress she'd worn when first they met; the wrenching jolt of grief and regret and wanting that almost stopped his breath as he slewed around in his chair . . .

And of course there was no one there.

The loss was worse than the recognition had been.

"Or there's this," said McKennon, drawing his attention back to her, he didn't quite see how. She had the same quality Arios did, of almost magnetic charm. "But please . . . I'm trusting you on this one."

As far as McCoy could tell, the Domina did not move, nor alter her expression, nor make a sound. She only sat with her hands folded, her face grave and a little sad. But McCoy felt a wave of absolute disgust wash over him, an utter revulsion as if the woman had just finished making some crass and bigoted remark about his manhood or his background, or as if he had, only a moment before, seen her pick a bug out of her unwashed hair and eat it. The involuntary thought flashed through his mind, *My God, how can anything that filthy sit there looking so sickly-sweet. . . .*

But she wasn't filthy. Her hair was clean, scented faintly of vanilla.

He couldn't imagine where the feeling had come from, or where it had gone.

"My God," he said softly. Kirk was looking at her with a kind of shaken awe, Spock with an eyebrow raised and a look of deep interest on his face.

McKennon laughed like a handful of chimes in an evening breeze. "My roommates and I back at the Institute used that when men got fresh on dates. But only—*only*—if we never wanted to go out with that man again . . . *and* if we weren't interested in any of his friends. I'm sorry, Doctor. Captain. Forgive me."

"Most fascinating," said Mr. Spock.

"Did you read that as disgust?" McKennon asked him interestedly. "The medullar cues are quite different for Vulcans, but you're half Terran, aren't you?"

Spock inclined his head in assent. "What I found fascinating," he said, "was the choice of emotion to be so demonstrated."

Her green eyes twinkled. "Did you think that, as a woman, I'd have made them both fall madly in love with me? It can be done." The color heightened, ever so slightly, along her cheekbones. "I just . . . have trouble doing it." She turned quickly, touched the white plastic instrument again. "But this is what I really came here to show you."

On the briefing table's central screen the grainy image of the *Nautilus* appeared, silhouetted against the sulfurous glare of the star Tau Lyra.

"We were at the extreme limit of our pickup," said McKennon quietly. "Far too distant to stop them. This is top-end magnification."

A slit of dull orange light marked the opening of the shuttlebay doors—something small, rusted, black-painted, and scarcely to be seen glided forth, silent and lightless as a metallic roach. A moment later, a flare of dirty yellow flame, and the thing sped like a dart, straight for the heart of that waiting sun. Almost immediately the battered vessel swung about, began to move off.

"You must have picked them up shortly after that." The Domina folded her well-manicured fingers, that sliver-thin flinch of pain still marking her brow. "A slaved missile like that has the advantage of leaving no evidence in the torpedo tubes. We know they've stolen such things on raids. Our own sublight drive was badly damaged coming through the Crossroad Anomaly. They were out of range before we could even begin pursuit. After that we tried to pick them up again, quartering the sector. We were four or five parsecs away when you registered on our sensors, with the *Nautilus* in tow. Are they on board still?"

Kirk and Spock exchanged a glance. Kirk nodded. "Yes."

"Confined?" And, the next instant, "No, they wouldn't be, would they? If you tried to confine them," she went on, intercepting Kirk's quizzical glance, "you would have . . . I don't know what kind of trouble."

McCoy started to speak; Kirk's small gesture quelled the remark unmade.

"They're under room arrest."

In fact, for the three days of the journey to Tau Lyra, the *Nautilus* crew had been rather laxly confined to the suite of rooms on Deck Four usually reserved for ambassadorial parties. At Arios's request as well as Kirk's, they had kept very much to themselves, though Thad and Adajia had learned to bowl, with Raksha along to make sure no further cases of temporal paradox developed. On the journey to Tau Lyra, Kirk had seen McCoy's face settle into new and bitter lines as he dealt with the knowledge of what would happen to the galaxy he knew; had seen Lao's bright eagerness quenched as the young man withdrew into feverish pursuit of his computer analysis, working far into the nights as if to outrun the dreams that sleep might bring.

A week ago he had known Lao would make one of the finest officers in the next generation of Starfleet. Now he doubted that the young man would re-up after this mission was done.

God knew what he would do.

In his bleaker moods Kirk wondered that about himself, though in his heart he knew. He would be what he was, do what he could—and, he had found in the five years of this mission, there was usually something that could be done, if you stayed ready.

Sometimes he would meet Arios late at night, observing the stars from the Deck Ten lounge; sometimes see the Master and Raksha sitting quietly together there, handfast, quiet after their work on the *Nautilus* repairs, lovers who had become friends. Two or three times he'd seen Chapel and Sharnas, talking together in the semi-gloom—Chapel another one, Kirk knew, who was sleeping little these days.

McKennon leaned forward. "Do they have—or have they ever had—access to the ship's computers? Through anything—library outlet, food selector, anything?"

"The library readers in their—prison," said Spock, "have been replaced by free-input visicoms, with no connection to the central computer."

She seemed to relax a little, and sighed. "You have to watch them," she said. "Even if you don't think they have, Captain, I would *strongly* recommend rechecking every line of every operations and information program in your banks and in the backup, and running a multiple virus sweep of the entire system. We can help you with that, if you like. They are ruthless, Captain Kirk, and both Arios and the woman Raksha are extremely clever. Have you been onto the *Nautilus?* You or any of your crew?"

Spock said nothing. His hands were folded, hiding the still-blotchy permaskin.

Kirk said, "Not yet."

"After five days? Surely you could get their transporter codes with lyofane."

"My science officer warned me about anomalous energy pulses in the ship's secondary hull," replied Kirk blandly. "Arios himself spoke of booby traps. We hadn't decided what the safest course of action would be when our sensors picked up the solar flares. At that point we put the *Nautilus* crew under restriction and started back to Tau Lyra with the ship in tow. Even if they gave us their transporter shield entry codes, at maximum sublight I wouldn't want to try a beam-through between ships."

"I see," said the Domina.

Kirk nodded toward the central screen, the image of the *Nautilus* like an angular black bird against the sun. The slash of light, the small black missile gliding forth in silence, then the flare of its propulsion; the hangar deck closing and the *Nautilus* engines glowing a dull red. No burn in the torpedo tubes. No evidence at all.

Only Arios's word, and his repeated warnings about this beautiful, sweet-faced woman who sat at his side.

"Were you down to the planet?"

McKennon shook her head. Her pink mouth tightened a little, as if to stop trembling. "We didn't realize they were armed with that kind of weaponry until the flares read on our scanners," she said. "The Shadow Fleet only has what it can loot from our arsenals, and pirate from the merchant ships they attack. If we had known, I think we would probably have . . . I don't know. Disregarded the Prime Directive. Warned them. Something . . ." Her hand described a small gesture, helpless.

"Why would they do it?" asked Kirk.

McKennon shook her head. "I don't know!" The words burst out of her; her fragile hand bunched in a fist of frustrated rage. "That's the horrible thing about this! They were a perfectly harmless people, from all anyone's ever been able to tell from the records. Simple, kindly . . . quite primitive in many ways, for all their moderate level of technology. Did they offer any explanation?"

"They said that you had done it," said Spock, after a glance at the captain. McKennon's face twisted in appalled disgust.

"According to Arios," said Kirk, "the Tau Lyrans were a psychically adept race whose help he was trying to recruit for the rebels."

"The *Tau Lyrans?*" McKennon stared at him. "The . . . what did they call themselves? The Yoons?" She shook her head, closed her eyes in disbelief. "No, Captain," she said softly. "Yes, the Yoons had a certain level of psychic connection, mostly in language, but they were . . . exactly what they appeared to be. A simple culture who had managed to invent the radio but never got as far as bombs. Believe me, the Institute has records of every psychically active culture, past and present, in the known galaxy. We're always on the lookout for further possibilities of refinement of our own teaching, our own technique. We would never have committed such an act of . . . of waste."

She passed her hand across her brow, her mouth taut, as if she had tasted poison. "I can only guess," she went on after a long moment, "that the location of Tau Lyra Three itself was the reason. We knew the planet was a wasteland, of course. Our records showed it as having been destroyed by solar flares sometime in this period. Having discovered a way to make the psion jump through the Crossroad Anomaly, Arios may have been seeking to set up some kind of . . . of safe base in this time period. Either for the Schismatics in the Fleet, or for reasons of his own. I have no proof of that, but it's the way he thinks."

"You sound as if you know him very well," said Kirk.

Her jaw tightened, and for a moment the dark lashes veiled her eyes. "Yes," she said softly. "I know him." There was a world of unspoken past, of bitter experience, in the sudden, careful blankness of her face as she looked down at her hands, the determined smoothness to the set of her lips.

Silence lay for a moment in the room, like a spot of light in water.

Then McKennon said, "You'll want to speak formally with the captain of the *Savasci,* Captain Rial Varos."

Kirk raised an eyebrow, but did not comment on the Romulan name. So in two hundred years the Romulans would be part of the Federation?

McKennon went on, "Nominally I'm in charge of this mission—of bringing Dylan Arios and his crew to justice— but it is Captain Varos and his men with whom you'll be dealing. I admit," she added with her fleeting smile, "that I wanted to . . . to see how the land lay here first. Like any of the Consilium Masters, I am more expendable than a Fleet captain or ship. For all I knew—for all Varos knew—

Arios could have gained control of this vessel by this time. Knowing Arios, that isn't an impossibility." The dryness of experience touched her voice.

"No," said Kirk consideringly. "No, it isn't."

The Domina hesitated, studying his face with a trace of anxiety in those beautiful green eyes. "Are you . . . satisfied with our bona fides?" she asked after a moment. "I know Dylan Arios. I know he's probably told you something that makes you unwilling simply to hand him and his crew over to us . . . that's his style. Something with just enough truth in it to be convincing. And got you to put modern shielding on your own ship. Whatever proofs you require, Captain, I shall try to provide, to the best of my ability."

"Thank you," said Kirk. He wondered if her pleasantly conciliating attitude had anything to do with the fact that she couldn't simply beam Arios and his crew off the *Enterprise,* or beam her own strike force on. He rose. "Mr. Spock . . . a word with you. Please excuse us for one moment, Domina McKennon."

"Captain," said Mr. Spock in a severe undervoice as they crossed from the briefing room to the turbolift, "in the course of that conversation you told quite an alarming number of untruths."

"Deck Three," said Kirk to the lift, and a single bar of green light passed down the black slit of glass. Hands behind his back, Mr. Spock followed his commander interestedly into the physics lab, at the moment occupied only by Dr. Maynooth, deep in an analysis of digitalizations of the records of the Tau Lyra solar flares. Like Lao, the physicist had the appearance of a man who hadn't slept in three days, but in his case he still retained his usual maniac buoyance: what had kept him awake was fascination, not despair. He didn't even glance up as the captain and first officer crossed through the lab to the small, heavily shielded utility room at the rear.

"I presume eavesdropping technology will improve in the upcoming centuries," said Kirk quietly, "so we can only hope the shielding around this room is sufficient. I'm going to ask Domina McKennon to remain on the *Enterprise* for drinks in the officers' lounge. During that time, I'd like you and Captain Arios to spacewalk—in blacked-out survival suits, since I also presume the *Savasci* is monitoring ship's transmissions—across to the *Nautilus,* where I'd like you to have a look at the floor of the hangar deck, and the hangar doors themselves. You said in your report the whole place was caked with moss and the resins extruded by the yagghorth. A missile like that would have left a mark, where they dogged it down at least. If you find anything—scratches on the floor, makeshift dogging clamps, scraping where the doors were opened, anything—I'd like an explanation from him."

Spock inclined his head.

"You'll have to go without a guard," said Kirk. "Two spacewalkers won't be noticed—more might be."

"I assume that even if Captain Arios is the villain Domina McKennon portrays, he still has sufficient logic to know that he cannot operate the *Nautilus* himself. And even a guard of six or seven would be insufficient protection, should he summon the yagghorth Nemo to overpower me."

Spock had a point. It was just as well, thought Kirk, that none of the security officers who had escorted Spock and Scotty in their repair trips to the *Nautilus* had known of the existence of the yagghorth.

Kirk started toward the door.

"Captain?"

He raised an eyebrow.

"I have frequently attempted to study the operation of subliminal cues in human motivation. Was the origin of your distrust her choice of repulsion, rather than the more obvious attraction, as a demonstration of a Consiliar Master's power?"

Kirk smiled crookedly. "You mean, she didn't want to make us 'fall madly in love' with her because that's what she was already trying—very subtly—to do?"

If Spock had not been Vulcan he would have smiled. "Indeed," he said.

"Nothing that rational, I'm afraid, Mr. Spock. So I may be wrong. But in the face of this level of lying—on one side or the other—I'd feel better if I had a little firsthand empirical evidence. Now McKennon has committed herself on how she says the missiles were launched . . . but I'll bet you three moves in our next chess game she doesn't know the state of housekeeping in that ship. And I'll bet you, too, that the faking of visual transmissions will improve a lot in three hundred years."

And he crossed back through the lab to the lift, to return to the briefing room and his lovely red-haired guest.

"It's aye a bit small, for a deep-space vessel." Engineer Montgomery Scott helped Mr. Spock on with his gloves, dogged the seals tight, and cast an inquiring glance over at Dylan Arios, just wriggling his thin form into the blacked-out survival suit.

"You don't need much of a crew in a jumpship," pointed out the Master. "That's a big ship, huge for what they need. Nobody gets tired of each other on a two-week mission from Earth to Rigel and back again, including travel time. You don't even need laundry facilities. Just take your underwear home and have your mother do it."

Mr. Spock looked puzzled at Scott's laughter, but did not inquire. The three men worked quickly in the small chamber beneath the hangar deck's control tower, adjusting the roomy helmets and affixing the jet packs to their backs. Spock had worked in open space before and, moreover, had the physical strength of a Vulcan; he observed from the labored way Arios moved that the Master had not.

"The packs work on the principle of action-reaction," he explained. "Control stick on the front points in the direction you wish to go to change direction. Sharp pressure to stop, pressure again to start, though on this occasion I advise simply thrusting off from the hangar doors in the direction of the *Nautilus* to minimize light flashes visible from the *Savasci*."

"Understood," said Arios's light voice in the helmet mike. Scott was dogging down the Master's helmet, and through the smoky one-way visibility of Spock's faceplate Arios was nothing, now, but a vaguely humanoid shape in matte, nonreflective black. "We'll make for the main tractor-beam hatch. I can get that open from the outside, and it's in a part of the ship where we shouldn't lose too much atmosphere before we can seal it again behind us."

Spock and Arios ran through the check sequence of their seals while Scott climbed to the control tower above, the hatchway sighing as it sealed behind him. In order to minimize the possibilities of temporal paradox, the engineer had cleared the area through the simple expedient of inventing a shiftlong make-work project in the main hull, and assigning to it everyone who ordinarily would be in this section.

Spock turned to the visual pickup, signaled an affirmative. The lights in the shuttlebay cut out, leaving only the small glow of a single emergency lamp in the tower's shelter. As they crossed toward the vast curve of the outer bay doors, the line of amber signals above the tower transformed one by one to blinking red, then to solid red as oxygen evacuated; a moment later the floor vibrated softly beneath their clumsy boots. In darkness before them, where the hangar doors loomed huge, a slit of more profound darkness appeared, sugared with isolated light.

Logically, Spock was aware that stepping from the thick lip of the hangar deck into space was no more dangerous than stepping from the edge of the ship's swimming pool into water. Less dangerous, in fact, because sometimes one *did* sink in water. At some distance to starboard the *Nautilus* hung in the night distance, lightlessly brooding against the smoky glow of the Crossroad. If all its ships were painted so, no wonder the rebels were called the Shadow Fleet.

To port, and above the level of the *Enterprise,* the *Savasci* lay, like the detached saucer of a starship but somewhat smaller, its metal smooth as glass, without visible plate joins and without windows, seeming to shine faintly in the reflected shimmer of the stars.

Their navigator had positioned her so that whatever serial numbers she bore would be out of sight of the *Enterprise,* either by visual pickup or by line-of-sight from the observation lounges. She hung like a pearlized moon, her smooth perfection the absolute antithesis of the age-scarred black junker she pursued.

Hands resting on the door metal on either side of him—the slit was less than four feet across—Spock turned his attention to the *Nautilus,* gauging the distance for what was, in vacuum, one single, springing jump across nearly a terrestrial mile of space, over the fathomless infinities of eternity.

To regard the literally bottomless space beyond the lip of the hangar deck as anything other than perfectly safe in weightlessness would have been illogical, so Spock did not. He knew it was impossible to fall, and stepped from the edge and into the sensation of falling with the equanimity of perfect knowledge. He braced himself against the lip of the deck like a swimmer treading water, orienting himself toward his target. The expression on the face of Dylan Arios was, of course, completely invisible behind the matte plex of his blacked-out helmet, but Spock noticed that he hesitated a long time before following into the void.

"I've given every crewman aboard orders not to address you with more than 'Good day, Domina,' and remarks about the weather in this part of space," Kirk assured McKennon, who turned back to him with a startled look and then laughed like a delighted girl. The double handful of junior officers in the Deck Five lounge did their best not to look like they were staring, but Kirk was aware of being the cynosure of a score of surreptitious eyes. McKennon would have to be blind not to miss it, too.

"And I can't even respond, 'Oh, in my time it's *so* much starrier,' for fear of telling someone something that will change history and make me—and the *Savasci* and Captain Varos—all disappear."

"Well, you *haven't* disappeared, so I guess you said the right thing." Kirk guided her to the section of the lounge usually kept clear for the entertainment of guests. It was well clear, now; a conversation square of slightly depressing blue-gray Starfleet couches and a low table had been enlivened by a silver-gray Starfleet-issue bowl containing some of the calmer inhabitants of the Botany section. As Kirk seated McKennon, the yeoman on shift for that purpose came over and asked what they'd like to drink.

"Sparkling water," smiled McKennon. Kirk asked for a beer. The food synthesizers on the *Enterprise* had the usual consistency problems with such systems, but thanks to the disreputable Yeoman Brunowski's tinkering, the quality of the beer was in general pretty high.

"Yet another temporal paradox," sighed the Domina comically. "Romulan ale hasn't yet been introduced, has it? I probably shouldn't even have asked you that, lest the information that the Romulans are going to enter the Federation one day somehow prevent that event from happening, or change how it happens . . ."

She shifted her position on the couch, and Kirk felt again, a little stronger, that urge of protectiveness toward her, and that sense of nostalgia. He found himself thinking how much she reminded him of Ruth, the woman he had loved at the Academy.

And he found himself, very slightly, annoyed. Did she really think he was that simple?

"I'm surprised Arios didn't try to reprogram your mixer to produce it anyway," she went on, smiling up enchantingly at the yeoman who brought them their drinks. "He has that arrogance. He'd say it was for your own good."

She sighed and shook her head just slightly. Past her, Kirk saw Mr. Sulu stand up from the table where he was having dinner and put a hand on the yeoman's arm. There were quiet questions and more stealthy glances from Uhura, Organa, and Chekov, who were with him, all clothed in off-shift gear of varying levels of informality—the prize for the evening definitely going to Chekov's startlingly embroidered Cossak shirt. They all saw that they had Kirk's attention and immediately became absorbed in their dinners, like children caught peeking through the potted palms.

Kirk mentally rolled his eyes. Everyone on the *Enterprise* had been consumed with curiosity about the crew of the black starship from the moment it had been sighted, and subsequent events had only fostered the growth of some of the most startling scuttlebutt Kirk had ever heard.

Kirk had refuted none of it. Not even after Maynooth and Miller had talked about the characteristics of the systems override Raksha had put through the central computer, or Yeoman Paxson had described what her lab reports had turned up about medical scans on Cooper and Sharnas. Better, he had reasoned, to let the occasional true guesses be buried under the avalanche of speculation.

But it was impossible, he knew, to keep the secret for long. There were too many clues, too many people who had worked on one aspect or another of the dilemma of the black ship. Maynooth and Miller had been ordered individually to keep their mouths shut about the incredibly complex systems that had broken the *Enterprise*'s defense codes, but everyone in the Deck Nineteen auxiliary computer room had had a crack at getting through the locks, had seen what they were up against.

It would only be a matter of time before someone else would guess, as he had guessed, as Spock had guessed, as Lao had guessed. They had to admit Mr. Scott to the circle, and though the chief engineer could be trusted, it would only be a matter of time before one person too many had to be told. Before someone asked the question he himself was itching, fidgeting to ask: *What happens to me in the future?*

Do I bring the Enterprise *in safe? Do I get myself—my crew—my friends—killed in month, or a year? How long do I live, and when, and under what circumstances, do I die?*

The person who, somehow, started the Consilium was aboard his ship.

No wonder McKennon hadn't attacked them; wouldn't try to take Arios off by violence if there was the smallest chance that there would be a fight. Even if that single person—that unknown X—survived, and for all Kirk knew it might be some minor clerk in Stores, the death of friends, the disruption of environment, might easily influence X's decision to . . . do whatever it was he—or she—later did.

"Captain." McKennon's soft voice brought him back to

the present. Her eyes had followed his, watching the little group at the table clearly engaged in another bout of speculation among themselves while the yeoman went to the wet bar in quest of hand-mixed drinks.

"You know—I know—that a temporal paradox must be avoided at all costs." She laid a cool little hand on his wrist. "If I know Arios, he's told you—things—about the Consilium, things about what he believes is going to be your future. Maybe things about—someone—on board your ship."

Kirk thought, *Ah.* He said nothing. The green eyes gazed up into his, searching his with a desperate earnestness, trying to make him understand.

"Captain," she said softly, "you must believe me. In spite of what Arios has told you, the Consilium is *not* some monster conspiracy that's taken over the Federation. We're an independent research and communications corporation contracted to assist with astrogation and the operation of psion jumpships. If it were not for the Consilium—actually, for the research organization that preceeded us, which was called Starfield—civilization in the Federation—in most of known space—would have been wiped out by the plague."

"I understand that," said Kirk, wondering if the pleading in her face was genuine, if his own belief was real, or if it was all something emanating from her wired and augmented brainstem as a series of submedullar cues.

"Did Arios ask you to—do anything—to some member of your crew? Or display any kind of specific interest in someone on the ship? Try to get them alone?"

Kirk was silent for a moment, thinking about temporal paradox.

About Edith Keeler, stepping off the curb into a New York street.

The person who started the Consilium . . .

About sheets of rain-pounded gray water, floating with crude electronics and round bubbles of melted plastic. About digitalized readouts of frantic radio calls, wondering in baffled horror what was happening to the sun. About charred corpses in a bunker, fallen where they were trying to carry all the treasures of their culture to a safety they could never reach.

Fleet-issue mind control. Holovision torture that could kill a man in agony a half-dozen times, then bring him back for more. Free-form reality that changed with the Consilium's requirements. And a space-jump technique that would take a ship from Earth to the Barrier in minutes.

There are people who don't believe they seeded Qo'nos and Khedros and Romulus with the plague . . .

He shook his head. Her eyes tried to read his, tried to gauge the possibility of a lie.

"Captain," she said, "I know from the records that you have experience with temporal paradox. I know—and you know—that there are so many factors that make up events, so many things that can be changed by the ripple effect. . . . Even my presence here, your knowledge, the fact that your crew is speculating, thinking, could lead to disaster that would wipe out civilization in the galaxy. And I know," she added softly, "that this can't be easy for you."

His eyes avoided hers, as if she had read the uncertainty, the indecision, the moments of despair.

"We have techniques now—I'm sorry, we *will* have techniques—to selectively remove memories. To take things out, to make it as if it had never been. To remove all memory of Arios, and whatever it is he's told you—to remove all memory of the *Savasci*—from your mind, and the minds of other crew members who might be affected. They don't take very long, but they're one-on-one techniques, and they need the cooperation and consent of the subject. I think they could help you, and others on board."

Bones, thought Kirk immediately, remembering the corroded weariness that even a few hours had etched deep into his friend's face. Lao, struggling with the massive horror of his despair. And, for other reasons, Miller and Maynooth, Spock—though he suspected Spock could be trusted to keep separate what was future knowledge—Chapel, Scotty.

The terrible indecision, the awful sense of wondering what he could do about events so far from his own reach, would be gone. And, if Arios was lying, if McKennon was telling the truth, perhaps events more terrible than the plague could be averted. All things would return to being as they had been before. It would all never have happened.

If he could be sure that was all McKennon, with her Consilium training, would go in and change.

Chapter Twelve

"ENSIGN LAO!"

He spun, saw it was Chapel, made his way swiftly for the door of the dispensary, but Chapel crossed the room in two strides and took him by the arm. He turned like a snake about to strike and for a moment, so vicious, so rage-filled, was his face that Chapel released him, stepped back, afraid for one moment that he was going to strike her.

Stillness lay between them. Then he turned away, wincing, half-raising one hand. "Jesus, Chris—Nurse—I'm sorry. I'm—I'm sorry." He looked back at her, his hand almost shaking as he held it out in apology, as if he could grasp her forgiveness like a tangible thing.

"It's all right," said Chapel, but her eyes were on his face.

Chapel had seen Lao three or four times on her way to and from the lab, where she had been working off her own sleepless restlessness on analysis of possible yagghorth-transmitted poisons in Spock's blood—which so far she had not found—and so knew that Lao had been as sleepless as she. Usually he'd been working in Central Computer, doggedly putting together the information on the burned-out planet of Tau Lyra III: it was always rumored around spacegoing vessels that somebody had figured out a way to get quadruple-caffeine out of the food synthesizers, and seeing him, she believed it.

He'd held up well, she thought, until planetfall that morning. Had it only been that morning? According to the visual logs, he'd done well enough on the planet itself.

But in the briefing he had sat silent and ill, as if what he had seen in that steaming, wind-lashed Hell had been the final straw, the last horror he could stand. He was only twenty-one, she thought, and had been working for three days not to think about what he now knew would be the future of his world. It had to come back on him sometime.

"Did you get some sleep?" she asked gently. "You left right after the briefing. . . ."

He shook his head. "I can't sleep, right now," he said. "I—I came here looking for—for some nedrox. I just need to complete the computer analysis of what we found on the planet. . . ."

"Tomorrow will do for that," said Chapel, but he signed again, more violently, as if waving the thought away. She saw he still wore his uniform, black trousers, gold shirt with an ensign's single band of braid on the cuff, though it was now well into the second shift. After the briefing she herself had gone back to her quarters and slept a little, though her dreams had not been easy, haunted by baking heat and the spectacle of those twisted, mummified bodies, their convulsed arms still clinging to withered and melted shards.

"No, I'll—I'll be fine." He made a move to go, then turned back, the lines deepening again around his dark eyes.

"Do you know what Thad told me?" he asked, in a voice cracked with horror and exhaustion. "I asked him—I asked him if it was true, that the Consilium gene splices, deliberately makes the Secondaries the way they are. He looked surprised that I had to ask. He said they get implanted when they're infants, before the sutures in the skull heal up—pleasure-pain stimulators. They work better, they're more contented . . ."

He shook his head, like an animal tormented by flies.

"They are on the ship now, aren't they?" he said, after a struggle to calm himself.

Chapel nodded. "One of them. The Domina McKennon."

He pressed his fist to his lips, his eyes squeezed shut. In spite of the exhaustion that aged his face, he seemed to her then very young.

"Zhiming." She stepped close, touched his arm, and this time, though he flinched, he did not pull away. "Zhiming, you're tired. Exhausted. I'm telling you, go to your quarters, and get some sleep. Here," she added. "I'll prescribe something for you, cillanocylene . . ."

"No," he said quickly. "No, that's all right. I—I will go to my quarters," he went on. "You're right. I do need rest."

He turned, and stumbled out the door. Chapel stood for a moment, hesitant, then went to the dispensary cabinet and checked the white readout on the container of nedrox. The glowing numbers on the window matched the contents as of yesterday, but Chapel recalled that Lao was a computer maven, probably capable of altering the readout. He was usually scrupulously honest, but she knew that he wasn't thinking clearly now. She keyed in her passcode, and counted the capsules of the powerful stimulant manually.

The numbers matched. He hadn't taken any.

She remembered, as she turned toward her own small cubicle, all Zhiming had told her about his older brother, Qixhu. No wonder he felt protective of Thad, furious that anyone would harm him. It was that knowledge, as much as anything he had seen on the ruined planet, coming on him by surprise at the end of the briefing, that had driven him from the room in silent despair.

She tried to put the matter from her mind as she logged in the measurements from the latest IPs of Cooper's, Sharnas's, and Arios's neural wiring. The growth of the cut areas was infinitesimal but definitely present—according to Arios, the wire healed itself every two to three months, "depending." "Depending" on what? McCoy had asked. Arios had looked momentarily blank, then shaken his head.

What would it be, she wondered with a shiver, to know that was inside you, growing inexorably? Wire ends meeting, until you began hearing the voices of the Masters—the sweet, reasonable voice of Germaine McKennon—whispering in your head?

And yet . . .

She picked up the IPs again, studied them more closely, and then punched up the transcription of her interview with Arios on the subject.

All she got was SECURITY CODE PURPLE.

The transcription—like everything else connected with the future as described by the *Nautilus* crew—was sealed.

It scarcely mattered, Chapel thought; she'd done the transcription herself. And to the best of her recollection Arios had said that Sharnas's wiring had been cut five or six weeks ago, Cooper's almost eight.

A theory stirred in her mind. Replacing the IPs in the security drawer of her desk, she made her way to the ambassadorial suite on Deck Five.

The suite was silent when she reached it, so much so—usually it was lively with the rebel crew's good-natured bickering—that for a moment, as she stepped through the outer door, Chapel wondered if the crew had effected another escape. But a moment later she heard Adajia's voice say, "Try the next channel," in the bedroom, and stepping to the doorway, she saw them clustered around the disabled comm-link panel in the wall, Raksha kneeling on the bed, listening to a communicator—which none of them were supposed to have—connected into the comm panel by a hank of wire.

"Pick up anything?" Chapel asked politely, and the Klingon's eyes glinted, half-suspicious, half-wry.

"Just the usual rumors." She unhooked the wires and unself-consciously slipped the communicator into the pocket of her doublet, then stuffed the loose cable back into the comm panel and closed the hatch. From years of friendship with Uhura, Chapel knew there was far more wire there than there should have been, which meant the Klingon had stolen or jury-rigged tools to cannibalize wiring out of some other portion of the walls.

"According to Yeoman DeNoux in the officers' lounge, your captain and the Domina are still drinking soda water and chatting. Tell him to watch out for her, Chapel. She's crystal poison disguised as mother's milk."

"I expect," said Chapel quietly, "that she's saying exactly the same thing to Captain Kirk about Arios. They're going to want that communicator," she added, holding out her hand.

"They took the Master," said Thad, coming over to her, his dark eyes pleading. If what Cooper had told them was right, thought Chapel uneasily, no wonder the poor man always looked half-terrified; no wonder the information that they were on a Starfleet vessel, back in the transporter room four days ago, had driven him to near-panic.

Chuulak, Adajia had said. Public punishment with the intention of deterring others. God knew what they'd done to him.

"Mr. Spock and a security guard came down here twenty minutes ago and pulled him out of here fast," said Raksha shortly. "He seemed to think it was all right. Told us to stay here, anyway . . ."

Chapel reflected that it was very like the *Nautilus* crew to have remained in prison not because there was a guard in the corridor outside but because their Master had told them to. "Can Sharnas get in touch with him mentally?" she asked. "At least to see if he's well? Because I'm sure you'll find he is." Above all, she thought, she had to keep this crew from panicking, since Raksha had very clearly found a way to cut into the ship's comm system, and that probably meant she could get into the computer from here as well.

"Not if the Domina's on the ship," said Cooper, perched beside Raksha on the edge of the bed. "We don't know how much your captain's telling her. She can pick up a call, a signal; if Sharnas reached out looking for the Master, she'd feel it."

"Could she detect passive listening?" asked Chapel. "If *you* listened for *him?*"

"If the Domina has him," said Phil, "he may not be able to extend his mind."

"But the Domina's still in the officers' lounge with the captain."

"She was ten minutes ago," pointed out Raksha.

Chapel walked into the sitting room, studied the laminated table on the wall beside the unviolated comm-link pad. A little hesitantly—the number was not one she signaled regularly—she touched 5–24.

"DeNoux here." It was the yeoman on duty behind the bar that evening.

"Neil, is she still there?" Chapel lowered her voice to a conspiratorial whisper. "What are they up to?"

The grin in his voice was almost visible. "From where I stand, I'd say they're up to her hand on his wrist and him tellin' her stories about his days at the Academy. You know anything about who she *is*, Chris?"

Poison disguised as milk.

"I *never* seen a ship like that, but if she's wearin' a translator, it's not one I can see."

"Only what Dr. McCoy told me in the briefing," lied Chapel. "A VIP of some kind . . . but if *you* find out anything . . . She didn't give you any exotic recipes, did she?"

"Fizzy water." A beer man, DeNoux sounded mildly disgusted. "Miller's putting it through the computer for analysis of probabilities."

"Let me know what he finds out."

She tapped out, turned to Raksha. Sharnas was already half-reclined on the other bed, his eyes shut, his breathing light and slow, face relaxing as if in sleep.

"You weren't far off when you said she'd be telling your captain the same things about the Master that we're saying about McKennon—and the Consilium." The Klingon folded her arms, her dark face somber. "Information—and slander—is the name of the game for the Masters. She's probably got him convinced even as we speak that the Yoons suddenly invented spaceflight and phasers, went on a genocidal rampage two years from now, and would have destroyed the Federation if they weren't stopped."

Seeing Chapel's clenched jaw, Cooper said, "You should

hear what they're saying about the Organians, now that they're . . ."

Behind them, Sharnas whispered, "Nemo . . ."

"I know she was one of the old Constitution-class cruisers, long before they discovered the psion jump." The scratchy echoes of Dylan Arios's voice whispered eerily through the sounding tube of the long cargo corridors of Deck Twenty-three. "You can tell from the engines. God knows where they got her—she'd been hauling ore for years, and you can tell from some of the metalwork that she'd been damaged as hell at some point. But whoever had owned her when the Consilium got the patents on the psion jump sewed up paid to have the engines refitted and put out the credits to have a Consilium empath on board. My guess is that was before the Consilium hiked the price, drove most of the small companies out of business, and took over the deep-space freight market itself."

The lift tube, Mr. Spock guessed, hadn't been in use even then, to judge by the amount of *vescens zicreedens* growing on the walls and on the corroded doors. They ascended the gangways beside it, like whispering traps of dead air and unidentifiable sounds. The small hatch beside the tractor beam was supposed to open at a coded signal tapped into the recessed hatch plate—the Master had gone straight to the manual opener, to let them in.

"Phil and I escaped the Academy in a ship called the *Antelope*, but when we went back to get Sharnas we got shot to pieces, no gravity and leaking air in twenty places. There's air up in the saucer, but I'm not taking guarantees on what it smells like."

Spock elevated an eyebrow. They had taken the headlamps from the suits they'd left in the machine room next to the long-disused tractor beam, and the feeble illumination showed him corrosion and stains as well as lichen, the metal of the steps slimy underfoot. In places, beneath the fungoid growths, he could see the metal of the walls dark with old charring or bright with patches; at some point the ship looked to have been nearly gutted. Battle? he wondered. The wars following the plague?

"It is conceivable that the air in the saucer would smell worse than that in the lower holds," he said consideringly. "But if so, I would be interested to see how it could."

Arios laughed, his breath a trail of steam in the firefly light. A deck or two above them, Spock knew, lay the steamy heat of the yagghorth's territory; down here, the crippled heating coils barely functioned. A fortunate thing, in a way, since the cold kept down the smells of the assorted fungi, low-level oxidation, and the vaguely ammoniac stink of boreglunches; Spock was thankful for the thin suit of thermal protection he wore under his uniform. Ahead of him, he could see the Master shivering. The saucer, he knew from his original scans of the vessel, was colder still.

"It doesn't seem to make any difference to the yagghorth how big or small their ships are," Arios went on after a moment. "To them it's all their cyst, their shell . . . their many-chambered home. *I could be bounded in a nutshell . . .*"

". . . *were it not that I have bad dreams,*" finished Spock softly. It occurred to him suddenly to wonder whether Nemo, mind-linked to Sharnas, had nightmares as well.

From the darkness below him he heard a sound, a very faint blundering, scratching noise. He turned his head, looked down into the infinite darkness of several decks' worth of gangway. His own shadow blocked most of the dim gleam of the lamp. Still, he had an unclear impression of something dark and huge floating weightlessly in the darkness below him, steering itself on its vestigial wings: hairless tarantula legs tucked, tentacles dangling, a sticky glister of claws and teeth and organs.

Logically, he was aware that Nemo was no danger to him. Arios could not operate the *Nautilus* himself, even if McKennon's version of events was the correct one—for him to murder Spock, or have Nemo murder him, would be the height of foolishness. Spock recalled his own calm as he'd stepped from the lip of the hangar deck into bottomless infinity, knowing he could not fall because there was no gravity. Recalled his own slight impatience with Arios's very evident—and completely illogical—fear. He tried to suppress the adrenaline reaction he felt at the sounds behind him, and the sudden ache in his cracked ribs—and experienced a small qualm of human annoyance at how long it took to do so.

"Nemo," murmured Sharnas. Long lashes threw crescents of shadow on his cheeks as he turned his face, fitfully, as in sleep. "He's—they're—darkness. Steps. Aft gangway." He drew deep breath, let it out. "The egg."

"They're in the *Nautilus*," said Cooper, frowning. He looked over at Christine, seated on the other corner of Sharnas's bed, almost crowded off by Thad and Adajia. Only Raksha had not left her position on the other bed, close by the comm link; her hands were folded, so as to hide the expression of her mouth.

Cooper explained, "Those turbolifts have been seized shut since God left for Betelgeuse. Most of the gangways don't go all the way, either. They've got to be heading for the Bent Zone—the original yagghorth haunt under the engines —or somewhere around there."

"What the hell is he doing on the *Nautilus?*" asked Adajia.

"Spock's with him," said the empath after a moment. "Nemo . . . breathes his mind . . ." A line of concern twitched into being between the slanted eyebrows, and he fell silent again.

"Maybe Spock left a plug driver when he fixed the engine?" suggested Thad brightly.

"I can see sending the Master over to the ship if the Domina's here," said Cooper, "but . . ."

"No," said Chapel softly. "They have to be looking for something."

"Voices," said Sharnas suddenly. "Nemo . . . absorbs . . . from the darkness . . ." He flinched, his face twisting in sudden pain. "I can't . . . I feel . . . They're the voices from the mine. Voices from the mine. I hear them . . ."

Raksha and Cooper exchanged a puzzled glance; Chapel

felt herself get utterly cold. She leaned forward, not wanting to touch Sharnas, not wanting to break his trance, but her heart slammed harder in her chest.

"What voices?" she asked, as gently as she could. "The voices of the dead?"

"Voices. . . ." His words came out as a hoarse breath; his hands had begun to shake. "I hear them. Nemo . . . drinks . . . them. Reaching with his mind he finds them, takes them to himself. Voices like those I heard in the mine. The Yoons."

He drew in a harsh breath, his features twisting with pain and horror; his hands groped out, and she caught them in hers. They were ice cold.

Impossible, she thought, impossible—yet she saw him again, standing knee-deep in filthy water in the deeps of the mine of Ruig, while all around her lay the heaped bodies, contorted in death. And in her helmet mike she heard him whisper hopelessly, *I hear their voices. Voices of the dead.*

"The Yoons are calling." His voice was thin, strained as it had been when in nightmares he had cried his mother's name. "The psychics, the savants, the teachers. They're alive. They're trapped. They're calling out for help."

From the darkness within the *Enterprise*'s hangar deck, the black infinity of space, dusted with a luminous powder of stars, seemed very bright. A crack of eerie light opening out of a denser night, even casting a pallid line of shadow, which stretched like an obscure allegory across the pale concrete of the floor. From the darkened control tower, Christine Chapel watched the two minute human forms darken the lowest fraction of that slit, awkward with the sudden reacquisition of gravity.

She knew, by his height and by the way he stood, which was Spock.

She thought she would know him anywhere.

Beside her, Mr. Scott tapped a key on the board. The dragon-eye slit of the hangar doors slipped closed, shutting out the dream of space.

Prosaic red warning lights came on, then began to blink

with the oxygen cycle. By the intermittent glare Chapel saw Spock and Arios stride clumsily for the shelter of the gallery under the tower, jet packs swaying like camel humps behind the anonymous, blacked-out spheres of their helmets. The lights had gone amber by the time they reached the tower door. Scott tapped the work lights on as the cycle finished, and Chapel followed him down the pierced metal slats of the stair.

"Ye find what it was ye're after?"

"Indeed we did, Mr. Scott." Spock lifted the clumsy headgear down, his own head emerging, sleek and dark and rather small-looking, in the gray metal of the shoulder ring. He saw Chapel and nodded her a polite greeting. "Nurse Chapel."

He had only once called her Christine—once, when he felt he owed her an apology, an explanation. Of course, he almost never called the captain by his name either, and over the years they had come as close to being friends as the Vulcan would admit. It was simply not in him to do so. It was not part of being a proper Vulcan.

She said, "Mr. Spock, when you have a moment there's an urgent matter I need to speak to you on. Captain Arios, too."

Spock raised an eyebrow halfway, but only asked Scott, "Are you aware whether the Domina McKennon is still on board?"

"Word has it the captain just walked her back to the transporter room."

Across the quarter-acre of open cement, the inner doors slid apart. Spock and Scott looked around sharply; Yeoman Wolfman had orders to keep everyone from the hangar. Chapel had only been admitted by application via comm link to Dr. McCoy.

Captain Kirk strode across the gray surface like a hunting lion, impatient power in every movement of shoulders and head. Chapel recognized the symptoms. Like poor Lao, he was a man fighting, in his own way, against what he knew. Scott, helping Arios with his clumsy glove seals, made a move to withdraw; Kirk signed him to stay.

"What did you find?"

"The doors of the *Nautilus* hangar deck were fused shut with rust and ciroid growths," reported the science officer. "The decking was covered in several centimeters of resins, lichens, and St. John's mold. All cargo dogs and cradles were thick with fungus, obviously unused for at least thirty-eight standard years."

Arios shrugged. "At the Institute they were always all over me for not keeping my room clean."

Kirk stood still for a moment. Then he closed his eyes briefly, and his breath left him in a gusty sigh. "Finally," he said softly. "Finally, some kind of evidence about who's lying, and who's telling the truth."

He held up a small device of white plastic. "This is faked, then." He extended it to Arios. "It's a visual record of the *Nautilus* releasing a slaved missile with high-compression fusion torpedoes via the shuttlecraft deck, to fire into the star Tau Lyra. The computers can detect no doctoring."

"Tcha!" Mr. Scott's mouth twisted in disgust. "So much for the butter not meltin' in *that* lass's mouth."

"You going to send another party back to check the doors tomorrow?" Arios eeled out of the pressure suit, rumpled the sweat from his hair. "Because I'll lay dilithium to little green apples they'll have been opened by then."

"I wouldn't even lay little green apples on it," said Kirk grimly. "I'm due to go aboard the *Savasci* at twenty-one-hundred hours, to speak with Captain Varos. If they have armament capable of destroying all life on a planet, God only knows what else they can do. The question is, how can we get the *Nautilus* away to the Crossroad and back through to your own time without the *Savasci* opening fire?"

Scott smiled. "Well, Captain, given you can get me ten minutes alone with her engines . . ."

"Captain," said Chapel. "There's another problem as well. Sharnas says Nemo has picked up mental transmissions that sound like those Sharnas felt in the mine on Tau Lyra. He's pretty sure some of them survived."

* * *

Nineteen hours, ten minutes. And beam-over to the *Savasci* was at 2100. Captain Kirk sighed, and rubbed his eyes, weary down to his bones.

"We'll need psychic amplification to get a strong enough link with Nemo from here," Arios was saying, folding his arms around his drawn-up knees. In the low light of the ambassadorial suite, sitting on the floor between Raksha and Phil, he looked very alien, seeming to have joints where humans did not, and the sweat still matting his green hair slicked it to the shape of an alien skull. Rembegil DNA spliced to enough human to stand the stress of empathic wiring, Cooper had said. True Rembegils had died at first mindlink with the yagghorth. Kirk wondered what else the "independent research and communications corporation" had done along those lines.

"How could the Yoons be trapped in mines deep enough to survive the heat?" Chapel, who stood beside Kirk in the doorway of the bedroom, leaned across to him and spoke softly below Arios's voice. "I was there. I ran a tricorder scan of the entire area. All the deeper tunnels were flooded."

"They could be trapped in the upper end of a sloping gallery, in an air pocket," Kirk replied, with an inner cringe at the thought of what it must be like in such a place, after five days. "I'm not a geologist, but I do know that high concentrations of certain metals can interfere with tricorder readings. I'd have to check what ores were present in the mine to be sure. There was heavy ion interference, too."

What he was wondering was how to get rescue parties down to the planet and across to the *Nautilus* undetected. How to explain such delays to the Domina.

". . . Oh, hell," Arios was saying. "The Yermakoff Psychic Index went out with antimatter. We'll need someone with a point-seven or higher on the Ghi'har Scale."

"Mr. Spock," said Sharnas, with a small inclination of his head. "It is, I understand, a serious matter, to ask you to enter mindlink with a yagghorth. Even with your help it may not be enough, to make clear contact with those trapped on the planet. But we have no choice. We have to get them away."

"I understand," Spock said softly, and took his place at the small table with Sharnas and Arios as Cooper turned down the lights.

Silence settled, their breathing deepening, as if in sleep. Spock flinched once; Arios's fingers tightened to keep him from breaking his grip. Kirk shivered, remembering the vids he had seen, the dark and terrible thing framed by fire, ripping men to pieces casually, like a gardener tearing up dead vines. It had almost killed Spock, materializing out of the *Nautilus's* clammy darkness, a mindless and silent hunter.

That thing was walking, with its bobbing head and spiky, insectile stride, down the corridors of Spock's thoughts.

Kirk glanced again at the chronometer. Nineteen hours twenty-one minutes. In a short time he would have to leave, to ready himself for the official reception on the Consilium ship. Twenty minutes, if nothing happened before then, he told himself. In the first year of the voyage, Spock had taught him techniques of relaxation, of meditation, to separate him from his emotional involvement in events, to put anger, or pain, or grief from his mind.

He'd used them on a number of occasions. He suspected he'd need them now.

Someone on the ship was responsible for the Consilium.

He wondered about that train of events, that person, that X, wondered if X was someone whose life he had saved at some point in the past five years—the past few months—making him responsible for Thad, for the swirling hell of heat and water and death on the planet below them.

To simply destroy, or to turn aside, the person responsible for the Consilium might condemn billions to death from the plague, as McKennon had said—and certainly McKennon and Arios both had been absolutely cagey about identifying anyone as responsible. And Kirk himself knew very well that the "let's kill his mother and then he won't be born" school of temporal paradox was absurdly simplistic and hideously dangerous—the kind of thing that only those who had no knowledge of human relationships, of economics and social forces, would invent.

There might be nothing he could do that could keep the plague from happening, that could keep cascading events from forming the chains that would one day bind the Federation. But there was jolly well something he could do to help those rebels, whose births all lay so many centuries after his own death, something distant enough from the center of events that it would not interfere with the halting of the plague.

"Nurse Chapel," said Kirk softly, and at his nod she stepped into the corridor with him.

"If they haven't made contact with the surviving Yoons before I have to go aboard the *Savasci,* let Mr. Spock know that my orders are to take whatever steps are necessary to send a rescue party to the planet." He spoke in a low voice, to exclude the guard posted a few meters away. "Tell him to keep information about what's going on to as few personnel as possible, on a need-to-know basis only. But tell him to get those people. Bring them back here and keep them alive, at any cost."

"Yes, sir." Chapel glanced at the guard also, and looked as if she would ask him something, tell him something. Then she seemed to change her mind, asked only, "Can the other ship trace our beam to the planet? Follow the rescue party down?"

"According to Arios they have limited personnel," said Kirk. "Tell Spock to send five parties down to different areas, four decoys as well as the rescue team. Tell him to send whatever security personnel he thinks he'll need."

"I'll tell him, Captain." Both were conscious that it was information that couldn't even be allowed into the computer.

"After we've gotten them off the planet, I'll work out the details of what to do with them, and of getting the *Nautilus* away. We'll probably have to keep them in some kind of shielded compartment, to prevent scanner identification. It'll be . . ."

"Where are we?" Sharnas's voice came from within the suite's parlor, harsh and breathless. Kirk stepped quickly through the door to see him bow his head almost to the table, his whole body trembling. "Where are we, Grandfather? What has happened to us?"

"The world screamed." Spock's brow furrowed suddenly with concentration, his dark brows convulsing together. Again his hands moved to pull free of the link, and again Sharnas and Arios kept the fingers gripped tight. In the low illumination, his face was ghastly with shock. "Sinaida, my beautiful one, my wife! Litas—Telemarsos—Indipen . . . My children. My beloved ones . . ."

"Dead," whispered Sharnas. "Dead, Grandfather, they died . . . they screamed out . . . *What has happened to us?*"

"Tell me where you are." Arios spoke without opening his eyes, his face filmed with sweat. "We are here, we are listening. Tell us what you feel, what you hear, what you smell. We can find you if you tell us. What is around you?"

Spock shivered profoundly; Sharnas's head sank forward again, long hair hiding his face.

"What do you see?" asked Arios again.

"Cold." Spock's voice was thick, like that of a man deeply hypnotized. Kirk and Chapel exchanged a startled glance. Even a mile below the surface, the mines had been like a slow oven.

"Cold . . . light," breathed Spock, as if fighting for every word. "Cold . . . walls. Cold air that smells of metal and chemicals. Nothing living, no plants, no trees. Hard bare walls, beds made out of things that never were alive."

"Others are here," murmured Sharnas. "Grandfather . . . I feel their minds crying. Other savants . . . Farmers, too, some . . . Aunt Tsmian the blacksmith and her son. All in little rooms. They're . . . near us. Cold, hard walls. They heard them die, too. Their families, their children, screamed out their names." His voice came suddenly fast, stumbling over the words. "Grandfather, I woke up in the night and there were things in my room, things that grabbed me. One of them just touched me on the arm and I don't remember anything after that. I couldn't fight, I . . . I woke up here."

"Iriane." The word came out of Spock's mouth a dreamy mumble, and he shook his head, like a man trying to come out of sleep. "Iriane, my child . . ."

"Grandfather . . ."

"Who are you?" Spock tried to raise his head. The lines of his face changed, altering it shockingly. His mouth seemed to widen and flatten; his eyes, though still closed, seemed somehow larger, rounder; his shoulders slumped. "I've been . . . drugged. We've all been drugged. This mind . . . this yagghorth that I feel dreaming of us. I was in my garden, on the balcony, I was just going to go inside with Sinaida. Then I was dreaming, dreaming about hearing her scream. Seeing her die. I know she's dead, they're all dead. Those of us who are here . . . a hundred, a hundred and five. Why us, why not my Sinaida, why not the rest? Iriane. Who are you who hears us?"

"Rest," whispered Arios. "Rest. We'll come and help you, come and get you out."

Raksha said something truly vicious in Klingon, and Cooper murmured, "I don't believe it. Those lying skunks."

"Where are they?" whispered Chapel. "They didn't say . . ."

"They didn't need to." Kirk felt his own body alight with a surge of rage. He, too, had his memories of the planet's heat.

"How are you going to find them?" asked Thad, looking at Kirk in puzzled shock, then from face to face to angry face. "If they're down on the planet someplace . . ."

"They're not," said Kirk softly. "McKennon sent someone down to the planet before the *Savasci* fired its torpedoes. They wanted to keep you from getting in touch with the savants of the Yoon, but they decided to go one better. They kidnapped a group of the Yoons themselves."

Chapter Thirteen

"THEY'VE DONE IT BEFORE," said Arios. He tried to turn his head to look at Kirk, who stood, arms folded, by the door of the ship's surgery; McCoy rapped his patient lightly on the back of the skull with his forceps, and Arios obediently resumed his original position, head rather uncomfortably held by the operating table's face cradle. His voice came strangely muffled.

"Everybody travels by transon net anyway—dial your destination, hit the switch, and you're in Cleveland. Places that aren't on the net just don't exist. Except there are *huge* stretches of territory with—officially—nothing in them. I know about this, I was brought up in a colony of Rembegils that had *no* contact with the outside world, aside from what the Consilium allowed it. Once they get the Yoons settled in one they probably won't know there are humans on the same planet."

"And you think you can locate them on the *Savasci?*"

"I think so, yes." Arios's body, naked to the waist and prone on McCoy's laboratory table, had been dyed the dark brown of a South Indian Dravidian native. Cut short and straightened by the ship's barber, his hair was now black, long enough to conceal most of the nape of his neck but short enough to reveal unblemished skin to the casual eye.

It was the skin McCoy was testing now, tugging very gently with the small forceps on the edges to test the permaskin's bond over metal and scars.

"I'll have to go by the layout of the ship rather than any kind of mental signals, though I can keep anyone from noticing me or Mr. Scott or Lao when we split off from the main group," Arios went on. "Sharnas burned out my wiring recently enough that McKennon can't detect me unless I signal her, which I promise you I'm not about to do." He spread his fingers, like a shrug, against the leather padding of the bench. "If the good doctor'll give us a dose of dalpomine and another one of adrenalase, I'll burn back Phil's wiring while you're getting into your dress uniform, just to make sure . . ."

"Can you manage?" asked Kirk, shocked. "My guess is he shouldn't be on his feet at all."

"It's only minor surgery," said Arios. "And Phil's made it through firefights ten minutes after I've pulled his wiring, without adrenalase, haven't you, Phil?"

"I have," said Cooper, from the corner of the surgery where he was admiring a very convincing artificial mustache in the mirror. "I'd rather not do it again."

"Sissy."

Cooper grinned. His hair had been lightened to a nondescript sandy brown to match the mustache, and in the red shirt and black trousers of a security officer he would, Kirk reflected, pass pretty much unnoticed.

Unless you looked closely. As a student of history, Kirk had always been fascinated by old portraits, and more than once had been struck by the difference in the faces from era to era. Seventeenth-century faces were different from nineteenth, which differed in turn from twentieth—none of them had quite the cast, the expression, of twenty-third. The differences were subtle but real: one barely noticed them except in contrast, when some strange ringer somehow got through. Out of dozens of Bellocq's photographs of nineteenth-century New Orleans prostitutes, one girl had a twentieth-century face; among pictures of twentieth-century rock musicians, there was one who looked like he should have been born in 1640 instead of 1940.

Dylan Arios and Phil Cooper did not have twenty-third-century faces.

Or maybe it was the wariness grained like dirt into a dilithium pocket miner's skin, the air of always looking over one's shoulder, that touched him with anger at the Consilium, that made him have to fight against despair. That made him willing to take this risk to help their cause.

A future when everyone had eyes like that.

"It may not be necessary," said McCoy.

Kirk, Cooper, and Arios all regarded him in somewhat blank surprise.

"I've been charting the regrowth of your wiring, and Sharnas's." The doctor returned the forceps to their drawer, passed his hands across the cleansing screen, and gestured to the latest internal photographs where they lay on the counter. "Nurse Chapel brought this to my attention about half an hour ago: in four days there's been virtually no regrowth of the wire. You said yourself the regrowth time 'depends.' My theory is that it depends on the presence of trace elements—iron, calcium salts, and minerals in the bloodstream—that the microprocessors in the wire itself use to rebuild. Now, it so happens that rhodon-gas poisoning—which all of you underwent when your coolant system blew—has the effect of stripping these trace elements out of the blood."

Arios sat up slowly on the table; Cooper put up a hand, almost subconsciously defensive, to cover the back of his neck.

"You mean if I take a big whiff of rhodon gas before I go across to that ship I'll be fine?"

"I mean if I give you a big shot of vitamin D-seven," said McCoy, holding up the silver tube of an injector, "the elements will remain in your blood, but they won't bond with the wire. You'll experience fatigue and you may get a little short of breath until your body readjusts, but it's better than the shock of having the wiring burned off the nerves."

"Is there any way to delay going over?" Chapel handed Arios the red shirt of a security officer and looked anxiously at Cooper. In the past four days she had grown very fond of all of them.

"McKennon would suspect something was up," said Kirk. "She thinks I have these men under lock and key." He glanced at the chronometer, something he'd been doing for the past fifteen minutes, the adrenaline rising in his veins. "I can't give her any reason to think I don't. We've got thirty minutes, and we need at least one person besides Arios who knows the layout of a Federation/Consilium jumpship."

McCoy grunted. "Sharnas is too young and God knows how we'd disrupt Thad's wiring, and McKennon will know there are no Klingons and damn few Orions in Starfleet."

"Right now, anyway," said Arios reflectively. His eyes, too, had been dyed dark. With his sharp features he had the appearance of an oddly half-caste Indian. "The first Klingon officer in Starfleet serves on this ship, you know . . . Not this *Enterprise,* but the *Enterprise*-D. After that there were a lot of them."

Kirk felt again that oddness that had come over him at Adajia's *Oh . . . That.* The knowledge that he was dealing with people who knew his future as past.

"They made—make—damn good officers, too. The Empire and the Federation—and the Romulan systems as well—were in a state of almost complete detente when the plague came along, though I can't tell you how it came about—we still don't know. If they hadn't been, I suppose the Romulans would have been completely wiped out. Their culture pretty much was."

He glanced over at Chapel, asked, "If Phil's going to get the D-seven and beam straight over to the *Savasci* with us, maybe he should have a hit of tri-ox and some adrenalase?"

Chapel glanced at McCoy, who nodded. As the door swished shut behind her, the Master turned back to Kirk. "The plague attacked the central nervous system, distorting mostly the sensory nerves, especially the interface between instinctive and cognitive centers of the brain. In most of its victims it produced violent rages, paranoia, random slaughter . . . hideous scenes. The endorphins from blind rage were one of the few things that lessened the pain. There was a wave of wars, because so many of the leaders—not to mention the troops in the field—were affected without anyone knowing. When the Consilium—only they weren't called that, then—finally got a med team down to Romulus, there was damn little left but smoking ruins. Ships can still pick up Remus on radiation detectors on the other side of the quadrant. That was . . . the damn thing about the Consilium."

Arios stepped aside, watched with interest as McCoy put the injector to Phil's arm and fired it with a soft *phut!*

"How is that stuff produced?" he asked, and, when McCoy raised his brows, added, "You've got to remember that for a hundred years now the Consiliar Institute is the only place where they teach medicine."

McCoy's mouth twisted in a wry grimace; he went to the terminal on the end of the bench, tapped in a sequence of commands. The printer hummed faintly, as if giving the matter thought, then extruded a sheet of pale green flimsiplast. "Simplest thing in the world."

"It better be," remarked Arios, "since we're going to be cooking it up in the galley. But you see, without the technology that made wiring cheap enough to be available on a wide scale—without nanocellular interfacing, and implants to the psionic centers of the brain—they'd never have been able to broadcast the low-level psionic alpha waves that kept people from going over the edge and killing everyone they saw. It was like a . . . a blanket of dust on a fire. Like turning down the volume on the pain that was driving everyone mad."

"But the price of healing," said Kirk softly, "was that everyone had to be wired."

"For a generation, yes," Arios said. "Afterward it wasn't as necessary—after the plague and all its little side viruses had been vaccinated against, and the thing mutated every couple of years for decades—but it was real common. By that time whole populations were showing major genetic damage. Half the population were Secondaries anyway, long before the Consilium started snipping people's DNA to get them that way. The wars left radiation everywhere, and there was incredible havoc from the side effects of early tries at medication. The Consilium were the only ones to have the facilities intact for cloning from the healthy genetic material that was left. Thad's one of about two thousand 'lines' on Earth. Every now and then new genetic mutations still surface, some of them pretty scary. Phil's not a clone," he added with a grin. "Makes it hard for him to buy shoes."

"You want to navigate your way back through the Crossroad with an astrolabe, or what?" retorted Phil. He had turned a pasty gray color and seated himself, rather quickly, on the operating table.

"Speaking of gene splicing," added Arios, "watch out for the Security Specials once we get to the *Savasci*. Lao and I will be able to shut down the doors and the gravity for a short time on the ship—long enough, I hope, to get the Yoons out of their prison and into the big cargo shuttle while Mr. Scott foxes the engines—but you'll probably have to hold them off us, at the end. Where is Lao, anyway?"

As he spoke, the door hissed open and Christine Chapel entered, carrying a tray with the injectors required. McCoy gave Cooper the tri-ox at once, and the *Nautilus*'s astrogator regained a little of his coloring. Mr. Spock, who had entered on Chapel's heels, said, "I have prepared launch and autopilot instructions, per Mr. Cooper's information, for the *Savasci*'s cargo shuttle; Rakshanes and I have also programmed a slicer program which should work on the *Savasci*'s computer, provided it is not a generation newer than two months before the *Nautilus* entered the Crossroad. However, Ensign Lao has not reported for briefing as instructed."

"I saw him an hour or so ago," said Chapel, handing the adrenalase to McCoy and turning, puzzled. "He said he was going to his quarters to try to sleep."

Kirk wondered about that for a moment, then realized with a start that at 0900 this morning—less than twelve hours ago—they had gone down to the steaming hell-pit of

Tau Lyra III, and seen all that remained of the civilization of the Yoons.

No wonder Lao was exhausted. He wouldn't even know, Kirk realized, that some of the Yoons had survived. That there was a chance, now, to help the rebels win.

"He did not respond to a signal," Spock was saying.

"Try him there again," said Kirk. "He may be deep asleep."

"He didn't look well," added Chapel.

"Brief him on the mission; have him meet me in Transporter Room Two at twenty-fifty." Kirk glanced at the chronometer. Twenty-thirty-six. Where the hell had the time gone? "Tell him he'll be able to sleep after that."

So will we all, he thought, and strode out of sick bay and around the corridor to the turbolift.

In twenty minutes, he thought, he'd beam across to the *Savasci,* to deal with the red-haired woman who had spoken so convincingly of the good the Consilium had done.

To see exactly what kind of people would—at least for a time—be his heirs.

To do what he could to remedy a situation almost three hundred years in the future, about whose ramifications he knew next to nothing.

As he donned his formal tunic, took from their boxes the small ribbons denoting the medals he'd won, he felt a queer disappointment, like a child realizing that the pirate's treasure he has achieved is only rocks after all. Whatever could be done in the meantime, the Federation was still in for some dark years.

The bright slips of color were memories: ten wounded men beamed up to the *Republic,* all alive; a Klingon ship exploding in a glare of white and yellow over the distant pink-amber surface of Thalia III. Another Klingon ship departing into the darkness of stars, its mission unfulfilled.

The smell of burned insulation and blood in the intermittent glare of the *Van der Vekken's* scorched-out bridge. The Kargite president shaking his hand.

Edith Keeler stepping off a curb . . .

Pieces of ribbon.

He closed his eyes.

And this—this impossible, crazy mission on the *Savasci* . . .

The door chime chirped. At his button touch, Dylan Arios stood in the doorway, almost unrecognizable with his dark skin and dark eyes, the crimson security tunic slightly too big on his narrow shoulders. No green showed at the roots of those eyebrows, and even the lashes were dyed dark. He said, "Before the fireworks start, I want to say thank you. Thank you for believing us. There's no reason for you to, you know."

Kirk sighed, and settled the green satin of his tunic on his body. "Somebody lied about those missiles. It wasn't you."

"No," agreed the Master. "But I don't know a whole lot of Fleet captains who'd check after seeing evidence like McKennon handed you. Especially not after being wrapped up in engine tape and shoved in a closet."

Kirk smiled. "I'll have to rewrite my recommendations for improvements in ship's design and training," he said. "In handwriting on paper, to keep Raksha from pulling it out of the computer when nobody's looking." He glanced over at the ribbons on the bureau. "Not that I'm a hundred percent sure it'll do any good."

The dyed eyes flicked to him, then to the ribbons, as yet unmounted on his shirt. Quietly, he said, "I did my best not to tell you."

"Was that for my benefit, or to keep us in the dark about your capabilities?"

Arios grinned. "Well, both," he said. "You *might* have been a Starfleet setup. It's been done before."

He frowned, leaning his narrow shoulders against the doorjamb. "Is there a reason you're planning to put the Yoons on the *Savasci*'s cargo shuttle to transport them over to the *Nautilus*, instead of trying to get them down to the *Savasci*'s transporter? We can run a scramble on the *Nautilus*'s transporter entry code to keep the *Savasci* computers from reading it."

"The Yoons aren't going on the *Nautilus* after they're

rescued—if we manage to rescue them." Kirk's voice was very quiet. "Spock has an autopilot program with the coordinates of that small planetary system—the one Mr. Scott calls Brigadoon—inside the Crossroad Nebula. From what you've told us about the continued isolation of the nebula in your own time, they should be safe there—from the Consilium, from the plague, from Starfleet—until you contact them, two hundred and eighty years from now, in your own time. By then they should have a fair little colony going."

"Ah." Arios considered the tips of his boots for a time in silence. "Is that because of the danger of us getting blasted before we reach the singularity point, or because you still don't trust us?"

"I trust you," said Kirk. "We'll give you the coordinates of Brigadoon, before we wipe them out of the computer so there'll be no way McKennon can get her hands on them, if she happens to get access to our mission log. I just want the Yoons to be able to make up their own minds."

Arios was silent for a few moments. Then he reached out a finger to touch the bright scraps of ribbon in their box. "That's what the Federation is really about, isn't it?" he said, suddenly shy. Without looking up, he went on, "At one time I dreamed about winning some of these. I can name every one you hold—and the ones you'll still win. You were the reason I went into Starfleet, you know."

Kirk stared at him. It was disconcerting to hear it, from a man not more than seven years younger than himself. From a man who'd managed to tie knots in his ship and had almost gotten away with it. For a moment he felt as if he were looking at himself as he would be in some unimaginable old age.

"I was conceived and gene spliced and more or less raised under the aegis of the Consilium," said Arios, "but it was reading about you—reading about this era of spaceflight, of the Federation—that made me fight to go into officer training, instead of just consenting to be linked into the mind of a yagghorth and being useful, the way they wanted me to be. You're . . . a kind of hero, to those who know their history," he went on. "Like Cook, or Patton, or Lee. I'd read about you—about the voyages of the *Enterprise,* and of the other starships—and I'd think, *That's what I want. That's what I want to be, and do."*

He grinned, with his old wry sweetness. "Of course, the minute I got into Fleet training I realized that being that kind of hero isn't possible anymore. That going out and finding new life, and new civilization—bringing them into the Federation, bringing the Federation into contact with *them*—doesn't happen anymore. Or if it does, they're probably pretty sorry. I can't even tell you . . ." He shook his head. "I can't even tell you what some of those instances were, because they might not have happened yet, but . . . You were an inspiration. And reading about you, and the way things were then—are now—made me look around at the Fleet in my own time and go, *Wait a minute. What's wrong with this picture?* I'm sorry if that sounds corny," he added. "It isn't meant to."

"No." Kirk remembered his own heroes, his own idols, Gordon and Ise and Reluki, whose footsteps he had followed as best he himself could. "No, sometimes we need to follow a line of footprints."

"I just wanted to tell you," said Arios. "You're known. You're remembered. Not just by me, but your name is known to a lot of the Shadow Fleet. The rebellion started in Starfleet, you know. It's still a place where idealists go, looking for the stars."

"So if you'd taken Raksha's advice and killed the life-support when you could," said Kirk quietly, "*you* wouldn't be the person you are."

He grinned, a little shyly, and said, "You heard about that?"

"Spock told me," said Kirk.

"It isn't that simple," said Arios. "It's never that simple. The person on your ship saved civilization, saved uncounted billions of lives, by doing the research that founded Starfield. It wasn't Starfield's fault that it got taken over by its founder's unscrupulous and greedy heirs. That it got merged with others who wanted to control, to rule—and those others were the only ones, at that time, who had the resources to do the good that Starfield couldn't afford to do by itself. Maybe there are cases in which you can kill one person, or tell them, *Hey, don't do that,* and change time for the better, but this isn't one of them. There's too much time involved, and too many factors. Too much good along with the evil. That's why I won't tell you who it is."

Kirk nodded. "Because he isn't now who he's going to be," he said softly. "And any change would turn him into a different person from the man who—who saved all those billions of lives." He folded his arms, regarded the thin, unprepossessing figure before him, rather small in the red shirt of a security officer with a phaser at his belt. "Like yourself."

"Maybe," said Arios, with his shy grin. "If I live. And things may turn out differently anyway.

"You're my past, Captain, but I am not necessarily your future. There are a thousand possible futures, my people— the Rembegils—used to say, and one degree of alteration in a trajectory can change a starship's path by thousands of miles, and destroy, or save, a world." He shrugged. "But mine is the only universe I'll ever know about. All I can do is try."

Kirk smiled, and picked up the ribbons to pin to his tunic. "So let's go try."

"Idiots," said Dr. McCoy, watching Phil Cooper— mustachioed, blond-streaked, and buoyant with adrenalase —disappear through the doorway en route for the trans- porter room. "Every single one of them. Nurse Chapel, I know you're off shift now, but . . ."

She shook her head, smiled. "Oh, come on, Doctor, you can't expect me to go to bed now."

He grinned back, crookedly. "The captain seems to think it'll all go off like clockwork, but we'd better have adrenalase, anticane, and the usual emergency kits on hand. Can I ask you to do that while I get things in train to have a supply of D-seven beamed across to that cargo shuttle along with the things we brought up from the planet? Damn, I wish we'd had time to even have a look at them."

Chapel made her way into the dispensary, blinking a little with tiredness in the bright glare of its lights. It seemed like days since she'd spoken to Lao here—crowded days filled with anxiety. Weeks since the morning, suiting up to go down to the scorched hell that had been Tau Lyra III. *Please, God,* she thought, *let them get them off that ship. . . .*

Over the general comm, she heard Mahase's voice say, "Ensign Lao, Yeoman Wolfman, Shimada, Watanabe, Chavez, please report to Transporter Room Two. Ensign Lao, Yeoman Wolfman, Shimada, Watanabe, Chavez, please report to Transporter Room Two. . . ."

And as she turned back to the wall of small plastic cases with their red, digitalized windows, Chapel noticed a nick in the plastic of one of the last containers on her right. A nick that she was ready to swear hadn't been there that morning.

Someone had forced a window cover plate.

Chapel walked over, frowning, and checked the infolabel.

Neurophylozine. A narcotic, carefully monitored and fatal in large doses. She touched the register switch; fifty capsules there yesterday, fifty there at the moment. Quickly she tapped in her code, slid the container itself from its socket.

There were not fifty capsules in it. She dumped them on the central table, made a swift count. Fifteen, sixteen, seventeen . . .

Thirty-three missing.

Thirty-three!

"Ensign Lao, please report to Transporter Room Two. . . ."

Chapel whispered, "Oh, my God. Oh, Zhiming . . ." She dumped the remaining capsules in their container, replaced it in the wall, Lao's haggard face, his trembling hands, his bitter despair, all flooding back to her with horrible clarity. He'd been in here—when? They'd come up from the planet at about 1400; the briefing had been almost immediate. Then the shining ship, the red-haired woman with her dazzling smile—Lao in here, looking for something to keep him awake, he'd said . . .

Even then, she knew he was lying.

Chapel strode from the room, heading at a rapid walk for Lao's rooms, dreading what she would find.

Very few people on board the *Enterprise* cared to visit the laundry and recycling facilities on Deck Eight.

Asked, most of them would say that there wasn't all that much to see: a big room with a line of particle shakers down the middle and folded heaps of red shirts, blue shirts, black trousers, and assorted articles of Starfleet clothing. Beyond it, an even bigger room full of clanking machinery, with the massive square conduit of the food conveyor from the engineering hull's even larger recycling facilities crossing the ceiling and necessitating a duck or a crouch every time you crossed the center of the room.

Even those who worked there—Lieutenant Dazri's two yeomen, Brunowski and Singh—had gotten Ensign Miller to rig them warning systems that would alert them to their supervisor's approach or hail, so they could return, or at least respond, from more congenial haunts.

Working L&R was the least desirable job on the ship. On Earth and on most of the major Federation planets, it was relegated to those incapable of any other task.

Qixhu worked the particle shakers in one of the massive facilities in Yemen City, thought Ensign Lao, stepping through the door into the dim, throbbing cavern of the recycling room. He was supposed to be very good at his job, having no hope of bettering himself, no qualification for any other task.

No wonder, Lao reflected bitterly, the Consilium would go on to create so many like him.

Darkness like a hand clutched at his heart.

"A *laser tennis* team? Whaddayamean, a *laser tennis* team?" complained a distant voice from the tree-grown chamber behind him, known to the entire crew—with the exception of Mr. Spock—as "Central Park." Track shoes scrunched on the gravel pathways; against the pungence of the hydrogen-carbon, oxygen-nitrogen mix came a drift, as the door closed, of water and grass. "The *Enterprise* needs a laser tennis team like I need a spare gallbladder. Now, if we could field a decent ball club . . ."

"Oh, come on, virtual baseball is like virtual sex. . . ."

Ensign Lao crossed the room soundlessly, musing through the darkness in his heart that the real reason people avoided L&R was that they didn't want to be reminded about what the food in the food slots was recycled *from*. Even that turned in his mind to darkness, to a memory that hurt like physical pain. People never wanted to be reminded that men like Qixhu existed, worked for them unseen in places like this. In the future, people would not want to be reminded of people like Thad.

Yeoman Brunowski was absent. Lao followed the massive pipe of the food conveyor down the length of the room, to where it ran into the wall, the bulkhead where the main hull attached to the ship's massive dorsal. Just beneath it, almost invisible in the gloom at that end of the chamber, a large access hatch permitted repairs.

With a bitter smile, Lao flipped the cover plate and released the hatch, crouching to crawl through. A jungle of wire and cable, of fiber-optic bundles and the plastic-covered hawsers of power lines, confronted him. A faint smell of dust and the thick residues of lubricants and the stink of the sludge that the conveyor brought up from below.

Above the access hatch the shipwide comm came into life with a muted, ambient hiss. Lieutenant Mahase's voice said, "Ensign Lao, please report at once to Transporter Room Two. Ensign Lao, please report to Transporter Room Two."

Her voice, he knew, would be everywhere in the ship.

From the pocket of the utility belt he wore, he removed a pale green flimsiplast chart, a series of bridge wires, a pin welder, and a cutting tool. Though the rest of the chamber was dim, there was a worklight here, among the massive ganglia that united the main hull with the engineering hull below. Feeling cold and strange and queerly perfect and no longer tired at all, Lao began to match up the schematic with the wiring before him, the spinal cord of the ship itself.

Behind his head in the quiet gloom, Mahase's voice sounded again. "Ensign Lao, please report at once to Transporter Room Two."

"Most curious." Mr. Spock folded his communicator and clipped it once more to his belt. "It is unprecedented in my experience with him that Mr. Lao should either be late or be without his communicator."

Kirk looked uneasily from the chronometer on the transporter-room wall, to the small group gathered beside the main console. Mr. Kyle. His assistant Mr. Oba. Mr. Scott, indistinguishable from the small squad of security guards, which also included the repigmented Dylan Arios and Phil Cooper.

"It wouldna take long to search the ship, Captain," suggested Scott, who, though he'd already had experience with the *Nautilus*'s impulse engines, had spent the past few hours studying Arios's schematics of more standard twenty-sixth-century technology. "If Spock's right, and it isn't like him to be late . . ."

"We're the ones who can't be late, if we're going to keep suspicion down," said Kirk quietly. "And I know just how long it can take to find someone on this ship." He hastily canvassed in his mind the computer mavens of the crew familiar enough with Raksha's programming to work the changes necessary: Dan Miller was taking Scotty's place in the engine room, and Lieutenant Maynooth was so physically incompetent that requesting his presence on such a mission as this would be tantamount to murder.

"Mr. Spock, I'm going to have to ask you to join the boarding party," he said at last. Spock inclined his head and reached for the small utility pack, which included a doctored tricorder, converted to a very efficient subminiature zip-and-record autotransmitter and data copier.

"Take the first opportunity you can to disarm the ship's transporter shielding—we may have to beam out of there fast. Don't black out the sensors until you're just about to get the cargo shuttle away. Take out the *Savasci*'s impulse engines before you do that. If there's trouble, rendezvous at the impulse-engine chamber; we'll cover you as well as we can. If you can do it, you're to tap the *Savasci*'s central files; Raksha has preprogrammed the likeliest file names in the autoslice file. Arios—you're sure you can get him and Mr. Scott away from the main party undetected? You're sure McKennon is the only Master on the ship?"

"Standard procedure is one." Arios was watching Phil, a little worriedly, but the adrenalase still seemed to be working. In response to Kyle's nod, Mr. Oba removed his red shirt and handed it to Mr. Spock. The arms were slightly too short, but would have to do. "It's the Specials you'll have to watch out for, but they're wired—and gene spliced—to make them receptive to psychic command, so with luck I can get them to look the other way when I need to. I don't like this business of Lao disappearing, though. . . ."

"Neither do I." Kirk crossed to the door and tapped the comm code, and a moment later a voice said, "Bridge here. Mr. Sulu." Despite the lateness of the hour, Kirk had requested that the helmsman remain, guessing that they might need some top-grade navigational work fast.

"Mr. Sulu," said Kirk, "Mr. Spock is accompanying Mr. Scott and myself to the *Savasci*. Alert Mr. DeSalle to institute a shipwide search for Ensign Lao; also to double the watch on the *Nautilus* crew."

Cooper started to protest, and Arios signed him silent.

"You have the conn, Mr. Sulu."

He turned back, and nodded toward the transporter disks. "Gentlemen . . . shall we go?"

Chapter Fourteen

"THEY'RE OFF." Raksha the Klingon opened her eyes briefly, her hands stilling on the deck of cards that she had been shuffling and reshuffling for half an hour. She reached to touch the wire, with its makeshift earplug cannibalized from parts of the disabled comm link, that ran from the comm, through the remains of the communicator, to her ear. "Transport circuits report nine beamed across, in two batches. Four humans and a Vulcan, first shot; three humans and an unidentified, second shot."

"Who's unidentified?" asked Thad, turning his attention from a holovid of a very bad Western. "And where's the Master?"

In the tank, a squad of Asiatic-looking cowboys fired a laser cannon at a horribly duped-in Cygnian belothmere—a creature which, though quite twelve meters high in the film, was in reality barely taller than a man's knee. Behind a foreground of a prop ranch house and a prop fence, what was quite obviously the Hindu Kush pierced the sky. The belothmere looked acutely embarrassed.

"The Master reads as unidentified on this computer because he hasn't been invented yet," Raksha replied patiently, laying out a ring of solitaire on the table before her. "Rembegil won't even be discovered until . . ."

She paused, bringing her hand to her ear again, her dark eyes sharpening suddenly and turning hard. Adajia hit the mute button on the remote, though Raksha could monitor the computer's small, tinny vocoder through worse distractions than *Terror of The Pecos*.

"That's weird."

"You talking about something the computer said, or that belothmere?" inquired Sharnas, who was lying on the couch, half-in, half-out of a subvocal mindlink with Nemo.

"Somebody's running my shield-slicer program." Raksha sat up straighter, covered her other ear. "Small keypad . . . deep-ops level . . ." She picked up the communicator, said, "Monitor and report all activity on flowline PN7995. Trace source of activity and report location."

Adajia got at once to her feet and collected a log pad, touching the button on its side to clear the games of tic-tac-toe and hangman that covered it.

"Does that mean Captain Kirk's gonna be sore?" asked Thad, but no one answered and he didn't really expect it. Sharnas, shaken free of his semi-trance, got to his feet and came over beside him, tapping the holovid off. Thad looked inquiringly at the Vulcan boy, but Sharnas shook his head. "Haven't the faintest . . ."

"They're setting up a link program with the transporter," said Raksha. "Damn this vocoder, it's cutting off half the sentences every time a new command goes through."

"Who is?" asked Thad, but softly. He'd interrupted Raksha before when she was concentrating and knew not to do it again.

Sharnas shrugged. "It can't be Mr. Spock, if he's gone across to the *Savasci*," he said. "Logically, it has to be Miller, Maynooth, or Lao. They're the only ones who studied the program."

Thad nodded, after a moment's cogitation. "So what are they linking to the transporter?" he asked. "And why?"

"It looks like," said Raksha after a moment, her eyes closed again in concentration on the small voice speaking in her ear, "they're setting up some kind of an automatic triggering mechanism to be tripped by the transporter's return transmission. In other words, when the captain beams back over, something's going to happen."

"Oh," said Thad. He frowned. "Like what?"

The first thing James Kirk noticed when he materialized in the *Savasci*'s transporter room was that the transporter chamber was separated from the main room by a circular, crystalline shield, with the tech's console on the other side.

Also on the other side was Domina McKennon, beautiful, fragile, and girlish-looking as ever, though she'd dressed her red hair up and wore a sable dress that completely failed to look severe. With her was a small, spare Romulan whose stance and eyes would have identified him as captain of the *Savasci* even if his uniform markings hadn't; a woman—Vulcan or Romulan, Kirk wasn't sure, but there was a strange glitter of madness in her dark eyes; and a fair and lanky individual whose red sleeve-bands were similar to, but more numerous than, those of the ten identical stalwarts in red-and-black uniforms ranged along the back wall of the room.

Their faces bore the marks of differing experiences; one had a small, sickle-shaped scar on his chin, another a short scar by his left eye. There were some differences in hair length, though head shaving seemed to be in favor, not only with the security guards, but with the Romulan captain as well. Some clearly spent more time in the weight-gym than others did, though all were well muscled. But the eyes were the same. Medium brown, narrow with suspicion, arrogant, and vicious.

The gray eyes of their fair-haired chief were like that, too.

Kirk wondered if this man had identical copies of him floating around the Fleet.

The transparent screen sank soundlessly into the floor.

"Captain Kirk." McKennon smiled and held out her hands. "Captain Varos, of Starfleet Interceptor *Savasci*. Security Chief Edward Dale—Karetha, astrogation tech."

The Romulan woman inclined her head. She had looked

almost normal, until she moved. But as she stepped forward she subconsciously gathered her arms up toward her chest, mantislike, and the scarred hands with their huge, curved fingernails spread a little in a fashion horribly reminiscent of the videos Kirk had seen of the yagghorth, backed and hissing in the flames. The way her head swayed, the slump of her back and shoulders—*Dear God, how long has she been mindlinked to the yagghorth who is her empath partner? Is that what it does to everyone?*

He felt a sick qualm of shock at the thought that one day—if he lived that long—Sharnas would move like that, look like that, too.

She looked like a human in her sixties, though given the longevity of the Vulcanoid races was probably much older. Her black hair, combed and braided into a knot the size of a man's two fists, was heavily shot with gray.

She held out her hand.

Kirk, mindful of the instructions Arios had given him, did not introduce either Mr. Spock or Mr. Scott. No one, not even McKennon, who had met them before and had reason to remember Spock, seemed to notice.

"Captain Kirk." Captain Varos extended his hand. He looked to be in his forties, older than Spock, certainly, though again, with a Vulcanoid it was difficult to tell. "It is an honor and a privilege to meet you."

"I only regret that it has to be under such unpleasant circumstances," said McKennon, stepping close. Kirk found it suddenly very difficult to look at the Romulan empath, difficult, almost, to remember that she was among the party as they left the transporter room, entered the curving, claustrophobically narrow corridor outside. Floor, walls, and ceiling were all covered with a kind of fiber, like spongy carpeting. Though it gave a different tread to his boots, Kirk could not see that it affected the opening of the oddly narrow doors.

"You must admit," the Domina added, seeing Kirk raise his brows, "that your main goal in coming on board was to see if Dylan Arios was telling the truth. Oh, come, Captain . . ." Her laughter brought to mind kites and picnics and summer days. "You don't think I have enough experience of the man to know that even as a prisoner, he'll have been telling you about how the Consilium has Starfleet in its pocket and has made lackeys of the Federation government? At least that was his story when last I heard. He may have come up with a new reason since then for raising a private army."

Captain Varos said, "I assure you, Captain, Starfleet takes its orders from no one but the Federation Council, as it always has." In his sloe-black eyes there was no deception, no nervousness. From his few encounters with Romulans he knew their culture prized honesty above honor, life, or any amount of social graces.

Or at least it had, almost three hundred years before this man's birth.

"Then who are the Shadow Fleet?" he asked.

Behind them, Security Chief Dale sniffed with laughter. "Cavalry and canvas," he said, and Kirk glanced back at Varos for confirmation.

"In a way, yes." The Romulan captain did not smile, but there was a sardonic light in his eyes. "They're the clipper-ship captains in your own world, Captain, who refused to set foot on a steam-powered vessel; the auto drivers in mine who boycotted bullet trams because they were nuclear-powered. Mixed with a smattering of those in both our worlds who tore out all the light sockets in their houses because they believed that the government could listen to them through electrical appliances. Spinal implants weren't designed to limit personal freedom or to allow the Consilium to take over the galaxy, you know. Civilians don't have them at all, except in certain jobs. They're to increase a ship's efficiency, pure and simple. They enable us to travel unheard-of distances, literally in the blink of an eye."

Kirk glanced sidelong, to where the empath Karetha was swinging her head nervously from side to side, her wrists still carried slightly raised before her. There was nothing human in her stance, her walk, at all. He looked back at the Romulan captain. Where the rucked trough of scar tissue gouged the back of Arios's neck, of Cooper's, of Sharnas's, was only smooth skin, not even marked with the tiny telltale flaws of surgical scars.

He'd have to tell Bones they'd either eliminated cutting altogether or had perfected the renewal of skin. In any case the surgery would have been a long time ago.

"If I'm going into combat," added Security Chief Dale, "and I'm given a choice of whether I want to serve officers who are wired—who can communicate among themselves and their empaths—or officers who're trying to do it by subspace and comm link, believe me, I know which league I want to be fighting in."

Spock raised a protesting eyebrow but said nothing.

"As I told you over that lovely mineral water on the *Enterprise*," said McKennon gaily, "I'm on board purely in an advisory capacity. Because Dylan Arios is a rebel Consiliar Master, and likely to use his powers against you; and because the Consilium wishes some questions answered about the methods of the rebellion itself."

Kirk wondered if having "some questions answered" involved the horrors of holo torture—unending and lethally real—which Cooper had described.

"Now, come," she went on. "It has nothing to do with the rights and wrongs of the rebellion, but purely as a commander I'm sure you'll be interested in the bridge. . . ."

Kirk followed. Sometime later he remembered to glance back at his own party, shocked at himself that he had completely forgotten to maneuver a situation in which Spock, Scotty, and Arios could discreetly slip away. It had been, literally, twenty minutes since he'd even remembered that they were there.

And they were gone, of course.

"It all still works on matter-antimatter flux." Arios neat-handedly put finishing touches on taping up the unconscious engineer's hands, mouth, and eyelids while Mr. Scott lovingly removed the hatch cover and contemplated the main power-conversion stem of the *Savasci*'s engines. "They finally cracked the problem of how to carry spare dilithium crystals about twenty years before the psion-jump drive was perfected, but as you can see, the warp engine is only a kind of auxiliary for emergency use. You want to pull that coil there immediately. It's the modulator that lets the empath hook the yagghorth through to the ship for the jump."

"Ach," said Mr. Scott. "Can't have 'em showing up ahead of you at the Anomaly, now, can we? Still," he added, sitting back on his heels to consider the impulse drive while Arios stowed the *Savasci*'s engineer in an inconspicuous locker, "it's such a beauty it's a shame to lay tool to her. Ye can't just cut her out by the computer, Mr. Spock?"

"With the existing shielding on the baseline operations programs," replied the Vulcan, glancing repeatedly from the tricorder's small screen to the screen of the engine-room terminal that he'd cross-wired in, "it's not something I would care to try."

He slipped one of Raksha's preset wafers into the tricorder and tapped through a code; a gratifying stream of numbers flowed down the screen, indicating that, indeed, the *Savasci*'s big cargo shuttle was being programmed for automatic launch, disengage, flight, and landing on the lush and pleasant world of Brigadoon. According to the screen of the engine-room terminal, none of the information was passing through to the ship's main computer, and Spock rather hesitantly tapped through a disconnect signal when the programming was done, in case *Savasci*'s computer had some kind of automatic cycle-and-backup mode, as many ships' computers did.

As Dylan Arios closed his eyes and entered a light trance of listening, Spock inserted the wafer containing Raksha's slicer program and started picking his way through the mazes of guards and locks to first disable the tractor beams, then remove the shielding by which matter-transmission beams could be turned back, all the while reassuring the computer itself—and anyone who might have been monitoring its operations—that nothing whatsoever was going on. It was a program Raksha described as the nobody-here-but-us-chickens function, though the connection between multilevel secondary directory installation and low-cholesterol sources of animal protein escaped him.

It had been, so far—even without the interruption whose statistical likelihood increased geometrically every few minutes—a most interesting experience.

Spock's quick hearing picked up the distant mush of boots in the spongy flooring of the corridor outside; at the same time Arios opened his eyes, raised his head sharply. He still looked slightly unfocused, as he had when they'd slipped away from the security officers; McKennon, absorbed in charming the captain, had not even noticed when they'd slowed their pace. Neither had the hard-faced, identical Security Specials; it was as if they had become, if not invisible, at least very, very inconspicuous.

In the corridor, boots halted. Voices greeted one another, the idle and unnecessary social contact forms of people who had nothing much to say to one another—the man could certainly have punched in a data reading from his own workstation had he truly wanted to know how things were in holo—but wish to establish the fact that they have spoken to one another that day. Two hundred and seventy-nine years had, evidently, not altered that. Early in the voyage of the *Enterprise* Spock had asked Lieutenant Uhura about this custom of "chitchat" and still did not understand it fully. Did Mr. Sulu, or Mr. Chekov, whose lives he had saved upon repeated occasions, actually believe that he, Mr. Spock, had forgotten that relations between them were cordial if he neglected to speak to them *every* time they came into proximity after absence?

Spock's glance crossed Arios's, then returned to the door. The Master's dyed brows quirked together; then his eyes slid closed again. Outside, one of the voices said, "Damn!"

"What?"

"I was supposed to meet Cane-Twelve for coffee!"

"Oh." The woman sounded just slightly miffed. Why, Spock could not determine, for she had not been insulted.

"Want to come?"

The footfalls retreated.

"Is this common to your people?" Spock asked, very softly, his eyes still tracking the flow of the numbers on the tricorder. "This ability to turn minds aside?"

"I think so," said Arios, equally low. "I never lived on Giliaren itself, mind you. Rembegil civilization—what's the polite phrase?—didn't survive contact with the Federation. The Consilium kept a colony of us going for about seventy-five years, like they intend to keep the Yoons—they kept an isolated colony of Vulcans, too. We—the Rembegils—had the highest psionic index, but as I said, the ones they tried to make into empaths died during first contact with the yagghorth. I don't look a whole lot like an authentic Rembegil, but they raised me till I was twelve or thirteen."

He glanced over at Mr. Scott, visible only as a slice of scarlet shirt through the hatchway into the impulse engine, then looked back at the outer door. Listening carefully, Spock could hear no one's approach; no one, in fact, anywhere near the impulse chamber.

He wondered how Vulcans and Romulans stood even two-week missions with so much ambient noise.

"They were pretty fragile, physically and mentally. I think they developed psi powers just to compete with whatever was big and mean and stupid in the original ecosystem, whatever that was; almost no records were kept. The Federation didn't have the funds to protect endangered civilizations like you do these days, after the plague. To my knowledge there wasn't even the equivalent of those boxes they're going to beam on board the shuttle in flight. . . . you did program in the pause at the reception point, didn't you?"

Spock nodded.

"I don't even know if there are any Rembegil left in the colony, or just frozen samples in the gene banks. But those don't do the Consilium much good, because all the techniques of teaching, all the exercises and the culture to develop the psi skills, are lost now. That it?"

Scott emerged from the hatch and gave him the thumbs-up sign. Mr. Spock, who had switched the tricorder over to data-absorption mode and was rapidly zip-copying the

entire contents of the *Savasci*'s central computer for
Raksha's use and analysis later, reluctantly disengaged.

There was now not a moment to be lost.

Yeoman Wein and Ensign Giacomo from Central Computer reached the bridge at the same time, the redshirt
standing aside to let the thin young woman in her blue tunic
step out of the turbolift ahead of him. Mr. Sulu looked up
from his console, where a digital readout of the relative
positions of the *Enterprise, Savasci,* and *Nautilus* hung in
black space wreathed in a galaxy of glowing green numbers.
The main viewscreen showed the real-time view of the
faintly shining disk of the *Savasci* hanging in darkness
above them and to starboard, like a luminous moon-
jellyfish, the barely visible shadow of the *Nautilus* below and
to port. Another screen depicted the three ships in a row
against the screen of stars, the ghostly blue shape of the
Crossroad like a blowing curtain of gauze. Half a dozen
people had made excuses to come onto the bridge and quiz
Mahase on the unknown ship's ID codes, and received only
her impassive reply that they were classified and she, sworn
to silence.

"Mr. Sulu, I thought I'd better come up in person to tell
you this," said Giacomo softly. "I just got a weird blip in the
readings on the central computer, the same kind we got just
before the lights went out." She glanced over at Wein,
knowing he was in charge of guarding their guests, then at
the screen, which showed a closer view of the *Nautilus* itself,
lightless as a ghost ship riding at anchor in eternal night. "It
went away immediately, but . . ."

"Raksha told me to come up to you and report," said
Wein, looking down at the helmsman. "She says she's
picked up evidence that someone's gotten into the computer
with her slicer program."

"How would she know that?" asked Sulu. "They don't
have computer equipment."

"I guess they . . . uh . . . got hold of a communicator and
rigged a voice breakthrough from that," said Wein, who had
noticed some time ago that his communicator was missing

but hadn't connected the loss with his charges. "She offered to surrender the communicator but said she was using it to track the interference. She says whoever it is has done a cut-in on the transporter ops."

Sulu muttered a reference to turtle eggs in Tagalog, then said, "Giacomo, get down to the physics lab and see if Dr. Maynooth is there. Wein, check Engineering for Miller. If he's not there check in the secondary hull, but don't use the comm link. Signal me on your communicator instead. Dawe, find out from Mr. Kyle if Lao ever turned up at the transporter room or if he's still missing, and if he is, get DeSalle to put out a search for him . . . quietly. Nothing over the comm link. Lieutenant Mahase, I'll be with our guests on Deck Four."

The auxiliary bridge at the fore part of the engineering hull had exactly the same dimensions as the main bridge up in the saucer; the same stations and capabilities; the same layout. Duplicate sets of controls linked each console with Engineering, Phasers, Shields, Torpedoes. In the Academy simulator, and later on the *Enterprise* itself, Lao had worked them all. He knew exactly which wires to cut, which bundles to isolate and relink with bridges so that no telltale blips would show up on the ship's self-regulating system. In the past few hours since the close of the briefing, he'd pulled the schematics files and studied them, even as he'd pulled the files on the precise attachments of the main bridge to this one. Since he was not an engineer, but a computer tech, it required intense concentration to do the job undetected by the ship's computer, even after he'd inserted all the careful baffle programs he'd taken or inferred from the backup recordings of Raksha's files.

Yet he knew he'd do it. He felt the strange, cold lightness he felt sometimes in kata training, or in sparring with Sulu—the sense of being unable to go amiss. This had to work, because it was the only chance he would get.

The only chance to stop the Consilium.

The only chance to save the Federation, and the world he knew, he wanted so desperately to believe in.

And he knew, in some isolated corner of his soul, that only by focusing his mind absolutely into the single cutting laser-point of what he was doing, could he accomplish this salvation.

His hands began to shake again with fatigue. He stopped them.

What he was doing took courage, and it took concentration. Through his exhaustion, he was well aware of this. He suspected that Kirk would approve, though of course his position as captain precluded him from even thinking of this obvious solution. He knew Arios would even assist him, if he had a chance. But it was a task that ultimately had to be done alone. By someone with sufficient courage. And sufficient skill.

Bridging-clips on green wire of the power bundle leading to the deflector pulse amplifiers; cut the wire; reattach. Bridging-clips on the wire to the main phasers . . . this bundle here, red wire . . . reattach. He tried to guess how much time had passed and couldn't, couldn't take his mind from his task. It couldn't be long, though with concentration, time seemed to stand still.

Genius is an infinite capacity for taking pains. . . . Who had said that? Bridging-clips on the yellow wire in the bundle along the back bulkhead under the gunner's console, that controlled the portside phasers, cut . . . no, check toggle . . . had he remembered to check the toggle on the transport connector? And there was something else he'd forgotten. . . .

A small alarm flag flared in the back of his mind but he repressed it, not daring to take his concentration off what he was doing. When he was done under here, he'd . . . he'd . . .

He remembered what he'd forgotten to do—which was lock the doors of the auxiliary bridge behind him—in the same moment that those doors swished softly open, and a woman's deep voice said doubtfully, "Zhiming?"

"Here." Arios's hands ran lightly along the edges of the door on the third level below the bridge, portside. Spock had been fascinated by the strange layout of the vessel, the oddly uneven spacing of decks and halls, the claustrophobic closeness of the walls. Even more fascinated by Arios's ability to keep the area around himself clear. Three or four times between Engineering and this corridor of guarded holding cells—the guards were sleeping peacefully in the first of them after attempting to give directions to Arios while Spock stepped around behind them—he had heard footsteps approaching in the corridors, and Arios had . . . done whatever it was that Arios did.

Every time, Spock had heard the footfalls hesitate, as if the approaching crew member had suddenly remembered something urgent, then retreat rapidly in the opposite direction.

What was it Uhura sometimes said? *Nice work if you can get it.*

An evolutionary plus for a fragile race of "glass fairies" if Spock had ever seen one.

The lock opened to the touch of Arios's hand— presumably coded to a Consiliar Master.

Cold light . . . cold walls . . . A flood of recognition washed over him, disorienting and a little alarming. A terrible familiarity, a sense of having been in this room before.

A sense, enormously strong, of having met the fat little toadlike creature standing now before him, stepping out from the midst of a clustered group of its fellow Yoons, blinking up at him with enormous, copper-colored eyes.

And of course, Spock reflected, he had. He knew this person, with startling intimacy in some ways: a long life of sorrow and joy, richly lived; scholarship, loving, delight in a wide circle of friends. He just didn't know his name.

The Yoon, he could see, knew him.

The Yoon made a gesture of raising his four hands— probably to show them empty—and warbled a ceremonious oratorio of whistles and trills. Spock, Arios, and Mr. Scott immediately repeated the gesture, and the Yoon toddled to a low table, on which rested a number of small brass disks. Down on the planet, the charring heat of the Götterdämmerung had seared away all but the naked skin of the dead;

Spock was interested to see that the Yoons were covered in long, coarse, silky fur, predominantly green or green-and-orange, though this Yoon, who approached him holding out a disk in its three-fingered hand, was bright yellow, tabbied with an intricate pattern of purple and blue. The fur feathered on the limbs, spread into splendid manes around heads and shoulders; loose-fitting robes, intricately decorated and lavish with pockets, added to the colors.

The fat yellow Yoon—the old man, the grandfather who had entered his mind, who had spoken through him to Arios—held out the disk again, insistent. Spock could not help observing that a long stripe of mane had been shaven from the back of the Yoon's neck.

He had already been wired.

Impatient, the Yoon took his hand—fingers hairless and mildly warm, after the iciness of human touch—and reached up to press the brass disk onto Spock's tunic just over the collarbone. Spock saw that a similar disk decorated the Yoon's robe.

The Yoon spoke again, and this time, in addition to the sweet alto trilling, Spock heard words, spoken very soft and clear, from the disk on his shoulder.

"You are he in whose mind I spoke," said the Yoon. "And he . . ." He turned, to regard Arios with those enormous, copper-colored eyes, their pleats of green widening and contracting. "He was there with you. He said you would come, to help us leave this place. Is this true?"

"It is true," said Spock. "I am Spock, of the world of Vulcan; this man is Dylan Arios, captain of a starship; and Scott, the engineer of yet another starship. I do not know if you can understand this, or comprehend what has happened to your world . . ."

"We know that our world was destroyed," said the Yoon, and for a moment, his eyes went bleak. "We know that there is no going back. The Domina explained to us all that she had saved us, and would take us to a place where we would be free to live. But then she took a number of us away—the savants, the sages, the healers—and put us to sleep, and when we woke there were cold metal wires within us, and strange voices coming out of them, whispering quite preposterous things."

He nodded toward Arios again. "According to this . . . this whispering . . . he is the one who caused the sun to erupt. But I have seen the inside of his mind. I saw no evil in him."

"This Domina," said another Yoon, mottled green and orange, with long black streaks in her mane, "she practices too much the . . ." Her word was a single looping whistle, but after a momentary lag the translator registered, "injecting the perfume into rotten fruit to sell it," and then hurried to catch up, "but you can see the rot in the pit of her."

The old yellow grandfather nodded. "I am called Cymris Darthanian," he said. "My granddaughter, Iriane, who spoke to your young friend, she is here somewhere. . . ." He looked around, and at his words a very much smaller Yoon female, bright green ring-straked with paler jade, slipped back through the outer door from where she had been in the corridor outside.

"Grandfather, if we're going to get out of here . . ."

She paused, turned considering amber eyes on Spock and Arios.

"It is they," she said. "Those who said they would take us out of here. Is this, indeed, what you will do?"

"It is why we came. We . . ." Spock halted, suddenly listening; aware, far off, of the drumming of feet.

He raised one eyebrow. "It appears," he said, "that we have been detected, and Security seems to be on its way."

Chapter Fifteen

KIRK KNEW the instant that things went wrong.

He was sitting in a café in Paris, the indigo night spangled and patched with molten gold and warm as bathwater. Violins dreamed to a crisp counterpoint of hoofbeats as fiacres passed through the darkness on the other side of the pale stems of the chestnut trees that edged the pavement. His own suit of brown striped wool blended in with the white-coated waiters, the city clerks in their homburg hats and the boulevardiers in natty black frock coats; across the small table, Germaine McKennon looked ravishing in dark green taffeta whose gleams in the gaslight brought out the emerald of her eyes. The air smelled of her perfume, of coffee, of horses and the river.

She was saying, "Holodeck technology has become increasingly sophisticated. If you were to drink that coffee it probably would keep you awake for forty-eight hours. Those who take a training program on the holodeck frequently develop psychosomatic bruises, if they take a punch or a kick or a blow from a sword. . . ."

She laughed, a beautiful sound over the soft babble of French, which he could understand far better than he'd ever comprehended it in school. "There are all kinds of stories of men falling in love with Honey What's-Her-Name . . . a tremendously popular character in what is politely called 'Men's Adventure,' or women developing *terrible* crushes on the heroes of Ms. Schindler's romances, but I've never actually met anyone who's done either."

He wanted to ask her if she'd met anyone who'd actually died from the holo-sims of having their intestines drawn out, or of being chewed to death by *mheerscha,* but he didn't. She'd only laugh that sweet laugh, and tell him exactly who in the Shadow Fleet was responsible for that kind of rumor, and he'd be overwhelmed again with how much Germaine McKennon looked like his first love, Ruth.

And naturally, nobody demonstrated the sex holo-sims, either: rough, violent, or simply impersonal.

"Mind you," she added roguishly, with a glance across at the next table, where Captain Varos, Edward Dale, and two identical security officers in the rough sweaters and berets of Parisian workmen watched them, "some of the historicals, and the views of far-flung planets, get a little . . . less accurate. There's even a holo adventure which takes place on the original *Enterprise.* I'd be curious to see how closely it matches . . ."

Then he saw it; the change in her eyes. They flared wide in the soft, white glow of the gaslight from the café, first startled, shocked, then filled with the devil's cocktail of triumph, spite, and rage. She opened her mouth to speak, but Kirk was faster, ripping the phaser from his belt and hitting her with a full stun charge. At the same moment he wrenched the holo remote—a thin rectangle of plastic half the width of his palm—from her nerveless grip, threw it to the granite-block flagstones beneath his chair, and ground it with his heel. Paris flickered, leaped, jarred, showing disorienting patches of pale gray wall and hatch covers beyond the luminous shadows of the nineteenth-century night.

It all took only seconds. He identified the exit door at the same moment he opened fire on Dale and Varos, but they were already diving in opposite directions, dodging among fleeing waiters and patrons and tripping over tables that were flickering in and out of reality. Kirk yelled, "Wolfman!," then remembered that of all the rooms on the ship, the holochambers, whatever their size or function, were the only ones completely soundproofed. The images faded around him as he reached the outer door, jabbed the opener; a bolt from a phaser seared the wall close enough to his head to catch him in the disorienting nimbus.

Outside, one of the guards was down, Wolfman supporting her while the other two tangled viciously with four or five Specials. Kirk ducked, turned, fired at the controls of the door, then put stun charges into the backs of three of the Specials before they had a chance to turn around. Red lights were going off everywhere, alarms sounding. Wolfman brought down another two Specials, then hoisted the downed woman to his shoulders in a fireman's carry and bolted for the end of the corridor, making it through the vacuum shield just before it shut.

Cooper pressed his hand to his head, wincing as if at a blow. "Shuttle deck," he said. "They got the Yoons. They're on the way down there."

"I thought your wiring was disabled!" Kirk fired at the shield as it started to open, then headed down the corridor at a run.

"It's just a locator signal! This way!" He veered down a gangway—there was something, Kirk realized, to what Dale had said about wired commanders and wired troops.

Which meant, of course, that the Specials would know exactly where to converge.

He was right. Twice they met parties of Specials, the faint scuff marks of the phaser fire on the gray walls telling Kirk that the phasers of their enemies were set on heavy stun. The corridors of the *Savasci* were narrow and full of odd turns. He took a hit on the leg and forced himself to run on, stumbling, sick with the pain of it, knowing exactly what would happen to him if he was taken alive for McKennon to deal with—memories excised, changed, altered, though presumably nothing that would cause a temporal paradox, he thought grimly, ducking back behind a corner and returning fire at yet another group. Maybe, he thought—remembering what Cooper had told him of the holo-sim chambers—other things as well.

And if McKennon had any way of finding out which crewman aboard the *Enterprise* was the Consilium's point of origin—or if she knew that fact already—nothing would save the security officers who followed him. Unless, of course, they happened to be X's friends. Then they, too, would be changed. And in either case Phil Cooper would be a dead man.

Kirk heard Spock's voice call out, "Captain!," and he turned, caught a glimpse of the science officer framed in the partly opened door of a gangway. He and his security team ducked through; Spock let the door slam shut, fused the mechanism with a burst of phaser fire. In the near-darkness of the stairwell he was aware of clustering, luminous eyes, of a strong, though not unpleasant, alien smell—of being surrounded by the living, breathing bodies of the race he had only known that morning as charred skeletons, mummified corpses.

"Where're Arios and Mr. Scott?"

"Flank guards," said Spock briefly, and handed him a translator disk. "They'll rendezvous in the shuttle deck with us; each of them has half a dozen Yoons with him, armed with phasers."

"My granddaughter Iriane," whistled Darthanian, "has a great anger in her, a terrible rage—and she has been trained as a warrior. Believe me, these human beings have no idea what it was that they brought on board their starship."

They streamed down the gangway, hearing, now and then, the thunder of boots in the corridors outside the doors, the hiss and zap of phaser fire. "My guess is that the Yoons' prison itself was booby-trapped," said Spock, as Cooper signaled a halt, removed a vent panel from the wall, and led the way into the duct. "A reasonable assumption on Ms. McKennon's part, if she knew Captain Arios as well as he says she does."

Kirk, helping the Yoons lift the unconscious Yeoman Shimada into the vent shaft, had to agree.

"Don't come any closer." From the door of the turbolift, Chapel could see that Lao had a phaser in his hand as he turned from the console beneath which he had been kneeling. "Move around to Navigation and have a seat. This shouldn't take long."

Even from where she stood, Chapel could see that his hand was trembling. On the floor beside the open console hatch lay an instrument pack; its light seemed very bright in the brown dimness of the auxiliary bridge. There was a strained harshness in Lao's voice, and the way he moved—tightly controlled, jerky with fatigue—frightened her.

She stepped very cautiously around the raised ring to the analog of the console where Chekov usually sat, took her place in the padded seat. The consoles on either side of her were alive with lights; so were two on the other side of the ring. Engineering was one of those, she thought, picturing Mr. Scott bending over its small, glassy squares of screens and readouts; Dawe manned the other, which would make it Subsystems. She was between Weapons and Central Computer.

Lao's face glistened with sweat. "What are you doing here?"

What am I . . . ? thought Chapel indignantly, but she kept her voice level and pleasant. "I saw you just getting into the lift near your quarters," she said. "I was worried about you, and I wanted to ask you about some medications that were missing. . . ."

Her eyes went to the instrument pack again, picking out the bright-red pills in their twist of plastic. A huge dose, lethal to a dozen men.

"Zhiming," she said, "don't . . ."

"Don't *what?*" He laughed, a cracked and horrible sound. "The Federation collapses, turns into a . . . an obscene nightmare where they cripple and lie and murder anyone who dares to even *seem* like a threat to their power, and you tell me *don't?* Chris, are you really that blind or are you just trying to get me to put down this gun and unhook the phaser implode?"

"Phaser implode?" It took a moment for the meaning to sink in. Why he was in the auxiliary bridge. The look on his face when he'd been in sickbay. The way he'd turned away, and hastened out. "Zhiming . . . !"

"Down!" he ordered, for she had begun to rise to her feet. "Don't even think about trying to stop me. I've set this for kill. It has to be done," he said softly. "I can't think about it much—I can't let myself—but even Captain Kirk knows that it has to be done."

Kirk and the security team—Wolfman, Watanabe, Chavez—reached the bottom of the gangway shaft to find, as they had expected, Security Specials waiting around its final turn. Phaser fire sizzled, stinking holes gaping in the gray sponge of the walls; then a confusion of sound below, cursing, and the fall of bodies. Kirk emerged into the vestibule of the shuttle deck to find Yoons everywhere, still springing out of the vent shaft through which they had come to take the Specials from behind.

The one that Darthanian pointed out as his granddaughter Iriane was systematically breaking the necks of the five unconscious Specials stretched on the vestibule floor. As a member of a tree-climbing species, she had massively powerful arms, and for a moment Kirk saw the actinic glare of lightning, the weaving waterspouts and hellish rain of Tau Lyra III, reflected in her copper eyes.

Darthanian himself was crouched over the unconscious Yeoman Shimada, eyes half-shut, hands on her temples and wrists. Cooper leaned against the wall next to them, gray-faced with exhaustion. Presumably, thought Kirk, the adrenalase was wearing off.

"She will be well," said the old Yoon worriedly, looking up. "But I cannot bring her to consciousness just now. An evil thing, these weapons."

The door that led from the vestibule into—presumably—a corridor was shut; Kirk noticed for the first time that Arios was leaning against it, his eyes half-shut, as if listening. Mr. Scott and Spock emerged from the blast doors of the main hangar deck at a run.

"Ship's checked out and aye ready to go," Scotty reported breathlessly. "Coordinates are in for transport of yon crates."

"More than anything," said Darthanian, as the Yoons streamed around them, scurrying, stumbling, running on four and sometimes all six limbs for the shining, bullet-shaped bulk of the enormous shuttle, "we thank you for retrieving those chests."

He straightened up, chubby and dignified, and looked up at Kirk. "I know what was in them. All the Trees had repositories of the old legends, the old treasures; of equipment and medicines and instructions on how to make more medicines."

"Why?" asked Kirk, curious, knowing that this was something, also, that all those bereft scholars would want to know. Never, he reflected, had his routine adherence to duty—*to seek out new life and new civilizations,* even if that civilization had perished—been more startlingly paid in the salvation of the future. "If your people never invented weapons of destruction . . ."

The savant looked surprised. "Who told you that?" he asked. "Of course we invented them—in laboratories. In theory. Of course we knew how to kill one another, in huge numbers, if we ever went crazy enough to do so. But what need? And the repositories, no, we only kept those as reference for people who went colonizing other lands; to learn the best ways of surviving under adverse conditions. So they will be glad to have them."

From a ripped-open wall panel into which he'd plugged the tricorder, Spock called out, "Sensors and scanners blacked."

Kirk said, " 'They'?"

Darthanian smiled. Five or six other Yoons, mostly as old or older than he to judge by the white streaks in their manes, were walking back from the shuttle toward the vestibule where Kirk and his party stood, and they, too, were smiling.

"They," said Darthanian. "These few friends and myself . . ." He gestured with one hand. ". . . are going to remain with the Consilium while the others depart to their new world; to go forward with them into their future, as their servants. As you see, all of us have had those silly wires put into our necks. I'm sure the Domina is under the impression that we're taking seriously the dreams and thoughts she sends through them, or that we interpret as pain and grief and rage the little tickles and twitters they register in the brain stem."

He continued to smile, but suddenly there was a molten grimness in his eyes. "And so we will be her servants," he said. "If we scatter ourselves about the ship, and cry that we were injured, and left for dead by our comrades because we would not go with them, she will undoubtedly believe our good faith. There is nothing, of course, which will avenge what they have done. Still . . ." He gestured, like a shrug. "It will be interesting to see how much trouble we *can* cause, before we are caught. Iriane, my granddaughter . . ."

He held out his hands to her, where she crouched beside Arios, still at the outer door. She had, according to Spock, immediately assumed duties as his second-in-command of the flank guard, keeping the small group of Yoons safe on their flight to the shuttle with vicious and single-minded determination.

"No." Iriane's voice was barely a purring from the translator Kirk wore. "Grandfather, I am sorry. You know what I lost—my beloved, and the children I had borne him, and the sister who was closer than a sister to me. Mother, Father . . ." She shook her head. "My vengeance is un-slaked, nor will it be slaked, by flight, and the building of a future life." Her hard, black, hairless hand reached out, and touched Arios's fingers.

Darthanian's face was sad—like the face of one, thought Kirk, who sees the future, the inevitable currents of time. "You have promise as one of the greatest of the savants, child; trained in all our arts. There are few enough savants in those who will build the new world."

"The pain I feel would only turn to poison," said the warrior softly. "I cannot teach poison to the children who will be born."

"They're coming." Arios flinched, brought his hand to his temple in pain. His voice was hoarse. "She's with them."

"Send the ship away," said Kirk.

Spock tapped commands into the tricorder; the great blast doors flashed shut, hiding the hangar deck, the smooth white gloss of the shuttle, from sight. Red lights went on, warning as the air cycled out of the deck behind those doors; the Yoon savants were already scrambling back into the vent shafts, to seek the places where they would let themselves be found.

Metal hissed as phaser fire concentrated on the lock of the vestibule door, like the curses of the Specials gathered outside.

Kirk flipped open his communicator. "Mr. Kyle? Get us out of here."

"Uh . . . I'm afraid there's a problem with that just now." Kyle's voice came scratchy through the speaker.

"*Just now?*" Kirk demanded. "We're backed into a corner. . . ."

"We're working on it as fast as we can, sir," said Kyle. "But somebody's linked a phaser-bank dump to be triggered by an incoming transporter signal, then jammed the dump safeties."

Scotty, standing beside Kirk, drew a harsh breath of shock.

Unnecessarily, Kyle amplified, "So if you beam over, the ship blows up."

The corridor doors gave, lurched open to reveal Dale, Varos, and serious reinforcements.

With them, like a black and copper storm, was Domina McKennon.

Kirk barely had time to duck back into the door of the gangway, crowding with the redshirts, Arios, Scott. He sent two shots into the crowd of Specials to cover Spock's dash for cover, but knew it was hopeless. Pain stabbed his head, searing him and taking his breath away; a Special made a dash into the room, heading for the controls on the launch-cycle, and Kirk shot him, twice, three times. Only concentrated fire from Arios and Scott as well brought him down.

"Stop it!" Kirk heard McKennon shout from the corridor. "Stop the launch, whatever it takes!"

A blast of phaser fire stung his hand; beside him, Cooper gasped and sank to his knees. Three Specials ducked into the vestibule, laying down a field of fire that drove Kirk and the others behind the gangway doors, and he glimpsed more, moving up in the corridor behind.

Then, over his head, he heard a harsh and terrible grating noise, like ripping metal, tearing insulation. The Specials stopped, gazing up, as a section of the ceiling above them peeled back.

A tentacle fell through, dripping something that looked like honey and smelled like the abysm from which nightmares crawl.

Kirk felt his breath stop.

Arios whispered, "Nemo . . ."

The next instant it dropped through, black and glistening, a horror the more obscene for the clarity of the vestibule light. The eyeless head swung around. A claw like a straight razor opened the nearest Special from windpipe to pubis in a single casual swipe, and the man made a horrible gurgling attempt at a scream as he pitched forward in a bursting wash of blood.

Kirk was close enough to touch the yagghorth, flattening back into the gangway as it swung around with that eerie birdlike bobbing motion. It made a noise, indescribably, and reached out with an impossibly long arm and tore the face off a Special who was too shocked, too stunned, to fire; Kirk could hear the bone crunch as it did something else to the body, crouching over it like a misshapen dog. Behind Dale, Kirk heard McKennon's voice scream "Stun only! Don't kill it!" and Kirk wasn't sure if Dale heard, or heeded, but he knew already that it didn't matter. No phaser in the galaxy had ever caused a yagghorth so much as a case of hiccups.

In any event, it didn't matter. Dale put one shot into the

yagghorth at almost point-blank range as the thing tore a
Special beside him into three mortal and shrieking pieces,
then with an almost whiplike flick of its claws opened the
security chief's throat, thorax, and abdomen, ripping the
contents forth like a handful of softened rags.

Arios and Spock dragged Kirk back into the shelter of the
gangway door, up the twisting metal stairs. In the narrow
space the smell of the blood sprayed from the dead crewmen
—gouts of it, soaking into Kirk's satin tunic sleeve and
trouser leg—was thick and clammy, sickeningly sweet.

As they ascended the steps he saw that the lights above the
shuttlebay blast doors had turned solid red. The shuttle was
out, bearing the surviving Yoons to their new and secret
home.

Then Scott tripped a wire, the gangway door closed; a
moment later came the hiss of fusing mechanism, and the
engineer came running to join Kirk and his party in their
flight.

There was no pursuit.

To those flattened, shocked, to the wall around the corner,
the silence in the vestibule was even worse than the
yagghorth's hissing had been. The air was thick with the
stench of blood and voided waste. Then a thin sound began,
a kind of hideous, buzzing rattle, speaking of a man not
dead who should have been.

"After them," said McKennon, catching Varos by the
sleeve. "Cut them off. They'll know where that craft is
headed! Now . . . !"

Varos looked around the doorway. The yagghorth was
gone. Even with the absorbent duraso, the walls dripped
thickly with blood.

In the middle of the vestibule, Edward Dale was still
trying to move.

Varos took one stride toward his friend, and McKennon's
small, vicious hand closed around his wrist like a vise. "He's
dead," she said. "It's Arios you need to catch, and Kirk. I
should have known he'd get Kirk on his side."

"Ed is still alive," said Varos, forgetting to use the formality by which he had termed his friend for twelve years.

"Go!" hissed McKennon.

"He needs help! We can get him to a freeze box. . . ."

And the pain hit Varos, pain slicing his nerves, his backbone, his brain; pain and horror that took away his breath, as if, for one second, it was his body flattened helpless before the claws, his flesh ripping. Pain that had no center and no source but those wide, furious green eyes. Pain and a crippling weakness, cold and a sensation in his wired nervous system that he could not have described, was incapable of describing. His eyes darkened and his mind seemed to shut down, as if he himself—the part of him that was Rial Varos, the part of him that had had a friend named Ed Dale—had been thrust into a small room and locked in, while someone else—something else—moved his limbs, his spine, his organs. He stumbled five or six steps down the corridor in the direction of his surviving men—in the direction of the turbolift to the upper levels—before he even realized what he was doing.

He told himself to turn back, to walk into that crystalline shredder of pain, the acid sea of those eyes. To walk to them to Ed's side, to get him, somehow, down to sickbay, to a freeze box . . .

And he couldn't.

He simply stumbled, staggering into the wall so that he had to catch himself, and without his conscious volition, turned again toward the lift, and the man she wanted him to take.

"Hurry, damn you! They'll get away!"

He heard his friend make a sound that could have been his name as he left him behind to die. McKennon followed, her footfalls a small, vindictive squeak on the gray sponge of the floor.

Chapter Sixteen

"I TRIED TO FIND OUT who it was." Ensign Lao leaned against the gunnery console, the phaser still pointed, his eyes seeming to glitter in the semidark. "I looked through the records—ran probability matrices. I've been doing that all afternoon. What could have caused that situation, what could have given rise to such an organization, given a galaxywide plague, given mindlink with yagghorth—about whom we know nothing—given power vacuums when key figures died or went insane. Trying to find out who it was, who caused it all."

The person who started the Consilium is one of your crew.

Sulu? wondered Christine, as she had wondered, on and off, for the few hours of her own fitful attempt at sleep. Miller, with that deadly combination of computer expertise and engineering know-how? The calmly efficient Organa? She could picture Organa taking over the Federation. Easily.

At one point she thought that it might be Lao himself.

Or was it someone unlikely: the feckless Riley, for instance, or Chekov? But surely Chekov was too sweet-natured . . .

"It would be easy then." Lao moved his hand, as if to

bring it up to rub his eyes. He did not, though. Did not let anything obstruct his view, his aim. "All I'd have to do is kill one person. Even if it was someone I cared for, I'd do it. I'd take the court-martial, gladly, and I wouldn't cause a temporal paradox by explaining. I'd accept my sentence. You know I'd have to do it. But there wasn't enough data to tell."

"And what about the plague?" asked Chapel, keeping both hands on her knees and her voice as calm, as gentle, as matter-of-fact as she could manage. To her own surprise, she found she could manage rather well. "From what I understand, the Consilium saved civilization from the plague."

"I'll—I'll warn them about the plague," said Lao, stumbling a little over the words, she thought. "There's something they can do. Quarantine, or—or finding another solution. . . ."

"What if there *isn't* another solution?" demanded Christine, forgetting for a moment that she was dealing with a man in a state of serious sleep deprivation. All her work with Roger Corby returned to her—studies of ancient epidemics, their spread and vectors through the history of civilizations long past. "Zhiming, I've studied this, and quarantines *never* work. Not on a galactic scale. Not if the incubation time is long enough. And you won't even be *alive* when . . ."

"Shut up!" His hand trembled on the phaser, his eyes burning with passion, with rage at what he had seen on the planet, at what he had heard from the *Nautilus* crew. "Maybe it isn't a fair solution, maybe there are other solutions . . . but it's best, Chris. Think about it and you'll know it's the only way! These people murdered the Yoons, the whole planet wiped out . . ."

"But some of them survived!"

Lao hesitated, blinking, shaking his head. "They couldn't have."

"They did. The Consilium took them . . ." Chapel broke off, seeing the change in his eyes.

"So they became tools of the Consilium, like everyone

else?" There was something—satisfaction? bitterness? regret?—in his voice, and something of Phil Cooper's weary cynicism in the lines of his face.

"Chris, we can't look away from it and pretend it's not going to happen. I wanted . . ." He shook his head. He looked exhausted, far worse than he had in sickbay a few hours ago.

"I wanted to do this the easy way. Set up the wiring, find a place to hide, take the neurophylozine . . . just fall asleep. I wanted not to know." He produced the parched rictus of a smile. "I guess I won't know anyway. Or you. It'll happen fast." He frowned, his brow folding in pain, and he looked vaguely around him for the chronometer.

"What time was it when they went over there?"

Chapel tried to calculate whether a lie would help the situation, and in which direction she should stretch the truth, but it was difficult enough to think as it was. "Twenty-one-hundred hours," she said truthfully.

"An hour and a half ago," he whispered in his hoarse, beaten voice. "It won't be long. And it'll be fast. I promise. Nobody—none of us—will feel a thing."

"Can he trigger it manually?" asked Sulu, regarding the shut—and locked—blast doors of the backup computer room from the corridor outside the Deck Nineteen briefing room. It had taken almost no time to locate Lao and figure out what he had done, once they knew what they were looking for. The auxiliary bridge was the logical venue for an attempt to cause a phaser backfire, and Miller and Maynooth had both been easily accounted for. In fact, both were standing in the corridor now, with Sulu, DeSalle, the redshirt who had initially ascertained that the doors wouldn't open—it happened to be Yeoman Butterfield—Dr. McCoy, and Raksha.

"Absolutely," said Miller, scanning the ceiling already for entrances to the vents. "My guess is he's monitoring ship's internal communications to let him know if somebody gets on to him, in which case he'll probably take his chances and pull the plug."

"He's cut out ops," reported Maynooth, who'd just emerged from the briefing room. As the door slipped shut behind him, Sulu could see the lines of amber readout on the triangular table vidscreen. "So we can't simply drain power from the phaser banks."

"We can do it manually," said Sulu. "That'll also keep him from being alerted to the drain itself until it's too late to do any damage. Any idea who's in there with him? Or what this is all about?"

Heads were shaken. McCoy looked around at the others —Maynooth and Miller, DeSalle and Butterfield—and said slowly, "I may have an idea of why." He sighed, and Sulu reflected that the doctor didn't look to have slept very well. There was a weariness in the slouch of his shoulders, and air of . . . not exactly hopelessness. A kind of resignation tinged with anger, the knowledge that there was nothing that could be done.

It was a look Sulu had seen lately, in other members of the crew. The captain. Certainly Ensign Lao.

But at Sulu's raised brow he only shook his head. "At a briefing yesterday, just before the . . . the new ship came into view, Captain Arios gave us a piece of information which may have sent Ensign Lao into . . . into a crisis. I know he hadn't been sleeping. I prescribed cillanocylene-six for him and come to find two-thirds of my total stock of neurophylozine is gone." He paused, with a look in his blue eyes as if sifting through some knowledge for portions of it that could be disclosed. Sulu saw his gaze cross that of the Klingon woman Raksha and saw the warning shake of her head.

McCoy sighed. "That's all I can say."

"That isn't enough," said Sulu.

Raksha raised a finger. "It's enough," she said. "Lao's actions are logical from his own standpoint. Trying to destroy the ship, and hooking it to the incoming transporter as a trigger. And I think," she added, as Sulu opened his mouth to protest, "that you'll be safe enough draining the phaser power. The last thing the *Savasci*'s gonna do is open fire on you."

Sulu hesitated, but the warning look was still in the Klingon's dark eyes. Sulu considered a moment, his glance going unobtrusively from the two computer mavens, to the doctor, the security chief, the guard beside him and the other one—near enough, possibly, to overhear—at the end of the corridor. Whatever that information was, that Arios had released at the briefing—and presumably this Klingon woman knew it, too—if it had provoked a crisis of this kind in Lao, it might easily trigger a similar unpredictable reaction in any of the others standing in the corridor with them. Sulu personally didn't think it likely, but he'd seen less likely things in deep space. He wouldn't have thought it of Lao, either.

"How long will it take?"

Miller shrugged. "Forty minutes, counting the time it'll take to put up safeguards on the gauges so no sign of it'll show up on the ops board for Lao to read in there."

Sulu's communicator chirped. Kyle, thought Sulu, flipping it open. The transporter chief had already been alerted not to use the ship's internal comm link.

"Mr. Sulu, sir, we've got another request from Captain Kirk to be beamed over," came the chief's pleasant baritone. "He sounded pretty urgent."

"Tell them we're working on it," said Sulu, and nodded to Miller. "Get after it. . . . Tell them we'll get them out as soon as we can."

And as the assistant engineer loped down the corridor, with Raksha at his heels, Sulu wondered what that piece of information had been, what that final riddle was that had proven too much to take for a man well on his way to becoming the best captain in the fleet. How could *information* unhinge a man? And he wondered if he really wanted to find out.

He turned to DeSalle. "Get your men out through the ship," he said quietly. "Try to find out who Lao's contacts were, if he told anyone else this . . . this piece of information, whatever it was . . ." He glanced curiously at McCoy, who looked away.

"I'll be in the briefing room here. No in-ship link—just

communicators. But I'd like to know if this—crisis—got him or anybody else to plant any other little tricks around the ship. And I'd like to know if that person in there with him is an accomplice or a hostage."

Great, thought Sulu, as DeSalle strode off in the wake of the vanished Miller. The captain leaves me with the conn, and in ninety minutes I've stranded him in enemy territory and gotten a maniac trying to blow up the *Enterprise*. If anything happens to the ship, Kirk'll kill me.

He went into the briefing room to study what readouts Maynooth could call up for him, and to await events.

"Forty minutes," said Kirk grimly, and snapped his communicator shut. "This ship isn't that big and they have a larger security force than the *Enterprise*." He checked his phaser. The batteries were down to ten percent. The low-roofed storage compartment in which they had taken refuge was poorly equipped as a fort, empty of contents and for cover boasting only the low hedge of a conduit box that ran the width of the room about two-thirds of the way back. Kirk wasn't even sure it would mask a prone man.

"How the Sam Hill did that—Nemo, was it?—get onto the ship?" demanded Mr. Scott. "Dear God, and they've got the Fleet completely hooked to those things?"

"Well," said Arios, sitting with his hands pressed to the unconscious Cooper's temples, "that's sort of the point of the yagghorth. Though I've never seen Nemo jump ship-to-ship like that. I didn't know . . ." He paused, and laughed, a little hysterically. "I didn't know he cared enough about us to try and help us." Cooper, lying beside him, looked grayish with shock; both Darthanian and Iriane crouched on his other side, conferring in soft whistling voices. Yeoman Shimada lay like a dead kitten in the ocean of her black hair, unconscious far too long, thought Kirk worriedly, for normal phaser shock.

For twenty-third-century phaser shock, anyway.

"If he doesn't care about you," asked Scotty, puzzled, "then what's he doin' flyin' your ship for you? What's he doin' in the rebellion in the first place?"

Arios straightened up and gave him a crooked grin. "That's the problem. And that's what drives Starfleet crazy. *We don't know.* He's helping us, but none of us—maybe not even Sharnas—has got the smallest inkling of an idea why."

"And where's he gone now?"

Arios only shook his head.

"They are currently searching compartment by compartment." Spock had pulled a hatch on the conduit and wired the tricorder in as a data-pull, tracking the search through the in-ship com channels. "More to the point, they have begun a systems clearance and replacement, which should close the gap in the transporter shielding in, at most, sixty minutes."

"And at least?" asked Arios softly.

"The soonest they could have their transporter shielding in place is five minutes," replied Spock, and the three conscious redshirts all stopped checking the batteries on their phasers and looked up in alarm.

"We have to move," said Kirk, stepping to the door of the compartment. "And keep moving." His right leg, where he'd taken the glancing hit, ached from instep to groin where it wasn't numb or sparkling with an agony of pins and needles. Iriane shifted over to listen with him as he pressed his ear to the door; he wondered how much the little green warrior heard, or in fact whether she heard the same things a human heard with the complex, petally clusters of her ears.

"They're coming." Spock removed the wire from the tricorder, stood with his head lifted, listening. "They're at the top of the gangway. There's a smaller party a level below us."

"Hmm," said Kirk softly. "Arios, where does that conduit lead, if we could get down it?"

"Anywhere," said Arios promptly. "It's one of the main lines. But it's a straight drop past that bulkhead, and no handhold but the main coil." He glanced back at Cooper, and reached to touch Shimada's icy hand. "They need anticane. Somebody probably gave the Domina a shot of it, to get her on her feet again this fast. Without it they'll be out for days, and sicker than dogs for weeks."

"The drop is not a trouble," said Iriane, moving back with an oddly froglike movement. "I will carry your friend down. He's no more trouble than a sack of flour to a higher branch."

"I, also," Darthanian added mildly. "In time I'll have to desert you—so that I can be found in suitably pitiful circumstances, you understand—but for the moment . . ."

"Don't be ridiculous," Iriane snapped. "You're going to have enough problems getting yourself down that tunnel."

"Captain," Spock called, from where he had gone to listen at the door.

Kirk scooped up Wolfman's and Cooper's phasers as he passed them, knowing none of them had much charge left.

Tucked in the waste space at the side of the *Savasci*'s disk, the gangway twisted and wound. Kirk sprang up two flights of steps, two or three at a time, crouched in the elbow of a turning, and fired upward as Varos and a squad of Specials came around the turning above. He ducked back as they returned fire, hearing at the same time more shots echoing below. The light in the stairwell wasn't good, quarter-power or less; had the well been as wide as the gangways on the *Enterprise* he knew he could never have held it. As it was, the Specials, trained fighters that they were, were bottled up.

There was another flurried exchange of shots, then silence.

Then pain hit him, pain and constriction in his chest, burning, dizzying, nauseating. He gasped and heard footfalls above him, forced himself to lean around the corner and fire again, though every move made it feel as if his rib cage were splitting. *It's illusion,* he told himself. *Or something close to it, something imposed from the outside. . . .*

Pain sliced up through his groin, his bowels; he leaned around the corner and fired again, and heard the clatter of a man falling, rolling down the stairs toward him. A charge caught his shoulder glancingly as he leaned around and put another heavy stun charge into the Special who rolled to a stop almost under his feet. The pain sickened him and he cursed Germaine McKennon, that pretty, fragile redhead who reminded him of Ruth, and struggled to keep his mind clear, his eyes free of the darkness that seemed to be creeping in around their edges. . . .

"Hang on," whispered Arios's voice in his ear.

The pain lessened. Kirk's mind was so thick with confusion that he had to put his hand back behind him, feel the Master's bony shoulder, before he was actually sure the man was in the gangway with him and not merely projecting his voice and his will.

After a moment, his voice halting, as if he spoke through intent concentration, Arios went on, "She's using the stairwell as a resonating chamber. Darthanian . . . take Spock with . . ."

From below came the hissing zap of phasers, two or three being fired at once. Kirk leaned around the corner again and sent bolts sizzling up at the Specials around the door above, covering Arios while the Master reached out and relieved the unconscious Special of his weapon and communicator.

There was another pause in the attack, and Kirk, his right arm almost numb, fumbled his own communicator from his belt and said, "Mr. Kyle? Any idea how long that transporter will be?"

A maximum of sixty minutes, Spock had said, which meant that in effect it could be more like half an hour or less before the systems reformat cleared the shield block, stranding them on the *Savasci*. At that point, Nemo or no Nemo, phasers or no phasers, capture . . . and whatever McKennon would do to learn the destination of the Yoon ship . . . would be only a matter of time.

Kyle's voice was apologetic under the strain. "We're working on it, Captain."

"Did you see their faces?" Lao's voice was little more than a whisper in the dimness of the auxiliary bridge, his face in the tiny glare of the red console lights now bathed in sweat. Christine could feel her own perspiration crawling down her back, her nape, waiting, sickened, for the flash and roar of the phaser banks going up, wondering if it would hurt and, if she died instantly, whether that pain would matter.

"Arios. Cooper," the young man went on. "Those eyes that don't trust anything. Those eyes that can't open with wonder because they've learned that anything they see could be a trap."

He gestured around him at the control room, the silent viewscreens, blank windows onto nothingness. "I entered the Academy, I joined Starfleet, thinking . . . it's all wonder out there. It's all new things, beautiful things. What is it the captain says? Where no one has gone before. Where no one has gone before," he repeated in a whisper. "And now it won't be like that, unless I . . . unless somebody stops them. Stops them before they begin. I'm not doing it just for Arios and those others, I'm doing it for . . . for everyone, Chris. Can you understand that?"

"And what else are you stopping?" asked Chapel reasonably. "Yes, the Consilium is one path leading away from this ship. What are the others? Maybe the one that stops the Consilium *after* the plague that was so destructive; *after* the discovery of the new jump drive. You can't know . . ."

"I do know!" insisted Lao. "I can see what's most important, and I . . . What's that?" He whirled, head coming up, listening, and Chapel's heart slammed hard in her chest with the thought, *It's starting. . . .*

The silence was like death, like darkness. Neither breathed.

Then after a moment Lao tapped keys on the Central Computer board, the phaser still pointed at her, his eyes leaving her for only moments at a time to check the readouts. She saw his hand fumble at the keys, hit the erase, tap in again.

"Zhiming, you're tired," she said softly, astounded that she could control her voice. "You aren't thinking. . . ."

"I know what I'm doing!" he screamed at her. He stopped himself, breathing hard, the phaser shaking in his hand. More calmly, he said, "It's been over two hours. What's taking them so long?"

"How strong is the structural steelwork of these stairs?" Kirk's sense of suffocation, of nausea and pain, had not departed; he felt that it was slowly growing, slowly closing in on him again, but couldn't be sure. He felt in the grip of a strange fever, disoriented and frantic to move, as he had been when he'd come down with river fever on Iakchos II; his joints aching and darkness seeming to come and go in patches before his eyes. The ache in the arm and leg that had been hit by phaser fire was almost unbearable. Was that, too, real, or only part of the illusion?

"Pretty strong," said Arios, who hadn't spoken for five minutes or so. "You couldn't melt them with phaser fire, if that's what you're thinking."

"Would a phaser overloading take them out?"

"On full banks," said Arios promptly. "Below thirty percent, I'm not sure."

Kirk thought for a moment. There had been no movement recently from above, but he'd felt the pain growing, and knew it was only a matter of time.

A matter of time. Like the shields closing off again.

"Are you in touch with Darthanian?"

The Master nodded.

"I've seen you generate small illusions. The yeoman in the bowling alley said you conjured up the image of a friend of his to put him off-guard. Can you work an illusion here?"

"McKennon would see through it pretty quickly."

"We'd only need it for a few minutes. Tell Spock to put one of the phasers on overload and throw it down at the troops on his side, at my command. I'll do the same up here. Can you and Darthanian work an illusion that the explosion is bigger than it is, the damage is greater than it is, and hold it long enough for us to get into the conduit and down? So at least they won't know which way we've gone?"

It felt strange to be asking. *Can you cast a spell . . . ?* Arios was a child of feys, raised to use their powers in a deadly game; created by the people whom he now sought to destroy.

"I think so," said Arios. He closed his eyes briefly, and at once the pain, the sense of suffocation, increased. Arios looked close to finished, the sharp brown features lined with stress and running with sweat, like the sweat that soaked Kirk's own face and blood-stiffened satin tunic. Kirk wondered if Cymris Darthanian's exhaustion was catching up with him, too.

"Right," whispered Arios. "Iriane says the last of them is down the shaft . . . a dark place, she says. Hot, and the noise of engines near by. A lot of cover. Whenever you say."

"Cover us as long as you can," said Kirk softly. "You and Darthanian get down the shaft first. Spock next. I'll go last. At least they can't kill me, if I'm going to affect whoever's on the *Enterprise* that starts up the Consilium. And I made damn sure I don't know the coordinates of the Brigadoon system."

"They can't kill you," said Arios softly. "But if they take you, we may never be able to trust you again. So don't let it happen." He was silent another moment, his attention turned inward, elsewhere. Then he said, "Ready."

Kirk's hand was steady as he flipped the sequence, essentially doing in miniature what someone (*Who?* he wondered grimly) had done with the *Enterprise* itself: programming a dump and blocking the ability to carry it through. The phaser emitted a high-pitched whistle, shrill and furious; through it Kirk counted "Three . . . two . . . now!" and threw.

And turning, plunged down the steps.

Even with the phasers at twenty-percent power, the blast shook the confined spaces of the gangway, hot air slamming him forward against the storeroom door, sucking the oxygen from his lungs. He was aware of Spock and the squat yellow form of Darthanian in the dark room before him, Darthanian swinging nimbly into the conduit hatch that seemed far too small for his bulk, like a gaudy-hued Denebian bolbos squeezing into an impossibly tiny hole. The flash of light in the gangway behind him seemed huge, and glancing back, he saw what Varos at the top, and the other Specials at the bottom, saw: a tangle of ripped metal and dangling shreds of plastic covering, gaping spaces of darkness where risers had been completely blasted away, flames licking half-melted plastic and curling back in a dying stink of fumes.

Then he slammed the door shut, crossed to the conduit,

gathered the hatch cover as he walked. He fitted it to behind him, clumsily, but he knew the room was dark. There was no further sign there that it had been a refuge, that anyone had passed that way. He wondered if there was some evidence, a sticky thumbprint of blood from his sleeve, a silky strand of yellow or green fur caught in the hatch . . .

But there was no time to wonder.

The conduit, as Arios had promised, dropped straight down a meter and a half along. The casings that enclosed the bundled wires were more than strong enough to support his weight as he shinned down them like a rope in the dark. The square shaft was narrow enough to brush his shoulders as he descended, filled with the smells of insulation and the fine molds that collected in the vapor traps on the vent filters, the minute bacteria of human lungs and human breathing, the dust of human garments and human food. His right hand was still weak, leaving his left to take most of the weight as he let himself down into darkness. Here and there, pale splotches marked the walls. Thumbprints, or the illusion of thumbprints, left by one of the Yoons to guide him . . .

A lateral vent. A long crawl in fusty-smelling darkness, and the scurry of boreglunches among the wires. Even two hundred years, he thought, had not served to eradicate those well-traveled pests.

Heat ahead, and the low red throb of light.

And a smell of alienness that lifted the hair from his nape.

"Watch it." Arios touched his shoulder as he emerged from the hatchway into the red-lit swelter of the chamber beyond. Labyrinthine coils and tanks loomed everywhere, dense with shadows; cables looped from the darkness of the ceiling, caught the glow of the bloody lumenpanels like the glistening bodies of snakes and retreated upward to darkness again. There was a wet sheen to everything, and when Kirk touched the wall it was sticky with resin. His mind saw again a drip like amber oil from a tentacle that snaked down from the ripped ceiling. His mind smelled again the terrible pungence of nightmares and blood.

"We can't stay here."

The three ambulatory security guards looked their agreement, kneeling over the bodies of Cooper and Shimada. Even Scotty, looking around him at the strange shapes and the low, burning gleam of the control lights, stayed close and didn't wander, as Kirk knew he would have in some other engine room, some other ship.

This was not the engine room, he thought. But it was the heart of the ship.

Through a dangling screen of hoses he could see a plex bubble, in which there nestled a sort of couch, designed for human contours. The bubble stood before an oval mouth of darkness, like a rat hole or a cave; the sides of it crusted with dried resin, and something brown that looked like stains of blood. More resin clotted the bubble's sides.

The empath sleeps there, thought Kirk. Sleeps during the jump. Sleeps in the mind of the thing that lies in that darkness.

Within the darkness something stirred wetly, and there was the squamous gleam of moving tentacles, moving bone. Then shifting, as if unwinding itself, it emerged: the yagghorth of the *Savasci,* eyeless, arachnoid, gleaming in the dark, like a great squid brought from its lair by the whisper of food.

Chapter Seventeen

"MR. SULU, do you have an estimate on how long it will be before the problem with the transporter is resolved?"

When Kirk had asked that question before, Sulu had heard the vicious crackle of phaser fire in the background, the suggestion of movement, of bodies taking cover. Now the only thing he heard was the dim pulse of machinery, and, briefly, a soft, ophidian hiss. The captain spoke quietly. There was no other sound.

For some reason that was worse than the clamor of battle.

"Between ten and fifteen minutes, Captain." Sulu, also, spoke quietly. From his post in the corridor outside the auxiliary bridge, he could see through the secondary computer room to the fore bulkhead of the ship itself, where Miller's legs projected from the service hatch. Maynooth knelt beside him, crouched over a patched-in terminal. Only moments before Kirk's signal, the bespectacled physicist had signed to him that thirty percent of the ship's phaser power still remained in the banks.

Behind him in the corridor, DeSalle exchanged a few quiet words with one of his redshirts, below the level of hearing. Dr. McCoy grumbled something in reply. DeSalle went to the door of the computer room and signed to the squad of officers grouped around the auxiliary bridge's emergency door, ready to break in as soon as the power level dipped below critical—or anything happened that might possibly alert the man within that the game was up.

Sulu recognized them from his martial-arts classes: Organa, Butterfield, Inciviglia. DeSalle's fastest and toughest, and the best shots, if it came down to beating Lao to the wires of the weaponry console.

Over the communicator, Kirk's level voice held a hint of strain. "Mr. Spock asks me to remind you that the *Savasci* is undergoing a sweep-replacement of all systems, which will eliminate our block on their transport shields, with a probability rate increasing all the time." Still he did not raise his voice, almost as if he feared to be heard. Perhaps, thought Sulu, he did.

In the background, something hissed again.

"It's for Qixhu that I'm doing this."

Lao raised his head, after a long time silent. Though he had stood bowed over the Central Computer console for a long time, tapping through display after display with the green and orange lights streaming up onto his face, he had not been so absorbed, or so tired, as to lose track of what happened in the room around him. Once Chapel, her shoulders aching with tension, had moved to ease them, and he'd swung around upon her with his phaser at the ready, his eyes like a cornered panther's.

There was no chance, she thought, of getting the phaser away from him.

"Qixhu . . . is one of about point-five percent, you know," he went on, his voice distant, as if he were reading the words with his mind on something else. "Most people—like him—they can do something about before they're born. Enzyme injections. Augmentation therapy as an infant. Implanted cerebral storage. But there's still that point-five percent they can't do anything about."

"Yet," said Chapel gently, and Lao gave a bitter laugh.

"Yet," he echoed. "Yet. He asked Mother once why if I was younger than him, I was smarter. Why I got to go into space, and he had to learn how to run a particle shaker. He said he wanted to go into space with me." He shook his head, trying to rid himself of the memory. Rid himself of the guilt of being a fourteen-year-old genius saddled with the care of a man of twenty-two whose mind would never be older than seven.

His dragging intake of breath sounded to Chapel like a frantic effort to loosen not only his rib cage but some bond around his heart.

"They have to be stopped, Chris." His face twisted with a kind of pain. "If I knew it was going to take this long I'd have just pulled the wire myself."

"Percentage of completed replacement up to seventy-two," reported Spock softly.

In the red darkness in front of them, the *Savasci* yagghorth swung its disproportioned head, the fragile-looking sensory fans waving as if in currents of water. Flattened against the curving side of the tank behind which the others had dragged the wounded, Kirk shifted the Special's captured phaser—turned up now to its highest setting—in his hand.

"Are the fronds sensory?" he whispered to Arios. "If I burned them off, could I keep it from finding us?"

Arios shook his head. "The fronds are sensory, yes, but it would find us without them. As long as the fronds are out it's not going to attack."

He wondered if there was a deeper place on the ship to go to. If there was any place but this left to run.

Darkness within the cave mouth stirred again, like the slow unraveling of snakes. Kirk's first thought, his heart in his mouth with horror, was that the *Savasci* yagghorth had reproduced. That there were now two.

Arios whispered, "Nemo . . ."

Most of the blood that had spattered the larger yagghorth's hide was gone, but the smell of it remained, thick and vile in the room's close air. Nemo moved his tentacled head, like an unclean snake, making small strikes at the *Savasci* yagghorth with his thick-clawed lesser mouths. The other yagghorth fidgeted aside, nipped back with a mouth like a handful of dripping razors. Kirk swallowed, sickened, but beside him Spock whispered, "Fascinating. On the *Nautilus* I observed Nemo engaged in the same kind of play-biting with Adajia."

Kirk remembered Karetha's curving fingernails, and the cuts on Sharnas's hands and arms.

From the head of the metal steps came a soft clanking, a dim exchange of voices. The *Savasci* yagghorth ducked its head, hissed, swung again in the direction of the *Enterprise* party, and Kirk heard the hot spatter of phaser fire on the other side of the door.

"Key in priority for beam-off," he said softly into his communicator. "Arios, Cooper, the Yoon Iriane, Shimada . . ." He glanced back into the shadows, the thin green light catching strangely in Cymris Darthanian's eyes where he crouched beside Spock, watching the numbers on the patched-in tricorder screen turn from green to amber.

"Grandfather?" said Iriane softly, and there was a stirring of fur and robes as she clasped two of his hands. "You will not come with us?"

The old Yoon put another hand to the side of her face. "On the whole, child, I think I—and my few friends—can do far more damage where we'll be."

"I'll take care of her," said Arios softly, and Darthanian concealed a smile.

"I think it far likelier that she'll take care of you, my son," he said, the soft whistle of his voice like a mourning bird behind the clipped words of the translator. "Only, if you can, keep her from killing herself until her anger is all spent. In three hundred years, when you find and speak to the descendents of our race on Brigadoon, she can be a witness to what you say."

Iriane opened her mouth, her yellow eyes filled with sudden grief, and her grandfather made a wry smile. "Really, child," he said—to her alone, but the translator picked it up anyway. "Can you really see me leaping about with pistols in three hands and a flaming torch in the fourth? Now I must go, and prepare myself for my own part in this little masquerade."

Arios winced, put his hand to his temple. At the same moment Kirk felt a wash of dizziness pass over him that then retreated—only not completely. The huge chamber, with its thick shadows and resin-sticky machinery, was already hot, and now the heat seemed to condense around him, drawing the air from his lungs, and behind him in the darkness one of the wounded redshirts gasped in pain.

"Spock," said Kirk softly. "You're on first beam-over. Whatever happens, keep the ship between the *Savasci* and the *Nautilus*. . . ."

"Understood, Captain," replied Spock. "On the other hand, since their computer has replaced eighty percent of its functions by now I feel it my duty to point out that the probability is very high that no one will beam over at all."

"Spock," said Arios, his breath laboring with the effort of breaking up the psionic resonance congealing almost palpably in the room, "you really are a wet blanket, you know that?"

The *Savasci* yagghorth lifted its head, all its sensors turning toward the doors, listening like a lover for some voice from outside.

The sharp clap of shorting electricity was unmistakable, even through walls; a vicious sizzle and a man's muffled cry. Lao whirled as if the current had gone through his own body. "What's that?" he cried, and then flung himself across to the subsystems monitor, slapping visuals to life.

Chapel's first blinding thought had been, *That's it, that's the transporter* . . . even as she saw past the young man's shoulder the in-ship screen, the image of Ensign Miller scrambling out of a service hatch amid a tangle of cable and sparks and a patched-in monitor screen.

The next instant she thought, *He's away from the weapons*

station. Even as she thought it she was on her feet, running at him like a tigress, her mind blocking everything but that broad gold back, the man turning toward her with his phaser in his hand. . . .

"Go!" yelled Sulu.

Chapel didn't even hear the bridge door cave open, but Lao did, and his head swung around in that direction just as Chapel collided with his gun arm. He'd already pressed the trigger, and the nimbus of the shot caught her, an icy emptiness in her chest and her knees turning to water. Somewhere she heard voices shouting, and the whirring of phasers on stun, meaningless over the terrible pressure she felt, the terrible light. . . .

With a faint, grating whine the engine-room door moved, a slit of cold light appearing. The *Savasci* yagghorth hissed again, head moving heavily, snakewise, and with a movement that seemed like a horrible sort of echo, the Romulan woman Karetha eeled through the red metal of the doorway and stood, her head bobbing from side to side, at the top of the steps. Her dark eyes were perfectly blank.

After a moment she, too, opened her mouth and hissed.

Kirk flattened back against the tank, phaser held ready. Behind the swaying Romulan woman on the steps appeared the slim shadow of Germaine McKennon, and, cold-faced as stone, Captain Varos, and one by one a slow, careful line of Specials who dropped over the platform railing to the deck, fanning outward in both directions with barely a sound.

"Whatever you do," said Arios softly, "don't shoot the empath. We can't . . ."

His words were cut off by a faint electronic twitter, and Kirk felt against his face the startled whoosh and stir of air into momentary vacuum. He heard one of the security guards say "Boy howdy," and Mr. Scott add, "Thank God!"

Kirk stepped back toward the shadow, readying himself for transport, noting as he did so that Nemo, too, had vanished, presumably back to the *Nautilus* as soon as he realized his nestmates were no longer in danger. McKennon looked momentarily startled, then said, "Take them."

Kirk ducked behind the tank as a phaser bolt whined off the metal, returned fire, wondering if Karetha the Romulan would send the yagghorth against them, as Nemo had gone after McKennon's guards. Wondering how long it would be before Kyle reset the transporter coordinates. *Come on,* he thought, as the headache, the sense of breathlessness that had been building in his chest since Arios's disappearance, mounted unbearably. *Come on, Spock said those programs were eighty percent fixed, time's running out. . . .*

Scott and the two remaining redshirts crouched at his side, taking it in turns to keep up a covering fire as the Specials closed in around them. The cramped darkness between the tanks was like the resonating columns of the gangways on the *Enterprise,* like the vent shafts where Arios had been able to set up fields of psychic interference. Kirk flipped open his communicator, said desperately, "Mr. Kyle? What's . . ."

"Their transporter shields are up again, Captain," said the transport chief in a frantic voice. "We can't get through."

"Beam Arios and his crew back to the *Nautilus* and tell them to get out of here," said Kirk. "Mr. Spock . . ."

"Here, Captain." Of course Spock would still be in the transporter room.

Kirk flinched a little at the sound of Mr. Scott's grunt of pain, and turning his head saw the chief engineer collapse against the tank, slide to the floor.

"Keep the *Enterprise* in line-of-fire between the *Nautilus* and the *Savasci* until the *Nautilus* goes back into the Crossroad Nebula and through the Anomaly there. And if . . ."

He glanced back again at the sound of one of the redshirts cursing. The man was clutching his numbed arm, gasping with pain, and in the red glare of the engine room past him, Kirk could see the ring of Specials moving closer: identical, flawless, dead-eyed.

Controlled by McKennon's will. Thinking only what she wished them to think.

"When we come back on board, Spock, I want you to be ready to do a mind-meld with me and possibly with all of us still here, even against my direct orders. If you deem it necessary, I hereby authorize you to remove me from command and place me in solitary confinement in the brig until end of mission. Understood?"

"Understood, Captain," said Spock softly.

"We'll hold them as long as we can. Kirk out."

He flipped the communicator closed, the pain in his skull suddenly blinding. No wonder Scott hadn't been able to keep cover in this ideal hidey-hole, with that hammering in his skull, that sense of not being able to breathe. He staggered to the narrow slit between the tanks, fumbling with his phaser, his hands barely able to move now.

The red light in the room seemed to thicken to blood in front of his eyes, and he felt his vision tunneling to gray. He was conscious of the yagghorth, still crouched, motionless now, between the resin-webbed hole of its cavern and the bubble where Karetha slept during the psion jumps. Conscious of Karetha herself, equally still, her face frozen in an expression only marginally human.

McKennon stood beside her on the steps, her pointed, childlike features wearing an expression of smug triumph, and behind her Captain Varos no more than a shadow in the doorway, his brown face like something wrought of boiled leather, the red light of loss and grief and bitter hatred in his eyes.

It was an effort to draw enough air to remain conscious, to remain standing. . . .

When the Specials sprang forward, like wolves around a dying deer, he found he could only watch them with a curious blank disinterest through sheets and curtains of pain. His hand would not respond on the trigger—the phaser slipped from his fingers as his knees buckled.

He thought, *I guess now I'll find out how long I can hold against her. . . .*

The headache stopped. He felt oxygen once more in his

blood, in his brain, as the Specials dragged him to his feet. It was like a sudden silence after a noise of which he had not been quite aware.

More of them were dragging out the other redshirts from among the tanks, pulling Scotty's limp form from shelter. Even in unconsciousness the engineer wore a faint, desperate expression of pain.

McKennon came slowly down the steps, the long, smooth-fitting dress she wore whispering around her like a black silk flower. If the Specials hadn't been holding him up Kirk thought he would have fainted, but fought unconsciousness as he had fought his way toward the shuttle hangar, desperately, knowing he must not give in. The green eyes met his, and like looking into a well of cold water, clear so that he could see to its very bottom, he knew that everything Arios had said about this woman, about the Consilium, was true.

From the darkness among the tanks the guards dragged out Cymris Darthanian, his hands bound with makeshift spancels of wire. The old Yoon sobbed piteously as he was untied, "My granddaughter! My beloved Iriane! They took her aboard the small ship, took her far away!"

McKennon stepped forward, and rested her hand gently on the bowed, silky head. Her lips were taut and there was a white look around her nostrils, and her eyes narrowed to slits of vicious fury.

"My lady," whispered Darthanian, his voice a dove flutter of pathos, "my lady, they have hurt me. . . ."

"And they will pay," said McKennon, with aconite softness in her voice. "They will pay."

But not, thought Kirk, for hurting an old creature whom McKennon considered her ally. Arios would pay—or she would try to make Arios pay—for thwarting Germaine McKennon.

The comm link chirped beside the door. McKennon turned, strode to touch the square, bright-colored panel, while two Specials came up and pulled Kirk's hands behind him, clipping them together with something that felt seamless and flexible and fitted like a strip of tape. Karetha had descended the steps and stood beside the yagghorth, and yes, Kirk saw with a feeling of queasy horror, the yagghorth did play-bite, nipping and nibbling at the woman's hands and nose.

And Karetha, shaking back her graying masses of hair, nipped and nibbled back.

Would that happen to Sharnas? Kirk wondered. Would he slowly sink into the mind of the creature he had been wired, trained, given to from earliest childhood, becoming less and less human until he was only able to associate with that strange, empathic partner? Until there was nothing left of his life but the yagghorth and the dreaming of the psion jumps?

Or was that something that happened to empaths who did not have human friends?

Over the comm link, a voice said, *"Nautilus* moving off, Domina. Bearing on the Crossroad Nebula. Estimate time to Anomaly, forty minutes. No sign of the shuttle."

"Where is the *Enterprise?*"

"Same bearing, Domina. Line of sight."

Up in the darkness of the doorway, Kirk thought he saw Varos move and start to speak, but in fact the Romulan did not.

"Downward five degrees," said McKennon coldly. "Prepare to open fire. Maximum burst."

"Yes, Domina."

Kirk looked down at Mr. Scott's unconscious form, the dark brows still drawn in pain, then back at McKennon. *And here's the proof of the pudding. . . .* He realized that in the confused scramble of the running fight to the storage hold, the slither down the venting to this red-lit hell that was the heart of the Consilium's power, he hadn't even asked Scotty if he had, in fact, managed to accomplish his goal in the engine room. If he hadn't . . .

If he hadn't, what? There would be no consequences whatsoever for him, at least not any that he'd remember. With a little tracking they could probably even locate the Yoons' shuttle: pick them up, take them back through the Anomaly. It would all be as if it never happened.

Except that there'd be some order, some directive, from

Germaine McKennon, sleeping forever in the back of his brain.

The comm link chirped again. "Domina?" The navigator was trying to conceal it, but Kirk knew the voice of a man badly frightened. That, too, told its story. Sulu might moan, *The captain'll kill me if anything happens to his ship. . . .* But Sulu would never think, *The captain will hurt me. . . .*

"The helm isn't responding, Domina. Power isn't getting through to the engines. Mr. . . . Mr. Jarmeen is in sickbay—they found him in the engine room unconscious. . . ."

McKennon said a word Kirk hadn't heard since his teenage days in survival training camp.

Her green eyes cold and furious with a will that had never been thwarted, she turned and struck him across the face.

Kirk smiled.

She slapped him again, harder, and by the look in her face he knew this was a habit with her, when she did not get her way.

"You think you've won your little victory," said McKennon savagely. "You won't remember any of this afterward, so I'll tell you now: once I've finished ripping the destination of that shuttle out of your brain—and believe me, Captain, it'll take a lot longer than it has to—I'll install such a set of commands in your brain that not only will you work for the Consilium's good in your own time, but you'll never be able to love again, you'll never be able to lie with a woman again, you'll never be able to sleep again. That I promise you."

"I would not advise that, Lady." Cymris Darthanian reached up with touching respect to tug the Domina's hand. "Not any of it."

Her head snapped around, her eyes celadon fire. "And what do you know about it?"

Darthanian bowed, four hands folded, somehow looking far older and meeker than he had when he was scrambling down the steps to help Spock hold off the attacking Specials. "It is our study, my lady. The futures—all possible futures —and all the various pasts. It is what the savants of Yoondri

248

were known for. If, as I understand, this man stands close to some cusp of time—some event, or person, necessary to your present—*any* tampering with his mind as it exists, any whatsoever, even to question him, or alter in the slightest the process by which he makes decisions, can serve to undo all that you have worked to achieve."

"Even if he's just programmed to . . ." She hesitated.

"Programmed to what, Domina?" inquired the sage. "We do not know—*none* of us knows—exactly what causes a decision to be reached. What causes an event to unfold in one way or another. What causes a man to turn right instead of left, just at the time when it is needed; a woman to say yes instead of no; a child to laugh at something instead of running away in fear. Just because we never invented spaceflight does not mean we haven't studied chaos theory. If you plan to step twice into the same river, you had best not do anything to alter, even in the slightest, the flow or composition of its stream."

McKennon stared at Kirk with eyes that would have frozen mercury.

"Better to let the shuttle go for now, my lady," said Darthanian softly. "My misguided friends spoke of the stars that were their destination. With a chart, I can find them for you in your own time. But without tools, without equipment, without the instruments of teaching or the mechanisms of survival, even if they reach their destination I cannot see how they will survive."

She swung sharply away, jerked her hand toward Mr. Scott. "Give him an injection of anticane," she ordered one of the Specials. "I take it," she added venomously, looking back to Kirk, "that you'll order him to repair the damage he has done, if for no other reason to enable us to get back through the Crossroads Anomaly as well?"

"If for no other reason," said Kirk politely.

He thought McKennon was going to spit in his face. But she only turned on her heel and stalked back up the stairs; a slip of white skin and black silk and hair the color of embers. She quite clearly did not see the silent form of

Captain Varos, still standing, like a shadow in the door, watching her out of sight.

It was the last Kirk ever saw of her.

Mr. Scott took his time fixing the *Savasci*'s engines. "We wouldna want to do a poor job on 'em, seein' as how they're goin' back through the Anomaly. Accordin' to the Master—er, Captain Arios—ships take a hell of a poundin' in the energy fields there."

He spoke to Kirk and Mr. Palahnuk, the assistant engineer, and the two flinty-eyed Specials who stood guard over him while he worked. Not that they, or Mr. Palahnuk, had any idea of whether the engines were being repaired correctly or not. Owing to the shortness of voyages with the psion jump, the engineer had been relegated to an almost custodial position, responsible for the vestigial impulse engines and warp drive that were only required to get the ship from one jump point to the next.

Palahnuk had already tried to fix the elegantly subtle havoc Scott had wrought, and had done a fair job on what of it he could find. But the ship still hadn't moved a single degree. On the small engine-room viewscreen, Kirk could see the dwindling yellow flare of the *Nautilus*'s warp engine like a tiny star in the center of the triangular window formed by the *Enterprise*'s engineering hull and nacelles. On the readouts, which he tapped into idly while watching Scott work, he could see the digitalized shapes of the three ships as points in a steadily lengthening line whose end aimed straight toward the heart of the Crossroad Nebula.

Despite the racking numbness still plaguing his right leg and right shoulder—in a burst of spite McKennon had forbidden the medics to give him any anticane—Kirk felt conscious of a job well done.

Mr. Scott was still working on the engines when Cymris Darthanian and Captain Varos came onto the small upper engine deck.

Kirk rose to his feet, uneasy in the presence of the Romulan captain. He had made sure that yeomen Chavez, Watanabe, and Wolfman, the remaining security guards, had not been out of his sight since their capture. Watanabe had been given a partial dose of anticane, which left him groggy and clumsy-handed but no longer in pain, and Chavez had stuck close by his side, ready to resist any attempt to get any of them alone. But none had been made.

It was Darthanian who stepped forward, bowed, and spoke, the soft whistling voice flowing into the words of the translator and beginning now to mimic their form.

"Captain Kirk," he said. His palate could not form the hard "K" and the sound was a sort of buzzing whine. "Domina McKennon has agreed that any attempt to interfere to the smallest degree in matters touching this branch of the time stream would be extremely ill-advised. By the same token, however, we realize that interference has already occurred—massive interference. Hope and despair are factors like any others; knowledge is a factor.

"The Domina has spoken to you already of methods by which your people can be caused to forget things which happened. These methods are also known to us, to the Yoons, to the savants who have studied the healing of the mind. I think that it would be best for all, if I and my friends came to your ship and removed these things from the minds of your crew—indeed, removed everything which happened from the moment that the *Nautilus* appeared on your long-range scanners. I understand that Mr. Spock will be able to perform a similar service for your ship's computers and logs."

Kirk was silent for some time, looking down into those round, amber-colored eyes. Thinking about the future—about the possibilities for the future. About the good the Consilium did, before it turned to evil; about the world that would be saved, and the gamble he had taken in the hopes that the scruffy little band of rebels could save it again.

About why a man turned left instead of right, why a woman said yes instead of no, why one particular child might laugh at danger instead of running away in fear. Once you started tampering, he thought, it would all change, and who knew the results?

"Captain . . ."

He looked up quickly, into the dark, brooding eyes of the Romulan Varos.

"I give you my word," Varos said, his deep voice halting, as if he found words difficult, "that these Yoons, these savants, will be the only ones who cross to your ship; the only ones who touch the minds of your crew. I promise you, I will see to that."

Varos held out his hand, and the seared black gaze met Kirk's, hatred settling out of the initial pain into long and waiting cold. And hatred, Kirk realized with a start, not aimed toward him at all.

"Captain, farewell," he said quietly. "To have met you was . . . an honor. And an enlightenment."

He departed, to prepare for the beaming-across of Kirk and his party, with the last of the Sages of Tau Lyra, the old Yoon, shambling in his wake.

Kirk felt a strange sense of loss at the realization that he could have known this man better, had there been time or better circumstance. And now he would remember not even what he had known.

On the viewscreen, the yellow star of Dylan Arios's ship lost itself in the vast field of eternity, swallowed up by the glow of the Crossroad.

Chapter Eighteen

"MR. SPOCK'S HERE to see you, Chris."

Chapel moved her head a little, so that she could see the chronometer, and her breath escaped her in a little sigh. It was twenty-one hundred hours thirty. It was foolish—and selfish beyond words—to feel hurt that he hadn't come earlier, for she knew that something very strange had taken place on the ship which could not be accounted for, even as she had no clear recollection of what had happened to her, though she knew in her bones that she had nearly died.

But she did feel hurt.

"Thanks, Diana, yes. Ask him in."

Somewhere, buried under a tangle of drugs and pain, lay a dim impression that she'd wanted to talk to Ensign Lao about something important, but about what, she couldn't recall. Uhura had told her that Lao was in sickbay, too, suffering the effects of a severe phaser hit—source unknown—and what appeared to be the aftermath of sleep-deprivation and stress.

She thought there might have been a phaser-line blowout but couldn't imagine why she and Lao had been the only ones nearby when it happened.

"Nurse Chapel."

He stood in the doorway, the brighter light of the corridor outlining sloped, slightly stooping shoulders in blue, glistening on smooth black hair. Hands behind back, head tilted just slightly to the side in a characteristic pose. She remembered the first time she'd seen him, standing beside Mr. Kyle at the console of the transporter room when she'd beamed aboard—remembered Captain Kirk introducing them. She remembered the first time she'd heard his voice.

She'd been too preoccupied with Roger—with her hunt for the man she had loved—to give him much thought. That hadn't come until later.

"I am glad to hear from Dr. McCoy that you are recovering."

Chapel nodded, and moved to hold out her hand to him, but she felt too weak to make much of a gesture. In any case, a true Vulcan, Spock tended to avoid physical contact.

"I don't . . . remember clearly what happened." She was surprised at how strong her own voice sounded. She suspected she looked appalling, haggard and gray and thin, her face printed with the spoor of dreams she could not now recall, but if she did he made no comment. There was only calm interest in his dark eyes, reserved and neutral and very slightly abstracted, as if his mind were on some other problem.

Natural, of course, for the science officer.

He was silent for some time before replying. "Of everyone on the ship, it is not expected that you would."

"Everyone . . . ?"

"There seems to have been a . . . a most curious and widespread . . . disorientation. Whether this is the result of the phaser burn-through, or of some unknown type of radiation given off by the star Tau Lyra when it went into flare-up . . ."

"Tau Lyra?" The name snagged in her mind, a shock and a small, cold stab of grief. Surely she had dreamed something . . . ?

Spock regarded her with sharpened interest. "The star Tau Lyra entered a brief phase of core instability some time in the past five days," he said. "We are now in orbit around its third planet, taking up what artifacts we can find of the civilization there."

He frowned, as if something worried him, and Chapel felt swept by inconsolable sorrow. There was no need to ask what had become of any civilization whose primary had "entered a brief phase of core instability."

"I dreamed . . ." she began. But the dreams were gone. Only the image of a broken, froglike doll floated to the surface of her mind, then sank at once into darkness, never to be retrieved again.

"There have been some . . . most curious effects," Mr. Spock went on. "All ship's logs have been excised for a period of five standard days, during which approximately half of the crew is able to recall events—the commonplaces of routine duties. Unfortunately, when compared, none of their stories agree—both the Engineering and the Security bowling teams, for instance, have clear memories of winning the final tournament match. And Dr. Maynooth and several of the physics technicians report the 'impression' that one of our probes in the Crossroad Nebula reported a small planetary system there, for which neither data nor probe coordinates can be found."

He remained for five or ten more minutes, conversing mostly on the subject of what might have happened during the so-called Time-Out, and his efforts to put together a theory of what had taken place during the missing days. Chapel offered a few suggestions about brain-chemistry testing and magnetic analysis of the rec-room game chips for possible clues, and the self-consciousness that had sometimes existed between them melted away; they had, as she was drawn into it, one of the better conversations of their awkward friendship.

Only as Spock was preparing to leave for a meeting with Kirk on the subject did Chapel say, "I know my logical abilities aren't anything next to yours, Mr. Spock, but if I should come up with anything that sounds like an idea I'll let you know."

Spock regarded her in surprise. "The ideas you have already given are as good as any presented at Science

Department briefings," he said. "Indeed, I have never considered you as anything less than brilliant—certainly your work as Roger Corby's student, at least the work with which I am familiar, bears this out."

"You read my work with . . . with Roger?" She wondered why it had never occurred to her that he might.

"Of course." Spock tilted his head. "In my opinion," he added slowly, as if reminding himself that Roger Corby might still be a sensitive subject with her, "within a few years you would have surpassed him, had you continued your studies rather than abandoning them to seek him."

She started to say, *I had to . . .* but could not finish. *I loved him.*

But when she had finally found him, or the android he had built to house his mind and personality, he had built for himself an android geisha, petite, submissive, gorgeous, and, as Uhura put it, dumb as gravel. *Which sort of indicated,* thought Chapel wearily, *what he was looking for in a woman.*

She closed her eyes, and drifted into sleep.

A little to her own surprise, she found herself in the observation lounge on Deck Ten. She was in her civilian togs, sweatshirt and tights, which meant it must be very late at night—she frequently wore them to do research, when she couldn't sleep.

Over this past year, there had been many nights when sleep did not come easy.

It had to be late, she thought. The ship's lighting was dimmed to night-watch power, a soft twilight gentle to the circadian rhythms of men and women forced to live for months at a time in an artificial environment, and conducive to late-night thought. With the lights dimmed in this fashion, the starfield on the other side of the crystalplex walls of the lounge seemed to fill the room, to fill eternity: burning diamonds sunk in the chasms of the sea, velvet and fire.

For some reason, she was with a Vulcan boy.

In the detached peace of her dream—for she knew that she was dreaming—she wondered if this were Spock as a youth, but even as she wondered she knew it simply *wasn't* Spock.

He wore a robe of gray toweling, Starfleet issue, knee-length and ugly, and he wore it like a knight's cloak, a king's robe. His black hair was tied back in a tail, as thick as her forearm and nearly as long, down to the center of his back. He walked with his hands clasped before him, one hand holding the other wrist, with all of Spock's withdrawn bearing, but in his case his reserve was not intimidating but conducive of something close to pity. His hands were marked all over with cuts and scratches, as if he'd wrangled with a huge cat.

"It is absurd to say I miss him," the Vulcan boy was saying. He walked to the windows; Christine followed, and thought she saw, in the deep seas of night, something dark hanging in the deeper darkness to port and below the ship itself, something huge that did not catch the light. "We are in mental contact, but that isn't the same." A wry smile touched his lips. "Certainly it is illogical for me to worry about Nemo the way he worries about me. But then, illogic is the foundation of empathy."

"Is it?" asked Christine. She felt she ought to know who Nemo was; felt, moreover, that she ought to be shocked, disconcerted, at his words. What was it about Nemo, she wondered? Someone had once told her who that was and she had been horrified.

"Of course." The Vulcan boy looked back at her over his shoulder. "At least, for empathy with someone other than another Vulcan. We are trained to think clearly, and to put the dictates of reason above the clamor of the heart. To empathize is to accept on the partner's own terms, to drink of that partner's soul and dreams, whatever they might be. Vulcans do not do this lightly. Afterward, one knows more than one would like to. Frequently, one feels . . . stained."

He looked away from her for a moment, stroking the leaves of one of the many plants that grew in boxes among the gray-upholstered couches and chairs of the lounge. His skin had an unhealthy pallor, as from long sickness, and there were pain lines in the corners of his dark eyes. She wondered who he was, and why she dreamed about him. Why she felt she knew him, in some ways better than she had ever known Spock.

Christine frowned, trying to understand. "But Vulcans are capable of bonding," she said. "That is . . ." She hesitated, not knowing quite what she wanted to say or if she wanted to go on. "Mr. Spock . . ." She could barely say his name. ". . . is—friends—with the captain, however much he avoids admitting it."

He is capable of love, she thought. *He is.*

"Friendship is not the same," said the Vulcan boy, his dark eyes meeting hers levelly. "It is not friendship of which we speak. You know that."

She knew that. He had read her feelings for Spock, when she had covered his hands with hers, trying to quiet the terror of his dreams. She wondered now how deeply he had seen into her own dreams.

"Mr. Spock's friendship with the captain would—and will—remain the same were they to be assigned to different vessels for ten years, or twenty. When I return to my own time, though I shall never see you again, we shall remain friends."

"Yes," said Chapel softly, knowing it, meaning it. "Yes, we shall."

"Love is different. In friendship—the kind of friendship Mr. Spock bears to the captain—there is no drive to proximity." His voice hesitated over the words. "No sense of peace in presence which vanishes with absence— illogical, but true. No hunger." He turned to look back toward the stars, toward the half-guessed dark shape looming in the wan glow of the Crossroad's streaming dust clouds.

"I do not know whether this is something the Consilium had to instill in me, or whether the process of bonding simply released what most Vulcans keep buried so deeply within themselves that they have forgotten its existence, its very name."

The starlight picked sudden lines of sadness on his forehead, in the corners of the too-young mouth.

"I do know that bonded as I am—illogically caring as I do—I am not a proper Vulcan. It is true that very few Vulcan empaths go ashore on their homeworld, and those who do, lie about what they feel."

Then the scene slipped away, and she was wandering through the darkened corridors of Deck Six, the lumenpanels dead slabs of cinder above her in blackness. All around her she heard, glimpsed, people blundering in the dark. Someone moved through a doorway ahead of her, glanced back over his shoulder as he vanished, and she saw that it was Roger. How she knew him in the dark she couldn't be sure, but the set of those broad shoulders under the blue-and-green canvas coverall could not be mistaken, the graying fair hair, the wide-set, intelligent blue eyes.

She cried his name, hurried after him, bruising her shoulder on a corner, stumbling into an unseen obstacle that hurt her shins. Doors refused to open for her that had closed behind him; she had to go around, up and down blind corridors, with the voices of other searchers muttering on all sides, the muted scuffle of footfalls everywhere in the dark. *They're trapped,* she thought. *We're all blind and trapped.*

Another figure passed her, dimly seen. Again, though she couldn't tell how, she identified the black hair, blue shirt, the flash of a gold Fleet insignia. She would know the movement of his body, the way he held his back, anywhere, fifty years from now. She called out, *Spock,* but there was no sound in her throat. Fearful, desperate, she started after him, her bootheels clattering on the deck, her heart thudding with fear that she would lose track of him, lose him completely. Like Roger he moved ahead of her, leaving her behind in a blackness as dense as the voids of space. She followed him as she had followed Roger, wanting only to know that she would be safe with him. That she would be safe somewhere.

Then a glimmering form materialized out of the darkness before her. She hurried to catch up, crying out a man's name, and this time instead of retreating the figure came toward her, reaching out for her as she held out her arms.

Only when she reached it did she realize it was a mirror.

The shadowy image that held out its arms to welcome her was herself.

"Naturally, it was necessary to implant pseudomemories in certain key members of the crew." The fat, daffodil-colored savant widened his huge eyes at Germaine McKennon, as if surprised she hadn't considered the matter for herself. "How else would we gloss over the loss of five days?"

"Why wasn't I told?" she demanded pettishly and thrust the tiny reader away from her, with the report it bore. "You said nothing would be changed, and now I discover you *have* changed things. . . ."

"Nothing which matters, Domina. Truly." Cymris Darthanian folded his hands, dipped in that little bow that made him appear even more insignificant and humble than he was. McKennon had ordered robes made for him in the colors of the Consilium, gray and white—his own loose-woven, brightly dyed garments from the burned-out slagheap of Tau Lyra III were already shabby, and with missions as short as they were, there were few laundry facilities on ships of the line.

"For the most part it is a technique akin to restoration of a damaged video image, duplicating what is already there. Most of the crew will believe that they went about their usual business for the past five days. Anyone who has ever worked in any sort of government installation," he added wryly, "will know how difficult it is to tell one day from the next under such circumstances. For the rest, they will conjecture . . ." He spread his lower pair of hands. "But to what end? What, after all, are dreams?

"Their conjecture will not affect Christine Chapel's decision to leave Starfleet and enter the Institute of Xenobiology. It will not affect her research into the nanosurgery of the central nervous system, or her eventual discoveries on the artificial augmentation of psionic receptors. It will not affect her founding of Starfield Corporation, and the research which at last saves the Federation from the effects of the plague."

He remembered her, the only glimpse he had had of the woman whose research would save a galaxywide civilization ... and whose heirs would consolidate the unexpected harvest of technological reward and unbelievable wealth to forge the weapons that would destroy his world and the minds that would fire them. Stringy and awkward, as all these humans appeared to be, he remembered her lying broken on the high bed in the strange-smelling healing-place, surrounded by her friends. He knew too little of the history of this timeline to recall whether she would ever know what others did with her work.

Somewhere, sometime, someone would say something to her that turned her feet from the current dead end on which she walked, to the new road of a different life. No one could tell when, or where, or who.

He could only touch her memory, and wish her well.

The Domina slouched back into the softness of her leather desk chair, turning a stylus over and over in her fingers, the silver click of it small as the snapping of bone on the obsidian hardness of her desk. Beyond the viewscreen—piped in from the bridge, but in all respects resembling a vast, dark picture window—the pastel gas-giants of Earth's system glowed against the blackness, orange or green-white, necklaced with moons or crowned with dazzling rings of ice.

Sometimes at night Cymris Darthanian would weep out of sheer exhaustion, torn between his grief for his family, for his people, for the world he had grown up on for ninety-seven years, and the wonder and delight of this dazzling and unlikely universe into which he had been catapulted.

It was very difficult to realize that Yoondri—Tau Lyra—his home—had been a charred ruin for two hundred and fifty years already, suddenly, in the blink of a yagghorth's hellish inner eye.

Iriane was out there somewhere, he thought. They were all out there, the descendants, the inheritors, of those friends and fellow-prisoners he'd last seen rushing onto the *Savasci*'s shuttle as the great steel doors of the bay slipped closed. The re-makers of his civilization. The new savants of the Yoons.

Soon, Dylan Arios would be contacting them, for help against the Consilium.

Needless to say, the world to which he, Darthanian, had directed the attention of this woman before him was very far away from the Crossroad Nebula. If no trace of a colony was found, well, it had been nearly three hundred years.

The only ones who had known Yoondri were his brother-savants here on this ship, and Iriane. He prayed for her nightly, hoping that the burden of her rage would burn itself out, as he prayed for the lifting of his own. Sometimes, in the living inner whisper of his mind, he would hear her far-off singing.

In time, they would meet.

"You're sure?" McKennon's voice was the sulky voice of a spoiled and vicious child.

Cymris Darthanian nodded. "Trust the unreeling of the future, Domina," he said quietly. "Events befell because it was their nature to fall that way. Duplicate the conditions, and they must and will fall that way again."

This was, he knew, an unmitigated lie—and absolutely preposterous for anyone who knew anything about the composition of Time. He had sensed, in his brief conversation with Dylan Arios, that the renegade Master knew it, too. The past was the past, but futures were infinite. The node at the Crossroad had been a major one, with branches of possibility leading in every direction. In some futures, he knew, he himself and the other sages had not escaped the cataclysm of Yoondri; in others, the shuttle with its survivors had not made it out of the *Savasci*'s hull. In others it was, in fact, Dylan Arios who had fired those torpedoes into the sun; Dylan Arios as he would or might or could have been, had other events changed or branched the treed bundles of pasts and futures along the way.

In one or two, it was James Kirk.

"There are a thousand thousand infinite futures," he said softly to the woman seated behind the desk against the glowing backdrop of those alien stars, the woman who was so young to have acquired such power, and who held the power without the wisdom that true savants acquired along the way. "But each of us possesses the key to only one." He bowed low, to take his departure. "Your servant, Domina."

Another unmitigated lie, he thought, amused, as he left her presence. But she wasn't going to find that out until it was much, much too late.

". . . so, I got tired of this after a while and I went out and bought the oldest, junkiest, nastiest old planet-hopper I could dig up." Ed Dale's big hands, callused and strong but well-formed as a woman's, gestured expansively, and the grin on his face was like the sun coming up. "I mean, this thing should have been made into a planter in some city park about fifty years previously. You'd need a slingshot the size of the Galactic Courts Building to get it out of the atmosphere."

He leaned across Varos's table, one elbow on the final printout of the Crossroad mission report. Behind him, Jupiter smoldered red and amber, a Polyphemus eye of wounded rage in the dark. A veil of asteroids sparkled like a chain of diamonds beyond Dale's shoulder, clouds of interstellar dust glimmered around his head. A careless war-god, a displaced Viking, joyful only to be alive. His voice had the slight slur it got when he'd had a couple of ales—like most Earthmen, he had little tolerance for ale.

"I did just enough work on it to get the engines running, lifted off, and headed back to that 'exclusive country club' of theirs, that 'private Elysium' . . ."

Varos reached out and keyed off the holo as the sensors in the corridor signaled someone approaching. He slipped the tiny cube out of the player and replaced it in its box, at the back of his desk drawer.

It was the only holo he had of his friend, telling that same absurd story of boyhood pranks and youthful wildness. Varos knew he should be ashamed for still digging into that bleeding wound.

But friends did not forget their friends.

McKennon had let him die.

The Consilium had let him die.

McKennon had forced him, Varos—Dale's sworn friend, his blood brother, the man whose life he had saved in the filthy swamps of Deneb—to turn away from Dale as he lay dying, ripped to bloody shreds but savable. Savable had they gotten him into a freeze box quick enough.

But she'd wanted Dylan Arios, wanted James Kirk. And there were more security chiefs in the Fleet.

Hatred—the bitter heat at the core of the Romulan nature—was iron in his belly, sulfur and salt in the cut wounds of his heart.

The Consilium would pay. They had the power of pleasure and pain over him, but he knew there were techniques to overcome that. His will was his own.

Anger is the heart of the will, his grandfather had said. Friends do not forget their friends. Varos had always thought himself a Fleet captain first, a Romulan second. Now he saw that this was not true.

It was Karetha's step in the corridor, and he touched the opener as soon as the uneven tread came to a halt. Many of the crew, especially the Secondaries, were terrified of her, more and more so lately. Dale had never been. "Come," Varos said, his voice welcoming.

She started to hiss a greeting, then recovered herself. Her head came back and her eyes returned to being a woman's eyes. An old woman, tired and troubled; wrapped in the soft black robe she wore off-duty, her black hair braided down her back, as it was when she slept. She took a seat in the chair Dale had usually occupied, and sat instead of crouched, which she did sometimes now when she forgot.

She said, "I weep with thee, Captain," and he nodded, and held out his hand. Her nails were like claws, long and hooked. She and Khethi—so named after the smallest species of sand lizard on their world—played scratching games and she didn't like always losing to him.

"You're abroad late."

She sighed and ran her claws through her hair. "I slept some, after the jump," she said. Her hands were smutted with chocolate and there was a coffee stain on the front of her robe. She had been neater, years ago. "In the jump—and afterward—Khethi . . . was with me about all he had learned from the yagghorth of the rebels."

"The yagghorth of the rebels?" Varos sat up straighter, interpreting the odd, roundabout speech she used to describe her dealings with her insentient partner's thought processes.

Stun only, McKennon had said. As if more would hurt a yagghorth.

Karetha nodded. "I did not realize that Khethi missed his own kind," she said softly. "He is—Khethi is . . ." She frowned, unable, as always, to divide what the yagghorth said or thought. Varos had discovered over the years that most empaths made up their own languages, their own terms for communication with their counterparts, *is* most frequently being substituted for *says* or *thinks*. It was difficult for them, he gathered, to think in any coherent terms except shifting colors and the smells of the stars.

Her hands moved a little, fingers cricking like the echo of claws. "He is not entirely of his own kind anymore," she said. "As I am not. There are . . . Romulan parts in his mind, as there is now a good deal of yagghorth in me. Yes, I know it," she added, and her smile was a woman's, and sad. "He was—pleased—to encounter Nemo, this yagghorth of the rebels. Thoughts passed from mind to mind. Khethi . . ." She hesitated, struggling to say what she had come to say.

"Khethi will join the rebels." She brought the words out very quickly, as if hoping Varos wouldn't actually hear. Then she flinched, as if expecting a blow, or worse. Knowing, thought Varos, that to tell any Fleet captain this would be signing Khethi's termination papers—Khethi, whose life meant more to her now than her own.

He also knew that as a Fleet captain, he should hit the Summons button at once, before the yagghorth vanished, as the *Nautilus* yagghorth had vanished from the red-lit darkness of the *Savasci's* hold.

He remained still, listening, watching.

"Khethi . . . wanted me to tell you," she said softly. "I do not understand why it was in him that you should know."

No, thought Varos, settling back in his chair. Under his stillness the anger raced hot, a scalding river. But Khethi understood. Khethi, whose heart was the heart of the *Savasci*, whose mindless awareness spread through the ship's fabric like the web of the swamp-spider, which could cover forty square kilometers in its deceptive silvery fragility.

He found himself wondering, not for the first time, just exactly what Khethi knew.

"And you?" he asked gently. "What do you want?" They were speaking in the up-country Romulan dialect they shared. After years of Federation Standard, it was still the language of their hearts.

"I go where Khethi goes, of course," said Karetha. "Does he choose to be rebel, then rebel I will be."

"Does he know how to find them?"

"I don't know. I think he can go to Nemo again."

"Ah," said Varos softly, and reached out, to take her hand. "Then, my old friend, once we reach Earth and this crew goes ashore, will we all be rebels together, you and Khethi and I. And then," he added, his voice sinking almost to a whisper, "the Consilium will be sorry that it ever ordered the *Savasci* to enter the Crossroad, or make contact with the ships and captains of the past. They have forgotten now—Kirk and his crew, who answer to no master but their duties as they see them, and the dictates of their judgments and their hearts. And this is as it should be. But I have not forgotten. Nor will I, so long as I live."

It would be illogical for us to protest against our natures, Spock had said to her once. At the time she thought he was referring to the problem then at hand, the appalling drive of Vulcan physiology, which forced him back to his home planet at a time appointed by Vulcan stars and Vulcan genes.

Lying in the twilight borderland on the far side of sleep,

Chapel realized that he had been speaking of the relationship between them.

And it *was* a relationship, she realized. It simply hadn't been the relationship she was after.

And wouldn't be.

There had been times in the past four years when she'd felt that if only she could get to the other side of that impenetrable wall, she'd see the real Spock. But now she knew that if she got around that wall, all she'd see was the back side of the wall.

A fading dream had whispered to her in sleep, a strange dream about walking in the Deck Ten lounge with a Vulcan boy, a boy with long black hair and strange, small cuts on his hands; a boy with a face like a young prince.

There is no drive to proximity, he had said, of Vulcan friendships. And, *I am not a proper Vulcan.*

Proper Vulcan or not—and she did not recall just why he had said this last—she had understood, finally, the depth of difference it made, to be a Vulcan.

When I return to my own time, Nurse Chapel, I will always be your friend, though we shall never meet again. And, *Love is something different.*

Her relationship with Spock was far from over. But it was what it was, and would continue, she understood, in the Vulcan fashion—a friendship, distant at times when they were physically distant, but lifelong. If she wanted it that way.

She had given up enough, she realized, pursuing shadows among the dark spaces between stars. Nine years, pursuing one man, and then another who was kind, only to find, upon catching up with them, that they were not what she had dreamed them to be.

In a way, she supposed, she had wanted Spock to be Roger . . . and God only knew who she had wanted Roger to be. But Roger was only Roger . . . and Spock was only Spock.

It was time to return to her own work. McCoy would help her—*had* helped her! God! All the practical experience she'd gotten in xenobiology . . . ! Spock would applaud, with genuine joy, her receipt of her M.D. and her specialized credentials, something she now guessed—had then guessed?—Roger would never have done. Spock would be her friend, her supporter, wherever he was.

Not the comfort that she sought, in her heart of hearts—but comfort, nevertheless.

After supper, when she felt a little stronger, Christine asked for a reader, and ran up the end-of-mission form she'd been putting off from day to day.

RETURN TO CIVILIAN STATUS?
   ○ Yes   ○ No

DESTINATION OF OUT-MUSTER?
   ○ San Francisco—Earth
   ○ Memory Alpha
   ○ Vulcan—Central Port
   ○ Other _____

She typed in FEDERATION SCIENCE INSTITUTE and keyed in for the application to that university. With luck, she calculated, she'd get the okay on it by the time the *Enterprise* returned to Earth in three months, its mission done.

Epilogue

IT HAD HAPPENED shortly after the start of the evening shift. Whatever "it" was.

Kirk remembered sparring with Ensign Lao in the gym, remembered—half-remembered, in a kind of misty dream—someone calling him to the comm link for a message from the bridge.

And the next thing he knew clearly had been waking at 0400 in a cold sweat, from a dream of horror, a dream of something dark and chitinous, something that ripped men to pieces with casual ease . . . eyeless, tentacled, winged, and glittering darkly. A dream of a yagghorth, seen clearly visible in good lighting, unlike the dim and flickery image on the warning vid.

But no one of the crew was missing or injured, save Lao and Chapel, in sickbay with extreme phaser shock.

And further back than that, his memory would not go. Alone in his quarters, Kirk screened through the compilation of reports.

Spock had done a hero's work. The moment the temporal discrepancy had been discovered—at shortly before 0800 hours that morning, when he himself had walked onto the bridge—Kirk had ordered every person on board, from Mr.

Spock down to the disreputable laundryman Brunowski, to write up what they remembered of the past five days. Most people had very clear recollections of business as usual, but unfortunately, when collated, the accounts did not match. For most of the day Spock had been laboriously extracting what data from them he could, trying to align it with circumstantial evidence and come up with a coherent idea of what actually had gone on.

And had come up with very little.

Sheets of flimsiplast had been found in sickbay, with handwritten admissions notes for Chapel and Lao, listing severe phaser shock for both, complicated in Lao's case by sleep deprivation and nervous exhaustion; the stardates given for admission fell just at the end of the five-day "Time-Out." The notes were in McCoy's handwriting. McCoy remembered nothing.

Fully 189 people—nearly half the ship's complement—remembered waking at or at about 0400 on the same morning, and of those, more than a hundred reported either a troubling dream or a sense of something deeply wrong.

Phaser banks had been down to fourteen percent, with no photon torpedoes gone and none of the damage a battle would have caused.

Thirty percent of the magnetic cover plates to the manual door latches and emergency kits were found to have been demagnetized, and were dangling uselessly from their hinges. The one on the door of the portside engineering head had been clearly forced by a makeshift degausser tinkered together from the electronic field controls of the flushing unit—apparently, according to fingerprints, by Mr. Scott himself, for what purpose even he was now at a loss to relate.

Mr. Bryant, the third-shift communications officer, was rumored to be making discreet inquiries among several female crew members concerning the ownership of a garment he had found in his quarters.

Yeoman Zink of Stores reported that she remembered an out-of-body experience and meaningful revelations about her past lives. Lieutenant Bergdahl of the anthro-geo lab gave a long and detailed account of being taken onto an alien ship by small, glowing beings of unknown origins and forced to undergo invasive medical procedures. Adams, his assistant, reported that Bergdahl had put her on report for not properly tidying up after experiments of which there was no record, on artifacts from regions of the galaxy that they could not possibly have visited in the past five days.

Yeomen Wolfman, Watanabe, and Chavez all reported dreams about yagghorth, though none of them knew the name of the creature, nor had any of them seen the vid.

"I don't get it, Spock," he said, as the Vulcan stepped into the room a moment behind the door comm's chirp. Kirk gestured at the screen. "It adds up to something. . . ."

Turning in his chair made his right leg ache, as if he'd strained a muscle . . . or, he now realized, as if he'd taken a bad phaser hit himself.

Mr. Spock held out a yellow info-wafer to him. "My final correlation of data, Captain," he said. The pinkish color of his palms caught Kirk's eye—permaskin, keyed to human tones and jarring against the science officer's slightly greenish complexion. Even deep hypnosis had failed to unearth memories of the injury. McCoy had reported more permaskin missing than Spock's hands accounted for, as well as large quantities of the rare but harmless compound D7.

"Any conclusions?"

Spock was silent for a moment, turning the wafer over in his pi-colored hands.

Something had happened. Something had happened shortly after the end of first shift on Stardate 6251.1, something that had touched every person on board to some degree. . . .

Yet the leaves on the small potted plant on his desk—which his personal yeoman, a hulking young man named al-Jasir, was in the habit of trimming every day—had in fact been trimmed. Yesterday, by the look of it. How disastrous could the Time-Out have been?

"I have found none," said Spock. "Only—some rather odd speculations."

He stood for a time, head bowed in thought, with the air of a man trying to organize some difficult information in his mind.

"The region of the Crossroad Nebula has long been marked as uncanny, prone to unexpected occurrences," the Vulcan went on. "As you know, the standard warnings include stipulations to recheck all data pertaining to bio-chemical or biological experiments performed in this part of the quadrant."

"Fine," said Kirk, his mouth turning down at one side. "I always wanted to make it into historical holovids; getting a footnote in the standard warnings wasn't quite what I had in mind."

"Perhaps not even a footnote," said Spock quietly. "In dealing with the crew I have generally attributed the Time-Out to long-range effects of the Tau Lyra flare, but all the evidence points to some kind of careful and deliberate erasure of an incident. It might be that it is better to close the case."

Kirk looked up at the Vulcan in surprise. "Close the case?" He'd seen Spock come within finger-touch of getting himself killed to retrieve small pieces of information or minor artifacts, simply out of the Vulcan's incurable curios-ity. "Without learning what actually went on?"

"I am not sure, Captain, that we *can* learn what went on." Spock sighed. "Nor am I entirely sure that we should. In addition to excising—or altering—the memories of every-one on board, whoever or whatever caused the Time-Out blanked the ship's logs as well."

Kirk nodded. His own had ended on 6251.1 after a mention of instrument packets sent into the Crossroad Nebula that morning, and a comment upon the standard warnings.

"Not only standard logs, but every backup and internal systems log on the ship, even private diaries among the crew. I have just finished examining the microcomponent imprints of those personal diaries, and of your own personal log. In every case, the vocal and retinal prints of those who erased the information were those of their owners. All the evidence I can glean indicates that I was the one who deleted everything—even routine transmission and energy readings—from all ship logs and backups, and that you yourself erased the Ship's and Captain's Personal Logs."

He set the wafer down on Kirk's desk, on top of the small pile of the stiff-covered paper books that were Kirk's hobby.

"It may be that coercion was involved," he said. "But it may be that at the time, we fully understood what we were doing; better than we understand it now. And I think that should be taken into account."

Kirk sat for some time, turning the wafer over in his hand, after Spock had gone.

To seek out new life, and new civilization.

To boldly go where no one has gone before.

It had only recently begun to occur to him that there were, perhaps, places where it might be better not to go.

He sighed, and shook his head, letting the thought go. Whatever it was, it had had its effects: when McCoy had first come up to the bridge after the Time-Out, he'd looked like a man who'd aged ten years—the lines of bitter weariness, of sleepless torment, were only now beginning to fade from his face. For the first twelve hours after he'd regained consciousness Ensign Lao had been quiet, struggling with the memories of dreams he could not describe; for a time Kirk had feared, not for his life, but for the bright ebullience that seemed to have been utterly quenched.

Only tonight, when he'd gone by sickbay to talk to Lao, and to Chris Chapel, had the young ensign seemed more like himself, coming up with half a dozen theories about the Time-Out and talking of ways to bend light waves and outrace visual transmissions—all totally impossible in anything but utter theory—to actually figure out what had taken place. Even the Vulcan mind-meld, which Spock had performed on both Kirk and Lao, had yielded no further information.

Kirk grinned a little to himself at the boy's enthusiasm, and got to his feet. In a few months the *Enterprise* would have finished her mission. In a few months he would be forty, and so what? It had been a hell of a mission.

And there were more to come, he thought.

He picked up the book he had been reading—Xenophon's *The Upbringing of Kyros*—and moved toward his bed. As he did so a folded sheet of flimsiplast slipped from between its pages, drifted like a large, pale green leaf to the floor.

It bore three lines of writing.

So unusual was it for anyone to write anything by hand, on plast, that Kirk opened the note and read it before he even wondered who had been in his quarters, and when. It said:

You are my past, but I am not necessarily your future.
There are a thousand possible futures, and one degree of
difference in a trajectory can change a starship's path by
thousands of parsecs, to destroy, or to save, a world. All
we can do is try.

A thousand possible futures. Whether one was thirty-four going into a five-year mission, or thirty-nine coming out of one, wondering what the future would bring.

Whatever the future actually was.

All we can do is try.

Kirk did not recognize the handwriting. Eventually he had the computer run a comparison with the handwriting of everyone on the ship. Out of 430 people, it never achieved a match.